Mrs. Williamson,
Ever since 5th gr
write and publis|                                                          to
in my spiral note                                                        riting
you taking it over spring break and reading it.                          nber
Mostly, I remember you calling and telling me
how proud you were. That stuck with over all
these years and I promised myself that
my first book I published would be dedicated
to you.                                                          So I
present **Stories of Nickada** to you
*The Beginning*. I'm still thinking about further
edits,                                                                   but
the **The Beginning** story
really isn't going to change. I'm really
glad you encouraged me to read and write.
They helped me get through tough times
and my husband **Emily Boyd** and I started
talking because of the books we love.
You're an amazing person and role model.
I hope that I can be a good teacher
like. Thank you for believing in me.

Your Williamson Winner,
Emily (Koballa) Boyd

This book is dedicated to my fifth grade teacher, Mrs. Williamson. She encouraged me to write, read, and follow my dreams. She was my first reader, taking her spring break to read my very first draft.

# PART ONE

## PROLOGUE

The dragons flew north over and between the towering Minda Mountains. The rocky inclines were covered in coniferous trees as the peaks were blanketed in snow. The dragons beat their wings against the crisp, dry air, carrying a saddle and rider on their shoulders. A violet dragon was at the head of the group. Her few lighter colored scales glittered in the morning sunlight. She turned her head so one eye could look back over her shoulder at her rider. He sat there with a frown as he stared blankly at the trees below.

*Lionel, what are you worried about?* asked the purple dragon through her thoughts.

The man met her eye and sighed, *New Quartz hasn't been heard from in a month. I'm hoping its nothing, but I can't help but fear that Solea may have come.*

*I'm for sure everyone is fine. When we get there you can talk to them about moving into the mountains.*

*Eltika.*

*Hmmm?*

*There's smoke.*

Eltika looked forward and saw a faint pillar of smoke rising between the mountains. She felt her heart skip a beat and her endar broil. She could feel Lionel's anger like an ache in her mind as he shifted in the saddle. Snarling, she flared her wings and sped up. The other dragons followed quickly behind her.

Soon the mountains gave way to an open plain with a small village sitting

1

not too far from the coast. The smell of salt from the ocean mixed with the tang of burning debris and flesh. Eltika snorted and began a quick descent as the other dragons split off, approaching the village from different directions. Eltika flew over the grassland, watching for any movement between the buildings.

*I don't see anyone,* said Lionel, leaning over her neck and pressing a hand on her warm scales.

Eltika landed on the edge of the village, tucking her wings in, and crouched. She stared in horror at the destruction before them. Lionel jumped off as another dragon and rider landed behind them.

"Orders, sir?" questioned the rider.

"Search for any survivors and beware any lingering enemies," replied Lionel, drawing his sword. The other dragon took off and Eltika followed Lionel into the village, debris crunching under her claws.

The buildings were burnt to their stone foundations and heavy wooden frames. Dry, dark blood was splattered on the roads. Some areas still had glowing embers amongst the rubble. Smoke and the copper tang of blood stuck to Eltika's throat.

Lionel growled as he knelt down by a body covered in blood and burns. He said, "It looks like this happened yesterday." He rolled the body over and checked for a pulse. "He's dead."

"Let's keep looking," insisted Eltika, nudging Lionel with her nose.

"We should have come sooner." He slowly stood up and motioned at the pile of bodies haphazardly stacked in an ally. "We could have prevented this." His free hand trembled slightly before tightening into a fist until his knuckles turned white.

Eltika led the way down the road, careful to inspect each building and roadway. Some of the houses had walls still standing. Light enveloped her for a second, leaving a tall woman behind. Her long purple hair was braided. She drew her sword and stepped into one of the houses.

Soot stuck to her boots as she walked, scanning the shadows and corners. Most items were burned into an unrecognizable state. Eltika entered a room where most of the walls remained standing. Hissing in dismay, she pressed the back of her hand against her mouth and nose at the smell of burnt flesh. A half burned corpse of a woman laid face down on the ground with her arm outstretched. Eltika looked about, seeing the burnt remnants of a crib. She pressed her lips together, feeling her gut twist inside.

"Anything?" called Lionel from outside.

"No, nothing," she replied, exhaling a rattling breath and turning to leave. She paused, her ear twitching.

A muffled whimper came from under the floor boards. Eltika knelt down by the deceased woman and carefully rolled her over. At the motion the burnt clothing crumbled and charred flesh cracked. A stain was left from her on the wood, but there were no scorch marks. High pitched whimpers came from below.

"Lionel!" yelled Eltika. Heart pounding, she started to use her sword to wedge apart the boards.

Lionel ran into the room, sword readied, and questioned, "What is it?"

"There's something under here." She pried up a board and the cries had stopped. "Little one."

A small one-year old was curled up in the tight crawl space. Her face and hands were covered in soot and dirt. Her brown hair was tangled and stuck to her forehead. Her big, round green eyes stared up at Eltika.

"Is she hurt?" asked Lionel worriedly, kneeling beside the dragon.

Eltika reached down a hand and whispered gently, "It's okay, little one. You're safe now." The toddler let out a cry and tried to hide under the remaining floor boards. "We're not going to hurt you."

"Mama!" wailed the small girl, tears leaving trails through the grime on her cheeks. Lionel pulled another floor board up as Eltika gently touched the toddler's cheek. The girl's crying paused and she stared into the older woman's lavender eyes. The toddler puckered her bottom lip, grabbing onto Eltika's hand.

"Come on, little one," encouraged the dragon, slowly pulling her hand back. The toddler crawled to the open space, holding onto Eltika's hand. "Let's get you out of here. You'll be safe with us."

Eltika gently rocked the toddler as she sat on a cushioned windowsill, within Stone Fortress. The immense structure sat on a slope of a mountain with a forest of pine trees surrounding it. The window overlooked the valley in the heart of Minda Mountains, where soldiers could be seen walking along the road. Some helped refugees to the safety of the guarded city walls at the foot of the fortress. The little girl smacked her lips in her sleep and Eltika looked down at her, feeling her heart swell and whispering, "My precious lotus." Eltika glanced about the small room that had been turned into a nursery. A wooden dragon hung from the ceiling over the crib. A teddy bear lay forgotten for the moment on the floor. She thought, *I would be happy if these moments together could go on forever.*

The door opened and Lionel stepped in quietly, grinning at the sight of them. He said, "I can't express how happy it makes me to see you two together."

Eltika, blushing, smiled and replied, "Many years of waiting and trying and we finally have our own little one." She looked at the paper in his hand. "Is that your letter to Blazen?"

"It's just a part of the report." Lionel pulled a chair up to the window. "I'll trade you."

Eltika placed the toddler in his arms and took the letter. "She's been sleeping a lot still. The healers said that it may be a while longer before the shock wears off. Then she'll be okay." Lionel nodded and kissed the little girl's forehead.

Eltika slowly read through the letter:

*Blazen,*

*New Quartz has been destroyed by Soleite raiders. Many of our people were unaccounted for from the dead and we can only assume that they were taken as slaves. There was only one survivor found in the ruins. I have ordered my soldiers to escort the other villages surrounding the mountains to Stone Fortress. So far two of the villages have moved.*

*As for the one survivor. She's at most one-year old and Eltika and I have decided to adopt her. She'll be safe here in the fortress and others will take care of her when we are away. The healers have confirmed that she is a barrun, though we don't know who her parents were from our records.*

*We have decided to name her Blāzzer Lotus Ozol. She is already very comfortable with us and will grow up to be a fine, young girl.*

*I know you have talked about your own son being put into a hibernation due to the increase in battles... Eltika and I have discussed this. I know it would mean sacrificing another dragon, but if the war gets bad... if Stone Fortress falls then we would want her to join him. She's already seen enough trauma for being so young.*

*Your Captain and Friend,*
*Lionel Ozol*

Eltika, feeling her heart become heavy, pressed her lips together and looked to Blāzzer. The toddler had nestled her face against Lionel's chest and held onto his shirt with her small hand. He looked up to Eltika and asked, "Are you okay?"

"I just don't want to miss her growing up," murmured Eltika, feeling tears well in her eyes and her endar ache.

"Me neither," replied Lionel, reaching out and squeezing her arm gently.

"That's why we're going to do all we can to ensure the mountains stay secure... for everyone, for us, and for our daughter."

The desert was a vast sea of red and gold sand, broken up by rocky outcrops. Eltika flew slowly through the dry sky as the heat from the sun beat down on her back. Her wing beats were labored and she could feel her exhaustion demanding she stop. She looked over her shoulder to Lionel, who was covered in dirt and had dark stains of weariness under his eyes. Tucked against his chest in a sling was Blāzzer. All that was visible of her was her brown hair caught in the wind.

*I'm going to miss her,* whispered Eltika. *A year was not enough time to be with her.*

Lionel pressed his hand against her neck and replied, *I'll miss our little lotus too... But we don't have any other choice. Stone Fortress has fallen and Solea has taken over the western coastline.*

Eltika sighed, facing forward. *She won't remember us.*

*The Sentinel Crows will tell her about us.*

The dragon didn't respond.

Soon they came to a large erg before a towering cliff face. A facade had been carved and painted into the rock, depicting dragons and warriors. In the middle were double doors and lying nearby was a purplish gold dragon. He looked up at Eltika as she landed close to him. She crouched down and asked, "Where are the others, Eros?"

"They're inside," replied the male dragon, crossing his forepaws over each other. "You're late."

"We had some unexpected company along the way," explained Lionel, stepping down onto the hard-packed ground before adjusting the sling holding Blāzzer. Eros twitched his ears, eying the small girl. Eltika shifted, her legs nearly giving out, and stood beside Lionel. She reached out and gently touched the toddler's arm. Blāzzer was still sound asleep.

"You should hurry," said Eros, watching the horizons. Lionel and Eltika met each other's eyes before walking side by side into the sanctuary.

Sunlight came through the doorway, showing thick sandstone columns and a brightly colored mural on the far wall. Before the painting were several people and two raised stone basins. Eltika's heart pounded inside her chest and screamed to turn away with her daughter.

"Eltika and Lionel, I'm glad you made it," said a man turning to them. Dark circles were under his eyes and a bruise discolored his jaw. A young boy sat in the basin in front of him.

"Is everything ready, Blazen?" asked Lionel, stepping up to the other basin. Inside were blankets and a pillow.

The other man nodded. "These two are Rubix and Zuzana." He indicated to two older teenagers. The boy, standing behind the stone basin in front of Eltika and Lionel, had bright red hair that was uncombed and had a stern face. The girl had long seafoam green hair and stood in front of the other basin, fidgeting with her fingers nervously.

"They volunteered to put Blāzzer and Tetricus into hibernation," informed Blazen.

"That is very brave of you," said Eltika to the young male dragon. "It means a lot to us knowing that you'll be the one to take care of her." He pressed his lips together. "Would you like to hold her?"

"We shouldn't linger," insisted the only other person in the room. He was older with a balding head and wore a black cloak.

Eltika winced, feeling panic rise in her chest as Lionel removed their daughter from the sling. Blāzzer whimpered, opening her eyes and looking between them. He gently laid her in the basin, tucking a blanket around her. She pushed the blanket away, pouting and fussing.

"It's okay, little one," assured Eltika, trying to steady her voice and brushing her thumb over Blāzzer's cheek. "You're just going to nap for a little longer."

"Mama," whimpered the toddler, grabbing hold of Eltika's hand.

Eltika tried to swallow the lump in her throat as tears blurred her vision. She whispered, "We love you, little one. We always will." She glanced up at Lionel, seeing her pain and sorrow mirrored in his face.

"Mama!" cried Blāzzer, fear contorting her face.

Rubix stepped forward and, crouching so his eyes were level with Blāzzer, gently removed her hand from Eltika's. He held Blāzzer's hand and she stared at him as he said, "It's okay. I'm here."

Lionel took Eltika's hand and began to lead her away. Her tears began to pour down her face and she struggled to move one foot in front of the other. As they stepped out of the sanctuary, Blāzzer screamed, "Mama!"

# PART TWO

## FINDING A FAMILY

## Chapter One

Beyond the window was a blurred view of the city Maro as rain poured from the sky. The gray clouds seemed to merge with the stone buildings. A few people ran through the rain, but most were inside. Sitting at her desk, Blāzzer rested her chin in her hand and watched the droplets roll down the glass panes. She thought, *How come when it rains I'm always not feeling good?* She sighed and looked down at the book she was reading. *History facts don't really help brighten the day either.* She got up and laid on her narrow bed, looking about the room.

The walls were bare plaster and the floor paneled wood. Besides the desk, chair, and bed there was a short dresser with notebooks on top. The door was shut, making the room feel smaller and isolated. The only light came from the dull sunlight filtering through the clouds.

*When I turn twenty I'll be free,* thought Blāzzer, staring up at the ceiling. *Just two more years here... two more years... I can do that, right?* She put her arm over her eyes with a groan. *Why can't my patron have me live somewhere else instead of in this ward house? This is supposed to be temporary housing and I've been here for eight years!*

There was a knock on the door and she peeked out from under her arm at it. She waited, thinking, *You got the wrong room again, girl.* After a moment the knock came again. With a sigh, Blāzzer got up and reluctantly opened the door. A small, old woman stood there smiling up at her.

"Mrs. Esther, is there something I can help you with?" asked Blāzzer, blinking in confusion.

"Oh, I'm good," replied Esther warmly. "I just wanted to check and see how you are doing."

Blāzzer nodded. "I'm doing good. Was just studying."

Esther frowned and eyed her. "I might be old and getting senile, but I know when someone isn't doing well."

The young woman rubbed her arm and looked over her shoulder at the window. "I promise I'm okay... It's just a rainy day."

Esther shrugged and said, "Well, I won't keep you from your studies. You have always taken them seriously." She turned towards other wards' rooms. "Oh, I almost forgot!" She held out an envelope towards Blāzzer, the sleeve of her dress falling back and revealing a black tattoo of a crow on her wrist.

*A letter? From who?* questioned Blāzzer, taking the envelope.

"Make sure to eat some dinner," called Esther, walking away. "You're too skinny!"

Blāzzer smiled softly, feeling warmth in her chest. She stepped back into her room, closing the door, and glanced at the envelope. Seeing her name and address written neatly, her smile disappeared as her throat tightened. She flipped it over and looked at the wax seal. It was dark gray with the imprint of an 'S'. She pressed her lips together, thinking, *From my patron... It's been almost a year since I heard from them.* She sat on the edge of her bed and opened the letter, reading:

*Blāzzer Ozol,*

*It's been arranged for you to move to Palator. You'll live with a family there. The head of the family is Angel Kinsela and she has two children of her own. You'll live there for two years, until you turn twenty, and are then free to chose where and how you live. During these two years you will study politics, history, writing, Drakken, and swordsmanship. Along with any subjects you are interested in.*

*On March 16, meet Captain Gorvi of the Palator Guard at the southern gate. He will escort you to Palator and ensure your safety along the way. Pack lightly. Any items left behind can be replaced upon your arrival. You can trust them.*

*Your patron,*
*Shadow*

Blāzzer sighed and laid back, holding the letter in her hand and thinking, *I'm leaving Maro... and going to Palator.* She felt her stomach lighten with excitement. *Don't remember much about Palator from my geography lessons. Probably should've paid more attention.* She got up and went to her dresser, sorting through the notebooks on top till she got to one labeled 'Places'. She opened it and skimmed a section about the new town. *So it's mostly an agriculture hub... Not for sure exactly why my patron would send me there. Guess I should start figuring out what I'm taking and what I'm leaving. March 16 is only a week away. Then I'll be in Palator with a family!* She smiled and spun around, giggling with glee.

Blāzzer walked down the hall of the ward house, passing bedroom doors. Some were open with girls hanging out inside while others were closed. A girl in the hall looked at Blāzzer, averted her gaze, and stepped into her room. As Blāzzer walked by the door she heard the girl ask quietly to another, "That's the girl that's been here forever, right?"

The older girl pressed her lips together and continued down the stairs into the main room, thinking, *Soon I won't be. Just a couple of days and I'll be gone.* Across the open space was another stairway leading to the boys' dormitory. In the room were tables and chairs where several other wards gathered, talking and laughing. None of them smiled or waved hello as she, trying to avoid their gazes and feeling uneasy, walked through and onto the street.

Blāzzer meandered through the streets of Maro until she came to the shopping district. The neatly laid stone pavers, clear of rubbish, made the trip easy. The sound of people talking and carts rolling down the thoroughfares echoed in the air. Countless people walked about as the sun continued its climb in the sky. They ignored her and she ignored them. She looked down the street at the looming palace in the heart of the city, thinking, *Maro is nice, but I'm not going to miss this place.*

She stepped into a small shop and relaxed at the smell of mixed herbs. There were only a few women inside, perusing blocks of soap on shelves and jars of lotion on a table. Blāzzer picked out a few bars of soap and a small jar before going to the counter.

"Quite a number you got there," noted the shop keeper, smiling softly. Her long hair was pulled back by a floral scarf.

"Yeah, I'm leaving Maro so I thought I'd take a few extra with me," replied Blāzzer, placing the items on the counter.

"Four copper. Where are you going?" The shop keeper began to wrap the soap in wax paper.

"Palator." Blāzzer counted out coins from her satchel.

"I've heard it's quite lovely there. We get many of our flowers from Palator too. There's supposed to be fields of flowers there. I hope you have a safe trip."

Blāzzer smiled and placed her items in her satchel before turning and leaving the shop. She walked along the street, thinking, *I've rarely gone outside the walls of Maro and there are few flower gardens here. Makes me kind of excited to see Palator.*

A single candle illuminated Blāzzer's bedroom in the dark of night. The curtains were drawn over the window, but a glass pane was cracked open to allow in a soft breeze. She carefully tucked some folded clothes into her bag, thinking, *Don't quite have enough room for all my clothes, but I can leave them here for the other girls and I still have some of my monthly stipends.* She grabbed the wrapped soap and jar of lotion and placed them in the bag. *I hope the shop lady was right about the flowers at Palator. It would be really pretty to see.*

Blāzzer pressed the back of her hand against her mouth, trying to stifle a yawn. She placed her bag and boots by the door before blowing the candle flame out. She laid in bed and pulled her blankets tightly around herself. Her heartbeat echoed in her ear against the pillow as she asked herself, *Will they like me in Palator? I hope I can make some friends... real friends that are around for more than just a few months.* She pressed her lips together at the hollowness in her chest and tried to take a deep breath. *This will be a fresh start. Everything is going to be okay.* She curled up on her side, hugging herself. *Right?*

## Chapter Two

The wards in the dormitories were still asleep as Blāzzer tiptoed down the stairs. She slipped outside, closing the heavy wooden door quietly behind her. Shifting her pack over her shoulder, she stepped into the courtyard where birds were chirping in the gray light of dawn. The metal gate squeaked as she went through it onto the street. Quiet noises of workers could be heard, and the smell of ovens and furnaces permeated the air. Her heart pounded in her chest and she tried to take deep breaths to ease the tightness in her throat. She glanced back at the building and thought, *I guess this is goodbye.*

Blāzzer walked along the main road towards the southern city gate of Maro. The few people she passed paid her no attention and she focused on the cobblestones in front of her, her stomach turning slightly with anticipation. As she neared the gate she looked up at the guards along the parapets and at the gatehouse. The large wooden doors, braced with steel plates, were open to the farmlands of the outer area of Maro.

One of the guards stepped forward as she came to the gate. He wore studded leather armor and had a sword at his hip. He asked, "State your name and business."

She answered timidly, "Blāzzer Ozol. I'm a ward of Maro and I'm supposed to meet Captain Gorvi of Palator here."

The soldier pressed his lips together. "He's at the outer southern gate. Just follow this road and you should find him."

"Thank you," replied Blāzzer, passing through the gate. Once on the other side of the wall, a gentle breeze brushed her cheeks, bringing the smell of grasses and crops. To either side of the road lay farmland with buildings scattered throughout. The road continued to be made of stone, except many of the pavers were worn and had ruts from foot traffic and wagon wheels.

Blāzzer pressed her lips together and shoved her hands into her pockets, holding her letter, and thinking, *Who are you Shadow? Will I meet you one day? Are you in Palator? Is that why I'm being sent there?* She sighed. *Probably not. I should focus on what I know, that I'll be living with a family in a house.*

When the sun had fully come over the horizon, Blāzzer came to a cluster of buildings near the outer wall. The wall was made of stone but wasn't as tall as the buildings or wide enough to walk atop. The only two-story building had a wooden sign of tulips hanging over its door. A man was securing gear to three horses in front of it.

As Blāzzer came near he looked up, met her eyes, and said, "I hope the walk wasn't too bad. Sorry we couldn't meet you in town. Housing was a bit more expensive than originally planned."

"No worries," assured Blāzzer, struggling to keep eye contact.

The man smiled and extended a hand to her. "My name is Gorvi, Captain of the Palator Guard."

"I'm Blāzzer Ozol." She took his hand, feeling the calluses on his palm. He squeezed her hand momentarily before letting go.

"I'll take your bag for you. We're waiting for my niece."

She nodded, handing her bags to him, and looked around as he secured them to one of the saddles. Some workers moved about carrying supplies and tools, but none were young enough to be Gorvi's niece. Out of one of the shops came a young woman, holding her chin up and walking with an unnatural grace. Her skin was pale, and her hair was white with streaks of light green. Blāzzer thought, *She's beautiful, but she also looks otherworldly... Like not mortal.*

"Hurry up Mae," called Gorvi.

"I'm coming," replied the young woman, quickening her step. "There was a line, but I was able to get everything." She handed a bundle to Gorvi before turning to Blāzzer with a smile. "You must be Blāzzer."

"Yeah, and you're Mae?" asked Blāzzer, meeting her soft green eyes.

The other young woman, grinning, nodded. "Angel is really excited you'll be living with us. She's been busy getting the house ready and making sure you have everything you'll need."

Blāzzer smiled. "That's really nice of her. I didn't expect that kind of welcome."

"Well, we don't get newcomers to Palator often," said Gorvi, handing a pair of reins to Blāzzer. "Her name is Strawberry." He patted the large, red mare's neck. "She's a good horse; you shouldn't have any difficulties with her." He turned and led the other two horses out through the gate. Blāzzer, leading

Strawberry, followed with Mae walking beside her.

"Palator's nice," said Mae, looking up at the sky and smiling softly. "Lot smaller than here, but good people."

"I'm just happy to be going somewhere," murmured Blāzzer. Mae glanced at her and tipped her head in question. "I've been here in ward-housing since I was eight... Don't really remember anything from before."

Mae frowned. "Well, I promise this: that you'll make new, good memories in Palator." They both smiled at this.

They walked for ten minutes before Gorvi turned to them and said, "Time to mount up. We'll stop at noon for lunch." He tied the lead of the pack horse to the other's saddle before mounting.

Blāzzer climbed up onto Strawberry, grateful the horse stood like a rock. She looked down at Mae, asking, "Are you riding with me?" The pale girl shook her head with a smile and slapped Strawberry's rump. The horse immediately started moving and followed the other horses as Gorvi directed them down the road. Confused, Blāzzer glanced over her shoulder where Mae had been left behind.

A bright light enveloped Mae and when it vanished the young woman was gone. In her place was a dragon about the size of a horse. Its scales shimmered white and green as it flared its wings. In a smooth motion, the creature jumped into the sky and flew higher. Blāzzer blinked, stunned, and thought, *She's a dragon... No one mentioned that.* She bounced in the saddle as Strawberry picked up speed, making her face forward to stay balanced. *I'll need to ask about that when we stop.*

When the sun was high overhead they stopped on the edge of a grove of trees. The horses grazed while Blāzzer and Gorvi sat in the shade. He pulled a loaf of bread and wedge of cheese from his bag. Mae landed nearby, tucking her wings against her sides and making the horses whicker. She walked up to Gorvi and Blāzzer, keeping her head low.

"I didn't know that there were dragons in Palator," said Blāzzer, accepting a slice of cheese and bread and keeping an eye on the dragon.

Mae shrugged, replying, "There's just two of us." She laid down, tucking her forepaws against her chest.

"You act like there's a dragon in every town," chuckled Gorvi. The dragon stuck her tongue out at him. "Palator is lucky to have you two."

"I've never seen a dragon before," mentioned Blāzzer quietly, examining Mae. The dragon's ears were somewhat large and could move independently of each other. Between them sat two small horns that had a yellow tinge and pointed back.

Mae flopped her ears to the side and closed her eyes slightly in a smile, saying, "Well, now you've met me and you'll meet Raffel when we get to Palator."

"We'll be busy with planting when we do get there," muttered Gorvi, chewing on some bread.

"Your favorite time of the year," teased Mae with a toothy grin.

"Same goes to you," said Gorvi, grinning back at her before turning to Blāzzer. "Ever done any gardening, Blāzzer?"

"A little," she replied, blushing slightly, "but the plants don't last very long. I either overwater them or don't water them enough."

Mae giggled, "Me too!"

"Guess you two can learn together then," laughed Gorvi. "Or kill the poor plants twice as fast."

Mae and Blāzzer laughed together.

That night they camped under a large tree, laying around a campfire. The embers glowed softly and hissed every so often as sap oozed from the logs. The horses could be heard moving about and grazing a short distance away. Blāzzer rolled over on her bedroll, glad that she had the heavy blanket to keep the night chill off. She thought, *I'm so sore from riding all day that I'll be hurting real bad when I get to Palator... where I'll be living with a family...*

"You awake, Blāzzer?" asked Mae in a whisper. Blāzzer looked over to where she lay as a human under her own blanket, her green eyes reflecting the glow of the embers. Her hair shimmered as something moved under the locks until her ears, near-identical to her dragon ears with several points, stuck out horizontally.

"Yeah," breathed Blāzzer.

"Trouble sleeping?"

"Yeah, my body hurts."

"Sleeping on the ground doesn't help."

"No, it's okay. It's actually kind of nice to have the stars overhead."

"Gryphun always says that too."

"Who?"

"He's my boyfriend." Mae smiled softly. "He likes traveling and camping under the stars."

Blāzzer nodded, looking through the tree canopy at the white dots in the sky.

15

After a few minutes of silence, Mae asked, "Do you have anyone special?"

"No," replied Blāzzer without hesitation. "No one ever pursued me and I never pursued anyone."

"I'm sure there is someone out there for you."

Blāzzer shrugged. "I usually don't think much about it... And I guess I've accepted that I won't."

Mae rolled onto her stomach, crossing her arms. Placing her chin on her arms, she asked, "Why? Why would you give up on love?"

Blāzzer sighed, rubbing her cheek as a tightness grew in her chest. "No one has been in my life long enough... People came and went from the ward house quite often. They'd return to families or stayed for short periods of time before entering the craftsman program... But I stayed. I continue my studies at my patron's discretion and I had no way of contacting them... To ask that they place me in a home... All I've wanted is to have a family." She pressed her lips together at the pain in her chest.

After a moment Mae said, "That sucks. I'm sorry."

Each day they got up at dawn, rode till noon, ate lunch, and traveled again until the sun began to set. There wasn't much time for conversations as they traveled across the plains, sometimes on roads and other times cross-country. On the eighth day they crested a hill, overlooking Palator in the valley below. Crop fields, orchards, and gardens surrounded the town with numerous people tending the plants. A large wall, that rivaled Maro's inner wall, enclosed the town and a single road led through a wide metal door into it. Flags and banners of different colors and designs fluttered in the wind atop the parapets.

"It's beautiful," breathed Blāzzer, for a moment forgetting her aching body.

"Home sweet home," replied Gorvi, glancing back at her with a smile. "Come on we'll get you settled in." He urged the horses forward and she was happy that Strawberry automatically followed so she could look around.

They rode along the worn road through the fields. Workers, wearing simple, colorful clothes with smudges of dirt, waved and smiled to them. The Palatites worked diligently while children could be seen helping out and running about. Mae flew over the field, landing near a woman. She turned into a human and the two embraced.

Blāzzer winced at a small pang of animosity in her chest and looked away. The horses passed through the gate into town, where small gardens and trees were filtered in-between the buildings. Some of the houses and stores were two stories tall, but all had stone foundations, plaster walls, and clay tiled roofs. People were working at the different businesses while others were walking through the streets. Those that passed smiled or waved at the horse riders.

*It feels so different here... like safe and welcoming,* thought Blāzzer.

Gorvi led them toward the center of town and stopped in front of a house with several flowerpots of tulips on the stoop. He dismounted and Blāzzer followed suit, leaning against Strawberry till the pins and needles left her legs. He said, "This is where you will be staying with Angel." He gathered her bag from the pack horse.

Blāzzer looked at the house trying to absorb all she could. Floral designs were painted on the door and window frames and evidence of plaster repair on the walls was marked by lighter patches. Yellow curtains could be seen through the glass paneled windows.

"Blāzzer?" asked Gorvi worriedly, hand on the door knob.

"Sorry," she said, quickly looking down at the ground.

"You okay?"

"I've never lived in a house before... it's just odd to wrap my mind around."

"Well, I think you'll like it." He smiled encouragingly. "I know we are all happy to have you here." He stepped into the house, holding the door open.

Blāzzer took a deep breath, held her chin up and walked into her new home.

# Chapter Three

Blāzzer, heart racing, stepped into the house and looked about. The living room was cozy with a fireplace and couch. A worn dining table with a vase of daffodils was behind the couch. On the other side of the room was a small kitchen that had a metal stove.

"You'll be staying in Mae's room," said Gorvi, leading her down the hall by the kitchen and into the first room.

Inside were two small beds, two trunks, a desk, and a chair. The window looked out on a small garden and had yellow curtains. Gorvi placed her pack on the bed that was made.

"The washroom is across the hall," informed Gorvi. "Angel's room is down the hall to the right and Lenny's room is on the left. He's Angel's son and will be turning nine this summer."

Blāzzer nodded, still looking about the room.

"If you need anything make sure to let them know."

"I will," she replied, fidgeting with her fingers.

"I live in the barracks at the gate so if they can't help you with something, you can always come and find me there."

"Thank you."

"No-"

"Blāzzer!" called Mae. "You here?"

"Yeah," answered Blāzzer, stepping out into the hall and walking into the living room.

Standing next to Mae was an older woman. Her hair was tied up in a scarf and she wore an apron over her skirt. "It is wonderful to meet you," she said, embracing Blāzzer.

For a moment the young woman didn't respond then she, feeling love emanating from the older woman, hugged Angel back and whispered, "You too."

Angel stepped back saying, "I hope the journey wasn't too tiring. I'm making potatoes and beef tonight so that should be a good pick-me-up food." She looked past Blāzzer at Gorvi. "Will you stay for dinner?"

"I have to get back to the barracks," he said, smiling apologetically. "Definitely another time though. I'll leave you three to get settled in." He squeezed Blāzzer's shoulder as he walked by and left the house, leading the horses away.

"Why don't you go wash up and take some time to relax," encouraged Angel. "There will be plenty of time to talk later."

"That sounds good," replied Blāzzer, her body remembering its exhaustion.

After she washed up, Blāzzer went to the bedroom she was sharing with Mae. The dragon sat at the desk writing. Blāzzer put her boots at the end of her bed and laid down with a sigh. Her body sank slightly into the quilt and she thought, *How I've missed real beds.* She looked over at Mae.

"What are you writing?" Blāzzer asked.

"A letter to Gryphun," replied Mae. "It takes a few weeks for mail to get to him so I usually write what's going on during the days I wait for his letter."

"Where does he live?"

"In Gilzar Desert. He's training with the Sentinel Crows." She smiled slightly. "They keep him busy so we don't see each other often. We always see each other for the winter and summer festivals though."

"That's good," smiled Blāzzer. Mae nodded and continued writing. Blāzzer closed her eyes and slowly drifted off into sleep.

She woke up to sounds from the living room. She slowly sat up, stretching her sore muscles. Mae and Angel's voices drifted to Blāzzer along with a boy's voice. She went out into the living room where Angel was cooking dinner and a boy was talking to Mae.

"What did Maro look like?" he asked excitedly. "Was it big? Did it have towers of white stone? Did it-"

"Chill Lenny," said Mae, exasperatedly, and sat on the couch, leaning against its arm. "It looked different than Palator with several towers of stone."

"And the soldiers? Did you meet them?" He was bouncing about with his brown curls following suit. "Were they in suits of armor with shining swords?"

Mae looked at him and her ears pinned back. "Why don't you ask Blāzzer?"

Blāzzer blinked as Lenny turned to her with a grin. Mae patted the cushion next to her on the couch. Blāzzer sat down beside her as he asked, "Have you met the soldiers?"

"Not really," she replied. "I tried not to bother them. They'd only wear full suits of armor on festival days."

Lenny nodded, holding his chin up. "I hope one day I'll be a soldier to help protect the town. What do you want to be?"

"I don't know yet, just that I want to be something."

"That sounds like a good plan," said Angel, placing a pot on the table. "That way, whatever life throws at you, you'll be flexible about it. Now all of you come and eat dinner."

They gathered at the table with beef, potatoes, and green beans to eat. They ate heartily till there was nothing left. Angel sat back and asked, "What do you want to do tomorrow, Blāzzer?"

She shrugged.

"I can show you around town," offered Mae.

"I can come too!" piped Lenny.

"You have work in the orchard tomorrow along with your studies," reminded Angel, looking at Lenny. He sank in his chair with a pout. "They can stop by and see you."

"That sounds good, Mae," smiled Blāzzer.

Angel looked to her, saying, "I know you have your studies to start, but you'll have a few days to settle in. Make sure you let me know if there is anything I can do to help that process."

"Same here," insisted Lenny. Angel looked at him lovingly.

"What?"

"You are your father's son. He'd be proud of you."


When night fell, Blāzzer lay in bed and stared at the ceiling, tracing the grains of wood with her eyes. Mae sat on the edge of her bed, brushing her long hair in the candlelight. Quiet voices could be heard from outside along with crickets. Blāzzer rolled over onto her side facing Mae.

"Can I ask you something?" questioned Blāzzer.

The dragon nodded.

"How did you join this family?"

"Well... Xavier, Angel's late husband, found me," explained Mae, pausing in her brushing. Her eyes glazed over slightly. "He was doing a tour with the Nickadian army, patrolling the southern border. I was only three years old, so I don't remember anything. He brought me back to Palator with him and they raised me since."

"What happened to him?"

Mae ran her fingers over the brush's bristles, frowning slightly.

"Sorry."

"No, it's okay... It was seven or so years ago. He got really sick and nothing was helping him. No one could figure out what was wrong... He passed away in his sleep." She continued to brush her hair, looking at the ground.

Blāzzer murmured, "I'm sorry."

"It's okay," replied Mae, placing her brush down and laying in bed. She looked at Blāzzer across the room. "I'm glad I had a couple of years with him... I know you weren't lucky enough to know your parents and I'm sorry for that. That really sucks."

Blāzzer sighed and rolled onto her back.

"You're here now, so you can be a part of this family if you want."

She nodded solemnly.

"I wish you could have come sooner."

"Me too."


The next morning, after a quick breakfast of toast and eggs, Mae lead Blāzzer down the street towards the center of town. The road was mainly dirt with some areas covered in worn stone pavers. Numerous people were about, heading out to the fields or other various professions within the wall. Many smiled and nodded hello as the young women walked by. Blāzzer and Mae came to a rather large square building with narrow windows.

"This is the library," said Mae, stepping through the door.

Blāzzer followed her in and was surprised to see numerous rows of neatly organized bookshelves. Tables and chairs were grouped in open areas with few occupants. She thought, *A library open to the public... Maro didn't have this.*

"We're allowed to check out fiction books," Mae explained, "but reference books are to stay inside the library. The librarian prefers that no books are taken out into the fields though. This is where those that are older than fifteen, who want to study, go." Smiling, she glanced over her shoulder at Blāzzer. "Also you'll be meeting Raffel here."

"Raffel?"

"We'll meet with him later... Do you like to read?"

"Yeah, mostly folktales."

Mae grinned. "Good, because I know a bunch of good reads." She walked down a row of bookcases with Blāzzer quickly following. Mae stopped at a shelf with several short, narrow books and pulled one off. "This is the first book in a series of Nickadian folktales. It's about the bear, Stiggress, and the Wildwood Forest." She held it out to Blāzzer.

The older girl took the book and flipped through the pages, stopping on one. An intricate ink drawing of a bear facing a pack of wolves covered the two pages. She said, "I think I'll like it."

Mae beamed. "Awesome! Now we just need to sign it out." She led Blāzzer back to the front door where a large book lay open. It had a table filled with entries of dates, borrowers, and book titles. Using the dip ink pen beside the book, Mae quickly filled out a row.

"Now you have the book for two weeks," smiled Mae.

"Thank you," replied Blāzzer.

The dragon nodded and led the way out. They walked through the town stopping at a few places such as the town square and bakery. As they neared the town gate the sound of wood hitting wood rang against the stone wall. A large dormitory was to one side of a spacious yard edged with a squat stone fence. Inside the yard were men sparring with wooden swords. Blāzzer and Mae stopped at the fence, watching them train. Gorvi walked around the sparring pairs giving instruction when needed.

When he noticed them, he called, "Take a rest! Ten minutes!" He walked over to Blāzzer and Mae as the trainees dispersed around the yard. "How's it going?"

"Good," replied Mae with a grin.

Gorvi looked to Blāzzer.

She smiled, "Mae has been a good guide."

He nodded. "You'll be doing your sword practice here in the training rooms. Start you off with a wooden one; Mae can help you with the basics."

"I'm not that good," said the dragon with a slight wave of her hand, feigning humbleness.

"You're better than you let on," assured Gorvi. "Where are you two headed off to now?"

"To see Lenny at the orchards," answered Mae.

"Raffel is there too. Supposed to be tearing some trees up."

"Awesome! We'll catch him when we're out there too."

Mae waved to Gorvi before turning away. She led Blāzzer out of Palator through the main gate and along the dirt road towards the orchards. People worked in the fields and carried supplies along the road. The two young women neared an apple orchard where a man was overseeing several children climbing ladders to collect the fruit.

One of the boys, Lenny, noticed them and ran over quickly shouting, "You brought Blāzzer!"

"Of course," replied Mae, putting her hands on her hips. "How's the picking going?"

"Good." He pushed his brown hair out of his eyes. "I'm going to bring some home for apple pie."

"That'll be good," smiled Blāzzer.

"My mom is the best cook," added Lenny. "She-" A large cracking sound of a tree breaking echoed deeper in the orchard. "They've had Raffel busy today. Apparently, some of the trees on the far side got some sort of rot or something." Mae pressed her lips together in a frown. "Don't know why they didn't ask you to help."

She huffed out a breath, saying, "You should get back to work."

"Oh yeah," replied Lenny with a carefree grin. "See you guys later!"

Once Lenny was out of earshot Blāzzer asked, "Would they normally have asked you to help?"

"Normally, but I'm helping you today," said Mae, ear twitching. "Don't worry about it. Let's go see Raffel."

Blāzzer followed her through the orchard, passing several groups of pickers. Soon a red dragon could be seen moving through the trees. His wings were tucked against his flanks and he held his head low to avoid the tree branches. The dragon dug at the ground around a splintered tree trunk as Blāzzer and Mae approached. His claws cut through the dirt and roots with relative ease. He looked up at them and Blāzzer's breath caught at his slitted pupils.

She thought, *He looks like a predator evaluating its prey.*

"Raffel," said Mae and he blinked, his pupils rounding. Raffel straightened up, standing seven feet tall at the bottom of his chest. Red light engulfed him for a moment, leaving behind a young man. His simple clothing was covered in dirt and sweat. His red hair was coming loose from where it had been tied back.

"Didn't expect you two to come out here," he said, walking away to a tree. He picked up a glass bottle, gulping water.

"Good to see you too," growled Mae. Raffel held his hands up and sat down in the shade.

"I apologize," he replied. "You have time to join me?"

"Thank you," smiled Mae, sitting down with Blāzzer next to her.

"Blāzzer, this is Raffel... not usually as grumpy." He snorted and Mae said something to him in a different language.

He narrowed his eyes at her before turning to Blāzzer and asking, "How was the trip here?"

"Good," she answered with a nod. "I'm glad to be here." She thought he smiled slightly.

"I'll be teaching you Drakken along with some history and politics," he said. "Not the most interesting, but hopefully not boring."

"But then we can't talk to each other without others understanding," whined Mae with a playful frown.

"That's never stopped you before with other Drakken speakers around. If anything it encourages you."

Mae stuck her tongue out at him.

"What are you two doing out here?" asked Raffel, pushing loose strands of hair out of his face.

"I'm showing Blāzzer around Palator," replied Mae.

He nodded, looking to Blāzzer. "What do you think so far?"

"I like it here," she answered. "It's simpler here, but in a good way. When I was in Maro, I heard that the fields around Palator are full of wildflowers so I'm excited to see that."

"Well, when they've bloomed we can go out onto the hills," smiled Mae. "I can show you how to dry and press the flowers. And I can show you how to braid them into your hair." She looked to Raffel. "She can practice braiding flowers into your hair!"

"Why not your hair?" he asked, drinking more water.

"I have to show her how to braid the flowers into hair and that's hard to do on my own hair."

Raffel looked to Blāzzer and she smiled, excited at the idea of learning how to braid flowers into hair. He sighed and slowly stood up, saying, "I need to get back to work. I'll see you tomorrow morning at the library, Blāzzer. You two have a good day." He walked away from them before shifting.

Mae led Blāzzer back through the trees and questioned, "So, what do you think so far?"

Feeling warmth in her chest, the older girl replied, "Honestly, I feel happier than I have in a long time."

The next day Blāzzer left the house early, walking down the streets in the weak sunlight. Clouds had rolled in overnight, blocking out the warmth of the sun.

She walked into the library and wandered around, thinking, *I've always been good in my studies, but I'm still nervous. Don't know if it's because he's a dragon or just everything in Palator is still so new.* She found him seated at a table near a window, writing in a notebook with a charcoal pencil. As she approached, he looked up.

"Morning," he greeted, indicating for her to sit across from him.

Blāzzer sat down and noticed the writing in the journal wasn't the common tongue. She asked, "You like to write?"

He shrugged, saying, "Notes... for your patron."

She nodded.

"Are you adjusting all right?"

"Yeah. Angel and Mae have been working hard to ensure that."

"Good... They're kind people."

Again she nodded.

They sat there for a moment in silence before he asked, "Do you have any questions for me before we get started?"

She pressed her lips together, trying to think of a question, and asked the first that came to mind, "How old are you?"

"Twenty-two."

"Where are you from? Mae told me she came from the south."

"I'm from Keeko in Wildwood Forest. My family lives out there and I came here to get some breathing room."

Blāzzer nodded slightly, thinking, *I haven't even heard of Keeko*, before asking, "What will we be going through today?"

"Today is just for me to figure out what you know," he explained, rubbing his jaw. "We'll start with the formation of Nickada and work up to recent history. Then current politics. I assume you don't know Drakken, the language of the dragons." Hope seemed to flicker in his eyes.

"I never learned any to my memory," she replied, shaking her head thoughtfully. *Though I'm not for sure why I should learn it.*

He frowned slightly. "What do you know about the formation of Nickada?"

"Originally the races had their own territories and fought over land. Then the dragons came from the west. The dragons allied with the farnircks... Then Nickada was invaded by the dragons' original homeland, but the dragons fought against them. They, the dragons, formed alliances with the other races to defeat the invaders. Through the alliances they formed the Council of Leaders and the first King of Nickada was crowned." She paused for a moment looking out the window where people were passing by. "He was a mortal since the largest population was mortal... I've heard that it was also because as a race they aren't as strong as the others."

Raffel shrugged, saying, "It's more of that they were widespread to most territories. What else do you know about the formation?"

"Not much else comes to mind of key points."

He nodded and jotted down a few notes in his book. Her eyes narrowed slightly.

"Do you have to report everything to my patron?" Blāzzer questioned. *My other tutors rarely took notes for him... at least in front of me.*

Raffel blinked and placed his pencil down before leaning back in his chair, meeting her gaze. His red eyes were like multifaceted garnets. He said, "I report on the progress of your studies, including writing and sword fighting. That's it, just academics. Angel sends simple reports on your health and well-being every other month."

She looked down at the table. "Do you know who he is - my patron?" She looked up at him when he didn't answer. "You know?"

Raffel sighed and said, "You're in good hands. They have your back no matter what... But I can't give you any information."

"They?"

"Did I say they?" he asked with a slight smile. "Anyways, what do you know about the current politics?"

Blāzzer pressed her lips together before saying, "Not much, besides the Council is kind of struggling because some races aren't communicating. In Maro, it's mostly mortals. No racial groups would really visit, so I didn't hear much."

"That's the basic gist of it. You'll meet more of the other races here during the festivals. As for the Council... Relations are strained because of some disputes in the last fifty years. The farnircks won't even send representatives to the meetings and the Sentinel Crows rarely appear."

"That reminds me," said Blāzzer. "The Sentinel Crows aren't a racial group, but they are part of the Council?"

"They're supposed to be a bipartisan group that has the sole focus of Nickada's safety and prosperity. When someone joins the group, that person forfeits any racial ties. So for example, if an elf joins, they aren't allowed to vote or have political say with any of the elven laws or rulings. Any race can join, it just tends to separate them from their own race."

She nodded. "So if a group focused on safety and prosperity won't attend Council meetings what does that mean about the Council?"

"It's unbalanced," answered Raffel. "There is supposed to be a leader of every race: forest elf, mountain elf, centaur, uleakite, rucho, Sentinel Crow, farnirck, and dragon... Except there is no leader of the dragons."

Blāzzer blinked. "But there are dragons."

"A dragon can't be the leader of the dragons." She looked at him in disbelief. "It sounds silly and counterintuitive, but dragons are the strongest race. We live up to a hundred fifty years and have a huge form that can beat out any other race in one on one combat. Since leaders sometimes settle their disputes that way, it was decided at the formation of the Council that a dragon's rider would be the leader of the dragons."

"Are there no riders?"

"There were a few, but now only one. My mother's rider. He's a Sentinel Crow so that cut him from the list."

"You and Mae don't have one?"

"No. Mae isn't old enough to have the ability to create the bond."

Blāzzer's face turned to more confusion.

Raffel explained, "Dragons have to be around twenty years old before they can share their endar with someone else... The endar is the internal energy source that lets us shift. Dragons don't have the same number of benefits as a rider would from forming that bond, so dragons over the centuries haven't been."

"You guys are complex," she breathed.

"Not as complex as Nickada's politics and history," he said with a grin. Blāzzer frowned, narrowing her eyes.

For a few more hours they went through some basic history, politics, and vocabulary of the Drakken language. By the time the sun was high overhead, the clouds had mostly dispersed and Blāzzer felt like her brain was going to burst. As her stomach growled she looked up from jotting down some notes.

"I guess we should stop for lunch," Raffel said, closing his notebook. They gathered their belongings and walked between the bookshelves. "What are you doing this afternoon?"

"Angel said I could help her in the gardens," she replied following him out of the library. "Not for sure where that is though."

"Let me get you lunch and then I'll walk you out there."

"Thank you."

He shrugged as he led her through the streets. People waved to them and she realized how he stuck out like a sore thumb. It wasn't even his fire-red hair, but something that his presence emanated. Smells of cooked meats and bread made her mouth water. They came to a small shop that was busy and

Raffel joined the line, motioning for Blāzzer to follow.

"It's busy," murmured Blāzzer. "I don't want to be late."

"It'll move quick," he assured. "They only serve one type of sandwich per day." She raised an eyebrow and he pointed to the chalkboard above the counter that read:

*winters wheat bread with smoked sheep, goat cheese, tomato, and fresh greens*

"Sounds good," she said and blinked. "I don't have any money."

"I'll cover it. You'll-"

An old man slapped Raffel's shoulder and questioned with a laugh, "Who's your lady friend?"

Blāzzer felt heat flush her cheeks in embarrassment. Raffel's ears folded back before he said, "Don't you have sheep to feed, Sam?"

"Edna's been pestering me about you," the old man said with a gap-toothed smile. "And I don't have to. I have the honor to feed the sheep." With that he walked away, leaving Blāzzer staring at the ground.

"Sorry about that," said Raffel, gently.

She nodded slightly.

"A number of the townsfolk have been wanting me to settle down in hopes I won't move."

Again she nodded.

Once they got the sandwiches, Blāzzer followed Raffel away from the crowd and to a quiet garden. They sat on a bench and slowly ate. After a few moments, she asked, "How long have you lived in Palator?"

Raffel shrugged, replying, "Since I was fifteen, so seven years."

"Why'd you move here from Keeko?"

"I needed some space from family."

Blāzzer looked down at her sandwich, trying to understand his feelings. "Do you and your family not get along?"

"We do, but at the time I just felt like it would be better for me to live elsewhere. There was a lot going on then. Anyways, what do you think of your sandwich?"

"It's good," she smiled. "Thank you for paying. I'll pay you back next lesson."

"Don't worry about it," assured Raffel with a smile.

Once they were finished eating, Raffel led Blāzzer out of the town and towards the gardens. Unlike the fields and orchards, these were smaller patches of land with a low stone wall bordering each. Narrow dirt paths wound in between them along with a few small irrigation ditches. Bees buzzed about the flowers and people worked tenderly alongside them.

When they came to Angel's, Blāzzer smiled as warmth filled her chest. The older woman was sitting on a low stool weeding a row of tomato plants. "Hi, Angel," said Blāzzer.

The Palatite looked up with a smile and asked, "How was your morning?"

"Good," replied Blāzzer. "My brain is tired."

"I'm for sure." Angel chuckled softly. She looked past Blāzzer to Raffel who had started walking away. "Good to see you too, Raffel!" He waved a hand over his shoulder. She turned to Blāzzer. "Well, I have some weeding to do then some seedlings to tend to. You can start over here." She motioned toward some plants near her. "All weeds go in the baskets for the goats."

They worked till the sun was setting overhead. Blāzzer had sweat rolling down her face. She washed the dirt free of her hands before watering the sprouts they just planted. She asked, "Can we come back tomorrow and work? I didn't get to pruning the flowers."

"Tomorrow I need to help with the fields," said Angel, placing her gardening tools in a basket. "I only get to come here every few days. You could come down though and finish up if you'd like." Blāzzer nodded and followed her out of the garden. Angel placed an arm around her shoulders, giving her a gentle squeeze. "Let's go home and make some dinner."

In the morning Blāzzer sat in the living room, pulling on her boots. The house was quiet, since Angel and Lenny had already left for the day. Mae came walking down the hall, braiding her long hair over her shoulder.

She smiled at Blāzzer and asked, "Nervous?"

"I guess," replied the older girl with a shrug. "I've never had sword training before. Besides some basics a few years ago."

Mae nodded, slipping on her boots. "I got us one of the small training rooms, so if you fumble no biggie." She grinned and Blāzzer glared playfully.

"It's expected that I fumble. However, if you fumble no biggie then."

Mae stuck her tongue out before leading the way to the barracks.

The drill yard held numerous teenagers being instructed through stretching exercises. Blāzzer and Mae walked along the barracks wall to an open set of double doors. The large hallway was lined with different wooden weapons, stuffed dummies, and leather padding. Mae handed a wooden sword to Blāzzer and grabbed one for herself before leading the way down the hall. Several of the rooms were open, showing dirt floors and high windows. They walked into one that was smaller than the rest.

Mae said, "We'll start with some basic stretching." They placed the swords against the wall and Blāzzer followed Mae through some stretches.

"How long have you been practicing with the sword?" asked Blāzzer, stretching her arm behind her head.

"About five years," replied Mae. "I didn't start practicing every other day until a year ago."

"Do you want to be a soldier?"

"Not really, but as a dragon I'm supposed to be trained. We have to answer if the king calls on us and since there aren't many of us, we don't have a choice." She trailed off with a shrug. "I want to travel and see more of the world. Have you put any thought into what you want to be? I know Lenny asked, but I just want to check."

Blāzzer stopped stretching and looked at the sky through the high window. "I still don't really know. I've always done what my patron requested."

"There's got to be something," insisted Mae, picking up the swords.

Blāzzer pressed her lips together, thinking, *I'm not for sure. Just want to be different than I am now.*

"Anything?"

"I think I'd like to travel too... and... be more than I am now."

"Well, let's start with training," said Mae, holding out a sword to her. Blāzzer smiled with a nod and grabbed the hilt of the sword.

# Chapter Four

Blāzzer walked alongside Mae as they followed a road within Palator. She thought, *This place is starting to feel more familiar.* She looked to Mae and smiled, saying, "Thank you for letting me come with you for your training."

Mae shrugged, replying, "Most townspeople have come out and watched us at least once, so it's really not that odd."

"I think it's kind of exciting. I wasn't really able to watch you fly when we were traveling here. How does it feel to fly?"

The younger woman smiled softly, looking up at the clouds. "It's freeing... and exhausting. Every time I train in dragon form I have to push my endar to its limits in order to strengthen it."

"So, kind of like a muscle?" asked Blāzzer, shifting her satchel over her shoulder.

"Yeah, like a muscle," answered Mae.

When they got to the town's gate, they saw Raffel leaning against the wall. He walked over to them and said to Mae disinterestedly, "You didn't mention that Blāzzer was coming."

She replied something in Drakken and he narrowed his eyes at her before turning and starting to walk out of the town. She smiled and said, "Come on, Blāzzer, we got a bit of a walk first."

The sun slowly rose as they walked down the road between the fields and orchards. Nearby workers waved at them. Once Raffel, Blāzzer, and Mae were past the outer edge of crops, he led them off the road and along a dirt trail. They climbed a hill and paused at the crest, Blāzzer smiling at the sight of the expanse of green hills and blue sky.

"You can sit in the shade under that tree, Blāzzer," said Raffel, pointing to a tree several meters down the hillside. Blāzzer nodded and slowly picked her way between the grasses and rocks. She glanced over her shoulder, seeing Raffel and Mae talking, before turning and stepping under the shade of the tree.

The lowest branches were just high enough for her to stand upright and the canopy was wide, creating an umbrella of shade from the sunlight. Grass didn't grow around the trunk, leaving dirt and roots. Blāzzer knelt down and pulled a blanket from her bag. She spread it out before sitting down and leaning against the tree trunk.

Raffel and Mae had shifted into their dragon forms and were walking to the bottom of the hill. She was a little over half the size of him and had to trot to keep up with his longer stride. Once in the valley, they turned and faced each other. Mae mirrored Raffel's movements as he moved through various stretches.

From her satchel Blāzzer pulled her notebook and a charcoal pencil. She flipped to the back thinking, *I feel like I should take some notes about dragons.* She looked between Mae and Raffel as he sat back and was slowly rising on his back legs. His wings crooned, holding him steadily upright. The younger dragon struggled to stay balanced as she followed his movements. She fell back onto all fours before trying again.

Minutes past as the dragons continued their stretches until Mae launched into the sky. Her narrow wings propelled her towards the clouds. Raffel jumped into the sky, his tail slamming against the ground, and followed her until they both disappeared into the clouds.

*I don't think I would like to be that high in the sky,* murmured Blāzzer to herself, feeling nervous for Mae. She scooted forward to the edge of her blanket, searching the clouds for any sign of either dragon.

Raffel shot out from the clouds, plummeting towards the earth, with his wings tucked in tight against his sides. A moment later Mae followed behind him. Blāzzer tightened her grip on her notebook, scared to see them crash into the ground. Raffel flared his wings at the last moment, zipping over the grass and up a hillside. At the crest he pumped his wings, launching himself back up into the sky. Mae flared her wings a safe distance above the earth. For a moment she struggled to keep her wings rigid as the air caught in the membranes. Then she flew over the grass and back into the sky.

Blāzzer let out a pent up breath, thinking, *I'll stay here on the ground thank you. Flying ain't for the faint of heart and I would have chickened out before reaching the clouds.* She looked down at her notebook and slowly sketched an outline of a dragon in flight.

As Raffel led Mae through different flight patterns, Blāzzer watched, sketching and noting how they flew. She thought, *Raffel makes flying look easy.*

Nearly two hours past before Mae glided down and stumbled as she landed near to the tree. Her wings drooped into the grass and she held her head low, nostrils flaring. She shifted before staggering into the shade and laying down beside Blāzzer. Her white hair was stuck to her face from sweat and her chest rose and fell as she took deep breaths. Raffel landed and shifted, sweat making his shirt stick to his chest, but not as winded.

"Thank you for bringing a blanket," whispered Mae, grabbing Blāzzer's satchel and putting it under her head.

"You okay?" asked Blāzzer, worriedly.

"Shhh... I sleep now."

"You're taking notes?" questioned Raffel, raising an eyebrow and sitting on the other side of Blāzzer.

"I thought it would be a good idea," she answered, frowning at him.

"Nerd," grumbled Mae. Blāzzer glared at her, but she had an arm stretched over her face.

Raffel leaned over slightly glancing at Blāzzer's notes and asking, "Got any questions?"

She flipped to a different page and questioned, "At what age can dragons change shape?"

"Puberty," replied Raffel, laying back with his arms crossed behind his head.

"Cause puberty ain't hard enough with one body," groaned Mae.

"It's not that bad. The dragon form just takes longer to grow. Normal age for being done growing is twenty-four or twenty-five."

"So you're not full grown?" asked Blāzzer, looking at Raffel. He shook his head. She made a quick note in her notebook. "Are your scale colors hereditary?"

"Yeah," replied Raffel, wiping sweat from his forehead with his hand. "My dad is blackish red and my mom is purplish blue. Then my sister is reddish blue."

"Is there a way to tell the gender of a dragon?" questioned Blāzzer, trying to not blush. "I honestly wouldn't be able to tell, except I know you two in your human forms."

"It's a good question. There really isn't a difference. Just scent."

Mae giggled and Blāzzer and Raffel looked at her.

"I probably shouldn't ask, but what?" questioned Raffel, narrowing his eyes at the female dragon. She grinned at him and said something in Drakken, making his face turn red as he snarled slightly.

Blāzzer looked to Mae and questioned, "What did you say?"

"Oh, nothing," assured Mae, rolling over so her back was to them. Blāzzer turned to Raffel.

"You don't want to know," he grumbled, running his hand over his face.

Blāzzer pressed her lips together and placed her notebook down. She pulled her knees to her chest, lightly wrapping her arms around them. Watching a breeze cause ripples in the grass, she asked quietly, "Did you not want me to come?"

"No, I was fine with you coming," replied Raffel, looking up at the sky through the gaps in the tree canopy. "Why do you ask?"

"You didn't sound very happy about learning I was coming."

"Just wasn't expecting you to come."

She nodded slightly.

Raffel sat up and said, "People tend to struggle with understanding that we're the same person in both forms... or get nervous around the dragon form."

"I was kind of startled the first time I saw Mae and you in your dragon forms," murmured Blāzzer, "but it isn't that odd now." She met his eyes. "I think the dragon forms have their own kind of elegance." Raffel smiled softly and she smiled back, before looking over the hills and feeling warmth in her chest.

It took a few weeks for Blāzzer to notice her strength and coordination with swordsmanship improving. She trained with Mae in a small practice room of the barracks, swinging her wooden sword as she stepped forward. Mae blocked the slow moving sword with her own as Blāzzer repeated the same strike several times.

"I can feel your hits getting weaker," smiled Mae, blocking another strike.

Blāzzer nodded, stepping back and pausing to catch her breath before saying, "Yeah, I'm worn out. My arm is starting to get too heavy to lift above my shoulder." She leaned against the wall and wiped away sweat that was dripping from her jaw.

"Well, I guess we can stop here for today," replied Mae, taking Blāzzer's sword and placing both on a rack. "If we head back now then we should have time to wash up before dinner."

"That sounds good." Blāzzer smiled softly and followed Mae out of the room. "I wonder what Angel is making for dinner."

Mae shrugged.

Noise of other people training echoed through the hall of the barracks.

Some rooms were open with a few soldiers inside training. The pungent smell of sweat and body odor hung in the air.

"So, how are lessons going with Raffel?" questioned Mae.

"They can get long," answered Blāzzer, rubbing the back of her neck and wincing slightly. "He's a good teacher for the most part, but sometimes it's information overload."

"At least the view is good."

"What?"

Blāzzer looked over her shoulder to see Mae standing at an open door. She walked back to her and glanced into the training room. Heat rushed to Blāzzer's cheeks.

Inside the room were straw filled leather bags hanging from the ceiling. A single man trained there, punching and kicking a bag with concentrated purpose. He only wore pants and bandaging on his feet and hands. Sweat covered his chest where lean muscle was defined and accentuated with each movement. His red hair was coming loose from its tie.

Mae giggled, breaking Blāzzer's focus and making Raffel look up. Blāzzer squeaked and quickly stepped back into the hall, pressing her back against the wall.

"You two need something?" asked Raffel with a ragged breath.

"No," replied Mae, smiling. "We were just wondering if you wanted to come over for dinner."

Blāzzer glared at Mae.

"Not today," answered Raffel.

"Like you have plans," retorted Mae, crossing her arms.

There was silence for a moment. "I prefer my solitude in the evening."

Mae rolled her eyes. "You're such a bore sometimes. See you later then." She turned and, passing Blāzzer, walked down the hall.

Blāzzer quickly caught up with her and questioned in a sharp whisper, "What was that?"

"Just trying to help you," said Mae with a sly smile.

"With what?"

"You like him, don't you?"

Blāzzer pressed her lips together, and nodded slightly.

"Really? That was just a hunch!"

"You can't say anything to him," insisted Blāzzer. Shoulder to shoulder, her and Mae stepped out of the barracks into the training yard. The town wall cast the whole area in shadows. "Promise me you won't tell him."

"I won't tell him," sighed Mae exasperatedly. "When did you figure out you liked him anyways?"

Blāzzer shrugged. "He's always been so nice to me and he looks out for me in his own way... I guess I just noticed one day that I had this growing warmth in my chest."

Mae giggled.

"What?" asked Blāzzer, glaring at Mae.

The younger woman grinned. "Doesn't hurt that he looks good shirtless too."

Blāzzer blushed, thinking, *Definitely doesn't hurt.*

The days grew warmer as spring turned to summer. The sun was almost directly overhead as Blāzzer followed Mae and Lenny along the main road away from Palator. Blāzzer and Mae carried baskets over their shoulders as Lenny skipped ahead of them.

"Come on, guys!" called Lenny, looking back at them.

"I don't think our picnic is going anywhere without us," replied Mae. "Especially since we're carrying it.

Blāzzer smiled.

They passed other Palatites working in the fields and orchards, waving to each other as they went by. Blāzzer felt her heart skip a beat as she saw Raffel walking along the road towards them. Dirt and some sweat clung to his clothes.

"Raffel, you want to join us?" asked Lenny, smiling excitedly.

"You haven't told me what I would be joining you for," answered Raffel, nodding to Mae and Blāzzer as they caught up to the boy.

"We're going out to the tree for a picnic," explained Mae. "Going to collect some of the wildflowers."

"I think I'll sit out on it this time. Need to wash up."

"We can just dump some water on you from the well," commented Mae with a wave of her hand. "We packed good food."

"Yeah, meat pies and fruit tarts!" exclaimed Lenny, grinning from ear to ear. Raffel narrowed his eyes at Mae before nodding. "Yay!"

"No one is dumping a bucket of water on me though," muttered Raffel.

"Race you!" yelled Lenny, running off. Mae winked at Blāzzer and ran after him.

*Wait! Don't leave me here alone with him!* thought Blāzzer, feeling panic.

"You want me to carry the basket?" asked Raffel. She blinked at him a moment before nodding and handing him the basket. He easily slung it over one shoulder and started walking down the road.

*Come on, a picnic with all of us won't be bad,* thought Blāzzer. *We've hung out before... with others around... and I've had one on one time with him during lessons. Just not social hangouts really.* She quickly jogged to catch up with him.

"How has your day been?" questioned Blāzzer quietly.

"Alright, repaired some irrigation and fencing," replied Raffel. "Work for me really doesn't pick up until after the harvests."

"What do you do then?"

"Burn the harvested fields and help turn the soil to speed along preparations for the next planting. What about your day?"

Blāzzer shrugged. "It was good, just prepping for this picnic."

Soon they caught up to Lenny and Mae at the edge of the crop fields. Blāzzer smiled at the sight of the hills covered in wildflowers. She stepped off the road and knelt, gently touching the petals of a yellow daisy and thinking, *It's beautiful.*

"Come on, Blāzzer," insisted Mae, grinning. "There are tons more on the other side of the hill."

Blāzzer followed them up the hill, letting her fingers brush against the flowers. At the crest of the hill, she paused in awe at the expanse of wildflowers over the hills. Butterflies and bees flew between the flowers. Mae and Lenny walked to the tree and spread a blanket under its canopy.

"Have you never seen the plains in blossom?" asked Raffel, standing next to Blāzzer and glancing down at her.

She shook her head and, not looking away from the beauty before her, replied, "I haven't been lucky enough to travel outside of Maro before."

"Well, in the future we could take a trip to other places. If you would like?"

Blāzzer smiled and nodded, feeling her heart skip a beat. She led the way over to the tree where Mae and Lenny were seated and setting out their picnic. Blāzzer sat down and Raffel, before sitting, handed her his basket. They set out eight palm-sized pies onto a kerchief.

"Oh, I'm so excited!" smiled Lenny, reaching for a meat pie.

"Hold up," insisted Mae. "There are different flavors too." Her brother looked at her in amazement. "There's chicken, pork, beef, and sheep."

"Um, which one is which?" asked Blāzzer, looking between the pies and unable to distinguish any differences. Mae frowned.

"I would think there would be a scent difference," commented Raffel, crossing his arms.

"We aren't going to sniff check each of the pies," muttered Mae. Blāzzer tried to suppress a laugh.

"Can we just eat?" pleaded Lenny, rocking back and forth slightly.

Mae shrugged, answering, "Let's eat. They'll be good no matter what."

They each took a pie and bit into it. Blāzzer smiled, thinking, *Where have these been all my life? I could have bought so many over the years with my stipend.*

"Why can't I eat these every day?" said Lenny with his mouth full of pie.

"Cause then there wouldn't be pies for anyone else," teased Mae, grinning.

"I agree with Lenny," replied Blāzzer. "I would definitely eat one every day if I could." She turned to Raffel. "What do you think?" He shrugged, continuing to eat slowly. Mae eyed him and Blāzzer frowned slightly. "Do you not like them?"

"They're fine," answered Raffel. "Nothing compared to the one Angel made last year for me."

Mae laughed, "Of course not. Mom makes the best meat pies. We got these from the bakery."

"Angel hasn't made one since I've moved here," noted Blāzzer.

"They're a harvest festival treat Mom bakes," explained Lenny. "She makes a bunch and always gives some away."

"I can't wait for the harvest festival," said Mae, blushing. "Gryphun always comes out for it." Lenny stuck his tongue out at her. "If you keep doing that, your face is going to get stuck like that."

"Yours is going to get stuck like this during the festival with Gryphun here." Lenny puckered his lips.

Mae's face turned bright red in horror. She quickly stood up, saying roughly, "I'm going to go pick some flowers. Blāzzer, comb Raffel's hair out." She stomped away with her shoulders hunched.

"Wait for me," insisted Lenny, jumping up and running after her.

"Go pick your own flowers!"

"But I don't know which ones to pick."

"Any of them will work."

Blāzzer looked to Raffel and, seeing his frown, said, "We don't have to braid flowers into your hair if you don't want to. Just easier to learn on someone else with Mae showing me."

Raffel grunted and turned so his back was to her, teasing, "My hair better look fantastic." She smiled and grabbed the comb from one of the baskets. She knelt behind him as he pulled his hair loose from the tie.

She said, "I appreciate you letting me learn to braid flowers into hair with yours." He shrugged and she slowly began to comb his hair, careful to tease any knots out. "Your hair is so soft, I wish mine was like that."

"Your hair is fine," he replied, watching Lenny and Mae pick flowers.

Blāzzer frowned at the back of his head. "I'd like to cut it short one day. Sometimes with it being long, it feels like too much hair."

"It would look cute short," noted Raffel, making her blush. "Course, if you cut it then you couldn't braid flowers into it."

"They'd just be tiny braids," murmured Blāzzer.

He looked over his shoulder at her. "Why haven't you cut it short?"

She glanced down as she held the comb in her lap before answering, "I don't know... just haven't." She started to comb his hair again as he looked back over the hills. *It's soothing to just brush his hair.* She looked up as Lenny and Mae walked up, both carrying a handful of picked flowers.

"So I was thinking we'd do side braids and join them together in the back," said Mae, sitting next to Blāzzer, and the older girl nodded. "Probably shouldn't put the red flowers in his hair, that would be redundant." Mae picked out some white and yellow flowers from the bundles. The yellow flowers had a soft brown center with broad yellow petals while the white flowers looked like small poof balls. "So you want the stems just long enough to be tucked into the braid, but not too long otherwise they'll stick out."

Mae showed Blāzzer how short to break the stems, before showing her how to start braiding the flowers into Raffel's hair. Blāzzer smiled softly as his ears flinched whenever touched.

Mae questioned, "Why is your hair so soft?" He didn't respond, only twitched his ear in disregard.

Soon Blāzzer braided the hair on the other side of his head, tucking small white flowers and slightly larger yellow ones into his hair. Once the second braid was done, she joined both braids at the back of his head. She used his tie to secure the braid at the end, smiling at the neat braid and flowers.

"That looks really good," complimented Mae, smiling.

"Not too many flowers?" asked Blāzzer, cautiously. Mae shook her head and Blāzzer grinned proudly.

"Am I allowed to move now?" questioned Raffel. Mae patted his shoulder and he stood up, turning to them.

Blāzzer blushed, thinking, *He looks really good with his hair braided.*

Mae laughed, "The girls in Palator are going to be coming after you." Blāzzer looked away, facing downward, and hoped Raffel wouldn't notice her deepening complexion.

## Chapter Five

Soon the first large harvest of the year came in and Palator was preparing for a festival. Different merchants had come into the town to sell their wares, setting up booths and stalls along the streets. Blāzzer walked with Lenny and Mae, looking at the items for sale as the sun climbed into the sky. Lenny stopped at one tent where various daggers were displayed on fine cloth.

The merchant asked, "Did one catch your eye boy?"

"All of them," Lenny replied excitedly, eyes wide. "Did you make these?"

"No, these come from the Green Valley. Some of the finest blacksmiths in all of Nickada up there."

"How much?" Mae stepped up touching Lenny's arm.

"They start at fifty silver," said the merchant, indicating a simple dagger with a leather-wrapped hilt. Lenny instantly deflated.

"It's okay," assured Mae, putting her arm around Lenny's shoulder and steering him away.

"It's only the first day the merchants have been selling so prices are bound to be high," insisted Blāzzer. Lenny nodded solemnly as they continued to move through the crowd. "Let's go get a honey cake. That'll cheer you up."

They sat on the barrack's stone fence, sharing the honey cake, as they watched people come and go through the large gate of Palator. Blāzzer noticed a head of red hair in the crowd.

Before she could say anything, Mae was on her feet on top of the fence waving her hand and yelling, "Raffel! Over here!"

He, along with many other people, looked up at her. He rolled his eyes and made his way over, glaring at Mae who still stood on the fence. She, placing her hands on her hips, smiled down at him as he came up.

"I see you're avoiding work," he said.

"Oh, please," replied Mae, hopping down to the ground. "If you're under eighteen years old you get the week off."

Blāzzer blinked and looked at Mae with concern, asking, "Am I supposed to be working? Angel didn't say anything."

"She asked that you have off since this is your first festival," replied Mae.

Blāzzer smiled. "I'll have to thank her."

Raffel said, "Well, as you three continue to lollygag around, I am-"

"Nereids!" exclaimed Lenny, pointing at a new group that walked in through the gate.

Blāzzer stared at the sight of them, having only seen depictions of elusive race. There were ten of them and they all stood around seven feet tall. From the waist down they had strong horse-like hind legs that were covered in thick fish scales, ending with a foot that had three dense toenails. A five-foot tail with a fin at the end followed them and was held above the ground. From the waist up the nereids looked like a mortal except for their ears that had a ridge that stretched up and back. They wore soft leather and beautifully woven fabrics. Each nereid carried a large basket on their back.

"See a blue dragon with them?" asked Raffel.

"Like a guy with blue and white hair?" questioned Lenny.

"Yeah, that's Tsunami. You see a brown-haired man with them?"

After a moment Lenny replied, "No... Just the nereids and the blue-haired guy."

"I'm going to go meet up with Tsunami," said Raffel, turning away with a wave. "I'll see you three around."

Blāzzer placed a meat pie on the table alongside others to cool. She turned back to the kitchen where Angel was placing the last pie into the oven to cook. The smell of cooked meat, dough, and herbs filled the house. A quiet rumble came from the young woman's stomach and she smiled as Angel looked at her.

"They smell really good," said Blāzzer.

Angel grinned and grabbed a basket from a shelf, saying, "I want you to take one to Raffel." She placed a cloth in the bottom before putting a cooled pie in the basket. "I'm for sure he's waiting for one."

"He mentioned that he likes your pies better than the bakery."

"Good, I'm glad he enjoys them." Angel covered the pie with the ends of the cloth before handing the basket to Blāzzer. "Do you know where he lives?"

Blāzzer shook her head.

"His house is along the south wall, so just keep going south until you can't anymore. Then follow that street. You'll know it's his house by the absence of any decorations or plants outside."

The young woman smiled, thinking, *Yep, that sounds like that would be his house.* She slipped the basket handle over her arm and stepped out of the house.

The streets were somewhat bustling with the sun nearly at its peak. As Blāzzer walked closer to the town square the more crowded the streets became; she was careful to not have the basket jostled from her grasp. She took several different streets to avoid the most crowded ones. The nearer she got to the southern wall of Palator the more excited she became, thinking, *I really hope Raffel likes the pie. I helped make them, so now I can make them in the future for him.* She smiled, imagining her pride in baking one on her own and giving it to him.

Very few people were walking about on the southernmost street. Most of the houses had painted window and door frames, along with potted plants on the porches. Blāzzer chuckled at the sight of the single house with no such decorations. She stepped onto the porch where a single bench stood. A dark-gray curtain was drawn across the front window. She knocked on the door and stepped back. Several moments passed with no response from within. She stepped forward and knocked again, straining her ears for any sound from inside the house. The door opened and Raffel stood there. He wore pants and an untucked shirt, which were both wrinkled. His hair hung loosely around his shoulders. He smiled softly at her as she blushed slightly.

"I didn't mean to wake you," apologized Blāzzer.

"No, it's okay," insisted Raffel. "I should be up anyways." He suppressed a yawn. "Did you need something?"

"Yeah, Angel wanted me to bring this to you." Blāzzer held the basket out to him. He took it and pulled back a corner of the cloth.

He grinned. "She's always so kind to make me one." He met Blāzzer's eyes. "Thank you." She nodded and turned, stepping onto the front porch steps. "Would you like to come in?" She looked over her shoulder at him, feeling her heart skip a beat in excitement. "For lunch? I seem to have acquired some pie."

"I'd like that." Her heart fluttered as he stepped back and she walked into the house. He closed the door, placed the pie on the counter, and opened the curtains. Sunlight filled the little house and Blāzzer looked about. The kitchen was a narrow galley with a small cast iron stove. The round table was stained and worn. Books and papers were stacked haphazardly to one side. The couch faced a small fireplace that looked to be rarely used. Over the mantle was a simple long sword. Through a door by the kitchen was a bedroom and, from what she could see, it needed cleaning.

"I'm going to go get dressed," said Raffel. "Make yourself comfortable. There are plates and cups in the cabinets." He walked into the bedroom and closed the door.

Blāzzer thought, *He lives really simply. I know he makes good money from his work, so I wonder why he lives like this.* She pulled the meat pie out of the basket and placed it on the table. She glanced at some of the papers, noting they were all written in Drakken. After a bit of searching in the kitchen, she found cups and plates.

"Good, you found them," said Raffel walking into the kitchen as she filled the cups with water from the sink. He had changed into clean pants and shirt, which was now tucked in. His hair had been combed and tied back. He opened a drawer and grabbed two forks and knives. "How are you liking the festival so far?"

"I like it," replied Blāzzer, sitting at the table. "It's nice that it's not as grand as the one in Maro. Doesn't feel like I'm going to get trampled."

Raffel nodded and cut two slices from the pie. They both smiled at the aroma of herbs and meat. He put a slice on each plate before sitting, smiling, and saying, "I've never really have had that concern before."

"You're taller and have bright red hair," laughed Blāzzer.

He shrugged.

She took a bite of the meat pie and grinned. "Better than the bakery by far."

He chuckled.

"Were you able to talk to Tsunami?"

His smile faded slightly and he nodded. "Yeah, we talked for a while. He said he'd come by later today to catch up more."

"Must be nice to have another dragon to visit."

Raffel, frowning slightly, shrugged. "Tsunami and I have known each other for a long time. He and his crew come out this way to trade and in the meantime, he checks in on me."

Blāzzer tipped her head in confusion.

"He's just doing a favor for my parents," explained Raffel, rubbing his neck. "Anyways... Have you completely settled into Angel's house?"

She nodded. "Yeah, it's really nice. Loads better than the ward house." She looked down at her half-eaten pie slice. *I feel like I'm actually home when I'm there. Not just waiting in limbo for my life to start. Angel, Lenny, and Mae all love me. They're the family I never had. Lenny and Mae my siblings and Angel my mother. It makes me so warm inside to think of them... But what about Raffel? The feeling I have for him is different. I thought it was just a harmless crush.*

"You okay?"

Blāzzer looked up, meeting his eyes, and blushed. She quickly nodded.

"Looked like you got lost in your head there," said Raffel. She smiled sheepishly.

They finished the rest of their pie slices in companionable silence. Raffel picked up their plates and placed them in the sink. When he turned back, he saw Blāzzer getting the basket together and he asked, "Heading out?"

"Yeah, I should probably get back," she replied. "Thank you for having me stay for lunch." He smiled softly and followed her to the door.

Raffel opened the door and swore in Drakken.

A tall man stood there with short white hair that had blue patches. He grinned and chuckled, "What kind of greeting is that?" He looked past Raffel to Blāzzer and his grin widened. "Hello. Are you Raffel's lady friend?" She blushed and he held his hand out to her. She tentatively reached out and took his hand. He bowed slightly and kissed her knuckles. Blāzzer, shocked, quickly withdrew her hand and stepped behind Raffel.

"She's my friend," growled the red dragon. "You said you were coming over later."

"Thought I'd come earlier to make sure you're taking care of yourself," replied Tsunami.

Raffel pinned his ears back. "I was going to walk Blāzzer home, so you'll have to wait for me to return."

"That's okay. I can sit out here on the porch." Tsunami stepped back and sat on the bench.

Blāzzer quickly followed Raffel out of the house, off the porch, and down the street. She blinked as she realized her hand was gripping his sleeve. Blushing, she withdrew her hand, saying, "You don't need to walk me back."

"I'm sorry for his behavior," grumbled Raffel, looking forward along the street.

Blāzzer rubbed her knuckles where Tsunami had kissed her, feeling the chilliness of his touch.

"I'm also being kind of selfish right now. Need a moment to get my thoughts together and walking you home was a perfect excuse."

"Do you and him not get along?" asked Blāzzer.

"He can be a good person, but he also... He thinks me moving here when I was fifteen was a mistake." He took a deep breath and let it out slowly. "Don't worry about it."

"Raffel." He stopped walking and looked down at her. She clenched her hands into fists, thinking, *I want to comfort him. Give him a hug or something, but I don't know if I should.* "It's okay to talk to me. I'd worry more knowing that a friend of mine is trying to bear something alone."

Raffel suppressed a smile and started walking down the street, saying, "Come on. Let's get you home." Blāzzer frowned and followed him.

By the next morning, all the merchants had finished setting up their booths and stalls. Blāzzer walked alongside Mae down a street as they looked at the different wares. Banners and flags, flapping in the gentle breeze, had been hung up on the different buildings. People were busy carrying wood towards the center of the town and crates of last-minute decorations.

"I wish Gryphun could come out for this," murmured Mae. "Tonight is when the dancing will start."

"Maybe he will come out next year," said Blāzzer, looking at her friend's solemn eyes. "When is the Gilzar summer festival?"

"Not till the end of summer," sighed Mae. "Half the time I feel like when I see him I just want to kiss him... And then the other half I just want to kick his ass!" She held her fist up.

Blāzzer pressed her lips together, suppressing a smile.

"You think I won't do it? I have kicked his ass before because he didn't write me back for two months."

"I'm for sure you did."

"Long-distance sucks, but we'll make it work."

"Why don't you move to Gilzar?"

Mae smiled sheepishly. "I'm poor. I can fly there, but I wouldn't be able to live there either. Since I'm not a Sentinel Crow apprentice they won't let me stay in the barracks for more than a week... Gryphun and I are still young... and I'm not ready to leave home."

Blāzzer blinked and nodded slightly. "I think I get your feeling of not wanting to leave home... I really like living here with you, Angel, and Lenny."

They smiled at each other and continued walking until they made it to the town square. A large bonfire was being constructed at the center and food merchants' stalls lined the perimeter. A group of children ran by with one excitedly yelling, "The dragons are going to fight!"

Mae glanced at Blāzzer and they both quickly took off after the children. Blāzzer did her best to weave in between the people but struggled to be as graceful as Mae. Soon she lost sight of both Mae and the kids. She stopped to catch her breath, looking about for any sign of them.

"You look lost," said Raffel.

Blāzzer looked up at him and replied, "Some kids ran by saying the dragons were going to fight and Mae ran after them. I tried to keep up but got lost in the crowd."

He looked down the road where she was heading. "You're almost there. It's at the barracks." She nodded and he turned to her, raising an eyebrow with a playful smile. "Shall I walk you there so you don't get lost?"

She blushed and murmured, "Maybe." Blāzzer walked alongside Raffel, noting how people seemed to move out of his way without thought as he approached. "Are you fighting?"

"Just wrestling," said Raffel. "It's not often another dragon comes around so I've asked Tsunami to a few bouts to see how I compare."

"You'll do good."

He shrugged.

"Is this one of his ways of checking in on you?"

Raffel grimaced, replying, "Kind of. My combat training was halted when I left Keeko. It primarily affected my skills in dragon form, but I have some shortcomings in both forms in regards to my fighting skills."

"You have Gorvi and the other soldiers here to train with," commented Blāzzer.

"They help, but dragons in human form are still stronger than the average mortal." Raffel rubbed his jaw, continuing quietly, "I just want to prove that I've continued to grow. That moving here hasn't put me behind."

Blāzzer pressed her lips together, unsure what to say. As they came to the barracks, they saw a large crowd had gathered along the yard's fence. Raffel led the way through the crowd to the low stone wall. Some water centaurs stood on the other side several yards away with Tsunami, who turned to Raffel and grinned.

"I was wondering if you'd show," said the older male dragon. He only had pants on, and his skin was tanned a deep caramel color. His hair was just long enough to be caught by the wind.

Blāzzer blinked as his sea-blue eyes locked onto her. She shrank back slightly and looked at Raffel as he took off his boots and shirt. He held his shirt to Blāzzer and asked, "Can you hold this?" She nodded and grabbed the shirt. Raffel turned away, swinging over the fence, and Blāzzer noticed some of the younger women glaring at her. Someone touched her shoulder and she turned to see Mae.

"I was wondering where you went," said Mae with a smile.

"Raffel found me," replied Blāzzer.

"I see." Mae raised an eyebrow, looking at Raffel's shirt in her hands then to the young man who approached Tsunami. Blāzzer looked to them and heat rose to her cheeks, noting how both were honed with muscle and little fat. Raffel was broader than Tsunami, but something in how the older dragon held himself made up for the lack of bulk.

Tsunami stepped forward so they faced each other with a few meters in between them and said, "Best two out of three. Each one to submission."

"Sounds good," replied Raffel, rolling his shoulders. "Whenever you're ready."

Tsunami grinned and they circled each other. He lunged first and people started cheering as they wrestled and grappled. Raffel tried several times to maneuver into an advantageous position, but Tsunami held firm. The older dragon moved to step forward and his foot slipped on the dirt. Raffel immediately had him in a choke-hold. Tsunami patted his arm and they broke apart.

"Seems like you have some beginner's luck," said Tsunami, grinning.

Raffel snarled something back at him in Drakken.

Blāzzer looked to Mae and she translated, "Tsunami purposefully slipped."

Blāzzer turned back to the men that had begun circling each other again and thought, *Come on Raffel! You can do this!* Her fingers tightened around his shirt.

"Whenever you're ready," said Tsunami, holding his hands out from his sides with his feet set apart. Raffel squared himself up with Tsunami and nodded. Tsunami charged forward and Raffel met him head-on. They wrestled, trying to gain an advantage over each other. Tsunami twisted around, throwing Raffel over his shoulder. The red dragon hit the ground, grunting as the air was knocked from his lungs. He slowly got up, but Tsunami didn't give him a chance to attack. Tsunami stepped into Raffel's stride and threw him again, catching his arm.

Raffel slapped the ground and Tsunami let him go saying, "Maybe next round, bud." Tsunami stepped back as Raffel slowly stood back up. The crowd was quiet except for the occasional murmur. Raffel's chest heaved as he tried to catch his breath. Dirt clung to his skin and pants as drops of sweat traced lines down his back.

Blāzzer's hands were tightened into white knuckle fists. Worry gnawed in her chest as she thought, *I know you can do this. Just hang in there.*

"Come on, Raffel," smirked Tsunami. "We don't have all day. As a whelp, you're always allowed to retreat."

Raffel snarled something in Drakken, making Mae wince.

Tsunami chuckled, rocking back on his heels. "Still sensitive. Maybe it's time-"

Raffel rushed forward, lips drawn back. Tsunami, grinning, stepped aside. Raffel swiped at him with his hand, but again the older dragon moved just out of reach. Raffel growled, ears pinned back, and charged again. In a flash of red he shifted. The crowd cried out, many falling back. Tsunami frowned before being enveloped in white light.

"This isn't good," muttered Mae, grabbing Blāzzer's arm.

A dragon, larger than Raffel, stood there. Blue streaks covered his white scales that shimmered opalescent in the sunlight. Tsunami rose onto his hind-legs and Raffel charged forward, his jaws aiming for Tsunami's neck. Tsunami pushed his head away, claws digging into his neck. Raffel, head pinned to the ground, snarled and beat his wings against Tsunami. Tsunami opened his mouth and blasted ice and frigid air across Raffel's back. The younger dragon squirmed and cried out. Tsunami snapped his jaw shut, ending the torrent of winter. He slowly stepped back and both shifted. Tsunami, frowning, said something in Drakken before walking away followed by the nereids. The crowd slowly dispersed, quietly chatting in disappointment and bewilderment and leaving Mae, Blāzzer, and Raffel. He slowly sat up with a trickle of blood running down his cheek.

"I'll go get some water," said Mae, hurrying off.

Blāzzer, feeling a tightness in her chest, jumped the fence and knelt in front of Raffel, asking, "You okay?"

He nodded and went to rub his face.

"You're bleeding."

He grabbed his shirt from her and wiped his face, smearing the blood.

"Here let me get it." She took his shirt and gently wiped away the blood and dirt.

"Thank you," he murmured, meeting her eyes. "I tried winning for you. I wanted to prove I'm good enough."

She blushed and looked away, feeling a flutter in her chest and her mind go blank.

"That's not what I meant... not like that."

She flinched.

Blāzzer quickly got up, dropping his shirt, and walked away, pressing her lips together. She could hear Mae asking Raffel, "Where is she going?... What did you do?" Mae then angrily scolded him in Drakken.

Blāzzer hurried back to the house and ducked into her room. She closed the door and paced about the room, clasping and opening her hands repeatedly. Emotions and thoughts ran through her as quick and turbulent as river rapids, *Does he have feelings for me?*

She stopped at a light tap on the door and Mae asking, "Can I come in?"

"Yeah," replied Blāzzer, sitting on her bed. Mae opened the door slightly and slid in, closing it behind her. She sat on the bed beside Blāzzer.

"You okay?"

Blāzzer shrugged.

"Raffel told me what he said."

She looked down at her hands.

"He's kind of an idiot when it comes to talking to girls."

"Do you think he meant it?"

"What part?"

"About... not meaning it like that?"

Mae answered, "I don't know. He isn't always forward with how he feels. Tends to be pretty stubborn with sharing anything." She looked to Blāzzer. "He has seemed happier since you've come to Palator... if that helps any."

Blāzzer took a deep breath and murmured, "I think I might have a serious crush on him, like falling in love with him."

"Really?" questioned Mae excitedly.

Blāzzer nodded, feeling heat rise to her cheeks and her heart flutter.

Mae giggled. "You two would be so cute together."

"Promise me you won't tell him," demanded Blāzzer.

Mae sighed. "I promise I won't tell Raffel that you have a crush on him... because you'll have to!"

Blāzzer followed Angel and Mae towards the town square, music echoing throughout the town. The sun had set, and lanterns were hung about, casting a warm orange glow. As they came into the town square the flickering flames of a large bonfire in the center created long shadows. People were dancing, laughing, and eating food.

"This makes me miss Gryphun," muttered Mae, glumly.

Angel smiled softly, saying, "Well, you'll just have to tell him how you didn't save him any sweet cakes. I know there are many people that would be happy to dance with you." Mae looked at her mother with a frown and Angel patted her cheek. "I'll leave you two to your own devices. Now, where did that little rag a muffin go?"

Angel walked away leaving them at the edge of the square. Mae smiled mischievously, turning to Blāzzer. The older girl asked, "What?"

"We're going to get you a dance partner," said Mae, grabbing Blāzzer's hand and dragging her along.

"I don't want to dance," insisted Blāzzer with a laugh. "You've seen me in sword practice. I have no coordination."

"Really? Not even with you know who?"

Blāzzer blushed and Mae grinned wider.

"There he is!" said Mae, seeing Raffel across the square.

Blāzzer dug her heels in, stopping Mae in her tracks.

"You okay?" Mae looked back at her.

"I don't think it's a good idea," murmured Blāzzer, feeling her heart flutter.

Mae twitched her ear. "Why?"

"He doesn't like me."

Mae rolled her eyes. "He likes you."

Blāzzer blinked. "How do you know?"

"He at least likes you like a friend and who knows where the future will lead with you two." Realization crossed Mae's face as Blāzzer pressed her lips together. "You've never danced with a guy, have you?"

Blāzzer shook her head.

"Well you are tonight!" declared Mae, dragging Blāzzer again.

When they got to Raffel, he looked between them before saying, "It looks like you kidnapped her."

"Have you danced yet?" questioned Mae, ignoring his statement and letting go of Blāzzer's hand.

Blāzzer thought, *I just want to melt.*

"No," replied Raffel cautiously. "I don't dance."

"So, no one has asked you to dance yet?" asked Mae, putting her hands on her hips.

"A few," he answered with a shrug, looking back out across the crowd.

"Would you dance with me?"

Raffel looked at her, raising an eyebrow. "No."

"What?! Why not?"

"Because if I did then you'd tell Gryphun and he would get jealous. Then next time he came to town he'd bring it up and then he would pester me about it. If he's feeling particularly angsty, then he would challenge me to some sort of feat of physical strength. You would ask me to let him beat me so that you two could get back to-"

"Okay!" cried Mae. Her pale complexion had turned pink. She pushed

Blāzzer towards Raffel. "You two can stay here!"

Blāzzer watched Mae stomp away before looking to Raffel. She blushed as she noticed him watching her. She said quietly, "That sounds like that's happened before."

"Yeah," he replied, turning his gaze to the crowd. "Those two are good together though."

"How long have they been dating?"

He shrugged. "A year at least. They were friends before then."

"Have you ever dated?"

When Raffel looked down at her, he blush grew and she looked away. He replied, "No... haven't found the right person. You?"

Blāzzer shook her head. "Same, I guess. No guy has ever asked me out either."

They stood there quietly for a while, watching the people laugh and dance. After a few seconds, Raffel said under his breath, "Those guys were stupid."

"Huh?" asked Blāzzer, looking up at him, as the crowd burst into applause at the end of the song. She looked back at the people, chewing on her lip. Soon the music started again, this time with a slow tempo. "Would you... be willing to dance with me?" She glanced up at him and he was looking down at her.

Raffel opened and closed his mouth before rubbing his neck, saying softly, "Next year, okay?"

"Yeah," replied Blāzzer, feeling her heart twist in pain. She hugged herself and stepped back. "I'm going to go get something to eat. I'll see you later." She walked away from him, not seeing the pain in his face.

## Chapter Six

Days turned into weeks as Blāzzer continued her training. She was in the library working with Raffel on the Drakken language, writing new vocabulary in her notebook. Pointing to a word, he corrected, "A not e." She frowned and crossed out the word before rewriting it. "Okay, now try writing simple sentences with them. Write out the translation as well."

She worked quietly and diligently as he looked out the window. The sun was setting and could be seen barely over the wall of Palator. She asked without looking up, "Are you coming over for Lenny's birthday?"

"I didn't know it was his birthday," replied Raffel.

"I thought Mae would have said something to you."

He shrugged but didn't say anything.

After a moment she looked up and said, "Will you come? It'd be nice to have you there." He raised his eyebrow at her and she tried not to blush. "It's just a small get-together for some cake."

Raffel glanced out the window and said, "Not today... I have somethings to take care of later."

She nodded slightly, feeling her heart grow heavy.

"Maybe some other time we can hang out. Go ahead and finish the sentences then we'll be done for today."

Blāzzer struggled through the sentences doing her best till they were satisfactory for Raffel. She sat there as he made some notes in his book before handing her notebook back. They walked out of the library together, Raffel saying, "Your grasp on the Drakken language is doing good. Tomorrow we'll work on history."

She nodded.

"I hope you have a good evening."

"You too," she replied, watching him walk away for a moment before heading home.

As she opened the door, Blāzzer called, "I'm home!"

"Ah good!" said Angel from the kitchen, dusting flour off her hands onto her apron. "Can you help me finish making the cake?"

"Yeah, let me set this down and wash up," replied Blāzzer.

Angel smiled and went back to mixing the batter. Blāzzer walked into her bedroom and waved slightly at Mae, who was tying a ribbon around a flat wooden box.

"How'd it go?" asked Mae, smiling hopefully.

Blāzzer sat on the edge of her bed before replying, "He's not coming."

Mae frowned. "I'm sorry."

"He said we could hang out some other time."

"Well, that's good."

Blāzzer nodded, picking at a loose thread on her quilt.

"I know it wasn't what you were hoping for, but it wasn't a complete no."

"I'll be okay," said Blāzzer with a soft smile. "You ready?"

Mae smiled, "Lenny is going to be so excited." Blāzzer nodded and led the way out, stopping at the washroom before going to the kitchen.

"Is Raffel coming?" asked Angel, checking the cake in the oven.

"He isn't able to," answered Blāzzer, tying on a waist apron. Angel frowned slightly. "It's okay - no worries. Anything specific you want me to do?"

"We still need to make the icing."

A little less than an hour later, Mae and Blāzzer worked on setting the table as Angel finished cooking dinner. Blāzzer placed the cake in the middle of the table and Mae poured water into the cups. The wooden box sat on the table next to Lenny's place. Soon the front door opened and Gorvi walked in with Lenny. The boy was glowing, wearing a new leather vest.

"Happy Birthday!" cheered Mae, Angel, and Blāzzer in unison. Angel embraced her son.

"I hope you're hungry," she said, stepping back so Lenny could see the cake and wooden box. His eyes lit up more. "First let's eat dinner."

Everyone sat around the table and started serving the food. Mae asked, "How was your day with Gorvi, Lenny?"

"He taught me how to fight with a sword," exclaimed Lenny, his meal forgotten. "He even let me hold a real sword! It was heavier than I thought it would be."

Gorvi grinned and said, "You did good. Didn't even drop the sword."

"Then we went and fed the horses in the barrack's stable. I got to brush the biggest horse there. Then we went and got me this vest."

"And you look very handsome in it," said Angel, smiling. "Why don't you open your present?"

Lenny quickly untied the ribbon around the box and carefully opened it. He stared open-mouthed and slowly picked up the item inside. He held a simple dagger in a leather sheath. He rotated the dagger looking at the angles of metals and corded rope wound about the hilt. Carefully he grasped the hilt and drew the dagger.

"Be careful when you have it unsheathed," instructed Angel. "It's very sharp." Lenny nodded and looked at how the light caught the blade.

He sheathed it and looked at his mother, grinning from ear to ear and squealing, "Thank you!"

"I'm glad you like it."

Gorvi patted Lenny on the shoulder saying, "I'll teach you how to use it, clean it, and sharpen it. Now let's have some cake."

The library was quiet except for the patter of rain on the roof. Blāzzer watched the water droplets streak down the window panes. There were very few people walking through the town on the mud-filled streets. She looked down at her closed notebook and charcoal pencil then across the table to the empty chair. She sighed, thinking, *This is really unlike him to be late.* Crossing her arms on the table, she laid her head down. *Did someone need his help? Did he get distracted with something? Someone?* She took a deep breath and closed her eyes. Slowly, she began to drift asleep.

"You doing okay?"

Blāzzer looked up as Raffel walked up. She sat upright and nodded.

"Sorry I'm late," said Raffel, pulling off his wet leather jacket before sitting down across from her. "Woke up and my roof was leaking in the kitchen." He sighed and leaned back. "Took a while to clean up and then put the biggest pot under it. Should be good for several hours."

"Will you be able to get it fixed?" asked Blāzzer.

"Yeah, just got to wait till it stops raining. Anyways, I wanted to come here for your lesson. I forgot my notebook, so remind me where we left off on Friday."

Blāzzer flipped through her notebook, saying, "We were talking about the Council and the different leaders."

"That sounds right." Raffel pushed his damp hair back. "So each of the races has their own way of choosing a leader. Some by family lineage, others by voting, and a few by combat. Both elven races use lineage. So the children of the leaders will become the new leaders. Usually, the eldest is the heir, but sometimes one of the younger children becomes the leader. The races that choose their leader by voting are the farnircks and the Sentinel Crows. Each of them has their own form of a council and they choose who leads their race. Then for combat, centaurs, uleakites, and ruchos use this method. Usually, they have a specific time of the year when challengers can come forth."

"The king goes by lineage too, right?"

Raffel nodded.

"Except King Nayax isn't married and doesn't have any children," muttered Blāzzer.

He shrugged. "Apparently he has an heir decided, but hasn't announced who for some political reasons. Also, the king has to accept each leader as a member of the Council. He's kind of like the last line of defense to make sure the leader is fit for the position."

"What about the dragons?"

"Well, we don't have a leader. Used to be democratic way back when there were enough dragons and riders."

"So a rider joins the dragon race?"

"Allegiance wise yes. Unless you're a Sentinel Crow like my mother's rider then you're part of that group instead."

Blāzzer frowned, writing down the information as quickly as she could before any details slipped her mind. There was silence between her and Raffel while she worked. Once she finished writing, she skimmed over the words and looked up at him asking, "What if a leader can't attend a meeting? You said that there were leaders not coming to them recently."

Raffel nodded, replying, "They can either send a representative in their stead or not show up at all. In both cases, the leader loses voting rights on any Council decisions unless the representative has a written vote from the leader. At least if a representative is there then the race's voice can be heard and information taken back. All Council meetings are closed sessions, so no outsiders unless requested by the king."

"Have you ever been to one?"

"A Council meeting?"

"Yeah."

"Once, long time ago. I was thirteen or so... wasn't very fun." Raffel took a deep breath as if trying to rid himself of a bad memory.

*Something happened then*, thought Blāzzer, worriedly.

"Anyways, let's take a look at Drakken, and then that will be it for today. Make it a short day."

An hour passed before the lesson was over. Blāzzer sighed with relief as she closed her notebook. She looked up at Raffel and saw him watching the rain. She asked, "Are you doing okay?"

"I'm fine," replied Raffel, rubbing his jaw. "Just tired... I think you're ready for more independent study."

Blāzzer felt her heart sink.

"You need to focus on your swordsmanship too. I spoke with Gorvi and he'll be training you. You're to meet with him every Monday, Wednesday, and Friday morning at the barracks."

"So we'll only have lessons on Tuesday and Thursday?" questioned Blāzzer, fiddling with her fingers under the table.

"Yeah. That way you have the afternoon to work in the gardens and do your independent studies. I'll be busy the next few months with prepping the fields for the next planting."

She nodded, looking down at her notebook, thinking, *Why do I feel so hurt by this? I shouldn't be taking this personally, but it still sucks. Does this mean we won't be able to hang out? He's kept his distance though since the harvest festival.* She blinked realizing silence was hanging about them and that he was waiting for her to respond. "Okay... sounds like a plan."

Raffel tipped his head slightly, looking at her, before standing up and saying, "Well, I need to go check on my house. Try to stay dry on your way home."

As he walked by, grabbing his jacket, Blāzzer turned and asked, "Do you want to get lunch together?"

He paused, but didn't look back at her.

"Like my first lesson. Go to the sandwich place."

Raffel's shoulders dropped slightly. "Not today. I got things I need to attend to."

Blāzzer watched him go, feeling her chest and throat tighten with each of his steps. She turned and laid her head on the table, looking at the raindrops slide down the windowpane. A tear escaped her eye and ran along her nose. She thought, *It's definitely a wet and dreary day.*

A few days later Blāzzer was helping Angel in the garden. The sun warm on her back, she carefully watered the sprouts that had been planted several weeks before. Angel sat in the shade of an umbrella, stitching holes in some of their laundry. Looking up at Blāzzer, she said, "You haven't said much since you got back from your lesson."

The young woman shrugged.

"Are you feeling okay?"

Again, she shrugged.

"Did you and Raffel have an argument?"

"No," replied Blāzzer, pressing her lips together. "It's nothing."

Angel placed the garment she was working on in the basket with the others and said, "You used to look at him quite fondly. Now I don't see that."

Blāzzer stopped watering the plants and went over into the shade, sitting on the ground next to her. "I liked him... like like liked him... but he doesn't feel the same way."

"Did you ask him?"

"He said it himself during the festival," murmured Blāzzer, leaning her head on Angel's knee. Her heart shuddered and she pressed herself against her adoptive mother.

"I'm sorry sweetheart." Angel stroked her hair. "You'll find someone."

Blāzzer nodded.

They sat there for a while with a soft breeze coming by until Blāzzer said, "He's a nice guy... doesn't talk a whole lot, but he's always kind and patient."

"Raffel has always kept mostly to himself, even when he first came here," said Angel, leaning back in the chair. "It was six years or so ago he came here. Just enough money to stay in the barracks... Worked hard... Bought a little house... But never really connected with anyone. He's always friendly when approached, but nothing beyond normal exchanges. Mae is the only one he connected with... She insisted he teach her Drakken." Angel smiled. "Now she yells at him in it."

Blāzzer smiled softly.

"I think you'll just have to give him time to open up."

The young woman nodded, then asked, "Was it like that with Xavier?"

Angel chuckled, shaking her head, and said, "Xavier was one of those people that could talk to anybody. He'd make sure everyone felt safe. We met through Gorvi primarily, even though we had seen each other in passing in the town. He'd bring me flowers every week... I ignored him at first."

Blāzzer looked up at her in astonishment and asked, "Why?"

"Didn't think I wanted a soldier for a husband... But then when I had the opportunity to build a garden plot, he was right there to help." Angel grinned at the memory. "He did most of the heavy lifting and digging... Made me laugh every day so I decided to give him a chance."

They sat there together listening to the others around working and feeling the breeze on their faces. Then an odd deep sound rumbled across the valley. Workers stopped and looked about. Angel stood up and Blāzzer questioned, "What is it?"

"I don't know," breathed Angel. The sound grew louder and Blāzzer pressed her hands against the ground to stand up and froze.

"There's a vibration in the ground," she said, pushing herself upright.

A bell rang out from the town just before a line of cavalry crested the surrounding hills. Screams and shouts rang out from the people of Palator. Blāzzer watched the horsemen charge towards the town with weapons raised. Her body froze in place.

Angel shoved Blāzzer and shouted, "Run!"

Blāzzer took off with Angel behind her. Other Palatites ran by, all heading for the safety of the open town gate. A large red shape launched from the wall and flew out to meet the riders.

"Raffel," gasped Blāzzer, glancing over her shoulder at the dragon.

"Don't worry about him," insisted Angel. "Keep running!"

The sound of the thundering hoofbeats, screaming citizens, and shouting invaders was deafening. Blāzzer's heart pounded in her chest as the air tore at her throat. She thought, *This can't be happening!*

Angel cried out and Blāzzer turned around. She quickly helped the older woman up from where she had fallen. Angel stepped forward, but her ankle gave out and she fell again.

"Keep going!" shouted Angel, pushing Blāzzer away.

"I'm not leaving without you!" cried Blāzzer, pulling Angel up and putting the older woman's arm over her shoulders. "We go together! A family!"

Blāzzer and Angel met each other's eyes and nodded at the same time. They moved as quickly as they could towards the gate, but soon all the other citizens were ahead. At the sound of near hoof beats, Blāzzer and Angel looked over their shoulders.

Angel screamed, "Run!", pushing Blāzzer.

The young woman, stumbling with tears streaming down her cheeks, took off as fast as she could and hated herself for not being able to fight back. Angel's screams filled the air as the wet crunch of metal on flesh cut them short. Blāzzer looked over her shoulder to see Angel fall onto the road in a pool of blood.

"Angel!" she cried. Her eyes looked up to as the rider charged towards her. She couldn't get in breath to scream before he was upon her. Pain exploded from her shoulder and she fell into the irrigation ditch.

Blāzzer laid there in a trickle of water as it mixed with her blood. She could barely breathe at the pain raking through her body. She whispered, "Angel... Mae... don't leave me.", before blacking out.

# PART THREE

## HEALING A WOUND

## Chapter Seven

Blāzzer listened but didn't hear anything except for her own breath and heartbeat. There was no smell when she inhaled. She slowly opened her eyes and blinked in confusion. All around her was darkness, except she could see herself. She was completely bare and the hairs on her arms stood on end at the chill in the air. She could feel hard, cold ground beneath her feet as she wiggled her toes.

*Where am I?* questioned Blāzzer, wrapping her arms around herself and looking about. *What is this place? Am I dead?* She took a deep breath and called, "Hello!" There was no echo as the darkness swallowed her voice. "Anyone here?!" She felt panic and fear creep up her spine. "Please! Anyone!" Her throat tightened as nothing changed in her surroundings.

Sitting on the ground, Blāzzer held her knees to her chest and wrapped her arms around them. She pressed her face against her knees and rocked back and forth slowly, thinking, *If I'm not dead yet, I'm going to die here... alone and cold.* She took a deep breath and the air rattled in her throat. *Please someone... help me. I don't want to die alone.*

Warmth spread across her arms and Blāzzer looked up. She stared in bewilderment at a floating flame the size of her fist. It hovered just a foot away from her. She watched the swirls of yellow, orange, and red make mesmerizing designs. A few sparks sputtered from the tongues of the fire. They glowed momentarily before joining the surrounding darkness. Those that landed on her felt like tiny hot kisses.

"Who are you?" asked Blāzzer in a whisper. "Are you here to help me?"

The fire bobbed slightly and moved towards her. She reached out a hand and a small tongue of the fire stretched out, touching her, holding her fingers. She sighed in relief at the warmth that moved up her arm. The heat though didn't make it past her shoulder. She shivered at the chill that had settled in her body, making her bones ache.

"Please," whimpered Blāzzer. The fire moved closer and reached out with little arms of flames. The fire sat in her palms and she could feel its weight shift with each movement of the colors in its flames. She hugged it against her chest, letting the cold inside her body crack and fall away. Soon there was only warmth through her body. Blāzzer felt her head rock against her knees as exhaustion pulled her eyes shut. Before sleep pulled her away, she whispered, "Thank you."

Blāzzer slowly opened her eyes. The world around her was blurred and it took several breaths before it cleared. The room smelled clean and of fresh-cut flowers. She stared at a wooden ceiling, lying in a bed. Her whole body resounded a deep, dull ache while her head felt like it was stuffed with cotton. The sound of someone softly breathing near her caused her to turn her head slowly. Mae lay asleep near her in the bed. A quilt lay over her with stitched patterns of delicate yellow flowers. Blāzzer blinked as the design tickled at her memories.

"Angel," she breathed. She and Mae laid in Angel's bed. "Angel." Tears began to trickle down her face as she remembered seeing the older woman fall. "Mom..."

Mae blinked open her eyes and, when she saw Blāzzer, she began to cry. She reached out a hand and touched Blāzzer's cheek, murmuring, "It's going to be okay." Blāzzer turned her head away, looking about the room. A vase of flowers sat on the nightstand along with a sketch of Angel, Xavier, Mae, and Lenny in a small frame. Light filtered through a small gap in the drawn curtains.

"She's gone," said Blāzzer, looking at the dust motes float in the light.

Mae cried out softly, clasping her hands to her chest, struggling to say, "She's gone."

Blāzzer ground her teeth together and tightened her hands into fists under the quilt. The pain that shot through her right arm was almost a relief to the pain in her chest. Slowly, using only her left arm, she sat up. Mae stopped crying and insisted, "You need to rest." The quilt fell away to reveal Blāzzer's right arm tightly bandaged to her chest. The bandages wrapped around her chest, leaving little bare skin. She looked down at her restrained arm. Her fingers hadn't closed into a fist.

"Blāzzer?" asked Mae, sitting up.

"They won't move," breathed Blāzzer. She looked up to the mirror above the low dresser. Blood had seeped through the bandaging on her shoulder coming from her back. Blāzzer quickly pushed herself out of bed, falling to the ground. A jolt of pain tore through her body, making her cry out.

"Blāzzer!" yelled Mae. Mae dropped to her side and tried to help her sit up, but Blāzzer pushed her away. "You need to rest!"

"Leave me alone," growled Blāzzer, trying to get her numb legs to obey her. *I have to... I have to save Angel.*

The bedroom door opened and Raffel ran over. He knelt in front of her, placing his hands on her cheeks, and said, "Stop." Blāzzer blinked at the fear in his eyes and stilled. "You need to rest." She looked to Mae then back to him.

"She's gone," whimpered Blāzzer pressing her face against the ground. She felt a warm hand grip hers and she looked up at Raffel.

"We're still here," he murmured. She laid her head down as the world darkened around her.

Blāzzer woke up to the sound of talking and looked about, seeing that she was back in Angel's bed and alone. She couldn't make out what the voices were saying, but soon they were gone. She stared at the ceiling, tracing the wood grains with her eyes and thinking, *I couldn't save her. I couldn't do anything to save her... and now I'm broken.*

The door opened and Raffel walked in carrying a bowl and a cup. When he saw her eyes open, he asked, "Do you think you can eat?"

She nodded and slowly sat up as he perched on the edge of the bed next to her. He placed the cup on the nightstand and held the bowl out to her. Blāzzer stared at the creamy soup with potato chunks but didn't reach out for the spoon sitting in the soup. She hugged her bandaged arm to her chest and thought, *I don't deserve this kindness. I couldn't save her.*

Raffel picked up the spoon and held it to her lips, saying gently, "Eat."

Slowly, Blāzzer ate as he fed her, not tasting the soup as she swallowed it. When it was all gone, Raffel placed the bowl on the nightstand, saying, "It's going to be a long recovery." Blāzzer looked at him, but he was looking at the ground. "Most of your shoulder was shattered." Slowly she laid back, looking at the wood grains of the ceiling. She felt like her body and heart were wrung dry. "Rest as much as you can." He stood up, grabbing the bowl and walked to the door.

"Wait," she croaked. He stopped in the open doorway. "What happened? Who were they?"

"They're gone," he replied and left, shutting the door behind him. Blāzzer felt the pain in her chest swell and she cried.

A few hours later, Mae and Raffel came in with Mae carrying a basket of clean bandages and Raffel carrying a stool. Blāzzer sat up and looked between them, thinking, *Why won't they just leave me? Can't they see I'm broken... that I couldn't save Angel.*

"We need to change your bandages," explained Mae, placing the basket down on the end of the bed. Dark shadows lingered under her eyes. "Your chest has a wrapping around it beneath the bandages. The other healers are busy, and it'll go quicker if Raffel helps."

Blāzzer nodded, barely registering her words.

Raffel placed the stool near the bed and held his hand out to her saying, "Let me help you up." She took his hand and did her best to stand up, but her legs were still very unsteady. He helped support her as she shuffled forward to the stool. "If at any point you are uncomfortable with me being here, just let me know and I'll leave." Nodding, she sat down before watching Mae and Raffel in the mirror as they slowly unwound the bandages.

Mae said, "Do your best to hold your arm in place."

Blāzzer winced at the pain caused by any jostling. Soon they were down to the last bandage and she hissed between her teeth as she could feel it pull at her raw wounds. Even with her breasts covered in a large linen wrap, she felt bare and exposed. She looked over her shoulder and quickly turned away. Trying to swallow the lump in her throat, she breathed, "That looks bad."

"It's looking better than it did," replied Raffel, carefully pulling off some cotton padding. "There's still some swelling, but mostly just the bruising." Mae applied an ointment over the stitches before replacing the cotton padding. Slowly they rebandaged Blāzzer's shoulder, securing her right arm to her chest. Mae gathered up the soiled bandages in the basket and left the room.

"How's the pain?" asked Raffel. "I can get you some medicine." She nodded and he left, returning with two cups. "It tastes pretty bad, so wash it down with this." She quickly drained the pungent liquid from the first cup, grimacing at the bitter taste.

"Thank you," coughed Blāzzer and drank the water from the other cup.

For several more days, she rested, never leaving the bed. In the middle of the night, Blāzzer woke with no one around and the world silent. She reached out for the cup of water on the nightstand and realized it was empty. Slowly she sat up, swinging her legs over the edge of the bed. A single low-burned candle illuminated the room in an orange glow. Pressing her feet firmly on the ground and using her left arm for support, she carefully stood up. She slowly walked to the door, holding herself upright with her arm against the wall. She opened the door and saw that the rest of the house was dark and quiet. Carefully she walked down the hall, leaning against the wall, and into the kitchen. She went to the cupboard and grabbed a mug. It clanked against the clay sink as she placed it in before pumping water. Slowly, she drank the water, leaning against the counter to stay balanced.

"You shouldn't be out of bed," said Raffel.

Blāzzer blinked, almost dropping the cup. A candle ignited next to the couch and he sat on the couch looking at her. A pillow and blanket were there with him along with books and a sword.

"You're staying here?" she asked, placing the cup on the counter and staggering over to him.

"You should go back to bed," insisted Raffel, standing up. Blāzzer sat on the couch and he looked down at her. "Shall I carry you back?"

She hugged herself, unable to meet his eyes. "I don't want to be alone."

He slowly nodded before saying, "Sleep on the couch. I'll grab a pillow and sleep on the ground here." As he walked down the hall Blāzzer laid back, pulling the blanket over herself. The couch and blanket were warm from his body. Raffel came back with a pillow and another blanket, tossing them to the ground in front of the couch where the rug was. He blew out the candle and laid down on the floor. She stared up at the darkness, listening to his breathing.

"Were you hurt?" asked Blāzzer quietly.

"Just some scratches," replied Raffel, tiredly. "Try to get some sleep."

"That's all I've been doing." *And I hate it. I can't do anything like this.* She blinked as he put his hand on her shoulder. The warmth emanating from him was soothing.

"The more you rest now, the better you'll feel soon... Try to be patient and kind to yourself right now."

Blāzzer pressed her lips together, feeling tears well in her eyes.

Blāzzer blinked at the morning light that filtered through the yellow curtains. Her body felt heavy as she stared up at the ceiling till her eyes focused on the wood grain. The sound of a page being turned made her look to where Raffel sat on the floor against the couch. He was reading a book with his ear twitching every so often. She reached out with her left hand and ran her fingers through his hair. He froze, fingers tightening on the book.

"Thank you for letting me sleep out here with you," murmured Blāzzer. He nodded and as he opened his mouth to speak a knock sounded on the front door.

Raffel turned his head quickly to the door, brushing his cheek against her hand before she could withdraw it. The knock came again and Raffel stood up. As he went to the door Blāzzer sat up, watching him. He opened the door slightly and a Palatite stood there.

Raffel asked, "What is it?"

"There are men here from the capital," answered the Palatite. Dirt covered his clothes and his sleeve had dried blood on the hem. "The one called Captain Teredana wants to speak with you immediately."

"Give me a minute to get ready and I'll be right there." With that Raffel, frowning, closed the door and walked back into the living room.

"Who is he?" questioned Blāzzer. "Are they here to help?"

"Captain Teredana is in charge of the king's personal army, the Lemay Army," replied Raffel, looking at her. "I'm hoping they're here to help." He sat on the far end of the couch and pulled on his boots. "Stay here, I'll be back as soon as I can. Wake Mae if you need anything." He grabbed his sword and left without glancing back. Blāzzer hobbled over to the window and, pushing back the curtain slightly, watched him and the Palatite walk down the street towards the main gate.

"Who was that?" yawned Mae, walking down the hall in a nightgown.

"Raffel was called to meet with Captain Teredana from the capital," replied Blāzzer, glancing at the female dragon. "Told us to stay here and that he'll be back as soon as he can."

Mae nodded and went to the cabinets in the kitchen, murmuring, "I'll make some breakfast while we wait."

"Where's Lenny?"

Her strides paused for a moment. "Staying with Gorvi... He didn't want to come back into the house."

Blāzzer nodded and shuffled back over to the couch.

"You seem to be walking good," said Mae, spreading some jam on bread. "Raffel feels pretty bad about your shoulder. He's been blaming himself."

"Why?" questioned Blāzzer, sitting on the couch and pulling the blanket around herself. *It was my fault. I couldn't fight.*

Mae walked over with a plate of bread and cheese, placing it on the coffee table. Sitting on the couch beside Blāzzer, she said, "He was the first one out there to defend. He didn't breathe fire cause he wasn't for sure if anyone was hiding in the fields or orchards."

"I don't blame him," insisted Blāzzer, picking up a piece of jellied bread. "I choose to help Angel."

Mae nodded and after a moment she whispered, "Thank you... for staying with her."

An hour later the front door opened and Raffel walked in. Blāzzer and Mae stared at him as he placed his sword down on the table. He looked to Blāzzer and Mae on the couch, saying, "Teredana is coming over very soon. Mae, find Blāzzer a tunic that'll fit over her arm."

Mae grimaced before walking down the hall and Blāzzer asked, "What does he want?"

"To talk to you, Blāzzer," replied Raffel.

Mae shouted something down the hall in Drakken. Raffel pressed his lips together before shouting back. He huffed a sigh and rubbed the back of his neck, baring his teeth slightly. She came back down the hall with a tunic and helped Blāzzer put it on.

"Just tell Teredana the truth and everything will be fine," assured Raffel, pulling out a chair. "Come sit over here." Blāzzer shuffled over, feeling her heart beat faster and struggling to keep her hands from trembling.

"What should I do?" asked Mae, looking to Raffel. When he didn't answer, she said something in Drakken.

"Stay in your room," he replied. "Don't come out unless told so." She nodded and started to walk away. "Also, if they ask, you don't know." Again, she nodded and went to her room, shutting the door behind her.

"You're making me nervous," murmured Blāzzer, a lump forming in her throat.

Raffel met her eyes and said, "It's going to be okay... I promise."

At a knock on the door, Raffel opened it to let in a man, who wore metal chest armor with Nickada's insignia of a rearing bear.

The man questioned, "Are you Blāzzer Ozol?"

She nodded, wanting to be anywhere but in the same room as him.

"I'm Teredana Kretin, Captain of the Lemay Army," the man said, sitting down across from Blāzzer. Raffel closed the door and sat down next to her. "You were injured during the invasion?"

"Yes," she replied, trying to read the captain's face, but struggling to. He seemed young, in his late thirties, but weathered with experience. Scars crisscrossed his hands as he folded them on the table.

"Can you describe them? The injuries?"

"Shattered shoulder blade... Injured muscles and tendons... Broken nerve connections... I can barely wiggle my fingers."

"Who was your healer?"

Blāzzer glanced at Raffel and then back to Teredana. "I don't know... I never asked. Mae and Raffel have been changing my bandages since I woke because the healers are occupied with others."

"And they haven't brought in a healer to double-check your wounds? Even with how severe they are." The captain's eyes narrowed for a moment.

She shook her head, hugging her arm through the tunic.

Teredana sat back and said, "As a ward, you have the opportunity for proper health care. There are healers in Stiggress who could see to your wounds, ensuring you the best possibilities with your arm. I and a few of my soldiers will be returning to the capital soon to report to the king, we could take you with us."

Blāzzer felt Raffel tense even though there was no visual cue. She looked down at the worn table, feeling the fingers of her right hand twitch slightly, and said, "I'd prefer to stay here." She took a deep breath and met Teredana's eyes. "This is my home. I'll do the best here that I can even if it means I don't have full functionality of my arm."

Teredana sighed and questioned, "You would choose this place? A place where you've been less than a year, over the chance to make the best recovery."

"Captain Teredana... I don't mean any disrespect, but this is the first place that has felt like home to me. I don't intend to leave it."

Teredana looked to Raffel and said, "You haven't told her."

Raffel closed his eyes and whispered, "No, I haven't."

"Understand that I tried to make this go easy," said Teredana and the dragon nodded solemnly. "Tell her."

Blāzzer looked to Raffel then to Teredana, questioning, "Tell me what?"

"You need to go with them," murmured Raffel, meeting Blāzzer's eyes. She opened her mouth to say something, but he continued, "If you refuse, it'll be worse."

"Why?" she demanded, feeling a spike of panic tighten around her heart. "Unless my patron tells me directly, I am allowed to choose where I stay and what I do. That is the agreement!"

"Blāzzer," breathed Raffel, sounding exhausted and defeated. "I-"

"Your patron is no longer your patron," said Teredana sternly. Stunned, Blāzzer looked between them. "King Nayax is your patron now and by his order, you are to be brought to Stiggress at once."

Blāzzer stood up quickly, toppling the chair beneath her and slamming her good hand on the table. She snarled, "I am not leaving! This is my home!"

Teredana looked up at her, not phased by her outburst. He turned to Raffel and ordered, "Have her things ready by tomorrow morning. I'll be by then to pick her up." The captain stood up and looked to Blāzzer. "I suggest you rest up. It's a ten day ride to the capital." Teredana turned and walked out the door.

Blāzzer turned to Raffel, feeling rage color her cheeks red. His face had lost most of its color. She demanded, "What are you not telling me?!"

"Blāzzer go rest," he insisted, slowly standing up.

"No! Not until you tell me what the hell is going on." Grabbing his arm, she bared her teeth at him with tears rolling down her cheeks.

"He broke the agreement," murmured Mae. Blāzzer turned to her, where she stood at the end of the hall. Mae's eyes were red from crying.

"What agreement?" asked Blāzzer, quietly.

"The agreement that kept you in the care of the Sentinel Crows," answered Raffel. "The agreement that stated you'd be free to do as you want on your twentieth birthday... given that certain requirements were met. One of them not being in contact with any dragons until eighteen... and the other not being a rider of a dragon until you were free."

"I've never heard that clause before and I'm eighteen," breathed Blāzzer, looking between Mae and Raffel.

"You're not twenty though," whispered Mae.

"What?" questioned Blāzzer, disbelief making her freeze. *No, I can't be!*

Raffel sighed and said softly, "You're my rider."

Blāzzer couldn't speak. She just stared at his face hoping to see he was lying, but she could see he wasn't. She barely asked, "Why me?"

"Your arm would have been amputated if you even lived through the blood loss." His hands tightened into fists as he struggled to withhold his grief. "I'm sorry... I should have talked with you beforehand... but you wouldn't wake." Raffel sank to his knees in front of her, pressing his forehead against the ground. "I'm sorry."

"Why didn't you tell me?"

"So that you could answer honestly... I had hoped that it may have gone unnoticed, but the injuries were too great to just have overcome in this short of a time." He slowly sat up and met her eyes. Blāzzer could see the tears in his eyes. "I promise everything is going to be okay. I will go with you to Stiggress."

"What about Palator?"

"We'll be okay," assured Mae, holding her chin up. "We're a strong people."

Blāzzer nodded slowly, turning and shuffling down the hall. She felt weak as she went into Angel's room, shutting the door behind her. She leaned against the door and sank to the ground, crying. *I didn't ask for any of this,* she thought, hugging herself. *I was so close to freedom... and now it's gone!*

Blāzzer laid in Angel's bed on her good shoulder, hugging a pillow to her chest. Her eyes were dry from her crying, but her throat was still tight. She thought, *I didn't ask for this. I didn't ask for any of this. If they had amputated my arm, I wouldn't have to leave. Wouldn't have to leave my home... If they hadn't amputated my arm, I may have not made it. I may have died.* She felt nauseous at the thought.

There was a knock on the door. Blāzzer didn't look up as the door opened and closed with a quiet squeak of the hinges. Mae walked over and sat on the bed with her back against the headboard and hugging her knees to her chest. Blāzzer's back was to her.

"I can't imagine how you feel," whispered Mae, looking down at the floral designs stitched on the quilt. "I'm sorry this is happening to you." She sniffled, wiping at her eyes with the back of her hand. "If I had been old enough, I would have given you my endar... but I'm not. I know that would mean you would still be leaving. But when they found you, a healer had bandaged you the best they could. You had bled a lot and were so pale. I had already learned that Angel had been killed... and I couldn't lose you too." She took a deep trembling breath. "So I found Raffel and told him you had been hurt. I was ready to beg and plead with him to save you, but I didn't have to. I've never seen him so determined. He went to you immediately and gave you part of his endar. Afterward, he could barely stand. Once you were stable, he sat by your side, holding your hand. He talked to himself really quietly in Drakken and I think he was talking to you. He slept on the ground next to you even. In the morning, he carried you here."

Mae looked to Blāzzer, pressing her lips together. Slowly, Blāzzer said, "I don't know how to feel about all of this... I'm glad I'm alive, but everything is so out of my control. I can't do anything right now to change my path." She rolled onto her back so she could see Mae. The young dragon laid down so they were eye level. "I'm really scared."

"I know," murmured Mae, touching Blāzzer's cheek gently.

"I don't want to leave. This is my home."

"It'll only be for a little while. You can come back. We'll be here waiting for you."

Blāzzer looked at the ceiling, thinking, *I want to believe that I'll be able to come back... but I don't even know if I can.*

## Chapter Eight

When morning came, Mae came in and changed Blāzzer's bandages. Mae helped her dress so that her arm was strapped to her chest on the outside of her tunic. Blāzzer touched the floral design that was stitched into the hem.

"Angel was working on it for you," said Mae, collecting the soiled bandages.

"It's beautiful," murmured Blāzzer, looking to her. "I'm going to miss you."

Mae hugged her gently and Blāzzer didn't mind the pain. Mae replied, "I'm going to miss you too." She stepped back. "I'll see you when I can, and I know you'll do the same. I'll help you with packing."

Blāzzer followed Mae into their bedroom. A bag was already placed on her bed. Blāzzer opened her trunk and started pulling out various clothes. Mae helped pack them into the bag, folding each item with care. Blāzzer went to the writing desk and picked up her notebook and pencils. She paused, looking at the book from the library, the fifth book in the folktales of Nickada series.

"Take it," insisted Mae.

Blāzzer looked to her and said, "What about the others?"

Mae waved her hand. "I think it's going to be a while before anyone goes looking for it."

Blāzzer smiled softly and placed them in her bag. Mae tied it shut and said, "Your toiletries are all packed already and are in the living room. I packed some extra lavender soap for you."

"Thank you," replied Blāzzer. "You've helped me out a lot."

"That's what sisters are for," said Mae with a sad smile. She picked up Blāzzer's bag and led the way down the hall.

Raffel, sitting on the couch with a pack beside him, stood up as they entered the room. His hair was tied back completely and he wore a heavy leather jacket with metal bracers. He had his sword tied to his belt and a hand resting on the pommel.

"Are you ready?" asked Raffel, slinging his pack over his back.

"I don't really have a choice," said Blāzzer, pressing her lips together. She turned to Mae and they met each other's eyes. "I guess this is goodbye."

They embraced and Mae said, "It's just see you later." Blāzzer smiled and stepped back. Raffel took the bag from Mae and Blāzzer picked up the satchel on the table.

"It's going to be okay," assured Raffel as Blāzzer walked by him. Mae looked to him and said something in Drakken. Taking a deep breath, he nodded before leading the way out. Blāzzer followed him and glanced back at the house, at the floral designs painted onto the door and window frames. Heart aching, she struggled to withhold a whimper.

The town was eerily quiet as they walked. Palatites, faces hallow and eyes hurt, stopped in the street and looked to them. Many turned, following them down the road. As they approached the gate, Blāzzer saw the crowd of people gathered. There were several soldiers, including Teredana, standing at the center, apart from the others with saddled horses and a few pack horses. Raffel led Blāzzer towards them.

"Please Raffel!" pleaded a woman stepping out from the crowd. "Stay here!" Many others took up her plea and pushed towards the dragon.

Raffel placed his hand on the middle of Blāzzer's back and guided her through the gathering crowd. Captain Teredana stepped forward and took her bag. He tied it to a pack horse's saddle.

"I can take your bags too, Raffel," said Teredana, extending his hand to the dragon.

"I'll keep mine, but this one is Blāzzer's as well," replied Raffel, handing over her other bag.

"Blāzzer, you'll ride with Will," said Teredana, indicating one of the soldiers with short blonde hair.

"I'll help you get in the saddle," said Raffel, walking towards Will. He stopped and looked back at Blāzzer. She stood there looking at the ground. "Blāzzer." She looked up at him, biting her lower lip. "It's going to be okay."

"Blāzzer!"

They turned to see Lenny burst through the crowd. Gorvi raced after him and grabbed his arm. "Blāzzer!" cried Lenny, trying to pry Gorvi's hands away. "Don't go! Please!"

Blāzzer stepped towards them, thinking, *I can't leave without saying goodbye to him... but I can't cry in front of him.*

Teredana stepped in her way, saying, "We need to get going."

"No! Blāzzer!" screamed Lenny.

"Now," said Teredana, firmly. Blāzzer blinked and looked to Lenny then back at Teredana.

"I'm going to say goodbye to my brother," said Blāzzer, holding her chin up and holding his gaze. She stepped around the captain and walked past him.

Gorvi let Lenny go and the boy raced to her, embracing her, and crying, "Please don't go! I don't want you to go!" He buried his face against her stomach, tears soaking her shirt.

Blāzzer held him close, ignoring the pain in her shoulder, and murmured, "I'll be back as soon as I can." She placed her cheek on top of his head as he cried. "It's going to be okay."

"No! It won't be the same!" His sob caught in his throat, making him cough.

Blāzzer took a deep breath and held Lenny at arm's length. "Lenny, I have to go." She wiped his tears away with her thumb. "I promise I'll come back when I can... Promise me that you'll do the best you can here. Palator will need you."

Lenny nodded and rubbed his nose on his sleeve. "I promise."

Blāzzer straightened herself and walked back over to Raffel. Her heart trembled, but she kept her chin up. He helped her get into the saddle in front of the soldier Will. She winced at the pain caused by her shoulder pressed against Will's metal chest plate. She glanced down to Raffel.

"I'll be following you overhead," he assured, stepping back as the Lemay Army soldiers began to ride out with Teredana at the lead. Blāzzer looked back at Raffel as he stood there.

"If you need anything, just let me know," said Will.

"Thank you," murmured Blāzzer, facing forward. She blinked at the sight of the gardens and fields.

They were torn and shredded from horse hooves. Dried blood splattered the fencing and sheds. People, working on cleaning the fields, stopped and looked up at the soldiers as they passed. Many of them saluted the soldiers with a fist over their hearts. Blāzzer looked up to see Raffel flying overhead.

When the sun began setting, the soldiers stopped off the side of the road. The surrounding land was flat with only a few trees stretching upwards. Raffel touched down a safe distance away and shifted as the soldiers began to dismount. He walked over to Blāzzer where she still sat on the back of a horse.

He helped her down as Will held the reins of the horse. She held onto Raffel's arm, waiting for the pins and needles to leave her legs. She could smell him, sweat and the scent of burnt leaves, and she thought, *Why does the smell of him make me want to curl up and sleep?*

"Are you feeling okay?" asked Raffel, looking down at her and gripping her elbow.

"I'm sore," she breathed, wincing at the resounding ache throughout her body. He nodded and guided her over to where the soldiers were setting up a campfire. She sat down heavily, hugging her arm to her chest, and he knelt beside her. He took off his pack and rummaged through it, pulling out a small canister and canteen.

Raffel removed a pellet from the canister and handed it to Blāzzer, saying, "Swallow this. It will take a little bit to take effect, but it should help and last through the night." She placed the pellet in her mouth and took a swig of water from the canteen.

She grimaced and gasped, "That tastes as bad as that tea." She glared at him and he frowned apologetically.

"It is the same."

A shiver ran down her spine and she quickly swallowed more water, trying to get rid of the bitter taste.

"You should rest," said Raffel. "Let us take care of everything and just sit here." She nodded and he stood up, walking away.

Soon the tents were set up, dinner cooking, and the pain from Blāzzer's arm was a faint ache. She sat next to the fire watching the stew simmer, appreciating the warmth of the flames and numbness of the medicine. A few soldiers sat around the fire, talking quietly. She looked up as Raffel sat down next to her, their shoulders almost touching.

"I've set up a tent for you," he said, indicating to one away from the others. It was only large enough for a single person while the tents the soldiers had set up were doubles. "I thought you might appreciate the privacy."

"Thank you," said Blāzzer, with a soft smile. "What about you? Where will you sleep?"

"I'll sleep in dragon form... it'll be safer that way."

"Don't trust our skills?" questioned a soldier stirring the stew. The dragon's ear twitched as he looked up.

"I don't trust your senses," answered Raffel.

After dinner Blāzzer got up and slowly made her way to her tent, leaving the soldiers at the fire. She ignored the twinge in her chest as the group broke into laughter. She ducked under the tent flap and was surprised to see that a bed roll and blanket had been laid out. Her bags sat in a corner alongside Raffel's. Slowly she sat down on the bedroll, staring at her feet. Pulling the blanket around herself, she thought, *I won't be able to put my boots back on by myself if I take them off.* Footsteps approached and through the tent wall red light could be seen for a moment. In the firelight, Raffel's shadow fell over the tent as he laid down beside the tent.

Blāzzer blinked at the warmth that came through the wall and relaxed more. Quietly she said, "Thank you for coming with me."

Blāzzer sighed in relief when the group stopped for lunch by the Snake River. Will helped her down and she stumbled for a moment as her legs tingled. Raffel landed next to the river, tail dragging in the water, and she walked over to him. The water-worn pebbles along the shore shifted under her feet. Sunlight glittered on the wide surface of the river.

Raffel reached out his head toward Blāzzer, saying, "Be careful. Don't need you to fall."

"I'm fine," she insisted, picking her way across the shore and sitting on a large rock by his head. The air was cooler by the water, a respite from the heat of the plains. "You're not going to shift?"

"No, I'm going to fish. I need to get some energy back. If you need anything while I'm under, ask the soldiers."

Blāzzer frowned and looked over her shoulder at the men. They were passing out bread and salted pork. She felt uneasy at the thought of being left alone with the Lemay Soldiers. She turned back to the river and watched as Raffel waded into the current. He dove under the surface with his tail disappearing last, water too murky to see him swimming.

The rocks crunched underfoot and Blāzzer looked up to see Teredana. He handed her some food before sitting on a different rock and saying, "Will mentioned that you've been quiet during our travel."

She shrugged and bit a chunk of bread off, thinking, *Yes, because I don't want to talk to any of you.*

"Is your shoulder feeling okay?" She nodded. He pressed his lips together in frustration and glanced at the river. "You and Raffel seem like good friends." She looked uneasily at the captain, meeting his eyes.

When he didn't continue, Blāzzer said, "He looks out for me."

They sat there quietly, listening to the river and the soldiers. Blāzzer slowly ate the rest of her lunch, thinking, *I don't trust Teredana. I know he's just following orders, but I still don't trust him. If I say the wrong thing, would they take me away from Raffel?* Her stomach twisted slightly, her lunch sitting heavy, and she hugged herself.

Large bubbles erupted from the middle of the river. The top of Raffel's head surfaced and he flared his nostrils. As he neared the shore his head rose above the water. In his jaw was a large catfish, thrashing about with its mouth gasping. The dragon's pupils were narrowed and his flanks heaved as he breathed. The soldiers whistled and cheered at Raffel as he stepped onto the shore. Slamming the fish's head against the rocks with one shake of his own, the men went silent. The catfish went limp and Raffel set it down. He snorted, spraying water, and turned so his back was to the others. In a short minute, the catfish was devoured, only leaving scales and a smear of blood. Raffel dipped his snout into the river before turning back to the shore. His eyes focusing on the Lemay captain.

Teredana slowly stood up and said, "We'll be moving out in twenty minutes." He walked back to the other soldiers.

Raffel laid down, tucking his wings against his sideS and looking to Blāzzer. He asked, "Did you get something to eat?"

"Yeah," she replied. "Teredana brought me some." He looked past her to the soldiers, his ears moving back slightly. Using only her good hand, she kicked off her boots, tugged her socks off, and rolled her pant legs up.

"What are you doing?" questioned Raffel as she stood up. Holding her arm out for balance, she walked over the rocks towards the river.

"I just want to get my feet wet." Blāzzer teetered a moment as the rocks shifted under her feet. Raffel stretched his neck out till his head was by her side. She could feel his warm breath around her. She pressed her hand against his muzzle to steady herself. "I'm not going to fall over."

Raffel flicked an ear and she stepped into the shallow water. The current tugged at her ankles, the coolness caressing her skin. She sighed and wiggled her toes, digging them into the sand. Her eyes closed as she listened to the river and felt her heart slow. At a shout from one of the soldiers, Blāzzer's heart skipped a beat and she looked over her shoulder.

"You're okay," assured Raffel pressing his muzzle against her hand. "We're not leaving yet. They're just arguing about food."

"You can hear them?" asked Blāzzer, looking into Raffel's eye, and blushed slightly. The lighter shades of red glittered and swirled in his iris.

"Yeah, I can hear a lot in this form."

Blāzzer pressed her lips together. "Can you hear my heartbeat?"

He tipped his head in acknowledgment.

"What about your other senses?"

Raffel twitched his ear and replied, "Touch doesn't change, though things feel different through a layer of scales. Like I'm wearing a heavy jacket. My sight is better. I can see much farther, and in good detail. Taste and smell are very advanced in comparison. It can be overwhelming at first if there are a lot of new smells."

Blāzzer nodded thoughtfully and ran her thumb over his scales absentmindedly.

"You should probably go to shore so your feet can dry."

She sighed, turned, and stepped out of the river. Raffel's breath followed her as she walked across the pebbles and stones. She grabbed her boots and sat on the rock with her socks. She laid back on the rock, enjoying the warmth radiating from its surface. He laid down next to her and slowly tried to stack pebbles using his foreclaws. Blāzzer watched as he carefully adjusted how his claws held the stones. His forepaws were structured like hands with an opposable thumb and each digit had a large, curved claw. When he tried to place the fifth pebble, the small tower toppled with a clatter. Raffel pinned his ears back for a moment before starting over.

*I wish we could stay here for a while,* thought Blāzzer. *Or just go back to Palator.* She watched the small stone tower reform. *But I wouldn't be getting to know him as much.* She looked up to Raffel's head. His eyes were focused on the pebbles. *Did he choose to come to Stiggress because he feels guilty? Or because he wants to make sure I'm okay?* She sighed and placed her good arm over her eyes.

"Blāzzer! Raffel! Let's get ready to move out!" shouted Teredana from where the soldiers were gathered.

Blāzzer groaned as she sat up, feeling a twinge of pain in her shoulder. She picked up her socks and looked down at her feet with a frown. Raffel shifted and knelt down in front of her, holding his hand out.

"You don't have to," said Blāzzer, handing him her socks.

"I have a feeling it will take you longer than Teredana wants to wait," answered Raffel, pulling one sock over her foot. His hands were warm against her skin and she looked away, hoping he didn't see her blush.

Blāzzer sat with her back to the front of her tent, holding her shirt in her left hand. A morning breeze tickled her bare lower back and a shiver ran up her spine. Raffel sat behind her, outside the tent, and carefully began unbandaging her shoulder.

"There are only enough supplies to change your wraps three more times before we get to Stiggress," he murmured. She gritted her teeth and nodded, helping him with the bandages over her chest. His warm fingers grazed her skin when he loosened another stretch of fabric. "I'm sorry Mae isn't here to do this."

"It's okay," breathed Blāzzer. She winced as the final bandage came off and air hissed between her teeth as Raffel pulled the soiled gauze off. "How does it look?"

"Better... slowly. It'll take time even with the liffen adding energy." A growl rumbled from him and before she could look over her shoulder, he had closed the tent flap. "What do you need, *captain*?"

Footsteps crunched on the grass as someone approached and said, "You shouldn't be seeing to her wounds on your own."

Raffel stood up, replying, "And why would that be?"

"We don't need others thinking you are taking advantage of her," said Teredana, his voice stern. "Myself or one of the soldiers should be present." Blāzzer blinked, anger catching in her throat.

"I wouldn't do anything to hurt her. I care enough about her to give her part of my endar. I would never violate her trust."

There was silence and Blāzzer listened to the pounding of her heart echo in her ears. She shifted, holding her right arm, and peeked through a gap in the tent entrance. Raffel's back was to her with the captain two feet in front of him. They were glaring at each other and Raffel's ears were pinned back.

"Upon our arrival to Stiggress you will no longer be in charge of her wounds," ordered Teredana. "I'll request that a *female* healer sees to her."

"That's if Blāzzer is comfortable with them," growled Raffel. "It's her choice, no one else's."

"It's the king's choice, not hers."


Blāzzer sat inside her tent, resting her chin on her knees, and watched the sun sink farther behind the horizon. Its rays warmed her cheeks as she thought, *The little fireball from my dream, what does it mean? I felt so lost, so alone. It found me though. I haven't seen it since, but I haven't dreamed much lately either. Too worn out.* The Lemay soldiers burst into laughter from where they sat around the cook fire. One of them heartily patted another on the back. Blāzzer frowned and scooted further back into her tent, before laying down on her bedroll. She stared at the fabric above her, feeling emotions twist through her.

A strong wind buffeted her tent, signifying Raffel's return. There was a flash of red light before he walked over to her tent and sat down at the entrance with his back to her. He looked out at the soldiers and asked, "You going to bed early?"

"Just feel like being horizontal," muttered Blāzzer. "Without the pain medicine, I'd be a lump of soreness."

"I can ask Will to not wear his chest plate if that would help."

Blāzzer pressed her lips together and looked at him. "What if I flew with you?" She watched Raffel's shoulders tense.

"It wouldn't be safe."

"Have you ever had anyone fly with you?"

He shook his head.

"If I'm your rider, then does that mean at some point I will?"

"Once you're healed."

Blāzzer looked at the wall of her tent, thinking, *I wonder what it would be like to fly. The ground passing fast and far below. I guess it would be cold up there, and lots of wind. How fast can a dragon fly? Can they-*

"Have you been having bad dreams?" asked Raffel, looking at her over his shoulder. His eyebrows were pulled together slightly.

"No," replied Blāzzer, sitting up. "I'm kind of surprised I haven't. You?"

He shook his head. "There's too much going on. Once things have settled down, they'll come."

"When will things settle down?"

He pressed his lips together. "I don't know, but they will. We'll get through this."

She hugged herself, struggling to believe him. "The last dream I had was right after the attack before I woke up at home."

Raffel shifted, facing her more, and frowned with concern. He questioned, "What did you dream?"

Blāzzer blinked and looked down at her feet as she answered, "I was alone. Everything was dark, but I could see myself. I was scared and cold. I tried calling out, but there was no response. I curled up on the ground. I didn't know if I was dead or alive." A shiver ran up her spine and the hairs on her arms stood upright. "But then this little ball of fire appeared in front of me. I held it and it kept me warm." She looked at him. "Was that because you gave me part of your endar?"

"It's very common that dragon and rider have a dream after the bond is made," muttered Raffel, looking over the plains.

"What did you dream?"

"I was in the same darkness. Except there were a lot of people walking around. Their faces were blurred and I couldn't identify any of them. Then I heard a cry for help, but no one seemed to notice. I tried pushing through the crowd, but I wasn't getting anywhere. I tried to shift..." He put his hand on his stomach, below his sternum. "But I couldn't. Like that part of me was gone. I yelled at the people. Some moved, most didn't. I got to the point where I lost my temper."

Blāzzer tipped her head slightly.

Raffel sighed, "I started punching and pushing them. They screamed and ran away into the darkness. All that was left behind was a woman made of fire kneeling on the ground. She was weeping. I knelt in front of her and pulled her to me, holding her close. Then I woke up." He looked to Blāzzer and she quickly averted her gaze, unsure what to say.

She murmured, "I think I should go to bed." He nodded slowly and stood up before moving the tent flaps to cover the entrance. She laid back and there was a flash of red light. She thought, *So the fireball was him. A part of him. But doesn't that mean that the burning woman was me?*

## Chapter Nine

Several days of traveling the roads along the northern rivers and Grapho Lake finally brought the sight of Stiggress onto the horizon. The large city had a wide harbor stretching along the lake shore where ships of varying sizes could be seen docked and sailing on the water. Massive walls surrounded the city, one stretching around the harbor. People and carriages crowded the roads leading into Stiggress. Blāzzer could only stare, trying to absorb every detail of the capitol of Nickada.

The soldiers slowed their pace as they passed citizens along the road. One of the soldiers raised a green and red banner that had a rearing bear with a crown above its head. Soon the people were stepping off the road, staring at the soldiers as they came by. Blāzzer, swallowing her unease, looked up and saw Raffel flying low. As they came nearer to Stiggress, she could see the soldiers standing along the outer wall and the Nickadian banners that flapped in the wind. The metal gate was open and several guards checked in and out people as they came and went. When they spotted the Lemay Soldiers, they immediately stood at attention and saluted.

The city had wide, cobbled streets and tall, brick buildings. People stepped aside as the soldiers rode through, not slowing their quick trot. Blāzzer looked up, but couldn't see Raffel around the buildings. It took a while for the group to ride through the city and reach the innermost wall that was heavily guarded. Again, the guards at the gate saluted, and the soldiers rode through. Inside was an extensive courtyard before a large fortress. Stable boys ran up and grabbed the reins of the horses as the soldiers dismounted. Blāzzer winced at the pain of dismounting and looked about for Raffel. He slowly glided down in a spiral and landed nearby. He shifted and walked over to her. His jaw was tight and when he met her eyes he quickly looked away. He took her bags from one of the soldiers before tilting his head for her to follow.

"This way Raffel and Blāzzer," said Teredana. They followed him up the stairs to the large wooden doors reinforced with metal plates. Guards, standing at the entrance, saluted him. Beyond was a vast great hall with tables and chairs spread out. On the far side were tall doors that were intricately carved, while along the side walls were several hallways. Teredana led them down one of these. Windows lined one wall, looking out on a well-tended courtyard with flowers and a fountain.

"You'll be staying in the Stone family suite," explained the captain. "You are to stay there until I come back. I'll let the king know you are here and have food sent up." He stopped at a stone staircase that had a small banner with a dragon next to it. "Raffel, I expect that you remember where everything is."

The dragon nodded and began climbing the stairs up. Blāzzer looked to Teredana and asked, "The king... when will he want to see us?"

"By tonight," he replied. "Head on up." He held his hand up, indicating the stairs.

Slowly she climbed the stairs, her legs sore from the days on horse back. At the top of the stairs was a small landing with a set of open double doors. Inside was a large living room with a fire place. Four doors led to bedrooms while another to a washroom. On the other side of the main room was a pair of open glass doors. Blāzzer walked through these onto the balcony where Raffel stood leaning against the railing.

"Didn't think I'd be back here for a while," murmured Raffel as she walked up to him.

Blāzzer stood next to him, looking out over the large city and to the lake beyond, and thought, *This place is massive and all I can feel is how small I am in comparison.* She pressed her lips together and turned her gaze to Raffel. "Can you help me with my bandages?"

He looked to her and raised an eyebrow, saying, "We changed them yesterday, so they should still be good. Are they bothering you?"

"No... I'd like to wash up."

After Raffel's help unbandaging her shoulder, Blāzzer undressed and scrubbed her skin, relishing the feel of the cleanliness. She washed her hair the best she could with one hand before wrapping herself in a towel. Standing before the mirror, she looked over her shoulder at her healing wound. Her shoulder wasn't inflamed or swollen as much, but the bruising was very prominent. She looked down at her right hand and closed her it into a fist. Pain raced up her arm and she gasped. Grinding her teeth, she took a slow deep breath.

*That's still better than what it was,* thought Blāzzer. She slowly dressed and once she had pants on and had her chest wrapped, she opened the washroom door to call for Raffel, but blinked at the sight of a woman standing there.

"Blāzzer, my name is Heather," the older woman said, smiling tentatively. "I'll be seeing to your shoulder while you stay in Stiggress. It is not appropriate for a man to see you undressed."

Blāzzer blinked and looked past her. Raffel was no where to be seen. She jerked nod and stepped back, letting Heather into the washroom. The healer closed the door behind herself and placed a basket on the counter.

"Does your shoulder hurt?"

"It's better now. I've been taking medicine for the pain."

"Do you know what it is?" asked Heather, gathering some bandages as Blāzzer sat on a stool. The young woman shook her head and winced when the healer touched her shoulder. "This is remarkable healing for your described injury. Do you have functionality of your arm?"

"Kind of... I can make a fist, but it hurts. Can't really move it."

"If the nerves are to reconnect you will need to move your arm. Even if it causes pain."

Blāzzer nodded and waited as the healer bandaged her shoulder. She stared at the tiles on the floor thinking, *Who sent her? Did Teredana? He was unhappy when Raffel changed them, but I hoped he wouldn't remember.*

"I'll come by tomorrow to check on you," said Heather, gathering the soiled bandages. She walked out, closing the door behind her.

"I would rather have Raffel do it," muttered Blāzzer. She pulled on a tunic and put her arm in the sling before leaving the wash room. She walked out to the balcony and looked to Raffel. His shoulders were hunched as leaned his elbows against the railing. "She talk to you?"

Raffel nodded and said, "Yeah... wasn't too happy about me taking care of your bandages and medicine." He sighed and straightened, looking down at her. "Everything okay with the healer?"

Blāzzer nodded, watching the waves on the lake, and whispered, "I trust you more than her."

Blāzzer and Raffel followed Teredana down the halls of the fortress of Stiggress. She struggled to keep her head up with her stomach turning from nerves. She glanced to Raffel, seeing his pinned ears, and thought, *I barely slept, couldn't with wondering when the king would call upon us. Didn't think that it wouldn't be till this morning... Did Raffel sleep at all?*

They walked down a hallway with guards lined on either side. Each soldier stood straight with a breastplate bearing the Lemay Army insignia and a sword at their hips. As Blāzzer neared the large double doors at the end of the hall her heart thundered in her chest. The nearest guards stepped forward and opened the doors.

The large room beyond had paintings and tapestries hung on the walls. Tall bookcases were crammed with countless books and scrolls. To one side of the room was a sitting area that had a fireplace before it. A map of Nickada and the surrounding countries was spread out on a broad table in the middle of the room. Near the far wall was a wide desk with a few chairs in front of it. Floor-to-ceiling windows behind the desk overlooked the city. Morning sunlight streamed into the room, dust motes floating about. A single man stood in the room, gazing out at Stiggress.

"My king, Raffel and Blāzzer," introduced Teredana with a salute before leaving. The doors closed behind him, leaving Raffel and Blāzzer standing there.

Blāzzer looked at the king, noting how straight he stood with his hands folded behind his back. His clothes were stitched with intricate designs and small stone beads. A simple crown of twisted gold and silver sat upon his brow. Raffel stepped forward and said, "King Nayax, I want to apologize for breaking the agreement."

The king turned and looked at them. Small wrinkles creased the corner of his mouth from stress and others the corner of his eyes from laughter. Gray locks mixed with his black hair and a thin scar crossed his jaw. Nayax asked, "Do you regret your decision?"

Raffel blinked, ears twitching. "No, sir."

Nayax turned to Blāzzer and she tried her best to not flinch. "Do you regret becoming a rider?"

She shook her head then said, "No, sir."

Nayax nodded and held out his hand, "Let's sit down and talk then." He sat down behind the desk while Blāzzer and Raffel sat in the chairs before it. "I want to apologize for what happened at Palator." Blāzzer looked down at her hands, throat tightening.

"Do we know who attacked?" asked Raffel.

Nayax nodded. "The raiders were from Snerx, but so far that is all we know. I assure you that Palator and the other towns will be well protected to prevent anything happening like this in the future."

"What will happen to Blāzzer now?" questioned Raffel, his voice strained. Blāzzer looked to him then the king.

Nayax turned to her and said, "You are no longer a ward of the Court of Crows, your original patron." At her questioning look, he explained, "They are a group of elite Sentinel Crows that make decisions for their group. You are now my ward, and therefore under my protection. The Council will have to meet to decide what happens next, but till then you will remain my ward."

"Why am I a ward?" she asked. "All I know is that I'm an orphan. That I've never been able to make my own decisions on major life choices."

He nodded. "Your parents gave you to the Sentinel Crows for your protection."

"Are they alive?" she questioned, leaning forward. *I always thought they were dead, but maybe...*

"No."

She slumped back and clenched her hands into fists, making pain run up her arm.

"I'm sorry. They died soon after you were given to the Sentinel Crows."

"Who were they?"

Nayax sighed. "I cannot tell you. There is limited information I can give you. Ultimately it is up to the Council what you are told."

"But you're the king!" demanded Blāzzer. Raffel reached over and squeezed her arm. "Sorry."

Nayax nodded and said, "As king, I act as a mediator between the races and am in charge of international affairs along with the wellbeing of mortals. Even I, as king, have my limits." Blāzzer pressed her lips together and looked down at her hands. "I know it can be frustrating... but try to hold on. It'll get better." He looked to Raffel. "I sent word immediately to your father when we heard about Palator. He should be here in a day or two."

Raffel nodded, murmuring, "Thank you."

"Did everything go well with the transfer?"

Blāzzer looked between them and Raffel explained, "The transfer of the liffen - um... energy from me to you... it's what makes you my rider." He looked to Nayax. "Everything went good, but she's still having a hard time with the nerves in her shoulder and arm."

"It's gotten better," she insisted.

"Has there been any telepathy so far?" asked Nayax, looking between them.

Blāzzer looked to Raffel and questioned, "Telepathy?"

"So you haven't explained much at all," said Nayax, raising an eyebrow and looking at Raffel.

"A lot going on lately," replied Raffel. He turned to Blāzzer and took a deep breath before continuing, "Over time the liffen enables a special bond to form. Think of it as a link between two people allowing energy to flow between them. There are a couple of abilities that come along with this bond. The first being telepathy, where rider and dragon can communicate via thought."

*What?* questioned Blāzzer, mouth slightly open.

Raffel looked to Nayax, asking, "How much can I tell her?"

"Anything about the bond is okay," assured the king. "Till your father arrives, I suggest you rest up."

Blāzzer laid curled up on her bed, hugging a pillow to her chest. She wasn't for sure how long she had laid there since she had returned from speaking with the king. The window was cracked open, allowing a breeze to come in. She closed her eyes as it brushed against her face.

There was a knock on the door and Raffel asked, "Blāzzer? You alright?"

She didn't budge.

Slowly the door opened, and he walked in, closing the door behind him. He walked over to her and sat down on the ground, leaning his back against the bed. The breeze made the curtains move slightly and brought the various smells of flowers and city life in.

"I'm sorry," murmured Raffel. "This is not how things should have been... You should have stayed in Palator with Angel, Lenny, and Mae... should have been a happy family."

Blāzzer buried her face in a pillow, feeling tears well up.

"None of this should have happened... I know nothing that I say can change what has happened, but... I promise that you won't be alone through any of this." He looked over his shoulder at her. "Blāzzer?"

She wouldn't look up, knuckles white with a death grip on the pillow.

"I promise everything will be okay."

She bolted up right, glaring at him, and demanded, "Is it!?"

Raffel blinked at her out burst. He pressed his lips together.

"You keep saying that things are going to be okay," she said, a sob catching in her throat. "But how do you know?"

"I don't," he replied quietly, looking away. "I just don't know what to say... But I feel like I should say something... try to say something to help you feel better."

"Then tell me this sucks!" She leaned towards him, eyes pleading.

He opened his mouth before closing it. After a moment he whispered, "This sucks."

Blāzzer's face softened slightly.

"Everything about this situation sucks. It's unfair... You didn't choose to be a ward or have the Council involved. They shouldn't and that sucks. It makes me angry to see how you are treated... You deserve better."

She laid down with her head near his as tears continued to slowly drip down her cheeks.

"I'm sorry I didn't give you a choice about the liffen. It was rude and unfair. It sucks that saving your life has now put your life in such turmoil." Raffel turned to her. "I know that there isn't much I can do... All I want is for you to know that I am here and that I'm not going anywhere." He dried her tears with his thumbs. "I'm going to stay by your side until everything is okay... That is my promise."

Blāzzer sat on her bed, staring at a page from the book of fairytales, but not seeing the words. She thought, *I'm stuck here. I can't go anywhere. I'm a glorified prisoner. Raffel can leave. Will he leave? No , he's promised to stay till I'm free. But is he staying because he feels guilty or because he wants to.* She sighed and closed the book before rubbing her cheeks.

There was a knock on the door before it opened and Heather, carrying a basket, walked in. Blāzzer frowned, trying to not glare at the older woman. As the healer closed the door she asked, "How are you feeling today?"

Blāzzer nodded and got up, thinking, *Better if I didn't have to see you.* Tugging the sling off, she pulled her shirt off and sat on a stool. Heather placed the basket on the bed before starting to unwrap the dressings.

"How is the pain?" questioned the healer.

"It's pretty mild," murmured Blāzzer. She winced as Heather pulled the gauze from over the sutures.

"The bruising is looking better, but there is a red tint coming through."

Blāzzer glanced over her shoulder noting that most of the bruising was green and yellow. A bright red shade covered the center of the wound. She muttered, "I guess that's the liffen. Raffel mentioned yesterday I would have a mark from it."

"Hopefully it doesn't become too apparent," said Heather, cleaning the sutures gently with a cloth.

The young woman blinked and questioned, "Why?"

"Well, it's a permanent mark left by a man. Some, or many men, wouldn't like their wife to be marked by another man."

Blāzzer pressed her lips together, feeling small and inferior.

"I wouldn't worry about it too much," assured Heather. "You'll find someone who accepts you for who you are."

*And what if I don't find that person?* Blāzzer asked herself. The healer rebandage her shoulder before helping her pull a shirt on. Blāzzer pulled the sling over her head and settled her arm against the fabric.

"There that should do it," smiled Heather. "Now make sure to eat some dinner. I'll come by tomorrow."

With that the healer left, leaving Blāzzer sitting on the stool. She looked up as Raffel knocked on the door frame. He smiled softly and said, "Your mobility seems to be getting better." She turned away, hugging herself. "You okay?"

"Heather says I'll have a hard time finding a man who wants to be with me due to the liffen," she murmured.

Raffel's jaw tightened and he walked over to her. He sat on the edge of the bed, lowering himself to her eye level. She met his eyes, seeing the swirls of red glitter. With conviction he said, "If someone can't look past a mark on your shoulder and see the person you are, then they don't deserve you... You deserve better than that."

For two days Blāzzer stayed in her room, only venturing out due to necessity. Heather came by each day to help with bandage changes and stretches. Otherwise, Blāzzer kept to herself, reading or looking out at Stiggress. She sat on the windowsill, doing the latter. Her temple pressed against the cool glass as she watched ships sail on the lake and people walk the streets. She thought, *It would seem prettier here in different circumstances. Maybe even-*

Blāzzer blinked, looking up at the door as she heard Raffel talk to someone in the living room. She pressed her lips together, not recognizing the other voice. After a minute there was a knock on the door and Raffel opened it enough for him to slip in. He walked over to her, frowning slightly as he noted her untouched breakfast on the table. He said, "My father is here... He'd like to meet you."

Blāzzer nodded and slowly stood up, her heart picking up speed.

"You doing okay?"

"Processing," she murmured, avoiding his gaze.

"I'm here for you... you know?"

Her left hand tightened into a fist and she nodded stiffly. Raffel took a deep breath before leading her out to the living room, where a man was unstrapping his sword from his waist. As the man turned to her, she blinked, thinking, *He's definitely a dragon.*

The older man was similarly built as Raffel, but his face was sharper and weathered by wind and sunlight. His hair was mostly red with patches of black and some speckling of gray. Ears pinning back, his eyes narrowed as he studied Blāzzer. Everything about him was intense and Blāzzer looked away.

"Doesn't look like you've gotten much sleep," the man said.

Blāzzer pressed her lips together, wanting to go back to her room and thinking, *Somehow I thought all dragons would be like Raffel and Mae. Different, but not... not like this.*

"Blāzzer, this is my father, Ash," said Raffel. "You don't need to be intimidated by him. That comes with being an old dragon." His father raised an eyebrow and Blāzzer suppressed a smile. "You mentioned speaking with Nayax?" She glanced between the two dragons.

"I'm speaking with him this afternoon," replied Ash with a shrug. "Till then you should pack and get something to eat."

"Is Nayax going to let Blāzzer leave?" asked Raffel.

Blāzzer stared at the older dragon in disbelief, questioning, "Will he?"

Ash nodded, saying, "He will. I just need to speak with him to confirm some details."

"But the agreement?"

"Let me worry about it."

Blāzzer, reading a book, sat on the couch in the living area. Golden sunlight spilled through the glass balconey doors as the sun sank farther behind the horizon. Raffel paced about the room, hands flexing with each breath. When he tripped against a chair, she looked at him and said, "Do you want to come and sit down?"

"No," muttered Raffel, clenching his jaw. He glanced at her, huffed a sigh, and sat on the couch. After a moment he quickly got up and was back to pacing.

"Why are you pacey?" asked Blāzzer, closing her book and turning so she could watch him move back and forth.

"I'm anxious and can't do anything."

"Your dad should be back soon."

He grunted and continued pacing.

"It'll be okay," whispered Blāzzer.

Raffel blinked, stopped in his tracks, and looked at her. He murmured, "That's my line."

She shrugged, opening her book and staring blankly at the pages, and thought, *Why did I say that? He's been telling me that since the attack. I even got mad at him for saying that... It'll be okay, right? As long as he's in my corner.*

Several minutes later the door to the hallway opened and Ash walked in. His face gave no sign of how his talk with Nayax went. He closed the door behind him and sat on the couch, saying, "Well, now you're stuck with us, Blāzzer."

"Really?!" questioned Blāzzer and Raffel and the same time. She looked to the older dragon in disbelief.

Ash chuckled and nodded. "You aren't allowed to leave the Stone family, so it isn't freedom."

"I'll take that," breathed Blāzzer, feeling a heavy weight lift off her shoulders.

"You mentioned packing earlier," said Raffel. "So we're leaving... with Blāzzer?"

"Yes, and I hope you did pack," replied Ash. "We'll be travelling to Shinda. There is a hospital there and they should be able to give some insight into the Blāzzer's healing."

"Is something wrong?" questioned Blāzzer, placing her hand over her shoulder.

Ash held up his hand in assurance, before saying, "I just want to make sure everything is okay with the transfer of Raffel's endar. The damage was extensive, including the nerve damage. The farnircks have countless records that should help."

Blāzzer nodded slightly and looked to Raffel. He smiled and her heart fluttered.

## Chapter Ten

The next morning, Blāzzer followed Raffel and Ash through the fortress. Raffel carried her bag and walked by her side. He asked Ash, "Are we taking horses to Shinda?"

Ash looked over his shoulder with his eyebrow raised and said, "We don't have time for horses, and we have wings."

"What about Blāzzer?"

"What about me?" asked Blāzzer, looking between them.

Raffel answered, "It's not safe to ride on a dragon bareback."

She turned to Ash in question.

"Nayax has a saddle that fits me so we'll borrow that," answered Ash, facing forward.

Raffel said, "You mean-"

"Yes," growled Ash, picking up his pace.

Blāzzer looked to Raffel and he mouthed, *Tell you later.*

They walked down a staircase and through a side entrance of the fortress. Stepping out into a sunny courtyard, Blāzzer shaded her eyes with a hand. Several Lemay Soldiers, including Teredana, stood there. On a large wooden structure was a specialized leather saddle.

"Let's get this done with," grumbled Ash. Light enveloped him, making the soldiers and Blāzzer step back. When the light faded, an enormous dragon stood there. He was several feet taller than Raffel and he had black scales scattered amongst the red. Lines of deformed scales formed ridges along his body. The horns on top of his head were long and striated, though one was broken in half. Slowly Ash crouched down and swung his head over to the Lemay Soldiers.

"Well? What are you waiting for?" questioned the older dragon, his sharp, yellowed teeth flashing.

The soldiers quickly jumped forward, carrying the saddle with them. Teredana walked around them and up to Blāzzer and Raffel, holding out a leather vest. He said, "Hopefully it fits. Extra rivets were added, but we don't have anything smaller."

Raffel nodded, taking the vest, and saying, "Thank you." He placed their bags down and turned to Blāzzer. "You'll need to wear this. It'll secure you to the saddle, so you don't fall." She blinked and hugged her right arm to her chest. "I won't let you fall." They met each other's eyes. "I promise." Pressing her lips together, she nodded and stepped forward.

Raffel helped her slip the leather vest on, tightening straps and securing buckles. He bandaged her right arm to her chest, then indicated three metal rings, one on each side of her ribcage and the last over her sternum. He said, "There are carabiners on straps attached to the saddle. You'll secure yourself using those to these rings. Okay?"

"Yeah," replied Blāzzer, trying to adjust how the vest sat over her upper chest and grumbling to herself, *This was not made for women*. She looked up to Ash and saw that the soldiers were securing the last few straps of the saddle. The saddle had a similar seat to a horse saddle and had large saddlebags, but that was where the similarity ended. The front part of the saddle extended up his neck with leather-wrapped handles at the top for handholds. There were no stirrups, but two pairs of rods. One was directly under the saddle, where stirrups would be. The other rod was towards the back of the saddle closer to the top. Thick straps around Ash's chest and neck held the saddle in place.

"I was hoping it still fit," said a voice. They all turned to see King Nayax walking towards them. Each of the Lemay Soldiers saluted to him. Nayax ignored them, his eyes on Ash. "I thought you might have gotten fat with age."

A laugh echoed deep in Ash's throat as he swung his head a foot away from the king. The Lemay Soldiers immediately put their hands on their swords. Nayax held up a hand and they relaxed.

Ash growled, "I thought age might have made you funnier."

Nayax grinned. "Seems like we both disappoint."

"My king," said Teredana in astonishment.

Nayax turned to him. "Merely banter between old friends, Captain Teredana." He then turned to Ash and spoke in Drakken. Ash nodded slightly and Nayax slowly reached a hand out, placing his palm between the dragon's nostrils.

"You still need to explain," whispered Blāzzer.

"Later," breathed Raffel.

Ash turned to them and lowered his body to the ground, saying, "Make sure she's secured properly." Raffel nodded and helped Blāzzer up into the saddle. He secured the carabiners from the saddle to the rings on the vest.

"You place your feet here," he said, indicating the rod directly beneath the saddle. "You won't use the other set. Then you hold on here." He tugged on the handles at the front of the saddle. "Between the rungs and the handle you should be balanced. It'll be a little tricky at first, but you won't fall. The straps will hold you on top of the saddle... Any questions?"

Blāzzer pressed her lips together and murmured, "How long does it take to get used to flying?"

Raffel shrugged and stepped back as Ash slowly stood up. She looked down and blinked. She was already twelve feet above the ground.

"Take some deep breaths and you'll be fine," assured Nayax. She met his eyes and saw sorrow tug at his face.

Ash turned to Raffel and said, "You go ahead and take off first."

Raffel nodded and light enveloped him. He stood there for a moment as a dragon before turning and jumping into the sky. His powerful wings quickly took him higher. Ash stepped forward and Blāzzer felt her heart pound so hard in her chest that she thought the dragon could hear it. His wings outstretched and in one fluid motion, he crouched, jumped, and flew.

It wasn't until their steep ascent leveled off that she realized she had a death grip on the saddle and her eyes tightly shut. She opened her eyes slightly and quickly shut them, feeling her stomach drop all the way down to the ground. Panic rose in her throat as she thought, *Shit! Why did I agree to this?!*

"Breathe," said Ash. "In through your nose. Out through your mouth... Again. In through your nose. Out through your mouth... Good. When you open your eyes, look forward along my neck."

After several deep breaths, Blāzzer opened her eyes, focusing her gaze forward. Ash had his head turned so one eye was focused on her. His large iris was primarily swirling shades of red with glittering flecks of black around the edge. She nodded slowly and he faced forward. She blinked at the expanse of blue sky and white clouds. Raffel flew higher and to the right. She closed her eyes and straightened her back, feeling the wind rush past her face and through her hair. The sun was warm and helped keep the chill from the wind at bay. Heat radiated from Ash and warmed her legs. She could feel his muscles move in strong motions, powering his wings beats between moments of gliding.

Flying felt like freedom.

Blāzzer leaned against Ash's neck, her back sore from sitting in the saddle. The sun was warm on her back and heat emanated from the dragon's scales. Her eyes were closed against the brightness of the blue sky and her lips were chapped from the wind. She groaned slightly as an air pocket jostled the dragon.

"We should land for lunch," said Raffel. Blāzzer barely opened her eyes, watching the young dragon glide closer.

"No, we'll continue for another hour then stop," replied Ash, his voice rumbling in his chest.

She groaned internally at this response.

"Blāzzer needs a break," growled Raffel.

Ash glanced back at her before descending and landing on the Seikal River bank. He crouched down and murmured, "You can get down if you want."

Blāzzer, still leaning against his neck, looked over his shoulder at the sand several feet below and thought, *Nope, not going to make that without hurting myself.* She blinked when an outstretched hand came into sight. She turned slightly and stared at Raffel, who stood by the saddle. He smiled sympathetically, reaching out his hand. Slowly she sat up and released the safety clasps on her harness. Sliding off of the saddle, Blāzzer dismounted and fell against his chest.

He wrapped his arms around her, saying, "I'm sorry I didn't realize you were wearing out so soon."

"It's okay," breathed Blāzzer, her breath catching in her throat and making her cough. Raffel frowned and helped her sit in the shade of the older dragon's body.

"I thought you had more endurance," said Ash, scanning the horizon. Glancing at him, Raffel handed Blāzzer an open canteen. She quickly gulped water from it, some drops running down her cheeks.

"Don't drink so fast," insisted Raffel, pulling the canteen from her mouth. "You'll make yourself sick."

"Already feel like I am," whispered Blāzzer, leaning back against Ash's shoulder. Raffel sat down in front of her, grabbing his bag, and rummaged through it, pulling some jerky out. He held a strip out to her and she shook her head. After a few moments, she asked, "Will I get used to it?"

Confused, Raffel raised an eyebrow.

"Eventually, but it'll take time," answered Ash, lowering his head so one large eye looked at them from only a few feet away. "Flying will be easier once you've had more experience and the liffen is at full strength."

"How do dragons learn how to fly?" questioned Blāzzer, her eyelids feeling heavy as her mind lost focus on the swirls of red and flecks of black in the old dragon's iris.

"It's like learning how to walk. There's a natural urge to do so, but it takes practice. The few morsels of freedom with each advancement drives the need to fly more. When Raffel was young, he'd jump out of trees and off of rooftops. Aurora was always worried he'd get hurt and Lydia-"

Blāzzer's eyes slowly closed as she listened to Ash talk. Her head tipped to one side and she fell asleep.

When night came they made camp near the bank of the Seikal River. A single tent had been set up a short distance from the campfire. Raffel, Blāzzer, and Ash sat around the fire eating rice, salted pork, and some greens. Cradling the bowl in her lap, she shoveled the food into her mouth and thought, *I really need to try to eat lunch tomorrow. Can't go all day again without eating. Course, have to see how my stomach-*

"Your mother is worried about you," said Ash without pause in his eating.

Raffel, frowning slightly, looked at him and asked, "Because of the attack?"

"Because you don't reach out. You haven't written in over three months."

Blāzzer pressed her lips together and focused on her bowl.

"Told her you were fine and just being an independent, young man," continued Ash. "Then we got word of the attack and she said I could sleep out in the rain."

Raffel blinked, murmuring, "I'm kind of surprised she didn't come."

"Cornin convinced her that going in as a big mama bear wasn't going to help the situation."

Raffel chuckled.

"Your mother's rider?" asked Blāzzer.

Raffel nodded, replying, "The only other rider in Nickada."

She felt her stomach tighten with unease. "I forgot that there was only one other rider, other than me."

"There aren't enough dragons in Nickada to have a good number of riders," explained Ash, putting his bowl down. "Not all dragons can find a person to share that bond with."

"So, you don't have a rider?"

The older dragon stared at the fire for a while before replying, "No... I wasn't one of the lucky ones."

## Chapter Eleven

A few days passed until on the horizon a town appeared surrounded by a low stone wall. The dragons slowly descended and landed along the road outside of Shinda. Raffel shifted before helping Blāzzer down from Ash's back. When she looked back to the town, she blinked at the two people walking towards them. Their stone-gray skin and poppy red eyes marked them as farnircks.

One saluted to the dragons, fist over heart, and said, "Welcome Stone family."

Both Raffel and Ash, once shifted, saluted back. Ash replied, "I need to speak with Durthuh and she needs to be seen by the healers." He indicated to Blāzzer with a jerk of his head.

The first farnirck nodded. "I can take you to Durthuh, while my companion takes her to the sanitarium."

Ash said something to Raffel in Drakken before following the farnirck into town.

"Please follow me," instructed the other farnirck, turning and leading Blāzzer and Raffel into Shinda.

Passing the low stone fence, Blāzzer looked about and saw farnircks smiling and waving to each other. Each interaction was genuine. The shindites wore primarily neutral colors with a scarf, ribbon, or belt of one solid color. Nested between the clay-brick building were small shrines, where a few farnircks were giving offerings or praying.

"Who is the god they pray to?" asked Blāzzer quietly, tugging on Raffel's sleeve.

"The thirteen household spirits," he replied. "Each family claims a spirit to make offerings to, but the farnircks pray to all the spirits."

Their guide nodded and added, "The sanitarium is a temple to LightRock and WitheringCloud." He pointed to a large two-story stone building ahead of them.

As they came up to the sanitarium Blāzzer noticed a shrine at the front with two small statues of a man and woman. There were coins, wilting flowers, and small pieces of quartz laid before the statues. They went up the stairs and through a large open door. A small reflecting pool of water was inside the main hall, making the air cool. Farnircks walked around and many had white or yellow tunics.

The farnirck that had guided Raffel and Blāzzer motioned to one of the women in white, "She will see to you." He saluted and left the sanitarium.

"Hello, do you need assistance?" asked the woman with a soft smile, eyes examining Blāzzer's bandaged arm.

"She needs her shoulder looked at," answered Raffel. "Preferably by someone with knowledge of the liffen."

"The liffen?"

"The dragon-rider bond."

The woman nodded and waved for them to follow. As they walked down the hall with many small side rooms, she said, "I will need to find Lillian. She will be able to help you." She stopped at an open door. "Please wait here."

Raffel and Blāzzer stepped inside and the healer closed the door behind them. The room was small occupied by some stools, a table, and a counter with various medical items on it. Blāzzer sat down and noticed that the two spirits of the sanitarium were painted over the doorway.

"The farnircks seem to be very religious," commented Blāzzer, quietly. She looked to Raffel, who was leaning against the wall and staring at the floor. "You okay?"

He looked up and replied, "Yeah."

"You seem nervous."

"I'm alright." He smiled softly.

Feeling anxiety gnaw at her stomach, Blāzzer glanced down at her hand. Slowly moving her fingers, she barely felt a tinge of pain. "I'm getting better."

He nodded, refocusing on the floor

"I-"

A knock on the door interrupted her. After a moment a female farnirck walked in, saying, "Hello, my name is Lillian LightRock. Your names are?"

"Blāzzer Ozol," said the young woman.

"Raffel Stone," answered the dragon, straightening himself.

"It is good to meet both of you," said Lillian with a soft smile. She placed a book on the counter and opened it to a blank page. "Atwood mentioned that you need your arm looked at, Blāzzer, and that you, Raffel, requested someone with knowledge of the liffen. Is that correct?"

Raffel nodded.

Lillian made a note in her book then turned to Blāzzer. "How old are you?"

"Eighteen," replied Blāzzer.

"How did you receive this injury?"

Blāzzer looked down at her hands, body tensing, and slowly said, "I was in Palator... when we were attacked... I was hit by a mace." She touched her arm then looked to Raffel.

"I give her my liffen to save her arm and stop the bleeding," he added, meeting her eyes.

Lillian looked between them, asking, "How long has it been since the transfer?"

"Three weeks and two days," murmured Blāzzer.

"If it is all right with you, I'd like to take a look."

She nodded.

"Raffel, if you can wait outside."

He looked to Blāzzer and said, "If you need me, let me know." With that he stepped out, closing the door behind him.

Carefully Lillian unbandaged Blāzzer's arm and shoulder. The farnirck asked, "Are you able to move your arm?"

"I can move my hand but anything above my wrist is too painful," replied Blāzzer. She looked over her shoulder and grimaced at all the bruising and sutures.

Lillian filled a bowl with water and began to wash the old ointment from the sutures. She said, "It looks like it's healing on the surface. The sutures will be ready to be removed in a few more weeks." She placed the bowl down. "If it hurts too much when I touch your shoulder, please let me know. I need to check if the bone is healing." Her hands were cool as they pressed against Blāzzer's shoulder.

The young woman winced at the pain and, biting her lip, forced herself to remain still. After a few minutes, she asked, "Is it okay?"

"The bone is all healed. Nothing broken. Possibly some fractures, but everything is in the proper place. Let's go ahead and rebandage it." Lillian opened a cabinet and pulled out clean bandaging. "Have you had any connection with Raffel through the liffen?"

"No," replied Blāzzer, quietly, holding the beginning of the bandage in place. "I haven't felt anything... just pain... Is that bad?"

"No, sometimes it can take a while to form. I wouldn't worry about it right now... What happened to you in Palator was traumatic and you'll need time to process it. Make sure to talk to someone and not hold your feelings inside."

Blāzzer looked down at her hands as her vision blurred with tears. "I just found a home... and they took it away." Lillian gently picked up her hands and Blāzzer met her soft, red eyes. "I feel lost... no control of where I'm going and no idea where I'm headed." A tear rolled down her cheek and her voice caught in her throat. "The world feels like it's against me."

Lillian let Blāzzer cry for several moments before saying, "The world is a big place and tends to not be very kind... That's why we have others in our lives to help us... and in return, we help them. Right now you have a young man out there who would do anything he could to make things alright for you. You are not alone... You are loved." Lillian squeezed Blāzzer's hands before giving her a handkerchief. She turned away as Blāzzer dried her tears.

"Thank you," the young woman breathed.

Lillian nodded and said, "Any time you are in Shinda and need to talk, I'm always here for you."

Blāzzer smiled slightly.

"Shall I let Raffel back in?"

She nodded.

Lillian opened the door and motioned for him to step in. As he did he noticed Blāzzer's puffy eyes and frowned with concern. Before he could say anything Lillian explained, "Overall her shoulder seems to be healing very well. There's some small coloring from the liffen, but it's still mostly hidden due to a large amount of bruising. I would like to do some research into the liffen's ability to heal nerve damage before giving my prognosis. If you have a few days of course."

"Yes, we'll be staying here," said Raffel.

"Good. Let me see you two out then." Lillian led the way back through the halls. "If either of you needs anything, please come by."

As they passed the pool in the front chamber, Raffel asked, "My father mentioned meeting with Durthuh DirtHound. Do you know where I can find him?"

Lillian smiled softly and answered, "My husband should be at the barracks just south of here." She stopped at the door. "May LightRock watch over you."

Blāzzer waved goodbye as she followed Raffel down the steps and onto the street. The town was busier now, but the farnircks didn't seem to notice them.

"Are you okay?" asked the dragon. She looked up at him and saw that he was watching her."You looked like you had been crying."

"Yeah... I'm better now," replied Blāzzer, turning her gaze to the street ahead of her.

He nodded slightly and continued to lead them through the streets for a few moments before saying, "If you ever need to talk, you know I'm here for you... Right?"

"I know."

Ears twitching back, he nodded again.

Soon they heard the sound of metal against metal and came to the drill yard. Young men were sparring with each other with blunted metal swords. Beyond them was a long, squat building with a black slate roof. As Raffel stepped into the yard a drillmaster noticed him and walked over to them.

"Can I help you, sir?" asked the farnirck with a purple belt.

"I'm looking for Durthuh DirtHound," answered Raffel. "My father, Ash Stone, was to meet with him."

The farnirck nodded and pointed to the building behind him. "Go through the front door, to the right, and down the hall at the end will be Durthuh's office. He should be there." The farnirck stepped aside and Raffel led Blāzzer through the drill yard.

The barrack's front door was propped open, letting sunlight pour into a large antechamber with a shrine. Along the front of the alter were twelve icons that had another one sitting above them. Blāzzer recognized the two idols from the sanitarium.

"Blāzzer."

She blinked and looked to Raffel, not realizing she had paused in front of the shrine. She glanced back to the spirits then quickly followed him. They passed a few people and several doors until they came to the end of the hall. Raffel knocked twice on the wood door.

"Come in!"

Raffel pushed open the door and stepped in with Blāzzer right behind him. Inside was a small office space with shelving, a desk, and several chairs. Behind the desk sat a farnirck with a gold sash hanging across his chest. In front of him was Ash, reclining in one of the chairs. Blāzzer jumped as the door closed behind her and noticed another farnirck with a pine green scarf covering the lower half of his face.

"Come sit you two," said Ash with a slight wave of his hand. "This is

Durthuh DirtHound, leader of the farnircks." He indicated to the man behind the desk. As the two sat down he continued, "My son, Raffel, and his rider, Blāzzer."

"It's good to meet you two," said Durthuh with a smile. Blāzzer noticed a canine skull sitting on a shelf. "Ash had been telling me of your adventures. I'm sorry times have been difficult for you two."

"Thank you," replied Raffel.

"How did it go with finding a healer?" asked Ash.

"We found one, Lillian LightRock."

The farnirck nodded.

"She said the healing is good," continued Raffel, "but she wants to research nerve damage recovery."

Ash looked to Blāzzer and asked, "How are you feeling?"

"Tired," she murmured, hugging her arm. "Just really worn out."

The older dragon frowned slightly, studying her, before turning to Raffel. "I'll let you two go to the inn while Durthuh and I finish up here. We'll be staying at the Rising Sun. It's just down the road."

As Blāzzer and Raffel got up to leave, Durthuh said, "May DirtHound be with you."

Blāzzer, staring at the ceiling blankly, laid on her bed in a small room of the inn. Everything was quiet, except for a soft breeze that carried the cool night air coming through the open window. She questioned, *When will this be over? Why can't I just go back to before?* She pulled the pillow over her face. *In two years I'll be free. Then I can go back to Palator and be home again... What about Raffel? We are dragon and rider now, but what does that even mean? I feel like we were closer before. We used to talk more and smile more. Now he just looks at me all worriedly... and me... I'm broken.*

It was two days till they got word of Lillian finding any information. Blāzzer felt her stomach gnaw on itself as she, Raffel, and Ash walked through the barracks to Durthuh's office. She held her arm and looked at the ground, trying to keep her breathing even.

"It's going to be okay," assured Raffel. She nodded but didn't avert her gaze. Ash, frowning, looked over his shoulder at the two. He knocked on the double doors at the end of the hall before stepping in.

Lillian leaned against the windowsill and Durthuh sat behind his desk. The farnirck with the green scarf closed the door once all three had entered.

Raffel sat in a chair and Ash motioned for Blāzzer to do the same. Slowly, she did, perching on the edge of her seat.

"We hope the news is good," said Ash, sitting next to her.

"Yes, it is," said Lillian with a smile, focusing on Blāzzer. The young woman pressed her lips together. "Thank LightRock that liffens are such powerful healing agents. The nerve damage should be repaired within two to three months." Raffel let out a big sigh of relief. Ash nodded. "However, the time for that decreases the better the bond is between the dragon and rider... and increases the weaker the bond."

Ash looked between Raffel and Blāzzer, neither meeting his gaze. The older dragon said, "I'll do my best to facilitate their bond." He said something in Drakken and Raffel stiffly nodded.

"How does this news make you feel, Blāzzer?" asked Durthuh, relaxing in his chair.

She shrugged, before saying, "I still can't go back home."

The room was quiet as Blāzzer bit her lip, trying her best not to cry. She blinked as Ash put a hand on her forearm; she could feel the warmth emanating from him. She looked at his face and saw his determination.

"I promise you will be home again," he said, squeezing her arm gently. "I know being with us isn't your ideal situation, but we're going to try to make the best of it."

Blāzzer nodded and murmured, "Thank you."

The thunder from the galloping horse hooves was deafening. Blāzzer ran as quickly as she could towards the walls of Palator, but they weren't getting closer. Screams were cut short as the Sernixites attacked the fleeing Palatites. The sound of a horse and rider chased at her heels. She cried out as something hit her shoulder, knocking her into an irrigation ditch. She laid there, her breath rattling in her chest. Water trickled by her, soaking the front of her shirt. The liquid was a little dirty from her disturbing it, but there was no blood. The sounds of the horses and warriors seemed to fade.

Blāzzer slowly sat up, trying to get her bearings. Her body was sore from the fall, but nothing scraped or broken. She looked about, noticing the stillness in the air. A body laid in the road, surrounded by a pool of blood.

"No!" screamed Blāzzer as she scrambled out of the ditch. She ran to the person and rolled him onto his back. His chest was smashed in from a mace. His red hair was plastered to his face from blood. "No, please. Raffel!" She pushed the hair out of his face. His eyes stared blankly past her. "Raffel!"

Blāzzer jerked upright in her bed, panting, and covered in sweat. The room was dark and quiet, except for the muffled sounds of the sleepy inn. She gasped as she realized pain was throbbing from her shoulder. She gritted her teeth as she slowly released her white-knuckled grip on the blanket.

"It was just a dream," she breathed, closing her eyes for a moment. She quickly opened them as the sight of Raffel's broken body appeared. "He's fine. We're safe." She looked to the door of her room and pressed her lips together. Her stomach twisted as doubts crept in her mind. *He's okay, right? He didn't get hurt... or die?*

Slowly, Blāzzer got out of bed and walked over to the door. The hinges creaked softly as she stepped out into the hall. The floorboards groaned as she tiptoed down the hall with a single lantern illuminating the corridor. At the end of the hall, the stairway glowed from the light of the fireplace in the main room. She stopped outside Raffel and Ash's door. She raised her hand to knock and paused, pressing her lips together and thinking, *I'm being silly. He isn't hurt. But why does my chest ache?*

Startled, she quickly stepped back as the door in front of her opened. Raffel, clothes were wrinkled from sleep, stood there, blinking down at her. He glanced over his shoulder before stepping into the hall and closing the door. He whispered, "You okay?"

Blāzzer fiddled with her hands, looking down at the ground. She murmured, "I couldn't sleep." She hugged herself, holding back a tremble.

"Me neither," replied Raffel, rubbing the back of his neck. "I was going to go sit by the fireplace. Do you want to join me?" She nodded and he led the way down the hall.

They went down the stairs into the main room, where only three other people were awake. One stood behind the counter cleaning dishes and the other two sat at a table drinking from mugs. None of the farnircks glanced at Blāzzer and Raffel as they walked by. He pulled a chair up beside the fireplace and motioned for her to sit. Slowly she sat down and pulled her knees to her chest, wrapping her arm around them. Raffel grabbed another chair and sat beside her.

"You warm enough?" he asked.

"Yeah, the fire feels good," replied Blāzzer quietly, smiling softly at the warmth. Raffel nodded. She watched the flames twist and turn as they chewed on the wood. "Were you having bad dreams?"

He leaned back in his chair and shook his head. "My mind just wouldn't settle. Just kept going in circles." He ran his fingers through his hair, pushing it out of his face. "When we travel, I'm at least tired enough to fall asleep. But now that things have settled some, all my mind seems to do is chase its own tail." He looked at her. "You have a bad dream?"

Blāzzer shrank in her chair slightly before replying, "It was the attack all over again." He frowned. "Except you pushed me out of the way and... was killed." She tightened her arm around her knees, ignoring the protest of pain from her injury.

Raffel reached over and gently placed his hand on her shoulder and she could feel his warmth through her shirt. She met his eyes, seeing the depths of red. He said, "We're both alive. We're both safe... and we're both moving forward."

On the edge of town outside a blacksmith, Blāzzer watched as a few farnircks worked on measuring the dimensions of Raffel's dragon chest and shoulders. She sat on a stool near to where the dragon saddle was laid out.

Ash stood beside her and said, "They are working on a harness for you as well. I know Nayax's didn't fit properly and I want you to be safe."

"Is it possible to ride a dragon without the equipment?" asked Blāzzer, noticing all of the straps required to hold the saddle in place.

"It's possible but it can be very tricky and dangerous. The saddle doesn't bother us once we're used to it."

The farnircks came over to the saddle and began adding more holes to the straps. Raffel stretched his legs from where he had been crouching. Slowly, he walked around in circles, shifting his wings.

"I'll leave you two here and catch up with you later," said Ash. He said something in Drakken and Raffel snorted. The older dragon walked away.

After a moment Blāzzer got up and walked over to Raffel, who was looking out over the hills. He lowered his head, so his eye was level with her. She asked, "Have you worn one before?"

"No," he replied, glancing past her to where the farnircks were working. "How's your arm?"

She nodded. "I feel better knowing I'll be able to use it again." Slowly, she reached out her hand and placed it on Raffel's snout. His scales were warm and almost soft. "Thank you for saving me."

The next morning Blāzzer, Raffel, and Ash sat at a table in the inn's common room eating breakfast. The farnircks food had an interesting spice to it that Blāzzer had not tasted before. She made sure to wipe up all the gravy with bread. Others sat in the room as well, eating, drinking, and talking.

"What are we going to do now that we're done with our business here?" asked Raffel.

"Hang tight until otherwise notified," replied Ash, drinking coffee. "Unless you want to go back to Stiggress." He smiled as Blāzzer and Raffel shook their heads. "We could be here a while. The Council has to meet and vote on where Blāzzer is to go." She frowned. "However, Nayax is preoccupied with the raids so you'll stay with us for while."

"There have been more?" questioned Blāzzer, placing her fork down and suddenly losing her appetite.

"A few, but nothing like what happened in Palator," said Ash. "The Snerxites seem to have backed off, but now the Budstarian border is becoming a hot spot." He drummed his fingers against the tabletop for a moment before looking up as a farnirck approached them.

"Excuse me, I have a message for you," he said, holding out an envelope to Ash.

The older dragon took it and the farnirck quickly left. Ash read the paper before draining his coffee, standing, and saying, "Go pack your things. We're leaving for Chamdal."

"Right now?" asked Blāzzer as Raffel questioned, "What's going on?"

"Nayax has called a Council meeting to address the raids and Budstarian unrest," replied Ash. "We need to leave as soon as possible. I'll meet you two at the north gate. Be ready to fly. I need to speak with Durthuh quickly and will meet you there."

As he left Raffel said to Blāzzer, "Meet you down here in ten minutes."

"Can you come by my room to help me with the harness?" she replied.

"Of course. You go ahead and head up. I'll be there in a few."

Blāzzer nodded, took one last gulp of water from her cup, and quickly left the common room. When she got in her room, she began packing her belongings. She grabbed her tunic that was laying on the bed and paused, running her fingers over the floral stitching on the hem. She held it against her chest, feeling warmth in her chest.

At a knock on the door, she put it in her bag and said, "Come in."

Raffel slipped in, closing the door behind him and asking, "You got your things ready?"

"Almost," she replied grabbing her soap, washcloth, and hairbrush from the nightstand. "Have you been to Chamdal?"

"Once, long time ago." He picked up the rider's harness off a chair as she finished packing. "Not personally too fond of elves."

She carefully slipped the sling off her shoulder, waiting for him to explain. When he didn't, she asked, "Particular reason?"

Raffel shrugged helping her slip the harness over her arm. "They can be very proud about their age and strength of their race... to the point of hubris." He helped tighten the straps across her chest and back. "That's not too tight?"

"No," answered Blāzzer. "This feels a lot better than the other one. It fits my-" She clamped her mouth shut. "Excuse me." She turned away grabbing the sling hoping that Raffel didn't notice her blush.

## Chapter Twelve

Raffel and Blāzzer stood by the north gate, waiting for Ash. She looked about, watching the farnircks walk by, and didn't see the older dragon. She said, "Your dad seems to have a good relationship with Durthuh."

"Well, my family lives in Keeko and that's the only town in Wildwood Forest that is occupied by farnircks," explained Raffel, shifting the bag on his shoulder. "In fact, the farnircks only have three towns. Here, Keeko, and Thy Minda."

"Why are there so few?" asked Blāzzer.

"History hasn't been kind to farnircks. They have been persecuted for centuries. Nickada is the first country not to."

Blāzzer looked about her at the gray-skinned people, thinking, *But they're so kind.*

It was several more minutes before Ash, face unreadable, walked up to them, saying, "Let's head out. We'll shift outside the wall." He led them through the gate following the road into the hills. "Raffel, You'll tire out sooner with her on your back. Make sure to land before wearing out too much."

Raffel pressed his lips together and shifted, stretching his wings before crouching. As Ash tied Blāzzer's bag to the saddle Raffel moved his head closer to her. He said, "I'll do my best to not hurt your arm during take-off."

"I'll be okay," replied Blāzzer, smiling. Ash helped her into the saddle and secured the straps. "It'll be nice when I can do this by myself."

"Just a little bit longer and you can fly until Raffel falls out of the sky," said Ash, slapping his son's shoulder.

Raffel snorted and stood up. Blāzzer blinked at the difference in Raffel and Ash's dragon form. Raffel was shorter and not as broad as his father. His muscles weren't as defined, though his scales were more reflective. She reached down and touched his wing membrane, running her fingertips over the velvety surface. In one fluid motion, Ash shifted and took off into the sky.

Raffel looked back to Blāzzer and asked, "Are you ready?"

"Yeah," she replied tightening her grip on the saddle. He jumped into the air and she gasped as she slammed forward onto the saddle.

As he straightened out she slowly sat upright, thinking, *I would have been a goner if it wasn't for the harness.*

"You okay?" questioned Raffel, with one eye looking at her.

She smiled.

It was only a few hours until Raffel grew tired from flying and the dragons switched to walking. Blāzzer looked about them taking note of the various types of wildflowers and murmured, "It's pretty out here." He twitched his ear. "Have you seen much of Nickada?"

"Not much," he said. "I haven't traveled much in recent years." He paused for a moment before adding, "Didn't have anyone to go with."

Blāzzer touched his neck and said, "I'll go with you." He looked back at her and he closed his eyes while flopping his ears over. "Is that a smile?"

He snorted. "Yeah, we really can't smile in dragon form." He shrugged and turned forward.

"Do you know why the king had a saddle for a dragon?" she asked, running her fingers over the etchings in the leather saddle.

Raffel looked to Ash who was a hundred yards ahead, before answering, "It was made for my father."

Blāzzer glanced at the older dragon. "Explains why it fitted... but wait... who was the rider?"

"King Nayax."

"Really?!"

"It was before Nayax was crowned king. Originally, he was second in line for the throne. He and Father met during border patrols of the southern border. Nayax was the commander of the group so he and Father worked very closely together. Eventually, they began to act as dragon and rider... basically waiting for the opportunity to pass the liffen. It can't be given without an unexpected injury. However, that didn't happen. Nayax's brother died from illness so he became the heir. Because he was to be king, he and Father couldn't be bonded. I guess Nayax held onto the saddle through the years."

"That sucks."

Raffel nodded. "Father rarely ever talks about it. He and Nayax are still good friends, but him being king stresses it."

"I know our situation isn't good, but I'm glad we don't have to worry about that."

Blāzzer ran as fast as she could. The screaming and shouting was deafening as the horse riders chased down the Palatites. No matter how long she ran the great walls surrounding Palator never got closer. She turned to make sure Angel was still behind her. A rider charged at the older woman and struck her with a mace. Angel screamed so loud that Blāzzer cried out, covering her ears and closing her eyes. When she finally moved her hands away, the world was quiet. When she opened her eyes, she saw Mae and Lenny standing in front of her. They had tears streaking down their faces.

Mae bared her teeth and said, "If she hadn't saved you then Angel would be alive."

"We didn't need you!" shouted Lenny.

"You should have died not her."

"Mother deserves your life!"

"You brought this upon us!"

"You killed her!"

"You killed her!"

Blāzzer screamed, pulling on her hair as Mae and Lenny continued their verbal assault. She cried an endless stream of tears that pooled about her.

"Blāzzer!"

Someone grabbed her arm and she pushed at them trying to break free.

"Blāzzer!"

She gasped, sat upright, and opened her eyes to see Raffel shaking her by the shoulders. She blinked as she remembered she was in her tent where she, Raffel, and Ash had camped for the night.

"Blāzzer?" Raffel asked gently, squeezing her shoulders. She slumped forward against his chest, burying her face in his tunic as she cried. "I got you." He held her close, placing his cheek on the top of her head. "I got you... You're safe."

It was several minutes until Blāzzer calmed down enough to sit upright. She scrubbed at her cheeks with her hand, trying to take even breaths. She murmured, "Sorry."

"Don't be," reassured Raffel, wiping away one of her tears. "You should try to get some sleep. We have a long day ahead of us."

Blāzzer nodded and slowly laid down, pulling the blanket around herself.

As he turned to leave she grabbed his hand. Raffel looked at her and she asked quietly, "Can you stay... until I fall asleep?"

After a moment he nodded and laid down beside her. She pressed her face against his shoulder, curling up on her side. Listening to Raffel's heartbeat, she took deep breaths and closed her eyes.

Blāzzer woke to voices arguing and blinked in the early morning light. She stretched out her hand to the empty space beside her thinking, *Raffel...*

"Were you even thinking?" questioned Ash from outside the tent. A growl resounded in his voice.

"She was having a nightmare," retorted Raffel. "You're being ridiculous."

"Am I? You slept in the same tent as her. Others, especially the leaders, would not perceive that well."

"I comforted her and she asked I stay until she fell asleep. That's it! Nothing happened."

"You stayed there all night, Raffel."

There was a minute of silence and Blāzzer felt her heart pound in her chest.

"Don't give the Council wood to put on the fire to take her away," growled Ash. She blinked, pulling the blanket over her head. "Or do you want that?"

"No," whispered Raffel, almost too quiet for her to hear.

Ash said calmly, "You and her actions can mean the difference between this working for you two or not. I won't be able to keep you two together as I did with Nayax if the Council comes with fire... If you have any romantic feelings for her, you better bury them."

There was a pause before Raffel answered, "I don't have any."

Blāzzer, watching the land pass by below, leaned against Raffel's neck as the dragon flew north. She thought, *I shouldn't have asked him to stay... It was selfish.* She closed her eyes, focusing on the warmth coming from Raffel's scales. *Does he blame me? Do they blame me?... No. It was just a dream... But his conversation. If we're too close then they'll take me away. I like him. He's a nice, caring guy, but he doesn't like me. Being near him though makes me feel like I'm home.*

"You okay?" asked Raffel, turning his head and looking at her with one eye. She nodded, continuing to stare out across the land. "I'm sorry you didn't sleep well. Do you want to talk about it?" She shook her head. "Blāzzer?"

"I just want to be left alone right now," she murmured, closing her eyes and feeling her heart ache.

A few days passed before a large forest loomed over the horizon. Blāzzer blinked at the expanse of greenery, unable to see any distinguishing landmarks. As they neared it she thought, *This is a very old... very ancient forest.*

The dragons landed on the edge of the woods, before walking under the boughs. Barely any light filtered through the leaves. Birds and squirrels could be seen moving between the branches. Some of them cried out as the dragons passed. With their heads lowered the dragons only dislodged a couple of leaves.

Blāzzer reached up and touched the leaves of a tree. She felt something in her chest and thought, *This place feels familiar somehow.*

A few hours slowly ticked by before they made camp under a large oak. Blāzzer sat in front of the campfire cutting potatoes into a pot. She looked up as Raffel walked up with an armful of broken branches. As he placed them down, she asked, "Where's Ash? He hasn't come back."

"He went hunting," replied Raffel, sitting across from her. "Nothing against your cooking, just being in dragon form drains a lot of energy."

Blāzzer nodded and went back to cutting potatoes.

"Are you warm enough?" he asked.

She nodded, focusing on cutting off a rotten part of a potato. She dropped the last chunk into the pot of water and hung the pot over the fire.

"What's next?"

"We have some carrots and salted beef."

"I meant about us."

Flinching, Blāzzer blinked and looked at him. He met her gaze and she had a hard time keeping eye contact with him. "I don't know what you're talking about," she said, grabbing a carrot from a bag and slicing it.

"You haven't talked to me for three days, not since you had that bad dream."

She ground her teeth together, trying to focus on cutting the carrot.

"I've respected your wish to not talk about it," said Raffel, "but you still won't talk at all. So maybe you should talk about it."

"I don't want to," murmured Blāzzer.

Raffel stood up and as he walked over to her, she looked up at him. He knelt down next to her and said, "Please."

She placed the knife down and, turning towards him, questioned, "Why should I tell you?"

He blinked.

At the hurt that crossed his face she looked into the fire, feeling shame rise to her cheeks. As Raffel reached out and touched her hands, she realized that she had been clenching them into fists to the point her nails bit into her palms. She didn't pull away as he slipped his hands into hers.

"I wish things were different," he murmured. "No politics... or battle. Us back in Palator... and you there from the beginning with Angel, Lenny, and Mae... Things would be better." He drew his hands back and she tightened her grip on them.

"I'm sorry," whispered Blāzzer. Raffel squeezed her hands. "I'm trying hard to be strong, but I don't know what that means." She wiped her cheeks with a hand, smearing a stray tear. "Maybe I'm just selfish."

"For what?"

"Do they blame me for Angel's death?"

Raffel blinked in surprise and said, "No. Mae and Lenny do not blame you. No one does." He sighed and shifted his legs. "It's not selfish to feel guilt... It's just being human. You shouldn't feel guilty; the attack was out of your control." He waited a moment. "I felt guilty for you getting injured."

"Mae had mentioned that," whispered Blāzzer, looking at him. "I had dreamed that Mae and Lenny were yelling at me... blaming me for Angel's death... how I should have died and she lived." She curled forward over their hands.

"They don't blame you and they don't think it should have been you. They're glad you're alive... I'm glad you're alive."

"Raffel?"

"Yeah?"

Blāzzer tried to swallow the lump in her throat and whispered, "I heard the argument you had with your dad."

Raffel grimaced slightly and murmured, "I'm sorry you heard that... Sadly, he's being honest. We just have to be careful."

She looked at him. "Do you like me – as a friend?"

He nodded. "Of course. You're very kind and caring."

She smiled softly.

"I like it when you smile."

## Chapter Thirteen

They continued to travel through the forest for several days till the trees began to thin out. The setting sun cast orange light onto buildings. All were made of wood with curved roofs and intricate designs carved into the support beams. Tall, long-haired people walked about and many glanced at the dragons.

"They're elves," said Blãzzer, noticing their pointed ears and prominent cheekbones.

"Welcome to Chamdal," said Ash, looking over his shoulder at her. Blãzzer blinked as the trees became taller and wider, holding buildings in their branches with interconnected walkways. No wall surrounded the city and stone roads led through with gardens and fountains at intersections.

Ash led them to the right, walking along the outskirts of Chamdal. Blãzzer studied the town, noticing centaurs amongst the elves. On several balconies stood elven guards in leather armor with longbows. Their critical gazes followed the dragons.

"They're watching us," breathed Blãzzer, resting her hand on Raffel's neck. He twitched his ear, but didn't make a sound.

Soon they came to a building that was set aside from the others. It was two stories tall with a balcony and covered patio. The primary roof beam was carved to look like a dragon with each scale defined. As Ash shifted and helped Blãzzer down a woman walked out to them.

"You're here!" exclaimed the woman with a big smile.

"Blãzzer, this is my sister Lydia," said Raffel, turning his head to the she-dragon. She placed her hand on his nose. Her long hair was the same red as his, except it had streaks of blue.

"It's nice to meet you," replied Blãzzer with a smile.

"Here are the bags," said Ash, handing down the bags from the saddle on

Raffel's back. "How are you feeling Lydia?"

"Good," answered his daughter, taking a bag. "Somewhat tired, but a lot better."

Ash smiled softly as he removed the last bag from the saddle, saying, "We'll take the saddle off later after we have some time to rest."

Raffel shifted and as the flash of light dimmed Lydia threw her arms around him, saying, "You're so tall now, little brother."

After a moment he smiled and hugged her back, replying, "It's good to see you too."

Ash grunted and, grabbing some bags, walked inside. Raffel grabbed the other bags and said, "Should probably head in. We have some observers."

Blāzzer glanced over her shoulder and noticed several elves blatantly staring, including a number of elven guards. A shiver ran down her spine and she quickly caught up with Lydia and Raffel as they walked into the house.

"Raffel, let's go to the bath house," said Ash, placing the bags down against a wall.

"I want to help Blāzzer get settled first," replied Raffel.

"Lydia can help her... and you smell." Raffel looked to Blāzzer and she smiled apologetically.

"Go, I'll take care of her," assured Lydia, squeezing his arm. He nodded and followed Ash back out.

Lydia led Blāzzer upstairs to a small bedroom, placing her bags on the bed. Blāzzer blinked as she noticed dragons carved into the headboard and into the other pieces of furniture.

"Lots of dragons," murmured Blāzzer.

Lydia grinned and said, "Our ancestors were a bit tacky." She pushed open a window to let some fresh air in. "I'll let you get settled. I'll be downstairs if you need anything." She walked up to Blāzzer and embraced her. "I'm really glad you're here."

For a moment the young woman tensed at the dragon's cool touch, but relaxed when she realized it was like the first sips of cool water on a hot summer day. Lydia stepped out, leaving Blāzzer to unpack.

*Part of me isn't for sure how much to unpack, because I might not be here long,* thought Blāzzer. She pulled her clean clothes from her bag and placed them in a drawer. Grabbing the bag, she went downstairs and found the female dragon sketching in a journal.

"Is there a place for laundry?" asked the young woman. "Most of my clothes are filthy from travel."

Lydia smiled softly and replied, "Place them in the hall closet and they'll get laundered."

Blāzzer placed them there before sitting on a couch across from Lydia, who was curled up in a large chair. The room was comfortable with chairs and couches around a small unlit fireplace. She watched Lydia's hands slowly work on a drawing and said, "I noticed your hands are much cooler than a mortal's. Ash and Raffel are so much warmer."

"Course they didn't tell you," answered the dragon playfully rolling her eyes. "Most dragons breathe fire, but some, like me and Mom, breathe ice. Pretty cool isn't it?"

"Yeah." Blāzzer smiled.

"Guess it's to be expected though. Men aren't as detail-oriented." Lydia shrugged. "Well now you have more dragons to ask and there's Cornin too. He's helped out the family a lot and, since he's a Sentinel Crow too, we get some extra support from them. You'll be able to ask him lots of questions about being a rider."

Blāzzer pressed her lips together, not wanting to think about the rider-dragon bond.

"Rough going?" When Blāzzer didn't answer, Lydia continued, "It's a big change and there's lots of stuff going on that it's understandable to not feel good... And I'm for sure my brother doesn't make it much easier."

"No, he's been very kind," insisted Blāzzer quietly.

Lydia smiled. "He really is a big softy, but stubborn." She closed her journal at approaching footsteps.

The door opened and a tall woman walked in followed by a man in a black cloak. The woman smiled greatly at the sight of Blāzzer and said, "You're here!"

Blāzzer blinked in response, thinking, *This must be Raffel's mom.* The older woman was beautiful with smooth skin and long blue hair that had highlights of purple. *The other must be Cornin.* The man was weathered, but not old, and had creases around his eyes from smiling. Blāzzer stood up and said, "It's good to meet you."

The older female dragon hugged Blāzzer and the young woman blinked at how cool, almost cold, she was to the touch. She stepped back and Cornin held out his hand saying, "I'm Cornin, and this is Aurora. Glad I'm not the only normal one now."

Blāzzer smiled and shook his hand, noticing a black tattoo on his inner wrist.

"Dad and Raffel should be back soon," said Lydia.

Aurora nodded and sat on the couch with Blāzzer. Cornin pulled up a kitchen chair before lighting a pipe. He grunted as if in response to someone, but no one had spoken.

"How is your arm feeling?" asked Aurora looking at Blāzzer.

"A lot better," she replied. "I'll be able to have it out of the sling all day soon. I'm just sore from traveling."

"We can go to the bathhouse," suggested Aurora. "It'll help with the stiffness. The hot springs are very nice here."

Blāzzer nodded.

"Us girls will go then. Cornin can you wait here for the boys?"

Cornin waved his hand slightly and leaned back in the chair. The three women headed out with Aurora leading them through the town. Blāzzer said, "An actual bath sounds really good."

Lydia smiled and replied, "The elven bathhouses are the best."

As they walked Blāzzer noticed how everything the elves made seemed elegant with few sharp corners and countless intricate carvings. She also noticed how the elves were mostly quiet and glanced or openly stared at the dragons. Some had disgust or contempt on their faces. Few children walked amongst the adults. She thought, *Raffel had said they were hubris. Now I'm starting to understand what he was talking about.*

Aurora led them into a short building that had pipes releasing steam along the roofline. Inside was a long hallway with sliding doors. Some elves, wearing silk robes, moved between the rooms and one approached them asking, "Are you here for the baths?"

"Yes, a private room if possible," replied Aurora.

The elf nodded and led them to the end of the hall. She slid open a door to a small stone room that had benches and towels. On the far wall was a curtained-off doorway.

"You two go ahead," insisted Aurora. "I'm going to get some soap."

"Oh, chamomile or tea tree please," said Lydia stepping into the room.

Aurora looked at Blāzzer.

"Lavender please," the young woman replied. Aurora followed the elf back to the entrance as Blāzzer turned, stepping into the small room. She slid the door shut and looked up at the sunlight that filtered through the frosted glass tiles in the ceiling. She undressed before asking, "Lydia, can you help me with the bandage on my shoulder?"

The dragon, already naked, nodded and carefully began to unwrap Blāzzer's shoulder. She said, "Does it hurt?"

Blāzzer shook her head. "Not really. There's some numbness sometimes." She looked over at her shoulder. The bruising was almost gone besides the yellow tinge. Bright red lines came from a central red spot. "It looks like a star bursting."

"You haven't seen it?"

"No. It's always been bandaged and the bruising... It's so... red."

Lydia smiled and led the way through the curtain, saying, "Well, a liffen matches the color of the dragon's scales. Cornin has his on his stomach, a big blue and purple lightning bolt."

Past the curtain was a pool of water with a small stone staircase leading down into it. Blāzzer stepped in, feeling her body relax immediately at the heat. She dropped under the surface and resurfaced pushing her hair out of her face, standing in the water that was a foot shorter than her.

"Why do the elves not like the dragons?" Blāzzer asked.

"Long history," replied Lydia, grabbing a washcloth from the rim of the pool.

"Because they ruled most of Nickada before the dragons came," said Aurora, stepping through the curtain. She had pale scars crossing her body like thin cracks in ice. She stepped down into the pool, handing the young women their soaps. "Mortals feared the elves back then. When the dragons and barruns came, they began forming a council that later became the Council of Leaders. Mortals were much more widespread and had a larger population. So, it was decided that a mortal would be king, acting as a mediator between the races. Except elves didn't like that. They tried to battle against the mortals, but the dragons beat them back. Keep in mind that elves hadn't known about dragons a decade before this. Elves used to be the strongest of the races, but dragons..." She shrugged. "So the elves agreed to an alliance as long as the dragon leader was a rider."

"But even after all these years?" asked Blāzzer, enjoying the smell of her lavender soap.

"They live a long time so they're good at holding grudges," grumbled Lydia, scrubbing her face.

Aurora's looked at her daughter from the corner of her eye before saying, "We currently live in Keeko with many farnircks. It used to be in elven territory and they have wanted it back for many decades." She sighed. "Basically, the elves tend to be racist." Blāzzer blinked at the bluntness of the words. "But let's not dwell on that."

After they washed, they stepped out of the bath and dried off. Blāzzer dressed up to the waist before asking, "Can one of you help me bandage my shoulder?"

Aurora nodded and picked up a roll of cloth that had appeared in the room while they were bathing. She worked quickly and efficiently wrapping Blāzzer's shoulder. She asked, "Have you been able to speak with Raffel through the liffen?"

Blāzzer shook her head, replying, "Lillian said it will take time... I'm not for sure how to even do it."

Aurora gently touched Blāzzer's chin, guiding her so they met each other's eyes. "Cornin and I will help you and Raffel."

Blāzzer nodded. The dragon stepped away and the young woman finished dressing. They wrapped the remainder of their soap blocks in parchment paper. As they left Lydia said, "I hope dinner is ready when we get back."

After a moment Aurora answered, "Cornin made a potato and pork stew." She smiled. "He's making sure Ash and Raffel don't eat it all."

Outside barely any sunlight could be seen over the treetops. Stars twinkled overhead and fireflies flitted about. Blāzzer followed Aurora and Lydia through Chamdal to the building the dragons were staying in. The two female dragons talked along the way, but Blāzzer was too lost in thought to listen.

*I'm feeling so tired,* she thought. *I needed that bath. I need food... Right now though, sleep sounds good. Don't know if I can stay awake while we eat.*

"Blāzzer, you okay?" asked Lydia.

The young woman nodded and replied, "Just tired. I think I'm going to go straight to bed when we get back."

"You should eat something," insisted Aurora with motherly concern. "You can go ahead and go upstairs. I'll have Raffel bring you up a small bowl."

When they got to the building, Blāzzer walked past the kitchen and went directly upstairs to her room. As she sat down on the bed to pull her boots off there was a knock at the door. She said, "Come in."

The door opened and Raffel walked in with a bowl of stew. He was clean with his hair hanging loose to dry. Placing the bowl on the nightstand, he asked, "How are you feeling?"

"Really tired," she replied. "Thank you for bringing the stew up."

He shrugged. "Well, I'll let you get settled in for the night." He turned and left.

As he crossed the threshold she thought, *Wait, I don't want you to go.* He stopped right outside for a moment before closing the door behind him.

Blāzzer sat on a bench on the patio, watching Aurora comb and cut Lydia's hair. The older dragon hummed quietly as she worked. Sunlight filtered through the vines that grew along the trellises overhead. Blāzzer looked up as Raffel walked over and sat down next to her.

"Do you want me to cut your hair?" asked Aurora, glancing at him. He shook his head. "You always have liked your hair long."

"It's so soft too," smiled Blāzzer. Lydia, surprised, turned her head to look at the young woman and Aurora pushed on the side of her head. "When the flowers had blossomed outside of Palator, Mae taught me how to braid flowers into hair. I practiced on Raffel."

Aurora chuckled softly and replied, "It's good that you're letting someone touch your hair."

Blāzzer blinked, glancing at Raffel and asking, "You don't like your hair being touched?"

"Not really," he replied with a shrug.

She frowned. "I'm sorry!"

"It's okay... I liked it when you played with my hair."

She looked down, letting her hair fall in her face, as she blushed deeply.

"Okay, your turn Blāzzer," said Aurora as Lydia stood up.

"I'll trade seats with you," said Lydia with a smile. Blāzzer nodded and got up. She sat on the stool as Lydia sat on the bench beside Raffel. "Just a trim?"

"Yeah," breathed Blāzzer. She sat quietly as Aurora combed out her hair, remembering the conversation she had with Raffel on the hill outside Palator. "Actually, can you cut it up to here?" She pressed the side of her hand to her jawline.

"Of course," answered Aurora. "You'll need to get scarves to hold it back for flying."

"That's okay."

"Shopping trip," insisted Lydia, smiling.

Blāzzer sat still and stared into the forest as Aurora began to cut her hair. She glanced down at the stone pavers, seeing her long brown locks mixed with pieces of purplish-red hair. Her head started feeling lighter. Aurora continued to comb and cut, asking, "What made you decide you wanted your hair short?"

"I've always wanted it to be short," replied Blāzzer, fidgeting with her fingers. "I thought it would be a good time to do so."

"It's going to look really cute," said Lydia. Blāzzer blushed slightly remembering what Raffel had said about her having short hair back in Palator.

A few minutes passed until Aurora said, "And you're done." Blāzzer reached up and ran her fingers through her hair, surprising herself with how it abruptly ended. "Do you like it?"

"Yes, I love it!" answered the young woman, grinning from ear to ear. She turned to Lydia and Raffel. "What do you think?"

Lydia clapped her hands, complimenting, "I think it looks amazing." Raffel had his mouth slightly open as he looked at Blāzzer. His sister elbowed his side and he, twitching his ear back, pressed his lips together.

He stood up, saying, "Come on, let's go get you some hair scarves." He walked past them towards Chamdal without glancing at Blāzzer.

Aurora patted Blāzzer's shoulder and said, "Go on. You can ask him on the way." Blāzzer nodded.

"I'll come too," offered Lydia, standing up. Aurora, frowning, looked at her daughter. "Fine, I'll stay here. Pick out some pretty designs."

Blāzzer hurried to catch up with Raffel, thinking, *My hair is so light now. It almost makes me feel giddy.* She caught up to him at the edge of town. The streets were bustling with elves, all much taller than her. She pressed her lips together in uneasiness and grabbed Raffel's sleeve. He glanced down at her and smiled softly.

"Do you know any of the stores around here?" she asked.

He shook his head and replied, "I thought we could find the main street and start there."

Large trees and balconies towered overhead. Several times the road led to courtyards with fountains and gardens. Some elves played musical instruments, filling the air with light songs. Most elves didn't pay attention to Raffel and Blāzzer. The only elves that did were the guards on the balconies above.

"This place makes me miss Palator," whispered Blāzzer, still holding onto his sleeve.

"Definitely does," replied Raffel.

"Are you going to go back to Palator after all of this?"

He shrugged. "I don't know. I should finish my dragon training. For that I'll need to either be in Keeko or Minda Mountains. Are you wanting to go back?"

"I think so."

He raised an eyebrow.

"I don't know. Angel is gone... and all I really want is a place to call home." Blāzzer met his eyes. "I think I'd like to be wherever you are."

Raffel jerked his head in a nod before facing forward and continuing to lead her through the crowds. Soon they came to a courtyard with merchant stalls set up under intricate cloth canopies. A variety of pottery, wood carvings, herbs, and fabrics were on display and being sold. Blāzzer couldn't help but take a look at the different booths. Most of the items had designs of animals and plant life with intricate detail. When she came to a booth selling scarves, she gently touched the fabric.

"All of the items are made here in Chamdal," said the elf behind the table. Her own long, silky hair was pulled back with a scarf.

"They're all so beautiful," commented Blāzzer, running her finger along the embroidery.

The elf smiled. "Are you looking for anything in particular?"

"Scarves to keep my hair out of my face when we travel."

"Over here I have some that are the perfect length for keeping hair back. They won't trail or get tangled."

Blāzzer picked up a soft blue one with red poppies. She held it up to show Raffel who stood a few feet behind her. He nodded slightly. She smiled and turned back to the other scarves.

"Here is one that will make your eyes stand out," offered the elf holding a scarf in her slender fingers. The fabric was yellow with green ferns.

Blāzzer took the scarf and asked, "How much are they?"

"Three for a silver."

Blāzzer nodded and looked at the other scarves laying on the table, thinking, *All the designs are so beautiful that I don't know which one to pick.* She turned to Raffel. "Which one do you think I should get?" He stepped forward and looked over the table.

"This one," he said, tapping a scarf. Blāzzer smiled and picked up the fabric. She pulled out a small silver coin from her pocket and handed it to the elf.

"Thank you," said the merchant, smiling. "Have a good day."

Blāzzer followed Raffel away before saying, "Wait a second." He looked at her and she handed him the first two scarves. "I want to put one on." She carefully wrapped the red fabric around her head before tugging it into a knot. Her fingers pressing against the gold embroidery of butterflies, she pushed it back to the top of her head. She looked up at Raffel and smiled. "What do you think?"

He reached up and tucked a loose hair behind her ear before smiling and whispering, "Beautiful." He blinked and withdrew his hand quickly. "We should head back." He turned and led the way down the street.

Blāzzer felt warmth in her chest as her heart fluttered and thought, *He called me beautiful.*

The following morning, Blāzzer followed Cornin and Raffel outside to a small covered patio on the side of the building. They sat on the benches as Cornin said, "Aurora and I want to help you with the liffen. Though most of it will take time, there are some tricks that can help facilitate it."

Raffel pressed his lips together and Blāzzer, feeling nervous, nodded.

Cornin continued, "Eventually the liffen will be strong enough to allow both of you to take on dragon qualities as humans." He closed his eyes and in a heartbeat his hair became rigid, horns grew from the top of his head, his ears became pointed, nails thickened and sharpened, and a purplish-blue tinge came to his skin in places. He opened his eyes and they matched Aurora's. "This half state is known as fatorana." He smiled and he had an extra set of canine teeth that were elongated compared to his others. "It's pretty useful... Draining, but useful." He sighed and reverted back to his normal self. "For right now we'll focus on the mental link. Go ahead and move so you are seated facing each other."

Raffel shifted to a different seat, his jaw tight. Blāzzer felt her insides turn at the prospect of trying to communicate via the liffen. She thought, *Is this something that will cause the Council to take me away?*

"Now, we'll start with simple impressions," explained Cornin. "Impressions are how you feel. There are no words to them. When you want to share an impression, imagine sharing that feeling with each other. Close your eyes and give it a try. "

Blāzzer took a deep breath and thought, *Share the feeling with each other.* She tried to imagine giving him a box of nervousness. When nothing felt different, she tried imagining showing him a picture of gray butterflies. *Nothing is happening.* She opened her eyes slightly and saw Raffel sitting across from her. His eyes were shut and his lips pinched in concentration. She imagined seeing steam coming out of his head as he tried to communicate.

His eyes flashed open and he looked at her with narrowed pupils.

"Something got through," said Cornin with the grin.

Raffel looked away with his ears pinned back and said something in Drakken.

Cornin blinked, his smile fading. He responded briskly in Drakken. He paused and, when the dragon didn't respond, Blāzzer looked between them in confusion before looking to Raffel thinking, *What's going on?*

He turned to her and she felt a wave of frustration that was not her own wash over. She flinched, wanting to hide. Cornin said something in Drakken before getting up and leaving them.

After a few minutes, Raffel's pupils rounded and he said, "I'm sorry."

Blāzzer didn't move her gaze from the cobbled stones at her feet. She felt a trickle of apology. She looked up at him, asking, "Why were you frustrated?" She blinked as she felt shame from him.

"I haven't been honest," he murmured. After a moment he continued, "I've been able to feel impressions from you for a while."

"Really?!" exclaimed Blāzzer, excitedly, then anger tightened her throat. "You felt it the other night."

He winced and nodded slightly. "I'm sorry."

"Why didn't you say anything?" She felt his uneasiness and lack of confidence.

"I didn't want you to be overwhelmed."

She raised an eyebrow. "Having you not communicate with me makes things overwhelming."

He raised an eyebrow. "Guess we're both guilty of that."

Heat flushed her cheeks and she looked away, mumbling, "I was processing." A rush of protectiveness came from Raffel and she looked at him. He was glaring over her shoulder. She looked and saw an elven guard standing there. She quickly stood up and Raffel stepped in front of her.

"What do you need?" questioned the dragon, his ears folded back.

"Lord Legorin has ordered I bring Blāzzer to him," said the elf, his face unwavering.

"Why?" asked Blāzzer.

The elf didn't remove his eyes from Raffel as he answered, "To meet you before you are brought before the Council."

"She's not going," growled Raffel.

The elf didn't budge and said, "I have my order to fulfill."

Blāzzer placed her hand on Raffel's arm and stepped forward, saying, "I'll come with you to meet Lord Legorin."

Raffel looked at her with astonishment. Before he could say anything she sent him a reassuring thought with a smile. She walked up to the elven guard and asked, "What is your name?"

"Leggauto," replied the elf, "son of Lord Legorin and heir of the Leader of the Forest Elves."

"Nice to meet you Leggauto. I'm Blāzzer Ozol." She held out her hand.

Leggauto blinked and turned away, gruffly saying, "Follow me."

Blāzzer, trying to keep her chin up, followed him away from the Stone family. She felt a warmth from Raffel spread in her chest, but before she could determine what emotion it was the sensation was gone. She had walked out of reach.

# Chapter Fourteen

Blāzzer followed Leggauto through Chamdal. The other elves silently stepped out of his way and bowed their heads slightly. He didn't seem to notice them. They went up a staircase and across a walkway to a double set of doors. Elven guards stood outside the doors and at Leggauto's approach, they opened them.

Blāzzer blinked at the large room with its high ceiling that rounded in an arch. Bookcases lined the walls where intricate tapestries hung. The far wall had floor-to-ceiling windows that overlooked a courtyard. In front of the glass panes stood a tall male elf. His golden hair was long and in several braids with beads made of precious metals and stones.

Leggauto led Blāzzer to the middle of the room as the doors closed behind them. He said, "Stay here." She watched as he walked up to a few yards away from the elf and knelt with his head bowed.

Moments past and Blāzzer looked about awkwardly, thinking, *This is ridiculous.* She stepped forward and said, "Lord Legorin, it's nice to meet you." As the moments continued to pass with no reply she blinked. "I'm-"

"I know who you are," said the older elf, not turning around. "You will speak when you are told to do so."

Blāzzer ground her teeth together, trying to suppress her anger.

Slowly Legorin turned around and walked up to Blāzzer, leaving Leggauto kneeling. His height made her crane her head back to meet his eyes. There were no wrinkles on his face but several strands of silver in his hair betrayed his age. He smiled slightly, but it wasn't friendly.

"Blāzzer Ozol you are looking well," said the elven leader, "considering the extent of your injuries just a number of weeks ago."

Blāzzer nodded slightly. They stood there in silence, his eyes studying her as if he was dissecting her. She struggled to keep eye contact with him and soon she looked past him at Leggauto, who was now standing and facing them.

"It was very kind of you to have Leggauto show me the way here," she said with a smile, looking back to Legorin. "I would have gotten lost otherwise."

Legorin raised an eyebrow at her and Leggauto tried to suppress a smile. A commotion came from outside the doors. They burst open and Ash walked in followed by Raffel. The elven guards that had stood at the doors surged in front of them, placing themselves between the dragons and their leader.

"We'll be taking Blāzzer back," said Ash.

"We were just getting to know each other," replied Legorin dismissively.

"It's okay," assured Blāzzer, looking between the dragons.

"Guards, return to your posts." The elven guards walked out with Raffel eyeing them. They closed the doors behind them. Legorin stepped away from Blāzzer, saying, "The little dragon boy isn't very little anymore."

Raffel pinned his ears back, his lips twitching as he struggled to rein in a snarl. He stepped forward and Ash held out his arm, blocking his advance. Raffel clenched his jaw, muscles straining.

*Raffel, please,* thought Blāzzer, doing her best to send him reassuring feelings even if they were shaky. Raffel's jaw relaxed, but his ears remained pinned back.

"In two days the Council will all be here," said Legorin. "Of course, no Sentinel Crow or farnirck will be present. How do you think the voting will go over her custody?"

Blāzzer blinked and questioned, "Wasn't the Council called to meet about the Snerxite attacks?"

Legorin shrugged, not taking his eyes off the dragons.

She stepped in front of him so he had to look at her. "What about the people?! Don't you care about them?"

"Those that were injured and died in those attacks were not my people."

Blāzzer felt her heart drop at the elf's words. She felt tears well and her hands clenched into fists. Before she could say anything Legorin turned and walked away, saying, "Leave. I have no further need to speak with you."

Blāzzer stood there not for sure what to do. She looked up at Raffel as he touched her shoulder. He guided her out with Ash following behind them, the large double doors closing after them. She didn't notice anything as they walked back to the building the dragons were staying at. When they got there, she went upstairs to her room and laid on the bed, burying her face in the pillow. Blāzzer didn't look up as footsteps approached. The bed sank slightly from someone sitting on the edge.

"You were very brave," said Aurora, rubbing the young woman's back gently. "Do you want to talk?"

Blāzzer shook her head.

"Do you want me to leave?"

Again she shook her head.

"Is it okay if I lie next to you?"

She nodded.

Aurora laid on her side next to Blāzzer, continuing to rub her back until she fell asleep. When Blāzzer woke, she was alone. She sat up and noticed that someone must've taken her boots off for her. Slowly she got out of bed and went downstairs. The house was quiet as she walked into the living room.

Raffel was asleep on the sofa and Lydia was in a chair with her sketchbook. She waved Blāzzer over and the young woman looked down at the drawing. "It looks just like him," she whispered with admiration.

Lydia smiled and responded quietly, "It helps to have a still model." She scooted over to one side of the large cushioned chair and patted the seat. Blāzzer sat down next to her and could feel the coolness of the dragon's body through their clothing. Blāzzer rested her head on Lydia's shoulder, watching her continue the final details of her sketch.

After a while, Blāzzer said, "I thought leaders were supposed to care about their people... All of their people."

Lydia paused her sketching a moment before continuing and saying, "Some leaders think that if a person isn't one of their subordinates then they don't need to care about them."

"That's not right," whispered Blāzzer.

Lydia nodded.

"I couldn't believe it when Legorin said that... how could he?"

"Because he's a pompous piece of shit," growled Raffel, not opening his eyes. Lydia glared at him. "King Nayax will make sure the Council discusses the attacks."

"Will I be going away?" asked Blāzzer.

Raffel pinned his ears back.

"No," replied Lydia squeezing the young woman's arm. "We are going to do everything we can to make sure you stay with us."

Raffel sat up and looked at them with his forearms braced against his knees, growling, "It doesn't matter what the Council decides. You will stay with us."

Blāzzer shuddered inside at his certainty, thinking, *This isn't good.*

Lydia said something in Drakken. Raffel responded. As they spoke back and forth their voices raised and tones sharpened.

"Enough!" said Blāzzer. Both dragons looked at her. "Please... don't argue. I don't understand what you're saying, but please... not right now."

"Sorry," murmured Lydia, looking at Raffel and he averted his gaze. "Why don't we go for a walk in the woods? It'll help clear our heads."

Blāzzer nodded and they soon left, heading away from Chamdal and the elves. She felt lighter the farther they went. Raffel led the way along a dirt trail winding between trees. Every so often he would look over his shoulder at Blāzzer and Lydia. It was one of these times that Blāzzer noticed he was specifically looking at her. She asked, "What?"

"Nothing," he replied quickly looking ahead.

Lydia chuckled quietly, before saying, "Just can't help but look when two pretty ladies are following you."

Blāzzer blushed and Raffel snorted. He said, "Making sure you two don't get lost."

"You're the one guiding us, so it would be you getting us lost," said Lydia with a smile.

As they walked, they came to a small grove of flowering trees. Bees and butterflies fluttered about the flowers that were soft pink with a yellow heart. Lydia reached up and plucked a blossom from a lower branch. She motioned to Blāzzer and the young woman came over to her. Lydia gently tucked the flower behind Blāzzer's ears and both smiled.

"Raffel," said Lydia, drawing his attention from the butterflies. She held out her hand to Blāzzer. "Isn't she pretty?"

"Yes," he said turning away, but not before Blāzzer saw his cheeks turn pink. She suppressed a giggle, her heart skipping a beat.

"Oh, look!" said Lydia, stepping off the path and walking up to a tree past the grove. Blāzzer quickly followed her as Raffel stood on the path. She walked up to Lydia's side and saw little, purple flowers nestled between the roots.

Blāzzer knelt down and gently caressed the delicate petals, whispering, "They're beautiful. Don't you think, Lydia?" When the dragon didn't answer, she looked up and saw that Lydia was staring blankly into the forest. "Lydia?"

The dragon collapsed, her body flailing about uncontrollably. Blāzzer, trying to grab her, yelled, "Raffel! Help!"

Raffel ran to them and pushed Blāzzer aside, ordering, "Stay back!" He grabbed Lydia and rolled her onto her side, hissing as steam rose from where he touched her. Blāzzer blinked and scrambled back as frost and ice spread out from Lydia.

She asked, "What's happening?"

"She's having a seizure," he replied through his teeth. Frost was starting to cover his clothing. "Her endar is leaking out." One of Lydia's arms broke free from his grasp and hit his chest, making him grunt. "Stay back."

"Should I get help?"

"No one can do anything besides hold her down. It'll be over soon."

Soon felt like hours to Blāzzer, but Lydia's seizing did stop. The frost stopped spreading and she lay still on the ground. Raffel sighed before carefully picking up Lydia. The ice cracked and popped under his feet as steam rose.

"We need to take her back," he said, walking slowly towards the path. Blāzzer glanced back where Lydia had been before starting after him.

The flowers had shriveled in the cold.


Blāzzer watched from the doorway as Raffel placed his sister carefully on her bed. He tucked the blanket around Lydia before turning to Blāzzer and walking to her. She stepped back as he walked out into the hall, closing the door slightly behind him.

"Will she be alright?" asked Blāzzer.

Raffel nodded, before leaning against the wall and sinking to the ground. He rested his forehead on his crossed arms over his knees. Blāzzer sat down next to him and wrapped her arm around her legs.

"How long has she had seizures for?" asked Blāzzer, quietly.

Raffel turned his head towards her, saying, "Since we were little... They got worse when she began to be able to shift." He sighed, closing his eyes. "She said that she had started taking some new medicine. That it was helping... I thought she meant they were gone."

"I'm sorry... I'm glad you were there to help her today though."

He opened his eyes. "Don't touch her if she starts seizing, okay? I know you want to help, but you'll get frostbite... and Lydia wouldn't be able to forgive herself if she ended up hurting anyone."

Blāzzer nodded, pressing her lips together. "Why does her endar leak?"

"Naturally endars leak to some degree," he said, tipping his head back and staring at the ceiling. "It's why I'm warm to the touch - beyond human normal... But what happens with Lydia's seizures is different. The seizures cause the leak, not the other way round. Just like her limbs spasm, her control of her endar spasms."

"What happens when she's in dragon form?"

"Well... being able to shift is having control of one's endar."

"She'll shift back to being a human?" murmured Blāzzer.

Raffel looked at her, nodding.

"But if she's flying..."

"She'll fall."

Blāzzer pressed her fist against her mouth, feeling fear well up inside herself.

"It's why Lydia won't fly without at least one other dragon in the air with her," said Raffel.

"Has she..." Blāzzer's words trailed off, unable to voice her question.

"Yeah, a few times. Mom and Dad have always caught her. They can't keep her from flying; it would be cruel... but they don't want her to be involved in any battles because of it."

Blāzzer nodded slightly, struggling to calm her racing heart.

"Lydia will wake up in an hour or so," assured Raffel. "She'll be worn out, but she'll be alright... She's not going anywhere. Lydia's a lot tougher than she lets on."

Blāzzer walked beside Ash towards the Council chambers. Her arm was not in the sling and she wore the shirt Angel had embroidered for her. She felt like her stomach was a bottomless pit and her heart was in her throat. She didn't notice anything as they walked, not even the stone path she stared blankly at. As they neared a building Ash touched her shoulder. She looked up at him and blinked, realizing she had tears in her eyes.

"Wipe the tears away," said Ash gruffly. Blāzzer did so with her embroidered sleeve hem. "Chin up. Shoulders back. You do not fear them. You want control of your future? Then show it no fear." She stood straighter and took a deep breath. "Whatever happens when you're in there, you will always be a member of the Stone family."

"Thank you," whispered Blāzzer.

Ash nodded and continued to lead her. As they entered the building several Lemay Soldiers stepped forward. Behind them was a large set of double doors that were intricately carved with a depiction of the Council. One soldier stepped ahead of the others.

"Blāzzer is to go alone into the chamber," he said.

She looked to Ash.

"I'll be here waiting," he assured. She nodded and looked towards the doors. She stepped forward and the soldiers opened them.

The chamber inside was large with a domed ceiling and glass panels. Blāzzer blinked at the Council in front of her sitting in half circle. She stopped in front of them, noticing Lemay Soldiers lining the walls. Captain Teredana stood behind Nayax who had a simple crown of gold and silver on his head. On both sides of him were empty seats. One chair had dragons carved into it while the other had crows.

"Welcome Blāzzer," said Nayax, inclining his head slightly.

"Thank you," she said softly, bowing her head.

"I know you've met Lord Legorin." He indicated to the elf on the other side of the empty dragon chair. "Leader of the Forest Elves. Next to him is Lord Caratin, Leader of the Centaurs." The centaur was laying down on a cushion. The gray hair on his body was broken up by scars.

"Next to him," continued Nayax, "is Lady Foxdur, Leader of the Uleakites."

*Foxdur,* thought Blāzzer. *Dragon in Drakken.*

The uleakite looked like a large wolf with gold and red fur. She sat on a raised platform with carvings of her race along the edge.

"Then Lord Pe'dah, Leader of the Mountain Elves," said Nayax, inclining his hand towards a dark-skinned elf next to the empty chair with crows. On the other side of the elf was another empty chair. This one had thirteen spirits carved into it. "And lastly Lord Meric, Leader of the Ruchos." The large elk laid on a cushion with his antlers held high. He was completely white with his blue eyes looking at Blāzzer.

"Well, let's get this over with," said Caratin, crossing his arms. "She shouldn't stay with the dragons."

Blāzzer felt her heart skip a beat, thinking, *What?*

"I see no reason for her not to stay with them," replied Foxdur, twitching her ear in disregard of the centaur.

"Of course you wouldn't," said Legorin.

Foxdur pulled her lips back slightly.

"Foxdur, let's listen to what they have to say," said Meric. "I'm sure Blāzzer has her own thoughts as well on her placement."

"She isn't to have a say until twenty years of age," said Pe'dah. "So having her here is against that."

Blāzzer opened her mouth to speak, but Nayax said, "Blāzzer is allowed to have her voice heard. She cannot decide, but she can speak her own thoughts." He looked at her. "Where do you want to live?"

"With the dragons," she replied, feeling her mouth go dry.

Caratin snorted.

"Tell us why," said Nayax, ignoring the centaur.

Blāzzer blinked, trying to think of what to say and wondering if her voice would stay strong. After a moment she said, "I've never had a family... When I moved to Palator I felt like I found one, but the Snerxites destroyed that. I was removed from Palator. Now the closest thing I have to a family is the Stone family."

"Do they consider you family?" asked Meric.

"Yes," she replied.

"What about the liffen?" questioned Pe'dah.

"Raffel and I can communicate feelings a little bit. But only over short distances."

"Do you understand that King Nayax didn't have the authority to send you to Shinda with the dragons?" asked Legorin.

Blāzzer shook her head, looking at Nayax. He didn't seem ashamed about this.

"With her injury as severe as it was," explained Nayax, "sending her with the dragons to the farnirck healers was the best option to ensure her well-being."

None of the leaders questioned him. For a moment they were silent then Legorin said, "I'm glad her well-being was put first."

Foxdur shook her head as if trying to rid herself of a gnat.

The elf continued, "But do the dragons have her best interests in mind, or do they have their own agenda?"

"Says the elf," laughed Foxdur that sounded like barking.

"What do you mean?" asked Blāzzer in confusion.

Legorin smirked, saying, "I'm for sure the dragons have mentioned how they have no leader."

She nodded.

"As a rider, you can become their leader once you are twenty-one years old. With the only other dragon rider being Cornin, and a member of the Sentinel Crows, you are the only candidate since three hundred years ago."

"It would bring the Stone family great political power," said Pe'dah.

"Too much for four individuals," grumbled Caratin.

"There are more than four dragons in Nickada," said Meric, twitching his ears.

"At most ten," retorted the centaur, jerking his head to the side. "No matter, ten individuals should not have the same political power as groups of thousands."

*Are they using me?* Blāzzer questioned herself. *The elves, at least the forest elves, don't like the dragons... I don't think they're using me, but how do I know for sure?* She pressed her fist against the ache in her chest. *Raffel... that feeling from before... what was it?*

"This is ridiculous!" barked Foxdur, her hackles raised. "You are only speaking such because that is how you see her!"

"And you don't," demanded Pe'dah. "Your own race is dwindling. You would use the dragons' power to your own advantage."

Meric snorted, saying, "Our races might be dwindling, but that doesn't mean our support of the other races has faded."

Caratin laughed, retorting, "Yes, it does. You hold onto your land even though others can use it for their growing populace."

"Leaders!" yelled Nayax. They quieted and settled in their seats. "I understand we must look out for our own people but you need to care about each other's people as well."

"That's why we want to get through this and figure out what to do about the Snerxite raids," said Legorin, smoothly.

Blāzzer felt bile rise in her throat at his word. She blurted, "You're lying!"

The leaders looked at her and Legorin, smiling slyly, said, "Do tell me how am I lying."

Blāzzer blinked, swallowing before replying, "Two days ago... you said that those injured and attacked were not your people."

"But I didn't say that we wouldn't discuss it."

She pressed her lips together. "You implied that you didn't care about them."

"If he didn't say it, he didn't say it," said Caratin, giving Blāzzer a look that made her want to hide.

"Any other input on whether Blāzzer should or should not stay with the dragons?" asked Nayax. None of the leaders answered. He looked to Blāzzer, but she couldn't find her voice. "All of those that agree to her staying with the Stone family."

"Aye," said Meric and Foxdur together.

"All of those opposed," said Nayax.

"Aye," said Caratin, Legorin, and Pe'dah in unison.

"It is decided then," said the king. He sighed before continuing, "Blāzzer will no longer stay with the Stone family."

Blāzzer didn't feel the tears fall down her face. Her ears became deaf as the

Council began to discuss where she would live. She grabbed her shirt in a fist over her heart at the pain. She struggled to draw breath in and the world felt distant. For a moment she felt like she was falling till she was kneeling on the ground. She struggled to grab her thoughts and process the vote.

She blinked.

A warmth slowly spread through her body. It pushed against her pain and sorrow like waves on a shore. Her trembling subsided and the last of her tears dripped off her jaw. The warmth settled in her chest and slowly began to burn stronger. She thought, *I do not fear them.* Slowly she rose to her feet. *I do not fear my future.* She straightened her back and held her chin up. *I control it!*

"I'm staying with the dragons!"

The leaders all looked at Blāzzer in astonishment. Before they could recover, she continued, "I don't care if you agree or not. I'm staying with them. They are my family!"

"You don't get to choose," said Legorin, shaking his head in amusement. "You-"

"Go ahead! Put me elsewhere! I'll do all I can to get away and back to my family. And I know they'll do all they can to get me back. I am a member of the Stone family!"

The chamber doors burst open and all of the leaders jumped out of their seats. Blāzzer looked at the older man that had walked in. His black cloak billowed behind him as he strode past Blāzzer and up to Nayax. The old man saluted with his fist over his heart, before saying, "Pardon me, my king, for my tardiness."

"Lord Shradur," replied Nayax with a tentative smile. "You are pardoned." The chamber doors closed. "Sit, my lords." Slowly, the leaders complied. Shradur sat at the left hand of the king. He looked at Blāzzer and she felt like her soul was being inspected by his gaze. "We were discussing where Blāzzer should stay. The Council voted that she would not stay with the Stone family."

"I ask for a revote then," said Shradur.

Caratin rolled his eyes.

Legorin sighed, saying, "We've already voted. You were absent for that."

Shradur shrugged and said, "Well then let's vote whether the previous vote should be overruled. That should be fine with you since majority is needed to change the vote."

"Sounds fair," said Nayax with a nod. "Shradur, do you have anything to add on Blāzzer's behalf?"

The Sentinel Crow shook his head.

Nayax said, "All of those who agree to the previous vote."

"Aye," said Legorin, Pe'dah, and Caratin.

"All of those who want the previous vote overturned," said Nayax.

"Aye," replied Meric and Foxdur.

All the leaders looked to Shradur. Blāzzer thought, *Even if he agrees, the vote won't be changed... I'll still be taken away.*

Shradur said, "Lord Durthuh of the farnircks and I vote 'aye'." He held up a piece of paper with a wax seal before handing it to the king.

"What?!" demanded Caratin, standing up, his hooves ringing out on the stone floor.

Nayax took a moment to read over the paper before saying, "Lord Durthuh has chosen Lord Shradur to be his representative in the matter of Blāzzer's wellbeing. He has specifically stated that she is to stay with the Stone family."

"You tricked us!" accused Legorin, gripping the arms of his chair till his knuckles turned white.

Foxdur grinned, showing all of her teeth.

"It is in the laws to call for a vote to turn over a previous one if a leader is absent," stated Nayax.

"I challenge you!" roared Caratin, stepping closer to Shradur. "I, Lord Caratin, Leader of the Centaurs, challenge you Lord Shradur, Leader of the Sentinel Crows, on you being Lord Durthuh's representative."

Shradur, hands relaxed by his side, stood up. He said, "I, Lord Shradur, Leader of the Sentinel Crows, accept your challenge, Lord Caratin, Leader of the Centaurs."

Nayax stood up and said, "Very well. If Lord Caratin wins then the majority vote is lost and Blāzzer will be removed from the Stone family. If Lord Shradur wins then the majority vote holds and Blāzzer remains with the Stone family. The duel will begin in an hour, till then the Council meeting is suspended."

The Lemay Soldiers opened up the chamber doors and the leaders walked out. Blāzzer watched them leave, not for sure what to do. She looked up as King Nayax walked up to her, saying, "Let's get you back to the dragons."

She wiped her cheeks on her sleeves before following him slowly out of the room. She asked, "Will Shradur win?"

"All leaders are trained in combat so it could go either way," replied Nayax. He looked down at her. "You were brave in there."

As they stepped out of the building Blāzzer saw the Stone family and ran to them. She threw her arms around Raffel. He held her tight as tears from stress fell down her face.

"In an hour Lord Caratin and Lord Shradur will duel," said Nayax.

Aurora looked at Ash.

"If Caratin wins, she'll be taken away?" asked the older, male dragon.

"Yes," answered the king.

"Is there anything you can do?" pleaded Lydia, touching Blāzzer's arm protectively.

"No, not this time," replied Nayax, shaking his head. He looked to Raffel, who was still holding Blāzzer, before turning to Ash. "Make sure they don't go anywhere."

Blāzzer followed the Stone family through Chamdal. Aurora had her arm around the young woman's shoulders, guiding her. Centaurs and mountain elves were scattered amongst the forest elves. All watched the dragons.

A centaur approached them and stepped into their path. His coat was gray with white stockings. He saluted them with his fist over his heart and said, "I apologize on behalf of my people."

"You're Naro," said Ash, "son of Caratin."

"Yes."

"We appreciate your sympathy, but please excuse us."

Naro stepped aside and the Stone family proceeded. Blāzzer looked over her shoulder and met his eyes.

Blāzzer sat on her bed, hugging a pillow to her chest. Lydia sat on the windowsill, looking out over Chamdal. Raffel paced about the room, slowly opening and clenching his hands repeatedly.

"I just want to know," whispered Blāzzer, looking up at Raffel, but he didn't hear. *Raffel?* He glanced at her and sat on the edge of the bed. She rested her head on his shoulder, relaxing at his warmth. "I don't want to go."

"I won't let them take you," promised Raffel, resting his cheek against the top of her head. "We won't let them take you."

"More people have joined the Lemay Soldiers," said Lydia. She looked to Raffel and Blāzzer. "It's almost time."

Blāzzer tightened her arms around the pillow, saying, "I feel like I've used up all my courage already... It doesn't make sense."

"What doesn't?" asked Raffel, lifting his head.

"Why are they so against me being with you?" When Lydia and Raffel didn't answer, Blāzzer continued, "Legorin said that I could become the leader of the dragons once I turn twenty-one. They said how that would be too much political power for so few individuals. Is that the only reason?"

Lydia and Raffel looked at each other.

"Answer me!" pleaded Blāzzer.

Raffel winced at the desperation in her voice, before saying, "Kind of."

"The other reasons go to you being leader," said Lydia, walking over to Blāzzer. "Even though we can't be specific, understand we don't want you to be leader unless you want to and are ready to." She touched Blāzzer's cheek.

Blāzzer sighed at the cool touch and relaxed, leaning against Raffel. Warmth came from him and she easily fell asleep.

Blāzzer followed the Stone family out of the house and staggered at the sight of all the people of different races gathered. Many of them looked at the Stone family, but most ignored them. Lemay Soldiers were forming an open space in the middle of the group. King Nayax stood at the center of the widening space. For a moment he met Blāzzer's eyes before continuing to look over the people. Someone squeezed her shoulder and she looked up to see Lydia.

"We're here for you," said the dragon. Blāzzer nodded, before looking up at Raffel. She followed his gaze and he was watching the king.

"My people," said Nayax loudly. Everyone quieted quickly and he continued, "Lord Caratin, Leader of the Centaurs, has challenged Lord Shradur, Leader of the Sentinel Crows. My leaders come forward." The crowd sidestepped as the two leaders walked forward. Caratin wore leather armor over his body and had two swords strapped to his flanks. Shradur wore a leather vest and bracers with his sword hanging at his hip. The two stopped six feet apart, facing each other with Nayax between them.

"The fight will commence when I say," said the king. "It will end at the first draw of blood." He looked between the leaders. "Take your places." He stepped back as the leaders turned away, walking away from each other. They stopped at the edge of the open space where the Lemay Soldiers stood between them and the people. Shradur and Caratin turned and faced each other, resting their hands on their sword hilts.

"Begin!" shouted Nayax.

Caratin charged forward, drawing both swords and kicking up dirt and grass. His face was calm and focused. Shradur stepped forward but did not draw his sword. The centaur cut straight at the old man. At the last moment, Shradur dived to the side, avoiding the blades and rolling back to his feet. Caratin, holding his swords at his sides, turned to Shradur. He moved to step forward, but his leg wouldn't move.

A matte black tentacle coming from the ground was wrapped around his lower leg. The black coloration followed along the ground to Shradur's shadow.

"What is that?" asked Blāzzer quietly.

"It's Shradur's mirazh," whispered Lydia. "Energy given shape. He's of the Shadow People from the north. They all have it."

Caratin glared at Shardur, saying, "Come on, old man."

Shradur stepped forward but stayed out of reach of the centaur's swords. As he moved the tentacle remained around Caratin's foreleg and branched off, wrapping around his opposite hind leg. Caratin struggled against the bonds, but could not free himself.

"Fight me! Fight me like a man!" shouted Caratin, lurching towards Shradur and swinging his swords.

As the mirazh released him the centaur fell forward. Shradur sidestepped as Caratin's momentum carried him past. Caratin was unable to catch himself and crashed to the ground. Shradur swiped his sword at the centaur's legs and held his sword up. Blood trickled down the metal. Blāzzer blinked; she couldn't believe Shradur had won.

"Lord Shradur drew first blood," announced King Nayax.

Some of the crowd cheered, while others swore. Blāzzer gasped as someone threw their arms around her in a hug and swung her around in a circle. When they put her down, she looked up and met Raffel's eyes. He was grinning and his eyes bright. She leaned her head against his chest, feeling warmth in her heart.

## Chapter Fifteen

The following day Blāzzer sat outside on the patio of the Stone family house, reading a book. Sunlight filtered through the tree leaves and left cool air under the canopy. She looked up and smiled as Raffel and Cornin approached. She said, "I was wondering when you guys would show up."

"Had to help Raffel with something," replied Cornin, shoving gently against Raffel's shoulder.

Raffel said something to him in Drakken. Cornin held both hands up innocently. They both sat down on the benches.

"Now that we're done celebrating," said Cornin, "We need to get back to training." He pulled out his pipe and worked on packing tobacco. "You have been able to still communicate emotions, correct?"

Both Blāzzer and Raffel nodded.

"Has it gotten stronger? More often?"

They looked at each other. She could feel his unsureness and she said, "It's gotten better. Don't have to really focus so much on it."

"Good," said Cornin with a nod. "Over time all of the communication will be a second thought."

"We'll still have our own private thoughts, right?" asked Raffel.

"Yes," answered Cornin, "it's just like talking except no one else can hear. You choose what to share through the liffen. The only time it becomes... blurred is during fatorana. Not just thoughts, but senses. It can be quite disorienting the first few times." Cornin lit his pipe with a match before continuing, "Today though we are going to try adding words to emotions. So for example when you send an emotion of happiness, also send a word that you associate with happiness." He leaned back in his chair, looking between Raffel and Blāzzer. "Go ahead and try. You first Raffel."

Raffel took a deep breath before meeting Blāzzer's eyes. She felt awkward trying to keep her mind open and holding his gaze. She couldn't hold back the small smile on her lips, feeling happiness at still being there with him. She thought, *You make me happy.*

Raffel blinked and looked past her, pressing his lips together. "Could we face away from each other?"

Cornin raised an eyebrow, before saying, "Okay. Sit on the ground then, back to back."

Blāzzer chewed at her lip as they moved, thinking, *Did he hear me?* She sat on the ground with Raffel behind her as Cornin had instructed.

"Scoot back," said Cornin, nudging Raffel's leg with his foot.

Raffel scooted towards Blāzzer till his back pressed against hers. She felt part of herself relax at his closeness.

"Now close your eyes," instructed Cornin. Raffel and Blāzzer did so. "Raffel try again." She waited silently with her hands resting in her lap, feeling Raffel's chest expand and contract as he breathed. After a few moments, Blāzzer felt an internal struggle coming from him. She tried to analyze it, but it slipped out of her fingers. She waited for another feeling, but nothing came.

She reached out to him with concern, thinking, *Okay?*

Frustration washed over her. She shivered at its cold, bitter touch. She held her breath as a word formed in her head, *Secrets.*

*That wasn't me,* thought Blāzzer. *That was Raffel... He sounded so vulnerable.* She remembered the warmth she felt in the Council's chamber and drew on that, cradling it in her chest. The goosebumps on her arms settled and her muscles relaxed. She sent him threads of the warmth. *That was you. You were there with me.*

*Yes,* came Raffel's voice in her head. The loyalty emphasized with the one word made Blāzzer clench her hands into fists. She opened her eyes and swiped at the tears trying to escape from her eyes.

"You alright?" asked Cornin, chewing on his pipe.

"Yeah," replied Blāzzer, shakily. She took a deep breath and closed her eyes, focusing on Raffel. *What secrets?* She felt him withdraw from her. *What secrets?!*

Guilt trickled from him. His voice came quietly in her head, *I can't tell you.*

*Raffel,* she sighed, feeling tired. *What are they about?*

*You're past.* There was fear in his voice. *I don't... I can't lose you.*

Blāzzer tried to draw her thoughts together to respond, but nothing came to her. She opened her eyes and stood up, saying, "I need to take a breather and get some water." She walked away and could hear Cornin ask Raffel something in Drakken. The dragon didn't answer.

Blāzzer sat on her bed, trying to focus on the book of fairy tales. Finally, she put it down thinking, *It isn't worth it. I can't focus anyways.* She walked over to the window and sat on the sill. She sighed as she pressed her forehead against the cool glass pane. *He knows about my past... My past that I don't even know. Why won't he tell me?* She watched the elves move about the streets of Chamdal. *He said he can't lose me, but the Council already voted and I'm to stay with them... with him. So why won't he tell me?*

There was a knock on the door and Blāzzer didn't turn from the window. The door opened slowly and Raffel stepped in, asking, "Is it okay if we talk?"

She shrugged, watching a leaf fall from a tree in a lazy spiral.

He sat on the edge of her bed. "I'm sorry that I can't tell you about your past... To be honest I don't even know much."

"It's more than me," she whispered.

Raffel pressed his lips together. *I'm sorry.* He rubbed his neck. "Would it help if I told you a little about your past?"

She looked at him.

"I really can't say much, but there are some things I can try to clear up." When she continued to watch him, he asked, "Would you like that? It wouldn't be complete answers."

"Yeah," said Blāzzer with a sigh, leaning her head against the window.

"Well, you think you're a mortal, right?"

She nodded slightly.

"You're not a mortal."

"I have round ears."

He shrugged apologetically.

"I'm not mortal," she whispered, then sighed. "What am I?"

"I can't say."

"What about my parents? Nayax said they weren't alive... Is that true?"

"Yes," replied Raffel.

"When?"

"Shortly after you were given to the Sentinel Crows."

Blāzzer took a deep breath. "Why was I given to them? Did my parents not want me?"

"They did," said Raffel quickly. "They loved you a lot... That's why they gave you to the Sentinel Crows to be raised. They knew that they wouldn't be able to come back."

"Why did they have to go?"

"They had to protect you... Protect Nickada."

"It's not fair!"

"I know."

She pressed the heels of her hands against her eyes, as her emotions rolled in turmoil.

"Your parents loved you more than themselves. They wanted to make Nickada a place that you could grow up happy... I know that didn't really happen and that sucks. I can't tell you much more about them. Just that they loved you."

Birds chirped in the trees as Blāzzer and Raffel sat back to back on the covered patio. Both had small wooden blocks before them. Cornin and Aurora, watching the younger pair, sat on the benches and Aurora said, "Raffel, now that you've built a structure, try to communicate with Blāzzer on how to duplicate it."

The young woman sat there, staring at the blocks before her. She rested her hands on her knees as she waited for the feeling of Raffel in her head. When a few minutes passed with nothing, she reached out with her mind towards him and asked, *You good?*

*Big block base*, he replied, his voice sounding muffled. Blāzzer grabbed the largest block and placed it directly in front of her.

*Okay. Next?* As she waited, she looked up at the flowering vines on the trellises overhead. Raffel's muscles tensed in his back and she felt frustration trickle from him.

"Relax, Raffel," encouraged Aurora, gently. "Try not to overthink communicating with your thoughts. Talk to her like you normally would, just not vocally." Blāzzer glanced at Cornin and he winked.

*So much to say*, groaned Raffel.

Blāzzer pressed her lips together, murmuring, *About yesterday's conversation?*

He sighed inwardly. *I want to tell you everything I know... but I can't.*

"Focus," insisted Cornin. "I can see you two getting distracted."

Raffel took a deep breath and said, *Place the half-circle in front of the first so that they're parallel.*

Minutes ticked by until Blāzzer had finished reconstructing his small structure. She turned and looked at his. She frowned, murmuring, "You said to put the triangles on their base."

"That is the base," replied Raffel, studying her blocks. "You also put the cube in the wrong place." She stuck her tongue out at him and he quickly looked away.

"As enjoyable as watching you two have a scuffle is," said Cornin, getting a glare from Aurora, "there is one more task for you two to do for today's training." He handed Raffel and Blāzzer each a folded piece of paper. "Read the poem to each other. You're missing every other line and the other one of you has the missing lines."

Raffel looked at his mother, asking, "How is this training?"

She smiled softly, "Remember the goal is to get you two practicing communication via the liffen. Continuously using it is the only way to increase distance." She stood up, grabbing Cornin's arm. "We'll let you two work. When your done, come inside for lunch." As she somewhat dragged Cornin away, he gave them a thumbs up.

"What was that about?" questioned Blāzzer.

"Don't know," muttered Raffel, shrugging. "I guess with the liffen, others miss the conversation and are left wondering." He turned so his back was to her. "You ready?" She settled in, leaning her back against his. "I think you have the first line."

She unfolded her paper and skimmed over it, noting the empty space between each line. She said, *First line: Falling Leaves.*

*Leaves floating down from the sky*, said Raffel.

*Spiraling till they touch the earth.*

*To never leave the ground.*

*Confined to waste away - This is a sad poem!*

*Cornin tends to only write sad or romantic poetry.*

Blāzzer blinked, happy that they weren't reading a romantic poem. *Um, your line?*

*Confined to become the foundation of new*, continued Raffel.

*Restricted from seeing the new.*

*Leaves floating down from the sky.*

*Remember the freedom of flight.*

*Remember the wind beneath you.*

*Carrying you -* She winced as a twinge of pain flared in her head. "Are you getting a headache?"

"Yeah," sighed Raffel. "Guess that means we're indeed exercising the bond. You okay to finish this?"

Blāzzer nodded and said, *Carrying you to your resting place.*

*Where you will stay till you are no more.*

*Your journey will be over.*

*But you will be the foundation for the new.*

*New growth will come forth.*

*And it will carry on without your memory.*

"That's it," murmured Blāzzer, her heart uncomfortable as her head ached. She leaned her head back against Raffel and looked up at the vines overhead. Lazy bumblebees moved from flower to flower.

"You okay?" asked Raffel, gently. He glanced over his shoulder at her. "Your head hurting badly?"

"I don't remember them... they helped make Nickada safe and I don't remember them."

A few days later, Blāzzer walked alongside the Stone family through Chamdal. Everyone in the town was heading towards a large courtyard. In place of the elven guards on balconies and walkways stood Lemay Soldiers. The air was tense with anticipation at the Council's awaited decision. The Stone family found a place along the back wall to stand. Blāzzer stood between Raffel and Lydia.

Several minutes later, the leaders began to walk out along the front of the courtyard. The people quieted as their leaders stood before them. King Nayax walked up to the railing of a balcony overhead. He looked over them before saying, "My people this is not a day for joy."

Blāzzer looked up at Raffel before looking back to her king.

Nayax continued, "Tomorrow our army marches for Budsta."

People began talking and questioning. Blāzzer felt fear in her throat and her vision narrowing. She blinked as Raffel touched her arm. She looked up at him and he whispered, "It's going to be okay."

The king held up a hand and they quieted before he said, "The Lord of the Tribes of Budsta was assassinated a week ago. Since then Budsta has been in a civil war. The majority want to remain with their traditions of nomadic life. Others want to begin building towns, putting their traditions into history. If these nomadic traditions are kept, the Budstarians will need more land. That is why they have been raiding our southern border. Snerx benefits from the nomadic lifestyle of Budsta as a main source of trade and commerce. Snerx has allied itself with the tribes who want to continue their traditions. We are not marching to war, but mobilizing troops as a precaution. However, if the Budstarians choose to attack we will be there." Nayax stood there as his words settled in. "If we do not stand and fight then our homes will be lost. In one month our army will gather at the southern border. Each leader is responsible for their own unit." He pressed his fist over his heart and the leaders followed suit. The Nickadians saluted them.

Blāzzer took a deep breath, straightened her back, held her chin up, and pressed her fist over her heart, thinking, *I do not fear my future.*

# Part Four

## Learning the Past

## Chapter Sixteen

As the people left the courtyard, Blāzzer asked, "So who is responsible for us?"

"Nayax," replied Raffel. "Normally at least." He glanced at Ash, who shrugged.

Blāzzer looked up as Shradur approached them through the crowd. He stopped in front of the Stone family and handed a piece of paper to Ash. As Ash read over it, the old man said, "Until the army has gathered in a month, Stone family you are my responsibility."

Cornin grinned.

"We'll go to Gilzar first," said Shradur.

Ash handed the paper to Aurora and she skimmed over it. Raffel looked to Blāzzer and she asked, "What?"

Raffel turned back to Shradur and questioned, "Are... Is Blāzzer going to learn about her past?"

*Please*, thought Blāzzer.

"The Council voted that all information should be given to Blāzzer," said Shradur.

"Really?" asked Lydia.

"How'd you swing that?" questioned Ash.

"I am Durthuh's representative in regards to Blāzzer's well-being," explained Shradur. "The Council-"

*My past*, thought Blāzzer. *I'll know who I am, where I'm from. I don't remember anything from before being a ward... being an orphan. Maybe I'll know who my parents were. Did I have siblings? Do I have siblings? They could be alive! Were they Nickadians? Uh...* She blinked as her vision began to speckle and she leaned against Raffel. *Breathe!*

"You okay?" asked Raffel, quietly.

"Yeah," whispered Blāzzer. "Just forgot to breathe." Raffel reached over and grabbed his sister's hand.

"What are you doing?" questioned Lydia.

He put her hand on Blāzzer's neck.

"Your warm," said Lydia, placing her other hand on Blāzzer's cheek.

"I'm okay," insisted Blāzzer, not pushing away Lydia's cool hands. "Just got a little overwhelmed." Blāzzer looked at Shradur, Aurora, and Ash, who were watching them. "Sorry."

"No worries," replied Cornin. "What time are we heading out, Shradur?"

"Tomorrow morning," said the older Sentinel Crow, "right at daybreak."

"What about Lydia?" questioned Aurora.

"I can fight!" said the younger, female dragon, withdrawing her hands from Blāzzer and standing straight. Aurora glared at her.

"She is to fight," said Shradur.

"No!" cried Aurora, with panic contorting her face. Cornin placed a hand on her shoulder. She looked at him and after a moment she nodded, solemnly.

"We'll be ready to leave at daybreak," assured Ash. "I'll make sure we are."

"You ready?" asked Raffel, stepping into Blāzzer's bedroom.

"Almost," she replied sleepily, grabbing her notebook by candlelight. "It's too early."

"Do you want to stay with the elves?" He grinned as she glared at him. He picked up her bag by the door as she blew out the candle. Carrying her satchel, Blāzzer followed him downstairs. The living room and kitchen were illuminated and busy. Aurora was setting out bowls of oatmeal on the table as Ash poured cups of water.

Lydia looked up at Raffel and Blāzzer and said, "Morning."

"It's not morning yet," grumbled Blāzzer, slumping into a chair.

"I agree," mumbled Cornin from the couch, where he had his eyes closed and head resting on his hand.

"Come on and eat breakfast," insisted Aurora. "You'll feel more awake once you eat."

Raffel sat down next to Blāzzer and pushed his oatmeal around with a spoon, asking, "Is there any meat?"

"It's at the bottom," said Lydia, digging into her breakfast.

"A meal without meat would be a sad one," commented Cornin, sinking into a chair.

Aurora handed him a mug of coffee, saying, "Says the mortal to dragons."

He chuckled. "Eat up before it gets cold."

As they ate Ash laid a map on the table. He pointed to a small dot in Wildwood Forest, saying, "This is where we are right now." He moved his finger southwest out of the bright green of the forest and over the softer greens of the plains to another dot surrounded by a tan area. "It should be an easy flight, but once we get through the plains the land will get very dry, rocky, and full of sand."

"Home sweet home," murmured Cornin fondly.

Aurora frowned at him and he grinned.

"Make sure to drink plenty of water," said Ash, ignoring Cornin's interruption. "Especially you two." He looked between Lydia and Aurora.

"I know, Dad," said Lydia, annoyed.

"I'm just reminding you. Also, keep an eye out for sandstorms. You-"

Blāzzer looked to Raffel, asking, *Normal dad thing?*

*Yep,* he replied.

"-and keep an eye out for mirages. Don't need anyone crashing."

Everyone sat there quietly for a few minutes before Cornin said, "Great pep talk."

"It wasn't a pep talk," answered Ash, with a slight growl.

"Honey," said Aurora, warningly. Both Ash and Cornin stared down at their bowls.

Soon they finished breakfast and headed outside with their bags. The dragons shifted before crouching down. Blāzzer fastened her and Raffel's bags to his saddle.

"Got it?" asked Raffel, watching her with one eye.

"Yeah, I think," she replied, stepping back so he could see.

"Looks good to me."

She smiled and swung her leg over the saddle before diligently securing all three carabiners to her harness. Raffel slowly stood up, stretching his wings, and walked over to the other dragons. Blāzzer looked at Cornin, who sat in a saddle on Aurora's shoulders. The saddle leather had been dyed black, but was faded from age. Ash jumped into the air followed by Aurora.

Lydia turned to Raffel, saying, "See you two up there." She turned and took off into the air.

"You ready?" asked Raffel.

Blāzzer, tightening her grip on the saddle handle, took a deep breath and replied, "Yeah." He crouched down and launched into the air. Blāzzer leaned forward over his neck as he flapped his wings, gaining height. As they stabilized out above the tree canopy Blāzzer punched her fist into the air with a shout, feeling exhilaration and freedom. Raffel roared in response, fire erupting from his mouth.

The dragons flew steadily southwest over the plains. Their pace slow compared to the speed at which they went to Chamdal. Blāzzer glanced below, where three Sentinel Crows rode horses at a swift gallop. She touched Raffel's neck, asking, "Do you know who the other two crows are?"

*No,* he replied, tipping his head down slightly. He then looked back at her. "What?"

*Nothing.* He faced back forwards.

Blāzzer pressed her lips together. *What?*

"You're a lot more stable with being able to use both your arms."

She smiled, enjoying the freedom of her right arm. "It's still kind of stiff."

"How are you feeling, though?" asked Raffel, cautiously.

*Huh?* replied Blāzzer, confused.

"About learning about your past."

She chewed at her lip uneasily. *I don't know.* She leaned against his neck, pressing her cheek against his scales. "A part of me is scared." She could feel him trying to comfort her. "Will it change who I am?"

After a moment Raffel said slowly, "I don't think so... You'll have an understanding of your circumstances." He looked back at her. "I'm sorry."

Blāzzer nodded and gazed out across the land. *I just want it to bring me some peace of mind. I want to understand why my parents left me with the Sentinel Crows. What danger was so great that made them choose to do so?*

For a while, they flew quietly until Blāzzer asked, "Raffel?"

*Hmmm?* he replied.

"Promise me that after the Sentinel Crows tell me about my past, there will be no secrets between us."

"I promise you till the end of our days that we will have no secrets between us."

She felt warmth in her chest from him and she closed her eyes to focus on it. "What is this feeling from you?"

*Love.*

Blāzzer blinked. *Love?*

"It's why I promise you that I'll be by your side to make sure that everything is going to be okay."

She placed her hand on his neck. *Love.*

The sun was setting by the time the dragons landed for the night. Blāzzer unhooked the carabiners on her harness as Raffel crouched in the tall grass. She swung down before unfastening their bags. Raffel looked up as the Sentinel Crows rode up to the dragons. The horses chewed at their bits with unease but didn't spook.

Patting his gray stallion's neck, Shradur said, "Dragons, I'll let you set up your portion of camp. Let us make dinner though."

"Sounds good to us," replied Ash, shifting into his human form.

It didn't take long for the camp to be set up with a few tents and one fire. Blāzzer sat alongside Lydia, watching the female dragon sketch. She asked, "How long have you been drawing for?"

Lydia shrugged, saying, "Since I was a kid. It's calming." She started to flip through her sketchbook. "I want to show you one." She held it out to Blāzzer.

"That's... Raffel and me," whispered Blāzzer, touching the sketch delicately. It depicted Raffel and her sitting back to back with their eyes closed. *It's so serene... as if nothing else is going on.*

"I couldn't help but make a sketch of you two," explained Lydia with a soft smile. "You two have a really special bond - and not just the rider dragon bond."

"Thank you for showing me." Blāzzer smiled.

"Dinner!" called one of the Sentinel Crows.

Lydia and Blāzzer joined the others around the campfire as bowls of sausage and rice were passed out. Cornin said, "I guess I should introduce the other two Crows. Everyone this is Inks and Argon."

"Always so courteous," teased Argon, who had a scar going down his cheek that tugged his lip into a permanent awkward smile. Inks grunted, reaching for some more rice and exposing a black tattoo on his wrist that matched Cornin's.

"Do all Sentinel Crows have the same tattoo?" asked Blāzzer.

"Yeah, we all do," replied Cornin, pulling back his sleeve. The black tattoo was in the shape of a crow. "Except if you're part of the Shadow Council, you get a little crown too." He chuckled. "Are you wanting to get a tattoo? Sentinel Crows are good at them."

She shrunk slightly. "No, I'm good and I wouldn't know what I would get."

"Cornin," said Aurora, looking to him, and he smiled sheepishly.

After a few minutes, Aurora asked, "How has Gryphun been?"

"Mostly staying out of trouble," answered Shradur, softly. "Another year and he'll be done with his training as a Sentinel Crow. After that I want to send him to you for training. He's growing too fast that he isn't steady in flight with strong winds."

"Will he be as large as his father?" questioned Ash.

"Possibly larger," replied Shradur.

"Has he been able to see Mae?" asked Blāzzer, thinking, *She misses him so much.*

Shradur looked at her. "Yes, he was there with her for a few weeks. He and several other Crows were helping with rebuilding gardens."

Blāzzer smiled softly. *I'm so glad it's all being rebuilt.*

After dinner Blāzzer sat inside her tent with the flap tied back so she could see the others. Raffel came and sat down at the entrance, saying, "Probably should pick up on your Drakken lessons soon."

She grinned, saying, "I remember the basics... like the really basics."

"It's not too hard," commented Lydia, sitting down beside Blāzzer in the shelter of the tent. "Most of it translates directly."

"Except for the grammar," mumbled Blāzzer, reaching for her bag and grabbing her notebook. She flipped to the pages on the Drakken language. "How did you two learn it?"

"We learned it alongside the common tongue," said Raffel with a shrug. "So, not too bad."

She frowned.

"We just had the difficulty that we didn't know it was two languages. We'd mash them together."

"What phrases were you learning in your last lesson?" asked Lydia, looking at Blāzzer's notebook.

"Basic ones, like introducing oneself and just vocab," answered Blāzzer, skimming her notes. She carefully pronounced in Drakken, "*My name is Blāzzer. I am from Maro. I am eighteen years old. I like flowers.*"

Lydia smiled and, turning to Raffel, said, "Not too bad, brother."

"I think Mae helped with encouragement," he said. "Always yelling at me in Drakken."

"What would she say?" questioned Blāzzer, eying him. "She always spoke too fast."

"Mostly how I was a gitarb."

"What's that mean?"

"It's like calling someone bird brained," explained Lydia. "Didn't you teach Mae?"

"Yeah," replied Raffel, rubbing the back of his neck. "But she looked up a lot of... other words in books. Then she'd start talking to Gryphun in Drakken when he visited... which left me to hear their sappy conversations."

"That's romantic!" exclaimed Lydia with her eyes glittering. "A secret language between lovers that no one else can understand."

"I could though! And I didn't want to listen."

"You're just not a romantic."

Raffel grunted looking away and Blāzzer suppressed a smile as Lydia giggled more.

"Don't stay up late you three!" called Ash as his wife ducked into their tent and he followed her in.

Blāzzer looked up at the stars and said, "The stars are pretty out here. No trees in the way."

"Do you know some of the stories behind the dragon constellations?" asked Lydia excitedly.

Blāzzer shook her head, studying the specks of white light in the sky.

Lydia pointed towards the sky. "That's Foxdur - the dragon. He is only out during the fall. His rider - Rideria - is a spring constellation. So they never appear in the same sky."

"Why?"

"Because others were jealous of the bond they shared, Rideria and Foxdur were forced apart. Their bond was so strong that, even though separated, they were still able to communicate." Lydia looked at Blāzzer and Raffel. "Some say they were even lovers."

Blāzzer blushed, glancing at Raffel, and saw that he was clenching his jaw.

"We should get some sleep," he said, getting up and walking away.

She looked to Lydia who was still watching her. Blāzzer said shakily, "We should go to bed." Lydia grinned before getting up and walking to her tent. Blāzzer scooted back into her own tent, closing the flap behind her. After taking her boots off, she laid on her pallet and pulled the blanket around her. A few minutes later she heard someone walk by her tent. Red light leaked from around the edges of her tent for a second before Raffel laid down outside her tent.

"You're sister is a romantic," said Blāzzer quietly.

*Yeah*, replied Raffel.

After a while, she said, "About earlier... when we were flying. What kind of love were you talking about?" She could feel him thinking through his response.

*It's up to you.*

She pressed her lips together. "That's not very fair."

*That's not what I meant... Let's talk about this later. Face to face without others.*

After a few days of flight, the grassy plains began to change into sandy dunes of gold and red. Blāzzer blinked at the rising sunlight as it hit the rocks far below. The distinct striations on the rocks glittered with small bits of quartz and mica. She thought, *I never thought that sand and rocks could look so beautiful.* She tried to swallow, but her mouth was too dry. Carefully, she turned and grabbed a canteen from the saddlebag. After taking several mouth fulls of water she asked, "Aren't you getting thirsty?"

Raffel, looking back at her as his wings beat against the warm air, replied, "No... I actually like this weather. I feel more comfortable in dry, hot weather."

She grimaced slightly.

"What?"

"No, just no."

"What?"

"The dry air I can do, but the heat is a no."

He blinked before saying, "I'm still lost."

"It's a compromise," said Blāzzer, placing the canteen back in the bag. "We can live somewhere dry just not hot."

He blinked.

"Cause we're stuck together."

"Oh... I think I get it."

She frowned. "After all this is over we can live somewhere dry, but not hot."

He nodded slightly and looked forward.

*We still need to talk,* said Blāzzer.

Raffel's wing beat stuttered a moment. *I know.*

## Chapter Seventeen

Blāzzer blinked as a city appeared on the southern horizon with the sun setting behind it. She asked, "That's not a mirage is it?"

"That is Gilzar," replied Raffel, "home of the Sentinel Crows."

As the dragons neared the desert town it became clear that all the buildings were made of sandstone. A large wall surrounded the town with aged evidence of attacks. Black banners flapped in the wind along the wall and on a large fortress in the center of the city. The dragons flew over the town before landing in a courtyard in front of the fortress. Sentinel Crows stepped forward as the dragons crouched down.

"You guys made it!" yelled one of the Crows, running down the stairs to them. His green hair with brown streaks was cut short. "Hopefully the flight was good."

"Oh gosh, Gryphun! You're taller again!" exclaimed Cornin, laughing and jumping down from Aurora's back.

The young dragon grinned as he stood head and shoulders taller than the rider. "Well, they keep feeding me so I don't know when I'll stop." He looked over to Raffel and Blāzzer; his smile fading slightly. He walked over to her before saying, "You must be Blāzzer."

She nodded.

He quickly bowed, saying, "Thank you for your friendship with Mae. I know she considers you a sister and that you two had many months of good memories together. She hasn't stopped worrying about you since you left Palator, but knows that you'll be okay." He straightened up and held out a letter. "She wanted me to give this to you if I saw you."

Blāzzer blinked and took the letter, murmuring, "Thank you."

Gryphun grinned before turning away as Shradrur, Inks, and Argon rode up. Shradur said, "Gryphun, show them to their rooms and make sure dinner is brought to them."

"Yes sir," replied the dragon.

After a couple of minutes, Gryphun led the dragons and riders through the sandstone halls of the fortress. Blāzzer held Mae's letter tight as she walked alongside Raffel. She thought, *Mae... are you doing okay? Is Lenny and Gorvi okay?*

"Here we are," said Gryphun, opening a set of double doors to a large room with a high ceiling. Several rooms branched off of it and narrow windows let in some sunlight. "I'll let you guys get settled while I grab some food. Any special requests."

"If there's any fresh-baked herbal bread," said Cornin as he walked into one of the bedrooms. Gryphun nodded before stepping out.

Blāzzer went into a bedroom and placed her bags on the floor as she sat on the edge of the bed. She opened the letter and looked at Mae's neat writing.

*Blāzzer*

*I hope this letter finds you well... Hopefully better than well. I know it's probably been pretty scary since you left Palator, but I know you can overcome anything that the Council throws at you. And don't let Raffel push you around either! You tell him when you have something to say. He's such a gitarb when it comes to women and relationships. Guess that's what happens to dudes who look like overgrown reptiles.*

*Anyways, everything is pretty good here. Most of the gardens are rebuilt... including Angel's. I've taken over care of it. I planted some tulip bulbs to bloom in the spring... Lenny won't step foot in the garden, or anywhere near. He's started sleeping in the barracks and training every day... I'm worried about him. Gorvi is watching out for him. He needs some more time to process I think.*

*No matter what, you'll have a place here in Palator. When you can, you should try to come visit. Angel has a small gravestone on a green hillside where all the wildflowers blossom in the spring. Take care of yourself and kick Raffel's butt for me!*

*Mae*

*P.S. Isn't my boyfriend hot!*

Blāzzer smiled and folded the letter. She slowly worked on unpacking some of her belongings. When the smell of cooked food reached her nose, she stepped out of her room and saw Gryphun placing food on the table from a cart. A black uleakite stood by him with his tail wagging slightly.

"You can come get some food," said Gryphun as he set plates on the table. Blāzzer walked over and immediately felt how short she was. He was almost two feet taller than her. She glanced down as the uleakite started licking her hand. "That's Bear, Shradur's companion."

"I didn't realize there were uleakites as Sentinel Crows," she said, stroking the canine's head.

"Just me," replied Bear, shaking his coat. His gold eyes fixed on Blāzzer.

"How has your training been, Gryphun?" asked Aurora, walking into the room, followed by Ash.

"It's been good," replied the young dragon. "Long days, but good." Bear chuckled and Gryphun bumped into him with his leg. "Well, I'll let you guys eat."

"Thornsten requested that Blāzzer and Raffel see him tomorrow," said Bear.

"The blacksmith?" questioned Ash, sitting at the table.

"Yeah, I can guide them," answered the uleakite.

"Won't you two join us for dinner?" asked Aurora, sitting beside her husband and grabbing a plate.

Gryphun looked down at Bear, before pulling out a seat and saying, "We can sit with you, but not eat. I'm at least on a special diet." He grinned sheepishly.

"I can eat," said Bear, nosing Blāzzer's arm as she placed some food on her plate. She gave him a piece of sausage and he swallowed it whole before laying down.

"Lydia! Raffel!" called Aurora.

"What diet are you on, Gryphun?" questioned Ash.

"Lots of protein," said the young dragon, "and calcium. I'm growing so much lately that I've been kind of struggling." As he spoke, Lydia and Raffel joined them at the table. "You haven't seen my dragon form yet... I'm almost as tall you Ash." Ash raised an eyebrow. Gryphun laughed. "I really suck at flying right now too."

"Where's Cornin?" asked Lydia, looking about.

"He went to go hang out with some of the Crows," replied Aurora. "He should-"

*Did you get a chance to read your letter?* asked Raffel, gently.

Blāzzer looked at him and, smiling softly, said, *It was really nice to hear from her. I should write back before we leave.* She could feel some of his tension ease. *Are you doing okay?*

*Really tired... and I'm excited for you to learn about your past.*

Blāzzer and Raffel followed Bear out of the fortress and down a street of Gilzar. People of various races filled the town, and most didn't take more than a glance at the red-haired dragon. Clothing and sheets hung on twine between buildings and crates were stacked between the sandstone walls. After a while, the buildings began to change into workshops and the smell of leather, metal, and wood filled the cool morning air. The pounding of hammers and scraping of saws on materials echoed against the walls. Bear ducked under a tapestry in a doorway and Blāzzer and Raffel stepped through.

Inside was a smithy with the far wall open to a shared courtyard. A man sat at a grinding wheel, sharpening a sword. Blāzzer looked about at the weapons and armor hanging on the walls. Everything was buffed to a shine and intricately stamped. A forge and anvil sat near the open wall, but the forge wasn't burning.

"Thornsten," said Bear, shaking his head.

The man stopped the wheel and stood up, turning to him. He had scars up and down his bare arms from fire and blades. He said, "Raffel and Blāzzer, I presume."

"Yes," replied Raffel with a slight nod.

Thornsten placed the sword down on a shelf and indicated to a couple of stools. Bear slipped out of the smithy as they all sat down. The blacksmith said, "How long have you been training with a sword, Raffel?"

"Almost fifteen years, if I remember correctly."

"May I see your sword?"

Raffel nodded, untying his sword from his belt and handing it the Thornsten. "I got that when I was seventeen."

Thornsten drew the sword and examined it closely. "Made in Palator?"

"Yeah."

He sheathed the sword and tapped his chin. "It wouldn't withstand a good number of fights." He handed the blade back to Raffel before getting up and going over to a tall cabinet. He opened it and inside were several swords, hanging on pegs. "You breathe fire, right?"

"Yes," answered Raffel, ear twitching.

Thornsten grabbed a sword and handed it to Raffel. "Try this one. It has a metal coil under the grip to help with not burning the grip."

Raffel stood up and drew the sword. "It's heavier."

"Well, you're not a boy anymore. That blade will withstand whatever you can throw at it as long as it isn't korsteel."

"Korsteel?" asked Blāzzer, vaguely remembering the name.

"It's a rare metal ore," explained Thornsten, grabbing a rock and handing it to her as Raffel continued to move about with the sword.

Blāzzer looked at the rock, seeing silver and a metallic red in the black rock, and said, "I've never seen it before."

"Most haven't," answered Thornsten, sitting down. "Comes from way up north. Primarily in Shadowfaire with some deposits south of their border. It's tricky to work with because it has to heat for a long time and cool for a long time. Not like other metals that need a bath to harden." He looked at Raffel. "Why don't you go out back and take a few swings with it? Then let me know if it's a good fit or not." Raffel nodded and walked out through the open archways. Thornsten turned back to Blāzzer. "What kind of sword were you training with in Palator?"

"A wooden short sword primarily," replied Blāzzer, thinking back to training with Mae. "A few times with a metal one."

"So you don't have one of you're own?"

"No."

"Well, that's no good." Thornsten stood up and walked over to the tall cabinet, looking over the swords. "Wait a moment." He went to a workbench and knelt down, pulling out a metal case with a lock. "A wood sword is much lighter than a metal sword." He pulled a key out from around his neck and unlocked the case. "A korsteel sword though is a little bit lighter than a wooden sword." He stood up and brought a sword over to Blāzzer. "Here, go ahead and draw it."

She gripped the leather-wrapped hilt and blinked at the pommel, saying, "There are rubies on it." A dragon was carved into both sides of the pommel with red gemstones inset for the eyes. The crossguard was designed to look like wings. Slowly, she drew the sword, moving the blade as it glittered in the sunlight. "It's made of korsteel."

"Yes it is," answered Thornsten, smiling. The blade was silver with red marbling its surface and the spine was engraved with runes.

"What does it say?"

"It's archaic lettering used by dragons way before Nickada was created," said Thornsten. "The runes say 'To the north a Flame burns'. The name of the sword is Flame. It's supposed to have three sibling swords and they make up the ensemble known as the Fire Compass." He shrugged. "Probably don't want to hear me rattle off the history of about it."

"No, it's interesting," assured Blāzzer, sheathing the blade careful. "But why give it to me?"

Thornsten grinned. "Well, korsteel is good against dragons."

"What do you mean?"

"Korsteel devours energy from the endars of dragons. It'll even absorb the fire and ice they breathe. Most other metals are not as strong as korsteel. It can also cut through a dragonhide easily."

Blāzzer swallowed uneasily, trying to keep her hands steady. "I wasn't planning on fighting any dragons... and I don't even know if I'll be fighting in Budsta."

"You're not going to be on the front lines, even if you are fighting in Budsta," stated Thornsten, crossing his arms. "In the future though - you'll be fighting. As a rider, it's your duty to fight alongside Raffel when Nickada needs you. It'll take many years of training to be battle-worthy. But with a sword made of korsteel, any blow you land will do damage. It'll help keep you safe. And then when you are trained you'll be fierce in battle."

"Thank you." She bobbed her head slightly still unsure.

"It won't need to be sharpened very often, maybe once a year if you're using it. You'll need to bring it to me for that though. It has to be reheated."

"You find a sword, Blāzzer?" asked Raffel, walking to them. His hair was damp from sweat and he carried the sword at his side.

"Yeah," replied Blāzzer. "It's a really good sword."

Raffel nodded. "Thornsten, this sword is a good fit."

"Keep it then," said the blacksmith. "Take your old one too until you get used to this one."

"Thank you."

"No worries. We'll get you both outfitted with some armor before you leave for Budsta. Till then we have some other matters to address. Shradur has put me in charge of informing you, Blāzzer, of your past."

She opened her mouth to say something, but no words came. She closed her mouth, gripping her new sword tightly.

"We'll need to travel west," said Thornsten. "Just a day out from here."

"You can't tell me here?" asked Blāzzer, feeling her stomach twist on itself.

"It would be better if you saw where you came from."

When night fell, Blāzzer sat at a small table in her bedroom. She held a dip ink pen over a piece of paper, thinking, *I don't know what to say, but there is so much to say too.* Slowly, she began to write:

*Mae*

*I miss you so much. I miss Palator and the gardens. I miss Lenny and Gorvi... and I miss*

*Angel.*

Blāzzer blinked as she felt tears start to brim her eyes and took a deep breath.

*I'm glad you were able to rebuild the garden, it gives me some peace of mind. I hope Lenny will be able to have some closure soon and I'm for sure he'll make a great warrior one day. It hasn't been too bad since I left, but I much rather be in Palator. I had to stand before the Council and it was really nerve-wracking. If it wasn't for Shradur, I would have been taken away from Raffel. I still feel like I haven't fully processed that I'm not going anywhere from him and his family. Things though have been kind of weird between us... We can now communicate through the liffen, but it feels like we've kind of drifted apart or at least there's a gap between us. Second is more true I think. You are right about him being a gitarb though with women and relationships. He said love is why he'll protect me and promises that everything will be okay. Then when I asked him what kind of love he was talking about, he wouldn't answer!*

*Anyways, tomorrow I'm going to find out about my past... and I'm not for sure how I'll feel or if it'll change me. Like is this going to be something afterwards that I wish I didn't learn? Raffel said that my parents loved me enough to put me in the care of the Sentinel Crows, but I still don't know. I'll try to write you again before we cross the border. When all of this is over, I will come by and see you and Lenny. I'll come see Angel... bring her some flowers. Please stay strong sister.*

*Blāzzer*

She glanced at Mae's letter beside her and smiled at the last line.

*P.S. Yes, your boyfriend is good-looking. I can understand why you fell for that smile.*

Blāzzer sighed before walking over to the window. The thick glass panes in the window were open to let the cool desert night air in. She looked up at the stars, noting how bright they were in the clear sky. She turned her head, searching for the constellation Foxdur.

There was a knock on her door and she looked over her shoulder, saying, "Come in."

Lydia stepped in carrying two small bowls, saying, "I brought you some pudding." The young woman smiled and took a bowl, sitting on her bed. Lydia sat in the chair, spooning some of the dessert into her mouth. "Raffel said you got a sword."

"Yeah," replied Blāzzer, searching for the bits of fruit in her pudding. "It's a really nice sword and I've never seen one like it. The blade is made of korsteel."

"Nice! That'll last you a long time. There aren't many of those." After a few moments, Lydia continued, "A number of years back we had thought of putting a small piece of korsteel in my body."

"Why? Your seizures?" asked Blāzzer, worried.

"It wouldn't stop the seizures, but it could theoretically stop my endar from leaking."

Blāzzer looked down at her bowl. "Thornsten mentioned that it devours the energy from endars."

Lydia nodded. "I've heard it feels horrible when it happens. My parents decided against it, because of the danger the metal causes... It's a struggle not being able to stop myself from endangering others." Her grip on her spoon had turned her knuckles white. "I used to hate myself for it."

"Lydia," breathed Blāzzer. The dragon looked up at her and there were tears in her fierce red eyes.

"That's why I want to fight. Because I don't want to be a burden. I want to be able to protect my home just like everyone else."

Blāzzer stood up and walked to Lydia, wrapping her arms around the dragon.

"I've tried hard to keep my chin up, but it's getting heavy. I'm a broken dragon." Lydia let out a sob and Blāzzer tightened her grip around her."

You're not a burden or broken," insisted Blāzzer firmly.

Lydia looked up at Blāzzer. "But I am."

Blāzzer grasped her hands and squeezed them. "If you were broken then they wouldn't be asking you to fight. They have faith in you, that you can protect Nickada. If they thought you were a burden they wouldn't be sending you to fight."

Lydia, taking a deep breath, leaned her head against Blāzzer's chest. After a while she said quietly, "I can understand why Raffel chose you to be his rider."

## Chapter Eighteen

In the morning, Blāzzer and Raffel followed Thornsten and Argon out of Gilzar and across the dry lands. The farther they flew from the town, the more her stomach ached with anxiety. She leaned against Raffel's neck and watched the land pass below. Thornsten and Argon rode their horses along a winding trail amongst the rock outcroppings.

"I wish they would just tell me," whispered Blāzzer.

Raffel looked back at her for a moment, saying, "I'm sorry this is being drawn out."

She pressed her lips together and tried to focus on their surroundings as they continued to fly. It wasn't until the sun was setting when they came to a large rock face. In front of it were three round huts and a corral with two horses. Raffel landed near the huts and two Crows stepped out of one of the huts. They looked at the dragon before turning to the Thornsten and Argon as they rode up.

"Are you okay, Blāzzer?" asked Raffel as he crouched down.

"There's carvings," she murmured, staring at the rocks. Raffel looked at the outcroppings and saw the faded etchings of dragons and people. They were slightly discolored compared to the surrounding rock as if at one point they had been painted. At the base of the outcropping was a set of wooden doors.

Raffel said, "I've never been here before."

Blāzzer dropped their bags to the ground, before sliding down herself. She looked up as Thornsten walked over to her leading his horse. Pointing to one of the huts, he said, "You two will stay in there. I'll let you two get settled. We'll talk in the morning."

As he walked away Raffel shifted, picking up their bags and asking, "You okay?"

Blāzzer looked away from the mural and nodded before picking up her satchel. She followed him to the clay hut and he held open the wooden door for her. She stepped inside and blinked at the limited light coming through the slatted windows. Raffel closed the door behind him, placing their bags on the ground.

"There's only one room," he said, looking around at the two cots, lantern, and low table.

Blāzzer sat down on one of the cots and gazed blankly down at the hard-packed ground.

"Here, drink," said Raffel, holding a canteen to her.

She took it, but didn't drink, saying quietly, "Something feels familiar about this place."

He sat down on the other cot, watching her.

"Like in my body... I've never felt this way before." She looked up at him with tears brimming her eyes. "It makes me want to cry, but I'm not sad." She took a drink of water. "I'm probably just tired."

Raffel nodded. "Why don't you rest for now? I'll go find us some dinner." He stood up and walked to the door. He glanced at her before stepping out.

Blāzzer sighed and laid down on her side, thinking, *What is this feeling? Like something in my body resonating with this place.* She rubbed her forehead as pain started to push against her head. *Why?*

After a few minutes, Raffel returned with two plates of food. He placed them on the table and sat on the ground, before saying, "Come and eat." Slowly she got up and walked over to the table. "You're looking kind of pale."

"I feel really weird," whispered Blāzzer, poking at her food with her fork. She felt his concern and closed her eyes as the connection brought some relief. *That helps.*

He tipped his head in question.

*The liffen it's helping... Like it's grounding me to reality almost.*

He nodded, though still confused. *Try to eat and then maybe you should get to sleep. You're probably just worn out from all of the excitement.*

Blāzzer woke in the night, feeling the headache coming back with vengeance. She slowly sat up and waited for her eyes to adjust to the limited star and moon light that came through the windows. Crickets could be heard outside, but otherwise everything was quiet. Carefully, she got up and walked over to Raffel. He was sound asleep on his back with an arm behind his head. She laid down beside him, holding onto his arm and watching his chest rise and fall.

She blinked as she realized tears were dripping down her face. He moved his arm away from her before putting it around her and holding her close. She closed her eyes and listened to his steady heartbeat. After a while her headache subsided and she pressed herself closer to him, glad for his warmth against the cool desert night.

"Couldn't sleep?" asked Raffel, drowsily.

Blāzzer gripped his tunic, afraid he would make her move.

"You're okay... I like having you next to me."

She pressed her lips together before saying quietly, "Me too." She could feel his happiness at that. "Raffel?"

"Hmmm?"

"What did you mean by love?"

For a moment he was silent and then he said, "Well... I love you, Blāzzer."

"But, what did you mean by that? You said it was up to me."

He sighed, squeezing her. "I don't want to be without you... It's why I always slept outside your tent. To just be near you makes me feel good. Feel stronger... Feel like a better person. You make me want to be a better person, Blāzzer." He rubbed his face with his free hand. "And the thought of you with another person..."

Blāzzer could feel his sadness and pain at that thought.

"It makes me upset. I want to be the one for you, but I know I can't force that... and I know that if you want to be with someone-"

"Raffel," said Blāzzer, sitting up slightly so she could see his face. "I don't want to be with anyone else... I love you." Relief washed over him and she pressed her face against his chest at the feeling. He rubbed her back slowly. "I'm not ready to be... intimate though."

"That's okay... me neither."

She laid down and pressed her nose against his jaw. After a few minutes, she asked, "When did you know?"

"That I loved you?"

She nodded.

"Back in Palator - before everything went crazy. One day I just noticed this feeling towards you. You smiled at me during one of the lessons and my heart... it just skipped a beat. Then when the festival came. I made such a fool of myself."

"Don't say that."

"It's true though," replied Raffel, pressing his hand against his forehead. "I told you that I had fought for you and then you ran away and then Mae yelled at me. Then when you asked me to dance, I said no and you looked so crushed... I should have gone after you."

"It's okay," assured Blāzzer, resting her hand over his heart.

"When the soldiers found you in the ditch... I couldn't even think straight. All I knew was that I couldn't let you die. That I couldn't let you be in pain. The only way I could fix that was to give you the liffen. I felt terrible at first about it, but when I gave you part of my endar all I could feel was love for you." He rubbed his thumb over her shoulder, over the liffen.

"So when you're father got mad about you staying with me after my nightmare and he asked if you had any romantic feelings..."

"It was a lie and Dad knew that."

Blāzzer nodded. After a moment she said, "And Lydia said you weren't a romantic."

Raffel chuckled. "Oh, she knew. She figured it out real quick."

"Really?"

"Yeah, she was pushing me to say something sooner."

Blāzzer smiled softly, feeling safe and warm.

"What about you? When did you know?"

"Well, after you said that you had fought for me I knew I had a crush, but I didn't realize that it went deeper than that. You have always been so kind to me and I always felt like you understood more of me than most. I knew for sure though when I was told the Council would try to take me away. I felt this horrible feeling like my heart was being squeezed... When I was with you though, things felt like they would get better. That I would be okay and that I'd come out stronger after all of this."

They laid there as the crickets continued to sing outside. Slowly Raffel pulled the blanket from under Blāzzer and covered them both. She whispered, "I feel so at peace."

"Me too," he whispered.


"Come on you two! Let's get this started before it's too late in the day!" shouted Thornsten from outside.

Blāzzer pulled the blanket tighter around herself, thinking, *It's too early*, as the first rays of sunlight came through the window. She pressed her face against Raffel's chest and listened to his heart steadily beat. She smiled softly then blinked and sat up, heart stuttering.

"What's wrong?" asked Raffel, sleepily, with his eyes still closed. When she didn't respond, he opened his eyes. "Blāzzer?"

"It's nothing," she whispered, laying back down. "Just had to remember where I was for a moment."

He nodded, pressing his cheek against the top of her head.

"I'm nervous."

"It'll be okay... No matter what, you'll still be you."

After a few moments they got up and left the hut. Thornsten was sitting on a rock outside. He looked up as they approached, asking, "Were you two able to sleep last night?" Blāzzer looked away, hoping she wasn't blushing, as Raffel nodded. "Good... Well follow me then."

Thornsten led them towards the mural and as they got closer Blāzzer began to feel the strange feeling from yesterday come back. She asked, "What is this place?"

"It's a sanctuary," replied the Sentinel Crow. "A sanctuary where a few children were brought to be kept safe."

"From what?"

Thornsten looked over his shoulder at her and said, "The invaders from Solea before Nickada was founded." He pushed open the wooden doors and stepped aside for Raffel and Blāzzer.

Inside were several lit braziers that illuminated most of the large room, leaving the corners in shadow. Thick stone pillars with intricate carvings of mountains and forests held the ceiling up. On the far wall was another mural of dragons and humans. The paint had not faded and it showed two dragons guarding two children. In front of the mural were two raised stone basins with runes carved into the rim. Blāzzer touched one of the basins and said quietly, "I was here before... I was really little."

"This is where you woke from your slumber," explained Thornsten. "You were brought here as a two year old to keep you safe from Solea."

"But that was centuries ago." She looked back at him and then to Raffel. The dragon nodded slightly. "How?"

"Dragons have the ability to transfer a portion of their endar to a person, creating the liffen. However, if a dragon were to transfer all of it to a person then it would force that person into a hibernation. They wouldn't age or decay. The dragon would die in the process and the person would wake up years later just as if they had gone to sleep."

Blāzzer felt her knees weaken and sat down on the ground, letting her head rest on the side of the basin. Quietly she asked, "So I'm not from this time?"

"No."

She tried to take a deep breath, but it came out shakily. She looked up as

Raffel sat down next to her, saying, "It doesn't matter that you weren't born in this time. You're here now." *And I'm really glad you're here too.*

"Your parents wanted you to live in a time when there wouldn't be a war," said Thornsten. "They knew that they weren't going to make it out alive, so they chose to put you in the care of the Sentinel Crows. It was agreed that you would be put into a hibernation and-"

"But the dragon," said Blāzzer, looking to him.

"He was a young dragon, probably fifteen years old. He agreed to sacrifice himself."

"What was his name?"

"Rubix. He was red and gold." Thornsten motioned to the mural. Blāzzer looked to the dragons protecting the two children, and saw that one was painted like Rubix. "Who was the other child?"

"That is Tetricus. He was seven when he was put into the hibernation. He woke one year after you. He went to stay with the Stone family."

Blāzzer looked at Raffel and felt his sadness.

"He struggled a lot," said the dragon, quietly. "My parents tried their best to console him, but one day when he was thirteen he ran away. No one has seen him since."

"I'm sorry," whispered Blāzzer.

"It's okay."

"When you woke," said Thornsten, "it was decided you would stay with the Sentinel Crows till you were older. But when Tetricus disappeared, the Council decided you would not live with the Stone family until you weren't a ward anymore."

"I thought it was because they didn't want me to become the leader," she murmured.

"The hope was Tetricus would. He was the son of the first leader of the dragons, Blazen."

"Who were my parents?"

"They were friends of Blazen's and acted as captains in his army. Your parents' names were Lionel and Eltika... They were dragon and rider." Blāzzer opened her mouth to say something, but closed it. "You're not part dragon. They found you as a baby in the rubble of a burned town. On the basin it says 'A lotus found in the ashes of ruins. A lotus to blossom into a great swan.'"

"So they weren't even my real parents," whispered Blāzzer.

"Blāzzer," said Raffel. "They were your real parents. They took you in as a baby and loved you enough to get you away from the war." He touched

Blāzzer's hand. "Do you understand? It doesn't matter if they aren't blood related... Like how Angel was a mother to you."

Blāzzer pressed her lips together, murmuring, "I know." After a while she asked, "What race am I? Raffel had said I wasn't mortal."

"That is correct," said Thornsten. "Have you ever noticed that you have an extra pair of ribs?"

"A healer mentioned that a long time ago."

"And your menstrual cycle is different too."

Raffel blinked and Blāzzer said, "I only bleed once every three months."

"The dragons that came from Solea brought another race with them," explained Thornsten. "They look like mortals, except for those two things, a third set of teeth, and 150 year lifespan. Those were the barruns... You are a barrun. The barruns and dragons are very compatible with each other. A larger chest means larger lungs, which is better for flying. The longer lifespan matches that of the dragons as well. Barruns also are able to hold more of an endar compared to the other nondragon races."

Blāzzer looked to Raffel, asking, "Did you know all of this?"

"Parts," he replied. "Not all of it."

Slowly she stood up. "I need to take a moment to think."

*Lionel and Eltika,* thought Blāzzer, *that was their names.* She rolled over onto her side on her cot and looked across the empty room. *Dragon and rider. Who was the dragon? Who was the rider? What did they look like? What did they feel when they found me in the rubble?* She squeezed her eyes shut trying to slow the tirade of questions without answers. *Why did you run away Tetricus? Where are you? Are you alive? Could you-*

"Blāzzer."

She opened her eyes to see Raffel sitting on the edge of his cot.

*You're not alone,* he said.

She rolled onto her back, saying, "Which one was the dragon?"

He blinked in confusion. "Of your parents?"

She nodded.

"Your mother, Eltika, was a dragon. She had light purple scales. Your parents were one of the strongest dragon and rider pairs... Tetricus told me that when we were kids."

After a few moments, Blāzzer said, "A part of me wants to be mad at you."

"I understand."

She sat up and they met each other's eyes. *But I don't want to be.* "It feels like I finally have some answers and yet I'm not for sure what to do with them." She looked down at her hands. "What am I supposed to do?" When Raffel didn't answer she looked up at him.

"I don't know," he murmured. "All I can say is to keep moving forward." He walked over to her and knelt in front of her. "No matter what I'll be by your side."

She leaned forward and rested her forehead against his. *I feel so tired.*

*I know. Go ahead and rest.*

*Will you lay with me?*

*Yes.*


Blāzzer watched the sun as it sank towards the horizon with the dry breeze pushing her hair back. Even though the air was cooling as the sunlight dimmed, the rock she sat on was still warm. She thought, *I wish I could remember them. Mother... father... who were you? I have your names, but you still feel distant.* She tapped the rock with a finger. *How bad was it back then for you to put me into that slumber?*

"I know it isn't easy," said Thornsten, sitting next to her, "but try to find strength in knowing who they were."

"I really don't know who they were though," replied Blāzzer, solemnly and looking at him. "Just their names and that they were dragon and rider."

"Well, sometimes we don't get to chose who our parents are and sometimes we don't get to know them. I know that might not be what you want to hear, but our parents don't make us who we are. We do."

"Did you know your parents?"

The man frowned slightly. "My mother raised me and my two brothers on her own. My father only was around when we were very little. He'd come for a few weeks then would leave for the rest of the year to return the following year. He always brought money and supplies. He fixed up the house, but he barely spoke to my brothers and me. One year though he didn't come... and same the next. My mother fell ill and told us that he was from Desla, and to not go looking for him. Before she passed away she called for the Sentinel Crows and they took us three. She died a month later."

Blāzzer blinked, gazing out over the rocks and sand. "I'm sorry."

"No reason to be. The fact is that it all made me stronger. It drove me to be a good person and to look out for others."

She nodded, looking down at her feet.

"It'll take some time for you to process and till then don't feel guilty about your feelings."

After a moment she said, "It's kind of hard not to. Like I know it must have been a tough decision to put me away, but I wish they had let me stay with them longer so I could remember."

Thornsten sighed and said, "If they hadn't put you into that slumber, you would have only had a few more weeks with them at most."

Blāzzer hugged herself. "It was really that bad?"

"Solea wanted to eradicate the dragons. It was so bad that there's still a country today with that mindset. Draig and Traig to the south beyond Budsta. Traig reveres dragons as holy beings and Draig sees them as demons. They've been fighting for centuries over the same thing that Solea invaded Nickada for. Except, Solea wanted to conquer the land and enslave the people. Be proud that your parents fought for the freedom of Nickada. That they didn't die in vain, because here you are. Free and... with a dragon looking out for you."

She looked up at him and saw his big grin. Blāzzer blushed. Several minutes passed before she said, "I want to continue their legacy." She stood up. "I want to make sure Nickada is safe and free."

Night had fallen, and a small lantern lit up the inside of the hut. Blāzzer sat on her cot, holding her knees to her chest and watching the little flame flicker inside the glass. She didn't look up as Raffel walked in, saying, "I thought you would have been asleep. It's late." She frowned. "You okay?"

*I'm going to miss the quiet time we had together,* replied Blāzzer, pressing her lips together.

He smiled softly and sat down next to her. "Me too."

She leaned her head against his shoulder. *Thank you.*

"For what?" He laid his cheek against her head.

"For being with me through all of this."

"I wouldn't want to be anywhere else."

They sat there for a while as the crickets outside chirped and the little flame grew smaller. Pulling off his boots, Raffel said, "We should go to bed."

Blāzzer wrapped her arms around him, burying her face against his back and asking, "Does me knowing where I came from... when I came from change who I am to you?"

Raffel blinked and squeezed her arm. "No. Not even a little. Does it change who I am to you?"

She shook her head.

"Come on, let's go to bed." He gently freed himself from her before getting up.

"Please... one last night?" asked Blāzzer.

He blew out the lantern before laying down next to her and holding her close. He whispered, "This won't be the last time we will be together."

"I know, but it feels like it'll be a while."

Raffel nodded.

"It makes me sad." She gripped his shirt over his heart.

He placed his hand over hers. "Me too. We'll still be together and we'll make new memories."

She relaxed. "I'd like that... I love you."

"I love you too."

## Chapter Nineteen

Blāzzer watched as Gilzar neared and felt excitement at being back with the rest of the Stone family. She touched Raffel's neck as he soared high above the ground, asking, *Should we tell your family about us?*

*Maybe not right now,* he replied, uneasily.

She nodded. *That's what I was thinking.*

Soon they landed in front of the fortress and Blāzzer untied their bags as the dragon crouched. She looked up and saw Lydia walking down the stairs to them. Blāzzer smiled and jumped down from the saddle.

"I was worried about you," said Lydia, embracing her.

"I'm good," assured Blāzzer. Lydia stepped back, holding her at arm's length. "I promise!"

"Okay, but I'll be checking later." Lydia turned to Raffel and asked, "So?"

Raffel snorted and shifted into a human, crossing his arms. "Lots of information."

Lydia frowned, looking between Blāzzer and Raffel, before smiling and saying, "I'm so happy for you two!" Blāzzer blushed as Raffel picked up their bags. They walked into the fortress as Argon and Thornsten rode into the courtyard.

Lydia said, "Mom and Dad were pretty worried about you two."

"Really?" asked Blāzzer.

Lydia nodded, leading the way down a hall. "Yeah, they spent a lot of time talking about how learning about your past would affect you two... and how the battles in Budsta will too. Then about whether or not I should be fighting." She frowned.

Blāzzer touched her arm, saying, "You should. You deserve to protect your home."

173

Lydia smiled then looked to Raffel, asking, "What do you think, Raf?"

He shrugged before saying, "I think they're just having to come to terms with us being adults."

She tipped her head slightly.

"It's like what we talked about before. They're used to being the ones that protect us. Now we're able to help protect others."

"What about Blāzzer?"

"What about me?" questioned Blāzzer.

Raffel looked at her, replying, "You can't fight... you're not trained yet."

Blāzzer pressed her lips together. "I might not fight, but I still want to help."

"I heard Mom and Dad mention you joining the medics," said Lydia. "Specifically for us dragons. We'll have to ask them."

They walked the rest of the way in silence. As they stepped into the family suite, they found Cornin sitting on the couch writing in a notebook. He looked up at them and grinned, saying, "They're back!"

Blāzzer smiled and said, "It's good to be back."

"I'll let you two get settled, then we should talk. Ash and Aurora should be here soon too."

Blāzzer walked into her room, placing her satchel on her bed. She untied her sword as Raffel placed her bag down and she said, "Thank you." He nodded and stepped out. She placed Flame on her bed before walking back out to the living area.

"How was the trip?" asked Cornin as she sat on the couch.

"It was good," she replied. "Still processing... but it's nice to have names for my parents now."

He smiled and nodded encouragingly. Lydia sat next to Blāzzer and questioned, "Cornin, do you know what Mom and Dad were talking about with Blāzzer training as a medic?"

"Well, as a rider it's important to know how to help dragons in battle," explained Cornin, closing his notebook. "Part of that is knowing what to do when fighting from the saddle, but also what to do on the ground to help." Raffel pulled a chair up and sat down. "As a medic, you'd stay well behind the battlefront. Aurora spoke about having you train with Truity Heart."

"She's awesome," exclaimed Lydia, turning to Blāzzer. "She's been treating my seizures since I was a kid."

"She was the midwife for you two as well," added Cornin. "Don't know any other healer that has as much knowledge about dragons as her."

Exhaustion tugged at Blāzzer's eyelids as she lay in bed, but sleep evaded her. A gentle cool breeze blew in through the open window panes and moonlight spilled on the floor. She pulled the blankets around her, trying to nestle against her pillow. She rolled over and sighed, thinking, *This feels lonely... Raffel?*

*Hmmm? h*e replied sleepily.

*I can't sleep.*

*Hmmm... I'm sorry.*

*I wish I was next to you,* she said, feeling her chest warm.

*Yeah, I was getting used to you being at my side.*

Blāzzer smiled softly. *Promise me that after Budsta, we'll be next to each other again like that.*

*I promise that we'll sleep next to each other again.*

*I love you.*

*I love you too.*

Bear led Blāzzer through several halls in the fortress of Gilzar before coming to a door at the end of one. He nudged it open and inside was an office space with narrow windows and bookshelves. Shradur stood up from behind the desk and smiled saying, "It's good to see you doing so well, Blāzzer."

"Thank you," she replied, smiling softly and looking to Thornsten, who sat in a chair, then back to the Sentinel Crow leader. "You asked to speak with me?"

"Yes, I wanted to check on you," answered Shradur, sitting down and indicating for her to follow suit. "How are you feeling?"

"Pretty good." Blāzzer sat on the edge of chair. "I'm still processing everything. I'm glad though that I finally know."

Shradur nodded.

"I never got the chance to thank you for what you did in Chamdal."

He raised an eyebrow and said, "Don't worry about it. I didn't mean to make a grand entrance-" Thornsten grunted. "-but we got behind on our travel."

"You fought Caratin to ensure I'd stay with the Stone family. You could have been injured."

"It'd take more than a scrape to keep him down," commented Thornsten, folding his hands behind his head. "His mirazh keeps him safe from most blades."

Blāzzer nodded, remembering the black, metallic tentacle that had wrapped around Caratin's legs.

"Do you understand why the dragons are not allowed to represent themselves in the Council, Blāzzer?" questioned Shradur.

After a moment she said, "Raffel had mentioned that since leaders can duel each other in order to settle disputes, it would be an unfair advantage for the dragons to represent themselves."

"Somewhat true. Back when Nickada was forming, the only way to get all the races to agree to creating the Council was through compromise. One of those being dragons not representing themselves. Think back to the other races at that time. Some new race has shown up and can shift into, what one might call, a monster." Blāzzer flinched slightly at this. "To top that off, the dragons had brought invaders on their heels into the land. The dragons and riders though needed to unite the races if they were going to fight off Solea. So the dragons agreed and the first rider was made leader of the dragons."

"Blazen?"

"Yes, he was the first. There were a few after him, but as the number of dragons dwindled so did the number of riders. No leader means that the dragons are at the whim of the Council."

"Remember how I said my mother called for the Sentinel Crows?" asked Thornsten.

Blāzzer nodded.

"It was because there's no leader of the dragons."

She tipped her head, trying to think of the correlation.

"My mother was a Nickadian mortal, but my father was a Deslian dragon."

She blinked in surprise and murmured, "You're part dragon."

"I'm what's known as a halfblood," explained Thornsten with an apologetic grin. "One parent a dragon and the other another human race. It's helped me be one of the best blacksmiths in Nickada. See halfbloods have an endar just like the dragon parent. Though we can't shift into a full dragon, we can shift into a fatorana state if trained. Because of the dragon heritage, my brothers and I would fall under the protection of the leader of the dragons. Without one though the Council would have had to decide what happened to us. Much like you're own situation. To avoid that my mother gave us to the Sentinel Crows."

"I was given to them too though," said Blāzzer. "But I wasn't protected."

"You were given to the Sentinel Crows for temporary protection," corrected Shradur, gently. "Thornsten and his brothers were given as trainees to become Sentinel Crows. Once they started their training, the Council couldn't touch them."

She looked down at her hands.

"Blāzzer, I want to offer you protection from the Council. The only way I can do that is by you becoming a Sentinel Crow."

She pressed her lips together, thinking, I *wouldn't have to worry about the Council anymore.*

"Keep in mind that you would have to complete five years of training here in Gilzar," added Shradur.

"So I would be away from the Stone family then?"

He nodded. "Afterward, you would rejoin them."

"I don't want to be away from them," whispered Blāzzer.

Shradur raised his hand slightly and said, "You don't need to decide now, but I do want you to think about it."

Blāzzer followed Bear back to the suite the Stone family was staying at. She stopped outside the door with her hand on the doorknob, thinking, *Should I join the Crows? I wouldn't have to worry about the Council anymore... but five years away from the them... my family.*

"You okay, Blāzzer?" asked Bear, nudging her leg with his nose.

She looked down at him and replied, "I'm just not for sure what to do."

"Well, I wouldn't worry about rushing into the decision. Shradur's offer will be there no matter."

"Why didn't my parents give me to the Sentinel Crows as a trainee? Instead of just protection."

Bear tipped his head to the side. "I suppose they wanted you to choose your future... even though it didn't quite work out completely that way."

Blāzzer nodded and said, "Thank you." As he turned to leave she opened the door and stepped into the living room.

The space was quiet and there was no one there. She called out, "Hello?"

"How was it?" asked Raffel, walking out of his room. When he saw her conflicted face, he said, "Not very good I take it."

"No, it was fine," insisted Blāzzer, wrapping her arms around herself and averting her gaze from him. He walked over to her and gently placed his hand on her cheek. "Shradur offered for me to join the Sentinel Crows."

He nodded slightly, pressing his lips together. "And?"

"I haven't decided... I would be away for five years and I don't want to be away from you." She leaned forward, pressing her forehead against his chest.

"I would join with you, Blāzzer," said Raffel, running his fingers through her hair. "I'll go wherever you go."

She took a deep breath and wrapped her arms around him, feeling safe and whispering, "How did I deserve your love?"

His ear twitched and he replied, "You didn't need to do anything to deserve my love. You deserve love just as you are."

"You're going to make me cry," said Blāzzer with a soft smile, squeezing him tight.

"But it's true," he answered, kissing the top of her head.

"Thank you."

They stood there for a few minutes, holding each other as if the world had stopped moving. Warm sunlight shone through the windows and little dust specks floated in the beams. The thick glass panes kept the dry heat out and showed the desert beyond.

Raffel took a deep breath, before saying, "We should probably go find my family. They'll be wondering where we are."

"Where are they?" asked Blāzzer, not wanting to step away from his embrace.

"They said they were going to a tavern outside the fortress. It's one of Cornin's favorite places to eat apparently." He held her tight for a moment. "We'll have more time together soon."

Raffel led the way out of the fortress with the sun high over head. Blāzzer blinked at the glaring light that bounced against the sandstone buildings, saying, "I still can't believe you like this heat." He grinned back at her and continued walking. They came to a building with a wooden sign of a pink pig. He held the door open for her and the cool air inside made her sigh with relief.

"Hey! They made it!" yelled Cornin from a table, holding up a mug and getting a glare from Aurora. Blāzzer sat next to Lydia with Raffel on her other side. "We'll get you two something to eat. Miss!"

"How'd it go?" asked Ash, offering Blāzzer some bread.

"Okay," she replied tentatively, tearing a chunk of bread off before handing it to Raffel. "Shradur offered for me to join the Sentinel Crows."

"Did you say yes?" questioned Lydia, looking at her worriedly.

Blāzzer shook her head, saying, "He told me to take time to think... I wouldn't have to worry about the Council if I joined, but then I'd be here for five years for training."

"The Sentinel Crows have been good to this family," said Aurora.

"You're making me blush," said Cornin with a chuckle before taking a drink. "But -to be serious- being a Sentinel Crow would mean you're training is high quality and you'll have access to all of our resources. Not a bad gig really. You'd probably be sent around Nickada for awhile since you're wings are going to follow you." He winked at Blāzzer and Raffel.

"I'd come visit you two," said Lydia quietly.

"What are your thoughts, Blāzzer?" questioned Ash, looking at her intently.

"I don't know," she murmured. "I just want to go back to some semblance of normal." Lydia squeezed her arm in reassurance.

"Whatever you choose, you'll be a part of this family," assured Aurora, looking to Blāzzer then to Raffel. "That goes for both of you." He nodded slightly.

"The Council wouldn't have to worry about you if you were a Sentinel Crow," muttered Cornin, resting his chin on his hand.

"What do you mean?" asked Blāzzer.

"Well, they're worried about you being the Leader of the Dragons, right?" replied Cornin. "If you're a Sentinel Crow then you can't be the the Leader of the Dragons."

*I really don't know what to choose,* said Blāzzer, following Raffel back to the fortress. She wanted to hold his hand for comfort.

*You'll know what's best once you have some time to process,* he said. *Don't try to overthink it.* He looked back at her and she smiled sheepishly.

*A wee late for that.*

He rolled his eyes playfully and grinned. They walked into the fortress and Raffel asked one of the Sentinel Crows, "Do you know where Truity Heart can be found?"

"Probably in her garden," replied the man. "I'll show you." He led them through the fortress and through a large door into a courtyard with numerous plants and a small pond. Across the courtyard was a greenhouse built into a sandstone wall. The Crow indicated to the glass panes. "She's usually in there."

"Thank you," said Blāzzer and the man left them. She led Raffel along the stone path, looking about at the plants. "I didn't realize there were so many different types of plants out in the desert." She reached out and gently touched a long plump leaf of a wide succulent. "And grew so large."

"Me neither," replied Raffel, eying some of the spiny cacti along the path. They walked up to the door of the greenhouse and saw a woman standing there tending to some of the plants. "Are you Truity?"

The woman turned to them and replied, "I am. I thought you might remember me, Raffel."

He smiled apologetically.

"No worries. You must be Blãzzer. You've grown a lot since I last saw you."

"Last saw me?" asked the young woman.

"You were just a small child then. Come on in."

Raffel and Blãzzer stepped into the greenhouse and she looked about at the various flowers and herbs. She thought, *Reminds me of Angel's garden.* She looked to Truity, whose short hair was pulled back with a scarf and had a kind face.

"What do you know about dragon anatomy compared to other races?" asked the older woman, sitting on a stool and wiping the dirt from her hands off on a towel.

"Not much," answered Blãzzer, glancing to Raffel. "Besides extra ribs, extra set of teeth, and mobile ears." He frowned and twitched his ears. "They have different body temperatures depending on if they breathe fire or ice. Hair and eye color match their scale color and they can't start shifting until puberty." She looked back to Truity.

"That's some of the basics. Raffel, show your teeth."

"Huh?" asked the dragon, taken aback.

"The best way to learn is with a model. Show your teeth. Blãzzer take a look a see what you notice that is different."

He awkwardly grinned, pulling his lips back as much as he could and saying, *I feel like I'm a specimen.*

*You make a very good one,* teased Blãzzer, looking at his teeth. "Do you have extra canines?"

"Dragons have an extra pair of canine teeth and a third set of teeth," explained Truity. Raffel closed his mouth, licking his teeth. "You as well Blãzzer have a third set of teeth. Helps with living to 150 years."

*Thinking of how long I'll live, makes me feel really young,* thought Blãzzer.

"Shirt, Raffel."

The dragon sighed and pulled his shirt off, saying, *Specimen.*

"Each dragon has an endar," said Truity, walking over to him and placing her hand under his sternum and making him tense. "While in human form it's condensed and housed under the diaphragm. Go ahead and see if you can feel it, Blãzzer." She stepped back and Blãzzer gently put her hand on Raffel's stomach.

"I don't feel anything different," said Blãzzer, not noticing him staring upwards. "Just a lot of muscle." Truity placed her hand over Blãzzer's and pressed it harder against Raffel's skin. Blãzzer blinked at the warm pulse that emanated like a ripple from inside him. "That's weird."

"Think of it as a second heartbeat. Stronger the endar, slower the pulse.

Weaker, faster. It's a good way to measure a dragon's energy when they're unconscious."

Blāzzer looked to Truity, removing her hand from Raffel and asking, "What happens if it stops beating?"

"It's no threat," assured Truity, sitting back down on the stool. "If the endar stops pulsing, it just means that they've used up all their energy from breathing fire or ice or flying around too much. They won't feel good, but once they've recovered some energy then the pulsing will start again. Raffel, turn around." He immediately did so. "Go ahead and put your hand on his shoulder, where your liffen would be."

Blāzzer reached up and placed her hand on his right shoulder blade. She blinked in surprise and said, "It's cool." She moved her hand across his shoulder, finding the defined edge of the cooler skin. Slowly, she mapped out what the area looked like by touch. "It's in the shape of my liffen."

Truity nodded, saying, "It's a match to yours. A liffen is given when a dragon transfers part of their endar. In the process of the connection being made, part of their body can no longer be heated or cooled by the endar."

*You never mentioned this,* said Blāzzer, glaring at the back of Raffel's head.

*I don't even notice it,* he replied, *except for when I wash.*

"Thank you Raffel," said Truity with a soft smile. "You can put your shirt back on, then you're free to go."

*I'll see you afterward.* He pulled on his shirt and quickly walked out of the greenhouse.

"If you need any medication let me know."

Blāzzer tore her gaze from where Raffel disappeared out of the garden to Truity, asking, "What?"

"Don't go to any normal healer for medication," repeated the older woman, still smiling. "Your cycle is different than mortals and the wrong medication could make you ill."

Heat rushed to Blāzzer's cheeks, muttering, "It's not like that."

"Yet." Truity inclined her head. "Go ahead and take a seat." She waited as Blāzzer sat down on another stool. "Have you been told what happens to dragons in time of war?"

"They fight."

"They fight... and fight. Think it through. A large creature that flies, can breathe fire or ice, and has sharp teeth and claws. Who would you send: one dragon or a group of soldiers?"

Blāzzer pressed her lips together.

"Dragons are used in battle... Even if wounded they are expected to fight. Dragons become thought of as weapons, not people in times of battle."

Blāzzer clenched her hands into fists, feeling her nails bite against her palms.

"They get up at dawn and fight till dusk. They land and are bedridden from exhaustion. Many times they are vomiting from exertion and swallowing too much blood. Healers do their best to patch them up and get food in them. The next dawn, they are sent back out to the battlefield. This repeats until the battle is over... or the dragon dies."

Blāzzer tried to find words as anger and fear welled up in her.

"When there was a leader of the dragons this didn't happen," said Truity.

Blāzzer looked up to her, questioning, "Then why now?"

"The Council decides to send the dragons out to protect their own," explained the healer. "If there was a leader of the dragons, then the Council couldn't make that decision. The leader of the dragons would work with the king without the Council present on when the dragons would fight."

"But there isn't one," whispered Blāzzer.

"Yet."

Blāzzer blinked before looking at the dirt, saying quietly, "It would be three years before I could become leader."

"That's sooner than anyone else... Yes, you would have a lot of work in those three years to get ready, but you could do it." Truity stood up and placed her hands on Blāzzer's cheeks, tipping her head up. Blāzzer looked up into her silver eyes and saw determination. "If you love that man, then you'll know what to do."

Blāzzer sighed, feeling her heart conflicting over her decision to come. She continued to brush out her hair while sitting on the narrow windowsill, looking out over the night covered city. Light could be seen coming from the buildings and people walked about the streets in the cool air. She thought, *If I join the Sentinel Crows, then Raffel and I will be safe from the Council. But then the other dragons won't. If I become leader then we'll have to wait three years... everyone would be safe then.* She sighed and placed the brush down.

There was a knock on the door and she said, "Come in." Raffel stepped in and closed the door behind him.

"You doing okay?" he asked, walking over to her. "You haven't really said anything since you got back from Truity."

"I've just got a lot to think through," murmured Blāzzer. "Truity told me about what happens to dragons during battle."

Raffel frowned and sat against the wall next to her.

"Aren't you afraid?" she questioned, sinking to the ground next to him.

He shrugged. "I don't put a lot of thought into it... I'm proud I get to fight." He looked at her and his face softened. "As long as the battle keeps you safe, I'll keep fighting."

Blāzzer felt agitation rise in her chest. "But I need you here."

"I'm not going anywhere."

She covered her face with her hands, trying to steady her breathing.

"Blāzzer... I need you here too."

She met his eyes.

"I can't face the world without you. You give me strength, you give me purpose."

Tears began to well in her eyes. "You give me strength too... and I think I know my purpose."

Raffel tipped his head slightly in question.

"I'm going to become the Leader of the Dragons when I turn twenty-one," said Blāzzer.

He blinked.

"I know it's going to be a lot of work and that I have a lot to learn... But I can't just let you and your family be used." She pressed her forehead against his. "Please help me."

"I will," replied Raffel, touching her cheek. "I'll be by your side through it all."

Blāzzer sighed and rested her head on his shoulder. "I love you."

"I love you too."

# Part Five

## Defending a Home

## Chapter Twenty

The next morning Blāzzer walked out of her bedroom and into the living room where Aurora and Ash sat drinking coffee. The older woman smiled and said, "You look like you're feeling better."

"I am," replied Blāzzer, sitting across from them. "I'm supposed to go talk to Shradur again this morning."

"Have you made a decision?" asked Ash, sipping his coffee.

She nodded. "I have... and I have a question for you two."

Aurora placed her mug on the end table, saying, "Of course."

Blāzzer swallowed before asking, "Would you help me become the Leader of the Dragons?"

Ash and Aurora looked at each other.

"I know I have a few years till I can and that I'll need to work really hard, but I can't let the dragons be used... I can't stand by and watch-"

"Blāzzer," said Aurora with a hand slightly raised. "We'll help you."

The young woman blinked.

"It won't be easy," said Ash, crossing his arms. "But we'll be here to support along the way."

"Thank you!" replied Blāzzer with a smile.

"We'll start with you're training once you get back from speaking with Shradur."

"That sounds good."

"Why don't you go talk to him now," encouraged Aurora. "We'll have breakfast ready by the time you come back."

Blāzzer nodded and left the suite, walking down the hall. She thought, *I feel lighter. Like the decision has lifted a heavyweight.* She paused at a window, looking out at the soft blue sky. *I'll make sure that I become the Leader of the Dragons. I won't stop.* She took a deep breath and continued down the hall, holding her shoulders back and chin up. She stopped outside Shradur's office door and placed her hand on it to knock.

"You're early," he said, walking towards her from down the hall with Bear at his side.

"I've made my decision," she replied.

Shradur nodded and opened the door to his office, motioning for her to walk in. Blāzzer sat down in one of the chairs in front of the desk as Bear settled onto a cushion and Shradur sat behind the desk. The old man asked, "What is your decision?"

"I want to become the next Leader of the Dragons."

He reclined in the chair and folded his hands over his stomach. "Why?"

Blāzzer fumbled for a moment before answering, "I don't want the dragons to be used by the Council anymore."

He raised an eyebrow, his steel-blue eyes pinning her to her seat.

"I don't want them to die... If I join the Sentinel Crows, Raffel would too. But that wouldn't protect the rest of the Stone family or any other dragons."

"You would have to wait till you were twenty-one before you could request that to the king, and he may not accept it till you were older."

Blāzzer pressed her lips together.

"You would need a lot of training to be the leader. You and Raffel both would."

"I - we know it would take a lot of work. Ash and Aurora have agreed to help us with the training."

"I'm not trying to dissuade you," said Shradur. "I want you to understand the road ahead of you." He looked to the uleakite. "Bear, can you inform Thornsten and Truity?" The canine stood up and left the room. "The Sentinel Crows will be here to support you."

"Thank you," replied Blāzzer with a smile.

Ash laid out a piece of paper on the table in front of Blāzzer. She looked at the list of tasks then up to him, saying, "This makes it look a bit more daunting."

He smiled apologetically before replying, "It looks longer than it actually is because I detailed out some specific topics for history and politics and such."

She nodded, scanning the list and noting several of the key areas of study: politics, history, sword fighting, Drakken, flying, medicine, archery, and writing. She chewed at her lip and asked, "Do you think I stand a chance to accomplish this in three years?"

"If I didn't, I would have told you already," he said seriously.

"Shradur mentioned that I'll need to request being leader to Nayax."

"Yes, you'll need to do that once you're of age."

"What would I need to do for that?"

"You'll talk to him and explain your reasons and qualifications. He may have you spar or such and probably require you to enter fatorana. Then you'll meet with the Council and they'll ask you questions. Afterward, they'll advise Nayax and he'll make a decision. You don't need the vote of the Council, but you want them to be supportive."

After a moment, Blāzzer questioned, "Would Nayax have been Leader of the Dragons if he didn't become king?"

Ash sighed and nodded slightly, saying tiredly, "Yes, he would have. He's fluent in Drakken and a great commander." He looked away for a moment. "Being crowned king was one of the toughest days in his life."

"I'm sorry."

"For what?"

She pressed her lips together, not for sure what to say. "I don't know... All I know is I would be sad if I couldn't be Raffel's rider."

"He and I have made our peace with it. Anyways, we should get started on your training. Raffel is going to go out later to hunt. Go with him and don't fall out of the saddle. Then we'll-"

A knock on the door interrupted him and the older dragon called, "Come in."

The door opened and Gryphun walked in, saying, "I got orders for you from Shradur." He handed Ash a piece of paper and stood there, hands at his sides, while the older dragon read the paper.

"We'll be ready," said Ash, folding the paper.

Gryphun nodded and left the room. Blāzzer asked, "Orders?"

"We're heading out in five days."

Blāzzer scanned the rocks and sand for any sign of life as they passed below. Raffel's wings propelled them forward fast enough that she had to squint. She leaned over his neck, tightening her grip on the saddle handle as he ascended further. She said, *I haven't seen anything at all. You?*

*Not yet,* he replied. *I can smell some animals, but just rabbits and such... You didn't have to come with me.*

*Did you not want me to? Ash said I should. Good practice for flying.* When he didn't answer she continued, *I know that you hunt, because you have to fuel your endar. If I'm going to be your rider, then I should know this part of you.*

Raffel shook his head. *Many people find it repulsive... I don't want you to be afraid of me.*

Blāzzer placed her hand on his neck and said, *I'll never be afraid of you for being you.*

He sighed in resignation and banked to one side heading north. After a few minutes, he said, *There.* Blāzzer looked past his nose and saw wild goats running and jumping amongst the rocks. *You'll need to put your feet on the back rods when we dive.* She looked down at her feet, moving them so the heel of her boots caught on the second pair of rods on the saddle. *You ready?*

She took a deep breath and replied, *Yeah.*

Raffel tucked his wings in and rolled forward. Blāzzer flattened herself against the saddle, already feeling her stomach fall. They began to hurtle towards the ground and the wind roared in her ears, making tears stream from her eyes. The goats noticed the approaching predator and began to run, scattering amongst the rocks. Raffel targeted one and streamlined for it. Blāzzer watched as the animal came closer and closer, hearing its hard hooves pound against the rock. It darted to the left and Raffel flared a wing, immediately correcting his course. She ground her teeth together as she held on tight. She could see the dirt and grass stuck to the sheep's hide. The sheep let out a shrill cry for an instant as Raffel clamped onto the sheep's neck. He flared his wings, making Blāzzer smash into his neck, and landed, holding the sheep in his jaws.

*You okay?* asked Raffel, looking back at her with blood dripping from the sheep.

*Yeah*, murmured Blāzzer, rubbing her nose. *That was a good catch.*

He flopped his ears to the side in a smile before placing the sheep down. Using a forefoot to hold the sheep down, he bit it in half and swallowed it whole before eating the other half. As he licked his lips he looked back to Blāzzer, noticed her watching him, and asked, "What?"

"I had wondered if you would swallow it whole or not," she replied with a soft smile.

"So... you aren't afraid?"

"No. Seeing it's definitely different, but I'm not afraid."

Leaving the blood-stained sand behind, Raffel walked to an outcropping of rocks and laid in their shadows. He said, "I have to lay down for a little bit."

"Make you sick to fly?" questioned Blāzzer, unhooking herself from the saddle and sliding to the ground.

He irritatedly sighed, "Yeah. Can't even shift for a while too."

She frowned slightly, sitting on his foreleg and stretching out her legs. "You don't sound happy about that."

"I don't really like the feeling of being pinned to the ground."

She patted his leg. "Now you have me to keep you company."

Raffel narrowed his eyes at her.

"What?"

He looked away.

"What?!"

"It's nothing," he replied, laying his head down.

Blāzzer got up and sat in front of his head, so he had to look at her. He closed his eyes. Irritated, she said, "Raffel, what is it?"

He huffed a sigh, blasting her with warm air, and saying very quietly, "You're very... touchy with my dragon form." He opened one eye slightly. Her face had turned pink and she lips pressed together as she stared at the dirt. Her shoulders were hunched slightly as she fiddled with her fingers.

Raffel lifted his head and said, "I didn't mean to make you uncomfortable."

She nodded slightly, still not looking at him.

"I'm just not for sure why," he murmured, placing his head back down. "I know part of it is probably because I'm not... human like this, but I still am."

"I know," whispered Blāzzer. Slowly he scooted forward till his nose touched her leg.

"I don't want you to feel bad about it."

She nodded stiffly before leaning against his nose. The scales there were soft and warm. After a while Blāzzer said, "I feel safe with you and this form-" She pressed her hand against his muzzle. "-watched over me every night... You're like a big teddy bear and I'm just recently getting to know that part of you in your human form. I know it may not make much sense."

*It's okay,* Raffel assured. *I like it when we're close. We don't really have the chance for that except when we fly.*

Blāzzer frowned slightly. "I wish we could be together more around others."

*I know, me too. The Council though could change their vote right now.*

"I'm coming with you hunting from now on. Have some quiet time with you, even if you're stuck in this form." She moved her head so she could look into his eyes. "You better not leave me behind."

Raffel said mischievously, *I'm going to have to go hunting more often.*

Blāzzer laughed, sitting up, and teased, "You're going to make them start wondering."

He snorted, lifting his head. "I don't hear you objecting to the idea though."

She grinned.

Blāzzer sat on a bench under the veranda to the side of a training courtyard. The cool morning air was already warming quickly. Sounds of the city beyond the fortress rose against the clear blue sky. She looked up as Raffel walked towards her. He wore a loose-fitting white shirt with the top button undone.

"I was starting to wonder if I got the time wrong for our training," said Blāzzer, smiling. He shrugged and sat down beside her. She pressed the side of her head against his shoulder. "You were gone early this morning."

"I needed some fresh air," replied Raffel, gently placing his hand over hers. *I'm quite restless without you next to me at night.*

She squeezed his hand. "After all of this... where are we going to live?"

Raffel rested his cheek on her hair. "I still have my house in Palator." She blinked as she imagined them together in the tiny house.

"It'll need some decorations."

He chuckled. "You can do whatever you want to it. The house is yours too now."

Blāzzer smiled at the warmth in her chest. After a moment it faltered and she said, "But for my training, I should probably be near your parents... so Keeko."

Raffel grunted with displeasure in response.

"I wouldn't want to live with your parents either, but I definitely don't have the money for a house."

He pressed his lips together and answered, "If I sold the house in Palator, we'd have enough money to build a house in Keeko." He absent-mindedly rubbed the back of her hand with his thumb. "It could be on the outskirts so you could have your own garden. I know it wouldn't be the same as Palator, but..."

"It would be home with you there," insisted Blāzzer, turning and kissing his cheek. Blushing, he looked down at her and smiled. He glanced at her lips and leaned towards her.

Raffel's ear twitched and his head jerked away as he looked to the doorway. He stood up as Cornin and Aurora walked in. The male rider said, "Sorry for our tardiness, had to take care of a few things." Aurora rolled her eyes and he leaned against a pillar, pulling out his pipe.

"How has the bond between you two been?" asked Aurora, looking between Raffel and Blāzzer.

The young woman dipped her head slightly while Raffel replied, "It's been steady, but the distance is limited. Basically just down the hall."

"That's good," answered Aurora as Cornin nodded. He packed his pipe before lighting it with a match. She sat on a bench near him. "The liffen doesn't just allow thoughts to transfer between you two, but also energy. When there is enough energy transfer, then you two can enter a heightened state." She glanced at Cornin and a minute passed before she continued, "When in fatorana, you be able to produce fire even as a human."

"An ice endar is very useful for cooling beer," grinned Cornin.

"Just like fatorana, it takes a lot of energy," said Aurora, ignoring her rider.

"Is there any way to increase the amount of energy available?" asked Blāzzer as Raffel sat down next to her.

"The stronger the bond, the more energy can be stored," explained the female dragon. "Remember, Blāzzer is now an additional pool for energy." Raffel glanced at his rider. "Typically a dragon cannot access a rider's energy unless they are physically near each other."

"Dragons can also strengthen their endar just from use," added Cornin, blowing out smoke.

"I didn't finish that training," whispered Raffel, sinking into himself slightly.

"I wouldn't worry about it," said Cornin. "You can do the strengthening training at any time. All the flying recently should help too."

"So dragons can't have wings or a tail as a human?" asked Blāzzer trying to imagine a human-dragon hybrid. Raffel glanced at her with an eyebrow raised.

"There are historical texts," said Aurora, "that say if the bond is strong enough between a dragon and rider, that a dragon can enter a half state. I've never met anyone who was able to do this."

"Half-bloods can enter their own form of fatorana," added Cornin. "Some get scales, a tail, or wings. Just depends on the individual." He tapped the mouthpiece of his pipe against his lips. "I think one of Thornsten's brothers has wings." He shrugged.

Blāzzer chewed at her bottom lip, saying, *I wonder when we'll meet his brothers.*

*Probably not for a while,* replied Raffel, before looking at his mother. "What is the training for today?"

Aurora smiled softly, answering, "You're going to lead each other around the fortress and the town." Blāzzer and Raffel looked at each other. "Except the one being led will be blindfolded, can't be touched, or verbally spoken to."

Cornin chuckled at the dismay in the young dragon and rider's faces and said, "You guys can practice in here first before venturing out." He held out a strip of black cloth. "You guys pick who goes first." Raffel took the cloth. "Have fun you two."

Cornin walked away with a wave and Aurora stood up, saying, "Be patient with each other." She smiled before leaving.

Blāzzer looked at the black cloth in Raffel's hand and asked, "You want to go first?"

Raffel held out the cloth to her, replying, "Ladies first." She stuck her tongue out at him before getting up and grabbing the cloth. She tied it around her head, covering her eyes.

*You can't see around it?* questioned Raffel, tipping his head as he studied her face.

"I can't see anything," murmured Blāzzer. "You better not run me into anything."

*I won't,* he promised. *Let's practice in here first. Step forward. Turn to your left... other left.* He chuckled. *Step forward.* She squeaked as she bumped into him.

"You're not supposed to touch me," she said, trying to contain a giggle and pushing on his chest.

*I'm not,* replied Raffel with a grin, stepping back from her. She tried to push him again, but stumbled forward into his chest. *That was completely on you.*

"You owe me, mister." She crossed her arms, turning away from him in a feigned pout.

*What do I owe you?* He leaned towards her and she could feel his breath on her cheek. She pressed her lips together as her thoughts slammed to a halt. She could feel the hairs on the back of her neck stand up as a blush crept across her cheeks.

"A new scarf for my hair," insisted Blāzzer, rotating so her back was to him.

Raffel smiled, replying, *So not only do you trust me to lead you through the city, but also pick out a headband for you.*

"Maybe."

It took them nearly an hour to wander through the city before they found a clother. Blāzzer sat on a bench under an awning, listening to the people walking by. She still had the cloth covering her eyes. Behind her was the store Raffel had gone into.

*What color are you picking?* asked Blāzzer, resting her hands in her lap.

*You have to wait and see,* replied Raffel, smiling.

*Just remember I have blue, yellow, and red ones.*

*So I should get one of those colors.*

She grinned. *You're a butt.*

He chuckled, making her heart flutter.

Several minutes past and Blāzzer continued to listen to the people walking by. They spoke with a sense of comradery towards each other. None of them approached her. She tilted her head at the sound of the shop's bell over the door tinkling.

"I thought you would have taken the blindfold off by now," commented Raffel, sitting next to her. Blāzzer shrugged and tugged the cloth off. She blinked at the scarf he held before her. Gently she took it, her eyes tracing the geometric patterns of red, orange, and black. The fabric was heavier and more durable than the ones she'd bought in Chamdal.

"Do you like it?" asked Raffel tentatively.

She nodded, replying, "It's beautiful." She folded the cloth into a long rectangle before replacing the one she currently wore with it. She turned to Raffel and smiled. "For a guy who had no decorations at his house, you're pretty good at picking out scarves."

Raffel grinned, bumping his shoulder against hers.

By the time night fell Blāzzer was exhausted. She closed her bedroom door and changed into her night shirt before sitting at the desk. She grabbed a piece of paper and pen and wrote:

*Mae*

*It's been so busy and so much has happened. I wish I could tell you everything in person, but I'll try to summarize it all here till I can. I learned about where I'm from... when I'm from. My parents gave me to the Sentinel Crows for protection and I was put into a hibernation by the endar of a dragon. I wasn't the only one either, but no one knows where he is. My parents' names are Lionel and Eltika. They were dragon and rider... but they aren't my birth parents either. They found me as a baby in a destroyed town. I'm still not for sure how to feel about them, because I don't feel a bond to them. I wish I could remember them. Did you know about any of this? Raffel did... and about him... we're kind of dating. I know you're going to have a ton of questions, but we're keeping it on the down low right now. Don't know if the Council will try to change their votes about me staying with the Stone family because of it. He's been so kind, but sometimes really awkward... Makes me just want to hug him!*

*We're leaving Gilzar in a few days. I'm going to be a medic for the dragons in Budsta so I have a lot of work to do. I'm not for sure I'm ready to see him and his family in battle. From what Truity said, it isn't going to be good. I'm going to do my best to support them. Please take care of Lenny and Palator. I'll come back as soon as I can.*

*Blāzzer*

She frowned for a moment.

*P.S. I have decided that I am going to become the Leader of the Dragons when I turn twenty-one. Ash and Aurora agreed to help me with training. It would be amazing to have you support me, even if it's across the country.*

Blāzzer sighed and fanned the ink. Once it dried, she folded the paper and crawled into bed, blowing out the candle. She stared at the ceiling in the dark and thought, *I can do this.*

The next day, before the sun made the air too hot, the Stone family walked through the fortress to a dirt courtyard. A covered stone walkway surrounded it with a water pump in one wall. Blāzzer held Flame tightly as the dragons stepped out into the sunlight.

Cornin patted her on the shoulder, encouraging, "No worries. We'll take it slow today." She nodded and followed him out.

"Stretches first," instructed Ash. They placed their swords on the ground by their feet and began working through some basic stretches. As Blāzzer reached down and touched her toes she noticed how Lydia was the most flexible. She could put her palms on the ground.

After stretching for several minutes, Ash straightened and said, "Okay. Raffel you're with me. Lydia and Aurora. Then Cornin and Blāzzer."

Cornin grinned, making Aurora rolled her eyes, before he turned to Blāzzer and asking, "You were learning basics before right?"

"Yeah," she replied, picking up her sword.

"Go ahead and draw it and show me what you remember."

Slowly she worked through the basic stances and strikes she had learned with Mae and Gorvi. Each time she swung Flame, it caught the sunlight on the swirls of red. Blāzzer thought, *It feels so natural.*

"Looks pretty good," praised Cornin with a smile. "How does the new sword feel?"

"Uh, really good. Like I was missing a part of my arm."

He chuckled and made a flourishing bow, saying, "Well, let me teach you how to not loose it."

Cornin worked with Blāzzer for an hour over more advanced stances, strikes, parries, and blocks. By the end she was covered in sweat and, even with the sword being made of light korsteel, she couldn't lift her arm above her shoulders. She sheathed her sword as he said, "Nice work. You're going to make a good sword fighter."

"Thanks," replied Blāzzer with a smile, plopping down against the stone pillar in the cool shade. She looked to the dragons. They were sparring each other in slow controlled motions. "When would I spar?"

"Not for a while with that sword," answered Cornin, wiping his face with a handkerchief. "Cuts from a korsteel blade takes dragons longer to heal." He tapped the side of his head. "Probably have you spar against Raffel, cause you can tell him where you're striking before you swing."

Blāzzer nodded, watching Lydia move gracefully from one stance to another as she swung her sword and blocked Aurora's. "How long has Lydia been training?"

Cornin sat down near Blāzzer before replying, "Both Raffel and Lydia started training as kids. She's always pushed herself though."

"That's enough for today," said Ash, sheathing his sword.

"I'm still good to continue," insisted Lydia, holding her sword ready.

"I know you are," replied Ash roughly, "but for today it's enough."

Lydia frowned before sheathing her sword and walking away.

Aurora looked to Ash and he said, "She's fine." She said something in Drakken before following her daughter.

*What did she say?* asked Blāzzer, looking to Raffel who winced at his mother's words.

He whispered, *To stop treating Lydia like a fragile child.* He rubbed the back of his neck. "Blāzzer and I are going to go meet with Truity to grab her supplies." She jumped up and followed him out of the courtyard, hearing the dragons talk in Drakken as they left.

"Should we check on Lydia?" questioned Blāzzer worriedly.

"In a little bit," Raffel sighed. "She'll want some time to herself."

"Has it always been this way?"

"Ummm, not always. Just when the seizures got really bad... before I left. She'd have one almost every day. Dad took it really hard. He'd stay by her side as much as he could. Even though we have endars and are used to our own fire or ice, it can still kill us." Blāzzer stopped walking, trying to process, and he turned to her. "He made sure the ice never got strong enough by using his own endar."

"But Lydia's better now, right?"

Raffel shrugged, replying uncertainly, "The medicine has been helping, but it could loose its effect over time. That's what happened to the first one."

She pressed her lips together, afraid for Lydia's wellbeing.

"She'll get mad at you if you pity her."

Blāzzer looked up and saw his soft smile.

"Come on let's go find Truity."

She nodded slightly and followed him down the hall, thinking, *There has to be something that can help her.*

# Chapter Twenty-One

The day had come for the Sentinel Crows to leave Gilzar. Blāzzer stood at the fortress entrance looking over the large crowd of black clad men and women, who sat on their horses. She looked to Raffel, who stood at her side, then to Shradur, who was walking down the stairs with Bear at his heels. The old man easily swung into his horse's saddle and sat there surveying his men. After a moment he nodded and Bear let out a howl. The Sentinel Crows turned their horses and began to ride out of Gilzar like a black river.

*Is it bad that the threat of Budsta is starting to feel more real?* asked Blāzzer, tightening her grip on Flame's pommel.

*No, seeing an army march is very rattling,* replied Raffel, frowning slightly.

"I've come to see all of you off," said Gryphun, walking up to the Stone family.

"You're not coming?" questioned Ash with a raised eyebrow.

"No, I'm staying here," answered the young dragon. "I'm to continue my training and assist in any border patrols."

"Take care of yourself," said Aurora, turning and walking into the still emptying courtyard.

"We'll bring you back a souvenir," teased Cornin with a grin. He, Lydia, and Ash followed Aurora.

"Blāzzer," said Gryphun, making her look to him. "Mae would want me to tell you to be careful."

She nodded slightly before following Raffel. He shifted and crouched down. She tied their bags to the saddle and secured her satchel in a saddle bag. She swung up into the saddle and connected the caribeaners as he stood up. They waited as the other dragons took off before he jumped into the sky. Blāzzer felt her heart pound against her chest at the thought of leaving Nickada.

The dragons continued to fly high over the marching army of Sentinel Crows. The horses kicked up large amounts of dust from the dry plains that left a trail behind. Blāzzer watched the Crows as they moved in a column four abreast. She whispered, *Lydia still hasn't really said much since the other day. Did you talk to her?*

Raffel drifted away from the other dragons, replying, *I tried, but she didn't want to talk. I think that she just needs some time to herself.*

*That's what you said before.* When he didn't answer, Blāzzer pressed her hand against his neck. *I'll try to talk to her later.*

After a while Blāzzer asked, *Lydia doesn't have a rider. Has she not met anyone she liked?*

Raffel shook his head. *She can't have a rider. When her endar leaks it could travel through the liffen and kill them.*

Blāzzer pressed her cheek against his neck.

Blāzzer felt awestruck when the large Nickadian army came on the horizon. Their tents were in neat rows with cook fires spread out. Sentries of different races were stationed around the perimeter. The Nickadian flag, green and red with a black bear, waved in the wind on poles around the camp. Tents of similar color were grouped together, making the camp have distinct sections. Raffel followed the other dragons towards the edge of camp where a few tents were setup aside from the rest. He landed and crouched down as Blāzzer began to unfasten the safety clasps.

"It is good to see you all arrived safely," said Nayax, walking towards the dragons. Some Lemay soldiers, including Teredana, followed the king.

"How has it been here?" questioned Ash, shifting and dropping his bag beside the only two-man tent.

"Not too bad," replied Nayax, sitting down on a log by an unlit fire pit. "We've seen a few riders, but they've all kept their distance." He looked between the dragons. "I'll need one of you to scout for me."

"Where was the last place you saw these riders?" asked Cornin, crossing his arms as Aurora shifted from one foreleg to the other.

"Several miles east of here. Just horses and men. No dragons."

"We'll be back in a few hours," said Aurora, jumping into the air and buffeting everyone with a blast of wind.

"Teredana, make sure the dragons have everything they need," ordered Nayax, standing up slowly.

"Yes, sir," replied Teredana as the king and other soldiers left.

Raffel and Lydia shifted and she said, "I'm going to nap." She ducked into a tent without a glance back.

"Do you need anything?" questioned Teredana, looking to Ash.

"Where is the food cart at?" asked the older dragon.

"I'll show you."

Blāzzer watched Ash and Teredana walk away before, saying to Raffel, "I'm going to check on Lyida."

"Okay, I'll put your bag in your tent," he replied with a nod.

Blāzzer walked over to Lydia's tent and stopped in front of it, calling out, "Lydia, can I come in?" After a moment the tent flap moved back a little and she stepped inside. Lydia scooted back to make space on the bedroll before picking up her sketch book. Blāzzer sat down on the bedroll, trying to keep her boots off of it. "Are you doing okay?"

"As good as I can be," replied Lydia, focusing on her drawing.

Blāzzer nodded slightly. "What are you working on now?"

"Just some flowers," muttered Lydia, not looking away from her sketch. "They're soothing to draw."

Blāzzer crossed her arms over her knees and placed her chin on her arms. She thought, *I don't even know what to ask. I'm just worried about her.* "Lydia-"

"So how's it going with my brother?"

Blāzzer looked up, blushing, and relieved to see that Lydia was still occupied by her sketch. "We're good... we're worried about you though."

Lydia closed her eyes for a moment, but did not answer.

Blāzzer sighed and looked at the dark fabric of the tent wall, saying, "I think you'll do good."

"Huh?"

"You'll do good protecting Nickada," replied Blāzzer sincerely. "I know that you'll be in danger, but it won't be from yourself. You'll be able to help keep everyone safe and you're willing to put yourself on the frontlines to do that." She looked to Lydia, who was stunned by her words. "You're not a burden and you're not broken."

Lydia smiled softly and whispered, "Thank you."

Blāzzer sat at the campfire with the sun setting in the west as she cut chunks of potatoes into some water. Raffel walked up with several logs and placed them near the fire, saying, "Some how you always end up cooking."

"I must be a good cook," replied Blāzzer, grinning. He raised an eyebrow in disbelief. "It's better than yours."

"True." He sat down next to her and looked at the different vegetables in a basket. "No meat?"

"Ash went to go find some. Apparently it's not kept at the food cart."

Raffel nodded, picking up some leafy greens and smelling it. He wrinkled his nose at the smell.

"That's parsley," said Blāzzer. "You can tear it up and put it in the pot."

"I thought you were the cook," he replied with a lazy smile.

"Wow."

Blāzzer and Raffel looked up to Lydia as she ducked out of her tent. Both blushed as the female dragon grinned, saying, "So smooth, brother." He dropped the parsley and looked away. Lydia sat down on the other side of small campfire as Blāzzer resumed cutting the potatoes. Lydia said something in Drakken, making Raffel tense.

*What'd she say?* asked Blāzzer, looking to him.

*She says we're cute together,* he replied sheepishly. She blushed.

"You need to learn Drakken so you can be in on the family discussions," said Lydia with a smile.

"Yeah, I definitely need to," answered Blāzzer with a smile. "Mae used to talk a lot in Drakken to Raffel. He wouldn't answer her though." Raffel crossed his arms.

"What would she say to you, Raffel?" questioned Lydia, barely able to contain her curiosity. "From my few encounters with her, she always has something to say."

"I don't want to talk about it," grunted Raffel, picking up the parsley and tearing it into tiny pieces over the pot.

"You're embarrassed," murmured Blāzzer, leaning forward so he could see his face. His face nearly matched the color of his eyes. She grinned. "Now I got to know." Very quietly Raffel said something in Drakken. Blāzzer watched as Lydia's eyes opened wider and mouth dropped. "What?! What did he say?"

"Wow... Who taught her all of those words?" breathed Lydia, rocking back slightly.

"Like I said, I don't want to talk about it," grumbled Raffel.

"This is unfair!" cried Blāzzer, shaking his arm. "You have to tell me!" He met her eyes and she let her hand drop to her side. "It was about me?" He nodded. "And you?" He nodded again slowly and Lydia was nodding vigorously with a wide grin. Blāzzer looked down at the fire, trying to control the blood that was rushing to her face.

"Again, like I said I didn't want to talk about."

Blāzzer and Raffel continued preparing dinner without looking at each other or Lydia. By the time the potatoes, carrots, parsley, and onion had all been added to the pot, Ash was still not back. Blāzzer said quietly, "So back on the subject of learning Drakken... I mostly just need to work on vocabulary. The grammar isn't too different."

"Well, there's linquint," said Lydia with a coy smile.

Blāzzer looked to Raffel and he sighed, "It means love."

"Oh," breathed Blāzzer.

"I wonder what sentence that could be used in," muttered Lydia, turning away from them, but still looking at them from the side.

*She's worse than Mae*, grumbled Raffel, hunching his shoulders.

"What has you all prickly?" questioned Ash, walking up with dark mesh bag and glaring at Raffel.

"Nothing," growled Raffel, standing up. "I need to stretch my legs." Blāzzer frowned as he walked away and she accepted the bag from Ash.

"You two get into a fight or something?" asked the older dragon, sitting down. Blāzzer blushed as Lydia laughed. "So something did happen."

"We're fine," replied Blāzzer stiffly, beginning to work on cooking the meat.

"Why did Aurora leave me to watch you three?" grumbled Ash to himself, looking up at the sky.

Once the meat was cooking, Blāzzer slowly stood up and said, "I'm going to go find Raffel."

"He's fine," said Ash, looking into the fire. "Remember you two need to be careful now. It isn't just the family anymore."

Blāzzer pressed her lips together and sat back down, thinking, *It's like the Council didn't vote for me to stay with them.* "When will we not have to worry?"

Ash took a deep breath before answering, "I would say not until after everything is resolved with Budsta. Right now, the Council is agitated and would be happy to have something to focus on." He looked to Blāzzer, who was staring at her hands in her lap. "Remember also to keep your chin up and shoulders back."

She looked up at him and asked, "Do you fear them?"

"The Council? No. I worry what they can to my family, but I don't fear them. As long as Nayax is king I know that there is someone who will rein in the impetuous leaders. You should not fear them either."

Blāzzer nodded cautiously and glanced across the fire to Lydia. The dragon was looking away and frowning. Blāzzer thought, *She's hurt by how he treats me.*

*He bolsters me... and tries to hold her back.*

After eating dinner Blāzzer stood up and said, "I'm going to get some rest."

"Sleep well," replied Lydia with a soft smile.

Blāzzer nodded and headed for her tent, stopping when she saw Raffel walking back from inside the main camp. She said, *Dinner is ready.*

*I ate already,* he muttered stopping front of her. *Decided to go out hunting.*

She frowned slightly. *Are you okay?*

He towards the plains, ears twitching back. *I'm fine, just needed some space.* He then looked to her. *Are you going to bed?*

*Yeah, I'm pretty exhausted.* She squeezed her hands together. *I want to hug you, but... Ash said we need to be careful.* She felt warmth from him and relaxed.

*I'll be out here if you need anything.*

She smiled at him and ducked into her tent, pulling the flap shut. She pulled her boots off and placed them next to her flying harness and sword. She sat on her bedroll and started to brush her hair. She could hear Raffel walking around outside.

"Raffel," called Ash. "There's a tent for you over there."

Blāzzer blinked, pausing in mid stroke.

"You need to conserve your strength," continued Ash. There was a pause and he added something in Drakken. Blāzzer could hear Raffel growl in response, but he walked away.

*I'll be okay,* promised Blāzzer, feeling Raffel's irritation. When he didn't answer, she placed her brush down and curled up on her bedroll, pulling the blanket around herself. *About earlier-*

*I don't want to talk about it,* he grumbled.

Blāzzer pressed her lips together, feeling her heart tighten in her chest. She laid there, listening to the sounds of the camp slow and settle for the night as the hour past. A gust of wind buffeted her tent and she sat up as the sound of something heavy crunched against the ground. There was a flash of blue light that even the dark fabric of the tent couldn't keep at bay.

"I'll be back once I give my report," said Cornin tiredly. "Save me some food." His footsteps faded as he walked away.

"Well, find anything?" asked Ash.

Blāzzer scooted towards the front of her tent and peaked through a small gap in between the flaps. Aurora sat down next to Ash at the campfire. She rested her head on his shoulder.

"We didn't see anything," replied Aurora with a sigh. "Just empty plains. If there had been riders, they're gone now. We were only able to patrol to the east, but we covered good ground. Someone should scout the west soon."

"I'll see to it in the morning," assured Ash, kissing the top of her head. "How are the kids?"

"Moody."

"All of them?"

Ash nodded.

"Are you being fair about your judgment?"

"Aurora, this isn't the first time I've been left alone with the kids."

She lifted her head and looked at him. His shoulders sank a little. "Where's Raffel at?"

Ash pointed to a tent across from Blāzzer's, saying, "Told him to save his strength."

"I doubt that worked," replied Aurora. "What did you say to him?"

"I told him that he needs mind his behavior around Blāzzer."

Blāzzer blinked, thinking, *Is that what he said to Raffel? Or just a summary?*

Aurora pressed her fingers against her forehead and murmured, "Ash, I know you have good intentions. But you need to back off and let them be."

Ash glared at her.

"They need to bond as rider and dragon."

"They aren't bonding as rider and dragon," growled Ash so quietly that Blāzzer barely heard him.

Aurora pressed her hand against his cheek. "I know you're afraid for them... that you don't want a repeat of your past for your son. But this is different. Their bond is something that will be unbreakable when it matures." Ash sank against her and she held him close. She turned her head towards Blāzzer's tent and her blue eyes met Blāzzer's.

Blāzzer scooted back quickly as her breath caught in her throat, thinking, *Did she see me? I think she did.* She tensely laid on her bedroll.

Inaudible to her, Ash said with a growl deep in his throat, "I wouldn't be able to stand by and watch the Council tear them apart."

Shouts echoed across the camp, jolting Blāzzer out of her sleep. She struggled for a moment to make sense of the shouts and other sounds. Then a voice yelled out, "We're under attack! To arms!" She quickly pulled on her boots and grabbed her sword.

*Blāzzer!* called Raffel.

*I'm here,* shouted Blāzzer, ducking out of the tent, and froze.

Soldiers were running through the camp, setting up a perimeter. Ash jumped into the sky with a roar and Lydia followed close behind him. Cornin stumbled out of his tent, pulling on his flight harness. Aurora shifted and crouched down before her rider. Blāzzer jumped as someone grabbed her shoulder. She blinked at Raffel, who caught her punch.

"Easy," he said, letting her hand go.

"Where are they?" questioned Blāzzer, feeling her heart pound against the inside of her ribcage.

"They're attacking from the west," replied Raffel. "Grab your harness." With that he shifted and crooned his wings.

Blāzzer stood there, frozen in place. The pupil of his red eyes were narrow slits and his lips were pulled back, showing white fangs that gleamed in the firelight. He swung his head towards her and she quickly ducked back into her tent. She grabbed the harness and slipped it over her head as she stepped back out. The tightness of the leather brought some clarity as she fumbled for a moment to secure the straps. Raffel crouched down and she swung into the saddle. As he stood she clipped the safety straps. He jumped into the air and quickly rose above the camp.

*There's so many,* whispered Blāzzer, looking across the camp and seeing horse riders charge towards the Nickadians. Ash dove at them and knocked several riders and horses to the ground with a sweep of his legs and tail. Ruchos and uleakites darted between the enemy soldiers causing the Budstarians' formation to break. Raffel veered away from the camp, heading in the opposite direction of the enemy.

*Wait! They're the other way!* cried Blāzzer, pressing her hand against his neck. A growl rumbled in his chest, causing her to quickly withdraw her hand.

*We're to check the rear and make sure there are no enemies coming around to flank us,* said Raffel, beating his wings hard and propelling them forward so fast the wind roared in her ears.

*What are we going to do if we find any?* questioned Blāzzer, leaning forward and trying to force her brain to think.

For a moment Raffel didn't answer, then he replied quietly, *It's just like hunting.* Blāzzer swallowed hard and tightened her grip on the saddle handle. *Let me know if you see any movement.* She scanned the plains, but even with the moon and stars out she struggled to see anything in the dark. She looked back as the sounds of the battling armies grew quieter.

Raffel let out a roar, growling, *There!*

Blāzzer turned to see horse riders galloping towards the camp. She blinked at the sight of fifty of them, hooves pounding against the ground as fast as her heart beat. She wanted to hide, but there was no where in the sky for her. Raffel let out a blast of fire that blinded her and warmed her for a moment.

*Stay low!* yelled Raffel. *Move your legs back!*

She cried, *Raffel, I can't-*

*Now!*

He began to roll into a dive and she leaned forward, moving her feet back. Her tears were torn from her face by the wind. As they neared she could see the soldiers individual pieces of armor and weapons. She yelled, *Archers!*

Raffel didn't halt as the soldiers fired arrows. The metal heads glittered in the moonlight as they arched through the sky. He rolled to the side, moving Blāzzer away from the danger. She held on tight, gritting her teeth. She watched as the arrows were deflected by his scales and scratched his wing membranes. When he righted himself he opened his mouth and roared fire down over enemy. Blāzzer held her fist out and screamed her own war cry. The enemy soldiers cried out and scattered, the horses spooking from the flames.

The dragon launched up to the sky before diving again. Blāzzer felt her body move in the saddle without her thought. Anger and determination flowed through her body; half of it was not her own. Her lips were drawn back in a snarl that mirrored Raffel's.

Over and over they dove at the enemy soldier, blasting them with fire and tearing them apart with tooth and nail. Soon the few soldiers that remained began to flee. Raffel landed and roared to the sky, flaring his wings and letting out a jet of fire. When the flames died in the dark, Blāzzer felt his exhaustion. She touched his neck gently and blinked at his trembling.

"It's over," she whispered. Raffel turned his head with his slit pupil glaring at her. Blood dripped from his mouth in globs and air hissed between his teeth. Blāzzer pressed her lips together, noticing the liquid that was splattered over his body. She touched her face and felt nauseous at the sight of blood on her fingers. She forced a swallow. "Raffel, it's okay... It's over. We did it."

He shook his head, still baring his teeth, and lashed out at a dead soldier. The wet crunch of breaking bone and tearing flesh echoed over the plains. His tail smacked the ground as he began to move among the corpses.

"Raffel, stop you're hurt," insisted Blāzzer, pushing on his neck. She tried to reach out with her mind and flinched. His mind was a torrent of fear and anger. "Please, Raffel!"

An injured soldier cried out as the dragon approached, but his cry was cut short. Raffel held the man in his jaws, crunching the metal armor and destroying the man. Blāzzer stared in horror as Raffel threw the soldier aside before continuing his search.

Blāzzer body trembled as the coppery tang of blood stuck to the back of her throat. She began to beat against his neck with her fists, screaming, "Stop it! You're not a monster!"

Another injured soldier was trying to drag himself away. Raffel prowled towards him, air hissing between his teeth, and lowered his head. The soldier pleaded, "Please! No! I don't want to die! I-"

Raffel struck the soldier with his claws, throwing him through the air and landing with a sickening thud. Blāzzer, sobbing, wretched over his shoulder. She struggled to unhook herself from the saddle and fell. She grunted as she hit the ground and looked up to see Raffel glaring down at her. She thought, *Your eyes... their those of a predator*. She closed her eyes and threw her hands out, waiting for pain.

Soft scales pressed against her palms as warm air bellowed around her in a sigh. Blāzzer opened her eyes and saw the fear in Raffel's eyes. Slowly he laid down in front of her, his wings hanging limply at his sides. She brushed at the blood on his lips, feeling lacerations. The red liquid was warm and sticky. She took a deep breath and said, "It's okay. It's over. They're all gone."

He whimpered and his pupils dilated to their normal round state. He pressed his nose against her chest, nearly knocking her over, and she wrapped her arms around him.

"We're safe now," whispered Blāzzer, resting her head against his. Raffel squeezed his eyes shut and his body shuddered as a suppressed sob escaped. Blāzzer reached out to his mind, feeling his fear that faced inward. She whispered, "You're afraid of yourself." She squeezed his snout, rubbing her cheek against his scales. "You're not a monster, you're human." He scooted forwards, stretching out his arms towards her. "I'm here. I'm not going anywhere."

Red light engulfed Raffel for a moment and he, stained with blood and gore, slumped against her chest. His shoulders shook as a sob tore from his throat. Blāzzer wrapped her arms around him and held him close. She could smell the blood, but under it was the familiar scent of him.

"I hate it," gasped Raffel against her neck. She rubbed his back, wanting to take him away from the violence. "Please... please." He tightened his grip around her and crushed her against his chest.

Blāzzer said sadly, "I have no words for you, but I'll hold you for as long as you need... I'll stand by you for as long as you need." She ran her fingers through his hair and let the warmth in her chest flow to him. "We'll make it through this together. I love you more than anything." She held him while the small grass fires turned into embers and the moon moved across the sky. "We should head back. Can you fly us back?"

Raffel nodded and shakily stood up. Blood was smeared across his face, his tears leaving faint trails. He shifted and crouched down, nudging her with his nose. She placed her hand on his shoulder for a moment before swinging into the saddle. When she was secure, he jumped into the air. His wing beats were slow and almost labored. The sound of battle was gone, but the smell of blood stuck to them. Blāzzer smiled softly when she saw the rest of the Stone family at their camp area.

Aurora walked towards them as they landed near and, when Raffel had shifted, embraced them both. Blāzzer let out a trembling breath and held her tight.

Aurora said gently, "Let's go get you two cleaned up." She led them to the campfire where a bucket of water stood by the flickering flames. She handed them each a wet rag, before resuming to clean herself.

Blāzzer wiped her face, wincing as red stains spread across the cloth. She looked up and frowned. Raffel stood holding his rag, staring into the flames. She walked over to him and, reaching up, began to wipe the blood from his face. His eyes focused on her and he opened his mouth to say something, but nothing came out.

"It's okay," she whispered. "You don't need to say anything. Let's get your shirt off of you." She helped him get his shirt off without smearing the sticky red liquid. She winced at the scratches on his torso before wiping away the drying blood. Raffel slowly undid the straps on her harness and helped her out of it. Blood speckled her chest, but mostly covered her sleeves.

"Let's get you to bed," insisted Blāzzer, guiding him to his tent. She ducked in with him and pulled off his boots as he laid down.

"Please," breathed Raffel. She glanced at him. "Stay." She nodded and looked about a moment before grabbing his bag and pulling out a clean shirt. She turned away from him and pulled her blood splattered shirt off, trying to not breathe in the metallic smell. As she slipped the clean shirt over her arms Raffel gently touched her shoulder where the liffen was.

She froze, trying to remember how to breathe. Her chest was bare and unmarred by the attack. Goosebumps rose on her skin as his fingers stroked her red bursting star. When he moved his hand away, she felt exposed and pressed her lips together to contain a whimper. Blāzzer quickly pulled on the shirt before taking her boots off. She slowly laid down next to him, resting her head on his shoulder as he wrapped his arm around her. His heart was beating fast against her cheek.

"We're safe," whispered Blazzer, touching his jaw. She closed her eyes, feeling exhaustion pull at them. "We're safe... We'll make it through this... together."

## Chapter Twenty-Two

Blāzzer groaned at the sound of voices and buried her face against Raffel's chest, inhaling his scent. Her eyes flashed open at the smell of blood, pressing her lips together as she remembered what had happened in the night. Slowly she sat up, rubbing grit from her eyes. Raffel's hand rubbed her back and she looked over her shoulder at him.

"Did you sleep?" asked Blāzzer, noticing the darkness under his eyes.

"I think," he murmured. "I just remember passing out with you next to me."

She smiled softly. "I'm going to go see how the others are doing." Raffel frowned and she leaned back, kissing his cheek. "Try to rest. I'll be back in a little bit." Before she could move back, he reached up and cradled her cheek. She met his eyes, there were different shades of red mixing together like the depths of a canyon.

"I love you," breathed Raffel. "I want you by my side for the rest of my life."

Blāzzer tried to inhale at the tightness in her chest. "I love you too."

He ran his thumb over her lips. "I know you said earlier that you weren't ready to be intimate, but-"

She leaned forward, her nose an inch from his. Her heart pounded in her chest and she wondered if he could hear it. She kissed him gently, lingering as their lips touched. His hand moved to cradle the back of her head. Slowly she pulled back, resting her forehead against his.

"Now, you should rest," insisted Blāzzer with a warm smile. As he closed his eyes she sat up and pulled her boots on. She glanced at Raffel, still feeling the softness of his lips, before ducking out of the tent.

Blāzzer blinked in the sunlight and walked over to the campfire where Ash, Cornin, and Aurora sat. Cornin looked up at her and said, "Well, you look worn out, but whole."

"Yeah, I feel like I have weights attached to my limbs," replied Blāzzer, sitting down heavily next to Aurora.

"Drink this," said the female dragon, holding out a mug of steaming water.

Blāzzer took it and sipped at it. "Mint?"

"That and a few other herbs."

"Helps with fried nerves," added Cornin. "Alcohol would be good too, but when you live with a bunch of lightweights." He shrugged.

"Lightweights?" questioned Blāzzer.

"Challenge Raffel to a drinking competition after Budsta," said Cornin with a wink. Ash glared at him.

"Thank you for taking care of Raffel, Blāzzer," said Aurora, squeezing Blāzzer's arm.

"I know we aren't supposed to be close right now," she replied, "but he didn't want me to leave last night... and I didn't want to leave him."

"Don't worry about it," grumbled Ash with a sigh, pinching the bridge of his nose. "Everyone was preoccupied with the attack last night to notice."

"How is everyone else?" asked Blāzzer, blowing on the tea.

"A few casualties and more injured," said Ash, leaning his elbows against his knees. "The Council is meeting right now. Nayax should be announcing their verdict soon."

Blāzzer looked up as Lydia sat next to Cornin, noticing the dragon's bandaged hand. He handed Lydia a mug of tea before saying, "No doubt this will mean war."

Ash nodded solemnly.

"We'll have to wait and see," said Aurora. "It's up to Nayax whether or not war is declared." She slowly stood up. "I'm going to wash clothes so bring them to me if you didn't leave them out."

"Just a moment and I'll grab them," replied Blāzzer, going to Raffel's tent. She ducked in and grabbed her shirt, taking it to Aurora. "Thank you."

"No worries," sighed the older woman, dropping the clothes in a basket. "Take some tea to Raffel." She met Blāzzer's eyes. "If you two need some quiet time together right now, then don't be concerned about others."

Blāzzer nodded stiffly and fetched a mug of tea before walking to Raffel's tent. She ducked inside and sat next to him. He was asleep, but his face was uneasy and his ears twitched. She touched his cheek gently and whispered, "Hey, I have some tea for you." He winced for a moment before opening his eyes. "Can you sit up?" He slowly sat up, the blanket falling away and revealing scabbed scratches. "Here."

Raffel held the cup with both hands as he drank deeply, draining the tea. He sighed and placed the cup down before saying, "Thank you."

She smiled softly and looked about the tent. Blāzzer noticed a folded piece of paper that had been torn from Lydia's sketchbook poking out of his bag. She picked it up and unfolded it, getting lost in the drawing.

"I asked her if I could have it," explained Raffel, looking at the sketch of Blāzzer and him sitting back to back. "I didn't have any memento to remind me of us."

"I can understand," said Blāzzer softly. "When I look in the mirror and see the liffen... the world seems to melt away and all I can remember is us." She folded the paper and placed it back in the bag. "Is that how you felt last night, when you touched my shoulder?" She met his eyes and saw warmth.

"I felt like even in the darkness... you're the one thing that guides me back to the light." Raffel rested his chin on her shoulder, his breath tickling her ear. He reached around her and pulled her into his lap, holding her against his back. She settled against him, closing her eyes.

*Can the world just stop moving right now?* asked Blāzzer, taking his hand in hers. Raffel smiled and trailed his nose along her ear. She shivered, tightening her grip on him. *Be good.*

*I am,* he whispered with a pout. *You're the one sitting in my lap.* She pressed her lips together, trying to calm the heat rising in her body. *Let me just hold you.*

They sat there for a while until a horn sounded across the camp. Blāzzer, heart skipping a beat, immediately stepped out of the tent with Raffel following. The rest of the Stone family was not alarmed. Ash said, "Aurora and I are going to go see what the Council has decided. Cornin make sure they don't wander off." Blāzzer walked over to the campfire as Raffel pulled on a shirt and his parents walked away.

Cornin frowned before, saying, "Stay here ankle biters. I'll be back." With that the Sentinel Crow left them, heading into the camp.

Blāzzer sat down next to Lydia and asked, "How are you feeling?"

"Alright," murmured the female dragon, touching her bandaged hand. "A little sore, but okay." Raffel sat down across from them, lifting the lid from a skillet. "If you're going to get some, can I have some?"

He nodded, picking up some plates by the fire and scooping oatmeal and sausage onto them. He handed a plate to Lydia before looking to Blāzzer and asking, "Want some? There's plenty."

"Yeah," answered Blāzzer.

They ate quietly, listening to the sounds of the embers hiss, soldiers talk, and breeze rustle the tents. When Blāzzer was finished with her plate, she watched as Raffel placed more food onto his and Lydia's plates. She smiled softly as Raffel searched for sausage in the skillet.

"I see you're wearing Raffel's shirt," said Lydia, making him look up.

Blāzzer looked down a moment at it, saying, "I forgot I had it on... It's comfy."

"Battle does bring out emotions."

"Huh?"

Lydia looked at Blāzzer with an eyebrow raised then Blāzzer blushed.

"Nothing happened!"

"Your voice is getting higher pitched," commented Lydia.

Blāzzer looked to Raffel and said, "Raffel!"

He sighed and said, "Lydia, nothing happened. She just didn't want to sleep in a blood spattered shirt." Lydia looked down at the fire and Blāzzer pressed her lips together. The young woman tried not to think of the battle or the fear in Raffel's eyes from last night. He rubbed his neck. "I'm sorry, I didn't mean to make either of you uncomfortable."

Lydia nodded stiffly, replying, "I thought I was ready to fight in a battle, but nothing could prepare me for... that."

"We'll make it through this," promised Raffel. After a moment he looked past them. Blāzzer looked over her shoulder and saw Cornin walking towards them with a slight frown.

When Cornin reached them he said, "Army moves out tomorrow morning at dawn. We're to travel east along the border and meet with the friendly tribes. Nickada has declared war against Budsta."

Blāzzer leaned against Raffel's neck as he flew over the Nickadian army marching east. She rubbed her hand over his scales, feeling his uneasiness. She looked over and saw Lydia flying just ahead of them. The dragon held her wounded foreleg tight against her chest.

Slowly Blāzzer sat up and said, *At least the fresh air is nice.* Raffel grunted.

"Stay alert!" yelled Ash, baring his teeth.

*What?* questioned Blāzzer, looking around and not seeing anything of threat.

*There's a group of horse riders moving towards us from the south,* replied Raffel with a rumble deep in his chest.

Ash began to descend towards the Nickadian army while the other dragons continued to fly. He landed in front of the army and it came to a halt.

Nayax rode out on a horse to him, followed by three Lemay Soldiers. After a few minutes Ash launched himself back in the sky and flew near to Aurora.

"It looks like friendly Budstarians," said Ash. "We're to land and wait for their approach."

Slowly all the dragons descended to the front of the army. Lydia landed roughly, trying to avoid using her wounded foreleg. Blāzzer watched as ruchos and uleakites spread out from the column of soldiers. A white rucho stood out from the others and at his side was a golden uleakite. Meric held his antlers high and Foxdur kept her nose low. King Nayax rode his horse up to Ash's side as the dragon crouched down. They talked quietly for a moment before looking to the southern horizon.

It took a while, but soon horse riders appeared and were cantering towards the Nickadians. There were twenty of them and they veered towards the front of the army. Banners flapped in the wind from their spears, bearing a red and yellow background with a black cobra posed to strike. One of the riders near the front raised a white banner. Nayax motioned to a Lemay Soldier and the soldier raised a similar banner. The king and a small group of Lemay Soldiers rode off towards the nearing Budstarians. Ash rose to his feet and followed behind them, ordering, "Stay here."

"Who are they?" asked Lydia.

"Looks like Budstarian warriors from the tribes that don't want to expand their territory," answered Cornin, standing in the saddle. "The tribes that are wanting to stick to their old ways changed their flag to be all red."

Blāzzer watched the others around her as she grabbed a canteen from the saddle bag. She took a drink and, noticing Raffel watching her, asked, *You thirsty?*

He looked away sheepishly, replying, *No, it's nothing.*

*It's not nothing. What are you thinking about?*

Raffel shook his head and she eyed him before drinking more water.

Nayax and his soldiers had arrived to the Budstarian soldiers. Ash stayed close to the king causing the Budstarian horses to shy from him. Minutes ticked by until an hour had past of them talking. Then Nayax turned and led the way back to his army. The Budstarian soldiers didn't move. As the Lemay soldiers neared they blew a horn and Ash launched himself into the air. The army started marching again and the other dragons took flight. Slowly the army turned south led by the Budstarian soldiers.

Blāzzer looked over to Ash and yelled out, "Where are we going?"

The elder dragon replied, "To Du Vent and to prepare for war."

The grassy plains gave way to dirt, rock, and scrubby bushes as the army marched for several days. Large hills rose in gray mounds from the flat land on the southern horizon. Blāzzer squinted as the sunlight starkly reflected against them. She could feel a drop of sweat roll down her back and thought, *I miss that elven bathhouse.*

Soon a city, nestled between the hills, came into view. Blāzzer murmured, "That's Du Vent." It had a large wall surrounding it and an immense palace at the center. All the buildings were made of gray clay with domed roofs. Brightly colored banners and flags lined the wall and palace. She pressed her lips together. "I have a weird feeling about this place."

Raffel looked back to her and replied, *I won't let anything happen to you.*

It was an hour before the army marched to a hillside next to the city. Budstarian soldiers could be seen watching them from the wall. The dragons landed nearby and waited as Nayax spoke with their guides. After a moment a horn was blown, signaling to make camp, and the guides rode off towards the city.

"Looks like we aren't invited in," grumbled Ash, eying the Budstarians.

"I'm not surprised," replied Cornin, crossing his arms with a frown.

Aurora slowly crouched down, saying, "Well, let's make camp."

Blāzzer helped Raffel pitch the tents for the dragons' small camp as the others worked on other chores. She tied a rope to a stake while Raffel hammered another one into the ground. He asked, "You okay?"

She glanced at him, tipping her head in question.

"You keep looking at the city."

"Oh," she murmured and looked back down at the rope, realizing she hadn't yet secured it in place. "I've never been outside of Nickada... so it's just all very different."

Raffel nodded, fastening the tent in place. "I've never been out of Nickada either. Guess I kind of knew one day I would, but I didn't think I would be as young."

"You're not that young. You're older than me."

He grinned. "Trying to make me feel old?"

Blāzzer blushed, distracting herself with placing bags right inside the tent. She brushed her hands on her pants and glanced around, thinking, *Well it looks like we got all of them set up... but where's Ash.* "Aurora, where'd Ash go?"

Aurora looked at her from where she was setting up a campfire and replied, "He went to go speak with Nayax. Should be back soon."

Blāzzer nodded and walked to her tent. She tied back the entrance flap and sat on her bedroll. She held her knees to her chest as she watched the other Nickadians continue to set up the main camp, thinking, *The more time that passes since that night... I thought I would feel better, but...* She closed her eyes at the memory of Raffel staring down at her with a predatory gaze. Slowly she took a deep breath and opened her eyes. *And now that we're here, we're even more on the battlefront.*

"You okay?" asked Lydia, sitting down next to her.

"Just uneasy," whispered Blāzzer. She looked at Lydia's hand, noticing the dirt and grime stuck to the fabric. "We should probably rebandage that."

"How much have you learned so far from Truity?"

"Eh, not a whole lot." Blāzzer grabbed her small medkit before unwrapping Lydia's hand. "She wants me to learn how to suture soon." Blāzzer carefully dabbed ointment onto the cut along Lydia's palm. "Does shifting help heal wounds?"

"I wish," grumbled Lydia. "Having scales prevents most strikes from reaching the skin, but there's still lots of soft spots."

Blāzzer nodded, wrapping a bandage around Lydia's hand. "Like noses."

Lydia raised an eyebrow. "Yeah. Noses, the bottom of the feet, armpits... and groins."

Blāzzer pressed her lips together, trying to not blush.

Lydia laughed, saying, "You blush so easily."

"I can't help it," whined Blāzzer, putting away her medkit.

"Don't worry, it's cute. Especially to dragons because we can't really. I'm for sure Raffel finds it adorable."

Blāzzer covered her face with her hands as Lydia continued to laugh.

"Stop mortifying Blāzzer, Lydia," called Cornin.

Blāzzer peeked over her hands and saw he was grinning at them. She mumbled, "I'm just going to hide in my tent from now on."

Lydia threw her arms around Blāzzer and said, "You can't do that! What would we do then?" She paused, smiling, and Blāzzer glared at her.

"Don't," growled Blāzzer.

"Guess we'd have to send Raffel after you." Lydia laughed louder and Blāzzer tried to scoot away farther into her tent.

"What would I have to do?" questioned Raffel, walking over.

"See!" yelled Lydia, laughing so hard she was gasping for air.

Raffel glanced at Lydia a moment before bending over slightly so he could look at Blāzzer. He blinked and said, "Why are you blushing so much?"

"Raffel!" called Ash, walking into the camp. Raffel turned to him and Blāzzer sighed in relief. "You and I have work to do."

"What work?" questioned Raffel.

"Digging trenches and preparing defenses."

Blāzzer sat with Aurora, Cornin, and Lydia around the campfire as the sun began to set. Aurora was focused on cooking meat and peppers in a skillet as rice cooked in a covered pot. Cornin chewed on the end of his pipe, watching others walk by. Blāzzer leaned over, looking at Lydia's current sketch, and said, "Even with your bandaged hand you're still way better at drawing than me."

Lydia smiled warmly, replying, "My lines aren't as straight as they normally are."

"You're your own worst critic, Lydia," said Cornin, blowing out smoke.

"Lydia, you can draw better than any of us here," commented Aurora, looking at her rider with a sly smile. "Especially him."

"I too can draw!" He grabbed a stick and drew a crude smiley face in the dirt. "See!"

"It's a masterpiece," teased Lydia and Cornin laughed. His laughter cut short as he noticed Nayax walking up with two Budstarian soldiers in tow. Their skin was tanned and hair long with braids and stone beads. Their clothing was made of fine fabrics and had intricate embroidery on the sleeves.

"Gentlemen, this is part of the Stone family," introduced Nayax with a tired expression. "Stone family these are two of the tribal leaders, Geartak and Vindeb."

Aurora stood up and extended a hand to them, saying, "It is good to meet you."

Both soldiers looked at her hand and frowned. One said, "We don't shake hands with women."

Blāzzer felt irritation rise up, and struggled to contain a grimace.

"Sirs, this is Aurora Stone," said Nayax, placing a gentle hand on Aurora's shoulder. "She is the wife of Ash, head of the Stone family. They are the only dragons within this army... and as I understand you do not have any dragons of your own." One of the soldiers reached out and gripped the tip of her fingers in a handshake but the other scowled further. "Understand, gentlemen, that I expect your respect of all of my soldiers- man and woman."

"King Nayax," replied the scowling soldier with a heavy accent, "we are warriors of Budsta. As of now women do not belong on the battlefront, but at home with children."

"Well, what's more terrifying than an angry mama bear," commented Aurora with a sickly sweet smile. Cornin winced.

The soldier that shook her hand quickly said, "Our old traditions are being changed... slowly, but are changing. Just as we are here to change our nomadic nature. One day, maybe, men and women will be equal here."

Nayax inclined his head slightly, replying, "Yes, traditions are changing. To a future when Nickada and Budsta see more eye to eye, wouldn't you say?"

The two soldiers nodded.

"Let's continue the tour shall we." Nayax led them away and Aurora slowly sat back down next to Cornin.

The rider said, "This is why I don't like it here. Budsta is the land of men who don't like women and don't like gays." He sighed. "Luckily for me that just meant no southern border patrol, but that meant northern border patrol in winter." He looked to Aurora with a charming smile. "But I did get to meet this pretty lady."

Aurora laughed softly, replying, "You always do know how to make me smile."

Night had fallen and the sound of quiet talking and crickets chirping hung heavy in the Nickadian camp. Blāzzer laid on her back in her tent, slowly dozing off to sleep. She rolled over as she heard footsteps approach and winced as someone moved the tent flap back.

"You go to bed so early," said Raffel, sitting at the entrance of the tent with his legs stretched out of the tent.

"I like sleep," mumbled Blāzzer, turning and pressing her cheek against his back. "You're covered in dirt."

"Yeah, digging trenches isn't fun."

She opened her eyes more and wrapped her arms around him. "Did you get some dinner?"

"Yeah, like two dinners."

"You're a pig." Blāzzer smiled softly, hearing his heart slowly beat in his chest.

"I heard you had interesting dinner guests," said Raffel, looking up at the stars. She squeezed her arms around him, feeling frustration at the thought of the Budstarian tribe leaders. "Promise me you'll be careful if you're around them." She glanced up and saw him looking over his shoulder at her concernedly. "I'm not saying that anything would happen. I just don't want anything to. And not all Budstarians are like that, I just want-"

"It's okay." She sat up more so her cheek was resting on his shoulder. "I'll be careful... and I think you're mom might have scared them away from our side of camp."

Raffel smiled softly, putting his arms over hers, and asked, "Is it okay if we sit like this for a little while?"

"I'd like that." She turned her head, burying her face against his neck. She jumped slightly when he tensed. "Sorry! Did I tickle you?"

Raffel turned towards her, a blush on his cheeks, and quickly said, "No, you didn't... It felt nice. Like when you lean against my neck when we fly." He placed his hand on her cheek. "I've never met anyone who makes me feel this way."

"And what feeling is that?" asked Blāzzer, pressing her cheek against his hand and feeling warmth throughout her body.

"Conflicted internally because all I want to do lay down by your side and yet I can't stay."

She puckered her bottom lip in a pout. "What if I asked you to stay?"

Raffel clenched his jaw, holding his breath.

Blāzzer blinked, worried, and said quickly, "You okay? I didn't mean to push you into something you don't want. It's up to you. I don't want you to just stay cause I want. It's not-"

"Blāzzer," breathed Raffel, pressing his forehead against hers. He trailed his thumb along her jaw and she pressed her lips together. "I would stay, but if I did I don't think I would be able to spend another night away from you." She whimpered slightly, curling her toes under the blanket. "And something tells me you wouldn't be able to either." She sucked in a breath between her teeth, trying to gather her thoughts. "So for now, we'll sleep separately. After we're back in Nickada though..." He trailed off as he kissed her lips. For a moment she froze then she kissed him back. She held onto the front of his shirt as his finger cradled the back of her head.

Warmth spread through Blāzzer's body from the liffen as their kiss deepened. The world seemed to slow down around them. She whispered, *Promise me that after all of this, you and I...*

*We'll be together,* he assured, resting his forehead against hers. *I promise.*

Blāzzer quietly said, "I love you."

Raffel smiled softly and kissed her forehead before replying, "I love you too. Sleep well, beautiful."

## Chapter Twenty-Three

It didn't take long for Blāzzer to find Truity the following day. The Sentinel Crows had set up their gray tents towards the center of the Nickadian camp. A battlefield hospital was under a large canopy with cots and medical supplies. Truity looked up as the young woman approached, saying, "You look like you got a good night's sleep."

Blāzzer nodded, hooking her thumb around her satchel strap that carried her medical supplies.

"You'll need it," said Truity, placing items in a crate. "We have a long day ahead of us."

"You let me know what I need to do and I'll do it," replied Blāzzer. Truity handed her the crate and motioned for her to follow. They walked away from the canopy to where four tents stood seperatre from any others. The tents were tall enough for a person to stand upright in and wide enough for three people to stand abreast. The entrance flaps were tied back, revealing a cot in each one along with a table and stool.

"Each dragon, and Cornin, has their own tent," explained Truity, walking into a tent. "Go ahead and place that here." Blāzzer placed the crate down on the table. "Each has their own healer assigned to them. You'll be seeing to Raffel."

Blāzzer felt her stomach tighten at nervousness and murmured, "I'm not a healer though."

"By the end of these few days, you'll be a good field medic." Truity looked at Blāzzer. "I don't expect you to take care of him on your own. Other healers will be here if needed, but as dragon and rider it is important that you can help him."

Blāzzer took a deep breath before replying, "I'm ready to learn."

Truity smiled. "Good. Well, let's get started with what's in the crate then we'll finish setting up in here."

Hours passed as Blāzzer worked with Truity. She took notes on the purposes of the different items and how best to help Raffel. Slowly, she felt more comfortable with the idea of being his personal field medic.

"Hello," said a voice.

Blāzzer looked behind her from her work in setting up another tent and saw a centaur. He was vaguely familiar with his gray coat. She asked, "You're Naro right?"

He nodded.

"Good you made it," said Truity, walking over from the main battlefield hospital. "Though I'm surprised you were chosen."

"There is more than just one way to contribute to a battle," replied Naro.

"Couldn't have said it better myself." Truity turned to the young woman. "Blāzzer, Naro has been assigned as your personal guard."

"My what?" questioned Blāzzer.

"Since you aren't trained to fight yet," explained Naro, "the Council deemed it necessary that you were assigned someone to ensure you're safety."

She frowned slightly.

He chuckled. "I understand you're distrust of the Council, but unlike them, I don't think poorly of the dragons. I'll do whatever I can to help you and the Stone family."

"I'm going to let you two get to know each other," said Truity. "Once you're done with the tents come see me."

"Okay," replied Blāzzer.

The older woman left and Naro questioned, "Anything I can help with?"

"The only thing left to really do is fetch water," murmured Blāzzer, looking to some buckets. "I haven't gotten any yet for the tents."

Caratin nodded and, grabbing a pole, placed two buckets on each end. He straightened up carrying the pole across his human shoulders, saying, "There that should work. Ready?"

Blāzzer nodded and followed him away from the medical tent. They walked through the Nickadian camp, passing different races and groups. After a while, she asked, "Aren't you Caratin's son?"

"Yeah, but I really don't think of him much as a father besides bloodline," replied Caratin with a shrug. People stepped out of his way as he walked. He looked down at Blāzzer. "I'm sorry he's such a pain in the ass."

"It's not your fault," said Blāzzer.

"Well, if I had been made leader this year it wouldn't have been such a mess."

"I guess you're his heir."

"Not really. A centaur leader is chosen based on battle prowess."

"So you have to fight him? Your own father?"

"I have and will again."

Blāzzer pressed her lips together slightly.

"Don't worry about it. Caratin isn't the best warrior and his popularity with the centaurs is faltering."

They arrived at a well, where a group of Budstarian soldiers were distributing water, and Naro placed the buckets down. They looked up at the centaur and disgust crossed some of their faces.

"We need some water for the medical tents," said Blāzzer, holding one of the buckets out to them. One soldier looked down his nose at her. Another soldier though took the bucket and began to fill it. He handed it back to her and she turned around to grab another when she noticed Naro. He was glaring down at the soldiers with his hands resting on the sword pommels at his flanks. She thought, *No wonder they aren't making any comments.*

The other three buckets were filled in a few minutes, and Naro carefully picked them up with the pole, placing it over his shoulders. As they walked back towards the battlefield hospital Blāzzer said, "Thank you for that. I don't think they would have given me water otherwise."

"You would have figured it out," replied Naro. "Or one of the Nickadian soldiers would have stepped in. Either way, you would have gotten the water." He glanced down at her. "You were brave to stand up to the Council."

Blāzzer smiled slightly. "I don't think it really crossed my mind like that. I just knew that I didn't want to go away."

"You spoke up, that was brave."

They walked into the area for the battlefield hospital and Truity waved them over. Naro placed the buckets down before following Blāzzer under the canopy. At Truity's worried face, Blāzzer asked, "Is everything okay?"

The healer shook her head before answering, "The enemy army is three days away. Snerxites have joined them too."

When the sun was setting, Blāzzer wandered back through the camp, heading for where the Stone family was set up. She didn't see the other soldiers as she walked by, thinking, *Make sure to wash all wounds. Then assess. If deep enough, I'll need to suture it. Otherwise, some ointment and bandages. Make sure he eats even when he doesn't want to. And-*

She squeaked when someone grabbed her arm and turned around to see Leggauto. He pointed behind her and she glanced to see a stack of wood she had nearly walked into. He said, "Maybe the army camp isn't the best place for you."

Blāzzer pressed her lips together, trying to swallow the irritation, and replied, "Thank you for saving me from crashing. I was lost in thought." She looked about slightly, noting more elves than other races.

"Then maybe you should stop overthinking," said Leggauto, dryly.

"I don't have the energy to be bothered by you if you're just going to critique me." She turned and began to walk away. "Good luck in the battle, Leggauto." She didn't see his momentary surprise as she walked away.

When Blāzzer got to the Stone family camp, there was no one else there. She tossed a few logs onto the coals of the campfire before gathering items for cooking dinner. She sat down at the fire, placing the skillet over the coals to heat. She looked up as Cornin walked over with a tired face.

"It's me and you tonight, kiddo," sighed Cornin, sitting down and pulling off his boots. He started to massage his feet.

"What about the others?" asked Blāzzer. *What about Raffel?*

"They're still preparing defenses around the camp, so they'll eat over there."

Blāzzer nodded with disappointment.

"How'd your day go?"

"Lot of information." Blāzzer cut sausages into the pan. "It's a bit overwhelming to be the one in charge of taking care of Raffel during the battle."

"I wouldn't worry about it too much," assured Cornin, pulling his pipe out. "Dragons react better when they know the healer. That's how I met Aurora."

"You were her field medic?" asked Blāzzer, pausing in her food preparations.

"That and her attendant. Anything she needed I made sure she got it."

"How long did you work with her before you became dragon and rider?"

Cornin took a twig from the fire and lit his pipe. "I think it was close to two years. By that time we were flying together... We were patrolling along the northern border and saw some Shadowfairites snooping around. We went to go speak with them, but a dragon came out of the clouds and nailed me pretty bad. You haven't seen my liffen yet, have you?"

Blāzzer shook her head, pouring some water into the pan along with rice.

He grinned. "Mine does make your's look pretty." Holding his pipe in his teeth, he pulled his shirt up so she could see his stomach. His liffen went from one side of his stomach to the other in a thick line. The edges splintered off like cracks in ice. The skin and muscle of his abdomen was pulled tight by the liffen and his flesh dimpled under his ribs.

She murmured, "I think I just lost my appetite."

Cornin chuckled, pulling his shirt down. "I nearly did permanently if it wasn't for Aurora." He chewed on the end of his pipe, looking into the embers. "I never thought I would be so attached to a woman as I am her."

"How was it when she met Ash?" asked Blāzzer.

"Well, Ash pursued her," said Cornin with a wink. "He came up to Green Valley in search of other dragons. Nayax had been crowned king a year or so. Poor guy tried really hard to get her attention, but she really didn't take a second glance at him."

"Really?"

"Yeah, Aurora was pretty focused on her work patrolling the border. I had to convince her to give him a chance. She was still pretty hesitant about it, but she did start talking to him." He shrugged. "They had a lot to learn about each other." He looked at Blāzzer, raising an eyebrow with a grin. "Building a dragon and rider relationship isn't that different than building a relationship with a life partner, wouldn't you say?"

Blāzzer blushed, replying, "Having the ability to communicate through the liffen helps."

"Trick is not to let your emotions show when you do," said Cornin with a chuckle. "I've never been good about that."

"I haven't really tried that."

"It's not a bad skill to have. Especially when speaking with officials, so you'll want to work on it for becoming leader."

"I thought leaders weren't allowed to communicate with others outside during a Council meeting."

Cornin smiled slightly, replying, "As stated in the Council charter 'Verbal and written communication with those outside the Council chambers is not allowed when in session'."

"So it's a technicality?" asked Blāzzer.

"Yep, and sometimes those technicalities are what helps you out the most."

Blāzzer laid on her bedroll staring up at the ceiling of her tent in the darkness. She put her arm over her eyes, thinking, *Where are you Raffel? I thought you would be back by now.* She sighed, feeling her chest tighten slightly. *Why do you make me feel this way?* She pressed the heels of her hands against her eyes. *All I want is to be next to you! Argh, this is frustrating.* She placed her hands on her chest, feeling her heart thump against her sternum. *I'm worried about you... I don't want you to get hurt, but I'll be there for you. I'll do my best to make sure you're taken care of.* She curled up on her side. *Just don't leave me.*

The army camp continued preparation for battle as the days wore on. Blāzzer worked at the Sentinel Crows battlefield hospital from dawn to dusk. She placed blankets and pillows on a raised cot in a tent for the dragons, before turning to double-check the supplies laid out on the table.

"Hey," said Raffel. Blāzzer turned around and heat rushed to her cheeks. Holding his shirt in his hand, he stood at the tent entrance and was drenched. His smile faded slowly. "You okay?"

She nodded quickly, feeling her thoughts slam into the front of her head.

He rubbed his jaw. "If you're busy, we can catch up later."

"No!" she cried out, stepping forward.

Hoofsteps rushed over and Naro stopped next to Raffel, looking to Blāzzer and asking, "You okay?"

"Yeah," replied Blāzzer quickly, bowing her head slightly and hoping the shade of the tent would hide her blush. "Raffel just scared me is all."

Naro, raising an eyebrow, looked between the two. "Okay, well I'm going to take a break and grab some lunch. You should probably do the same."

"Thank you."

Raffel watched Naro leave before turning to Blāzzer, saying, *I didn't scare you.*

She crossed her arms, replying, *Well I wasn't expecting you.*

He narrowed his eyes, studying her. *Looks like you got sunburned.*

Blāzzer frowned, relieved to feel some of the heat leaving her cheeks. *Really?*

*Does it hurt?* He stepped forward and touched her cheek gently. She felt heat rush right back to her face and her eyes glanced down at his bare chest that was lithe with muscle. Understanding dawned in his eyes. *You're blushing.*

She turned away, busying her hands with moving some jars and bandage wraps. After she took a deep breath she said, *You surprised me... you're soaked and shirtless.*

Raffel looked down at himself and chuckled softly before sitting on the edge of the cot. *I was helping with the trenches. Last time you mentioned me being covered in dirt so I thought I'd wash off.*

Blāzzer looked at him seeing his grin. *I appreciate that.*

*The washing off or me being shirtless?* He laughed as she glared at him.

She looked away and quietly said, "Both." She sat down next to him. "I'm going to do my best to take care of you."

Raffel laid his hand over hers, replying, "I know."

She looked up at him. "I don't want you to get hurt."

"I know."

She pressed her forehead against his shoulder, squeezing his hand.

"Knowing that you are the one that will be taking care of me gives some peace of mind. It may not be fair for me to expect you to, but it does make me feel better. I'll at least be able to see you and know that you're okay."

"Hearing that makes me feel better," whispered Blāzzer. She sat up and looked into his eyes. "I'm going to do everything I can to take care of you." She began to lean forward to kiss his lips.

"Blāzzer! Raffel!" called Truity.

Blāzzer jumped up, missing the irritation that flashed in Raffel's eyes. He followed her out and to the main hospital. Truity was busy putting supplies in satchels as other healers worked on the final touches of the supply setup.

"What is it, Truity?" asked Blāzzer. Truity pointed out of the tent and Raffel and Blāzzer followed her finger. Blāzzer felt her heart drop at the sight of an advancing army in the west.

Truity said, "They're here."

"I need to go get ready," said Raffel, turning away.

Blāzzer grabbed his arm and he looked down at her. She could see her fear mirrored in his eyes. She whispered, "Please be careful." He nodded and quickly walked away. She wrung her hands together a moment before turning to Truity. "Tell me what I need to do."

## Chapter Twenty-Four

Blāzzer helped Truity prepare battlefield medic bags when she saw the dragons fly overhead towards the gathering Nickadian army. She took a deep breath before continuing her work, thinking, *Please be careful.*

Other Sentinel Crows walked up to the battlefield hospital and Truity, said, "Hand each one a bag." Blāzzer nodded and began distributing the medical bags.

After a while, Truity said, "It looks like Nickada is calling a parley." Blāzzer looked up, squinting to see through the glare of the sun against the gray dirt. A group of soldiers with a white flag was riding out towards the enemy Budstarian army.

"Why?" asked Blāzzer, resuming to pass out bags.

"Officially to see if a compromise can be made without bloodshed," replied Truity, continuing to watch and holding onto a small gold locket around her neck. "It won't work, but it'll give our soldiers time to get in place."

Soon all the medical bags had been distributed and there wasn't anything to do but wait. Blāzzer sat on a stool, watching the Nickadian army assemble alongside allied Budstarians. The enemy had formed their ranks. The area between the armies was wide and at its center were representatives from each. She could see the dragons standing on the frontline of the Nickadian army and her stomach tightened.

"Here, you should eat," said Naro, holding a bowl out to her.

She looked up at him, seeing him fully suited in leather armor. She blinked saying, "I don't have my sword."

Naro placed the bowl down on a table. "We should go get that then. Here, get on." He turned and she stared at him. "Come on, it's like getting on a horse." Blāzzer smiled softly and quickly stood up. Using the straps of his armor, she easily swung up onto his back. He grabbed her hand and placed it on his shoulder. "Don't need you falling. Hold on."

He cantered away, kicking up dust. Blāzzer held on tight, feeling her teeth jar against each other. Naro moved quickly between the tents with the few remaining soldiers jumping out of his way. He stopped when they came to the Stone family tents. Blāzzer jumped down, happy to be on her own two feet, and ducked inside her tent. She grabbed Flame and stepped out, tying the sword to her belt.

"Do you have any armor?" asked Naro.

Blāzzer paused for a moment before ducking back in her tent and grabbing her flight harness. She slipped it on and as she tightened the straps she felt more steady. She looked up to Naro and saw his face contorted with focus as he watched the armies. She questioned, "Is everything okay?"

"The parley is being withdrawn," he replied.

She followed his eyes to the battlefield and saw the soldiers in the center returning to their respective armies. Once they were within their own ranks, horns were blown, the blasts echoing against the hills. War cries followed and the armies began to march at each other. Blāzzer's chest squeezed painfully tight as the dragons took to the sky, flying ahead of the Nickadian army.

"They'll come back," said Naro calmly. She looked at him, struggling to keep her body from trembling. "He'll come back. Have faith in them."

The last rays of sunlight disappeared behind the hills and horns were blown. Blāzzer stood alongside Naro outside the medical tents, waiting for the dragons. She felt relief the fighting was over for the day even though it would resume at first light. She could barely make out the dragons as they flew, only seeing them as they eclipsed the stars. Other healers gathered to receive the dragons.

Lydia landed roughly, falling to one side due to her injured foreleg. Blood dripped from her mouth and covered her sides. She hissed, spraying red globs, at the healers that tried to approach. Blāzzer focused on taking deep breaths, feeling nausea try to take hold. Lydia was enveloped in light for a moment, leaving behind her battered human form kneeling on the ground. Healers rushed to help her to a tent and clear the area for another dragon.

Raffel landed next, his mouth open as sticky blood hung from his lips. Blood was hard to see against his scales, but there was a thick stream of it dripping down the inside of his foreleg. He swung his head, searching with his narrow slit eyes. When he saw Blāzzer his pupils rounded and light flashed around him a moment. He stood there pressing his hand against the side of his ribcage under his arm.

Blāzzer and Naro rushed to the dragon. Naro helped guide Raffel to a tent as she began to assess his injuries. When they got to the tent, Blāzzer said, "Naro help me undress him." Naro nodded beginning to unbuckle the leather chest armor on Raffel. She wiped the blood from Raffel's face, trying to avoid meeting his eyes. Once the armor was off Blāzzer saw the large stain down Raffel's side. Naro removed Raffel's bracers, shirt, chainmail, undershirt, and sword. Blāzzer winced at the cuts all over Raffel's body.

"Should I help him with his pants?" asked Naro.

"No, I need to take care of that cut under his arm first," replied Blāzzer, guiding Raffel to sit on the cot. "Thank you, Naro. I'll call for you if I need any help." Naro nodded and stepped out of the tent, closing the flaps.

"I need to vomit," groaned Raffel. Blāzzer blinked and quickly held a bucket in front of him. He vomited blood and water, coughing as it caught in his throat. She gently brushed the hair out of his face. He looked up at her and she met his eyes. They were tired but relieved.

"Hey," she said softly. He smiled for a moment before dry heaving, saliva dripping out of his mouth. He groaned and rested his chin on the rim of the bucket. She grabbed a cup of water. "Here, rinse your mouth." She helped him with the cup and he swished the water around before spitting it in the bucket. She grabbed a smaller cup. "Drink this."

Raffel sniffed the silvery liquid and wrinkled his nose.

"It's fermented herbs," replied Blāzzer. "It'll help with the nausea." He threw his head back and swallowed the liquid. He grimaced, coughing. "And some water."

After he drank some water Raffel slowly laid down. Blāzzer placed the bucket under the table and grabbed a washcloth. She moved his arm and began to wipe away the blood on the side of his chest. There was a deep cut in the muscle and it was still oozing blood.

"You'll need to roll onto your side for me to suture this," said Blāzzer, setting out the suture kit on the table. Slowly Raffel rolled over, his back to her. She moved his arm and grabbed a small bottle of alcohol. "This is going to hurt." She dampened a cloth with alcohol and wiped the cut gently. Air hissed as he sucked it in between his teeth. After carefully threading a needle she began to stitch his cut. Raffel's knuckles were white as gripped the pillow.

Blāzzer touched his back gently and said, "Breathe." Once he started breathing evenly again she resumed the suturing. "Breathe in... Breathe out..." She repeatedly said this phrase until the stitching was finished. She wiped the area again with alcohol. "Okay, you can lay on your back."

With a sigh, he rolled over onto his back. She cleaned the scrapes on Raffel's chest and face before applying ointment. She got up and pulled his boots and socks off, glad to see no cuts. She looked up at him and saw he had lifted his head to watch her with a worried expression.

"You okay?" asked Blāzzer.

"Yeah," breathed Raffel, laying his head back down. "I guess you're supposed to take my pants off."

Blāzzer blinked, her focus broken, and blushed. She looked away, murmuring, "Well, any cuts need to be cleaned and you shouldn't sleep in bloody pants."

"It's okay. I'll take them off." He slowly stood up and unbuckled his pants.

She poked her head out of the tent, seeing Naro standing guard. He looked at her and she asked, "Can you go get Raffel some food?"

"Yes," answered Naro, turning to face her. "I'll bring you something too. You need to keep your strength up." She nodded and he walked away.

Blāzzer stepped back into the tent and looked to Raffel. He sat on the edge of the cot in dark undershorts, staring at the ground. She went to the table and picked up a comb, saying, "Go ahead and sit on the stool." He moved over slowly and she undid the string that was holding most of his hair back. Gently she teased out the knots, dried blood, and dirt from his hair.

"I feel kind of helpless," murmured Raffel. Blāzzer paused before setting the comb down. She touched his cheek, tipping his head so she could look into his eyes.

*I'm here*, she said. "You're not helpless, but right now it's my turn to help you." He leaned forward, burying his face against her chest. She cradled his head, stroking his hair. "I got you." His arms tightened around her and she could feel the wall holding his emotions back break. "I'm here. I'm not going anywhere." A sob escaped from his mouth and his body shook.

*I was so scared,* cried Raffel. *I'd be fighting and for a moment I forgot where you were.* Blāzzer blinked. *I thought they had you.* She squeezed him before unwrapping his arms, forcing him to look up at her face. Tears were falling down his face.

"I'm not going anywhere. And tomorrow, when you are done fighting, I'll be here again to help you." Using her thumb, she brushed away his tears. "Have a little faith in me." She kissed his forehead and felt his body relax.

Blāzzer and Naro helped Raffel put his armor on before daybreak. Afterward, Raffel sat on the stool as Blāzzer worked on tying his hair back and Naro pulled back the tent flaps. She could feel Raffel's determined focus, but underneath his nerves were still frayed. Once she finished his hair, she wrapped her arms around his shoulder, pressing her head against his.

"Come back once the sun has set," whispered Blāzzer. Raffel nodded before standing up and grabbing his sword. He walked away towards the other dragons in the open space between the tents. She followed for a moment but paused beside Naro. All the dragons shifted and took to the air except for Aurora. She crouched down and Cornin walked up to her. He pressed his hand against her shoulder before swinging into the saddle. When he was secure, she stood and jumped into the sky.

The sky, still holding onto its blanket of stars and darkness, was pink and orange at the horizon. Blāzzer watched the dragons fly away towards the gathering Nickadian army. She clenched her fist for a moment before turning away, saying, "I need to get the tents set for this evening."

"What do you need me to do?" asked Naro. She looked up at him.

"More water."

He nodded before walking away.

Blāzzer looked to where the dragons were flying and thought, *Please come back.*

"Blāzzer and Naro!" called Truity.

Blāzzer looked up from one of the dragons' tents, placing the soiled towels and bandages in the basket. She carried picked up the basket before stepping out of the tent. Naro took the basket and followed her to the battlefield hospital. Several of the cots had wounded Sentinel Crows that were either resting or being treated by healers. Truity was checking the sutures on one as Blāzzer and Naro walked up.

"Go ahead and place that basket there," said Truity and Naro placed the basket alongside others. "I need you two to take supplies out to the battlefront." She indicated two large bags by the edge of the canopy. "Deliver it to the red crow flag. It'll be well behind our lines and should be safe."

"Will do," replied Naro as Blāzzer walked over to the bags. They were stuffed with bandages and ointments. She looked to the centaur. "Here, tie the straps together and it can then sit across my back." She tied the straps together as best she could and with his help placed them across his back, with one hanging on each flank. "Now you."

"That's not going to be too heavy for you?" asked Blāzzer, putting a hand on his armor.

Naro chuckled, "No, I'm sturdy."

She nodded and swung up onto his back. She checked to make sure the bags were secure before saying, "Let's go."

Naro cantered off towards the west, towards the battling armies. When Naro rode past the last tents, Blāzzer saw the soldiers lined there. Their faces were hard set with their hands resting on bows and arrows. Naro's hooves rattled the makeshift wooden bridge across a wide trench before hitting compact gray soil. The sound of battle echoed dully against the hills, but as they neared it became an incessant drone.

"Hold on!" yelled Naro. Blāzzer gripped the back of his armor tighter and he broke into a gallop. She blinked in surprise at how fast he could run. The pounding of his hooves accentuated the sounds of battle. "Keep an eye out for that flag!"

She saw the dragons over the battlefield. They dove at the enemy army with tooth, claw, fire, and ice. They tore the enemy lines and scattered their soldiers. Friendly soldiers took advantage of this and pushed forward. Naro veered south to stay well behind the army. At the back of it were several large tents. Flags flapped in the wind over them with the Nickadian flag being the highest. As he neared the tents the individual designs of the flags became clear.

"There! To you're left!" called Blāzzer. Naro turned slightly and headed for a black flag with a red crow. He slowed as he came to a wide trench with spears at the bottom and crossed a wooden bridge. Lemay soldiers stood abreast on the other side of the trench. They let Naro and Blāzzer through without question.

The screams and cries of battle grated against Blāzzer's ears. She saw wounded soldiers being carried on stretchers and sheets covering still bodies. She felt lightheaded and let her head rest against Naro's back.

"Hey, don't pass out," he said, looking over his shoulder. "Breathe. Focus on your task." She took a deep breath and slowly lifted her head, focusing on the black flag.

They arrived at a gray canopy where Sentinel Crows were being treated. A healer walked up to them and Blāzzer swung off of Naro's back. Blāzzer said, "Truity sent these supplies."

"Thank you," replied the healer. Blāzzer helped her remove the bags.

"Is there anything you need us to take back?" questioned Naro.

The healer looked around for a moment before grabbing a piece of paper. She held it out to Blāzzer, saying, "Take this to Truity. It's the names of the deceased and wounded."

Blāzzer took the paper and tucked it into her medical pouch, answering,

"Will do." She swung up onto Naro's back and he trotted out of the camp.

As they crossed the bridge Blāzzer looked back to see Raffel roll into a dive. She thought, *Please come back to me.*


Blāzzer double-checked that bandages and ointments were set out on the table of Raffel's tent before stepping out. The setting sun tinted the sky orange and red as darkness crept overhead. She pressed her lips together in worry when she didn't see the dragons. Naro placed his hand on her shoulder and she looked up.

"He'll come back," he assured. Blāzzer nodded and they waited.

Stars winked into existence as the night sky heralded them. Slowly the colors of the sun faded into the darkness. A horn blasted across the hills and Blāzzer felt her heart skip a beat. She stepped forward as the dragons flew near. Their wing beats labored as they struggled to stay aloft.

Aurora landed first with a foot-long tear leaving a gaping hole in her wing membrane. She crouched down, her legs shaking. Cornin slid down, collapsing on the ground. His thigh was roughly bandaged and his chin rested on his chest. Healers rushed to them as Aurora shifted. Blood trickled into her eye from a cut on her brow.

Once they were clear Ash landed heavily. He opened his mouth, dripping with blood and saliva, and flames could be seen in the back of his mouth. He bared his teeth and the fire licked around the gaps of his teeth, showing that some had been broken. Light enveloped him and a flash of fire sizzled over him before the light disappeared. He crouched there, on hands and knees. As healers went to him he retched blood.

Blāzzer clenched her hands into fists, trying to stop the trembling that was taking over her body. She looked up, seeing Lydia and Raffel circling overhead. Lydia landed awkwardly, barely catching herself. She shifted before she had tucked her wings in. Healers quickly helped her away before Blāzzer could see the extent of her injuries.

Finally Raffel landed, his claws digging into the dirt to hold himself upright. He snarled at the healers, swinging his head and scattering blood. A broken spear shaft was sticking out of his thigh muscle. Blāzzer rushed to him and Naro followed. Raffel snapped at the centaur, causing him to rear. She stepped in between them with her arms out stretched. Raffel eyes fixated on her, his narrow pupils studying her.

"It's okay," she whispered, reaching a hand out and placing it between his nostrils. "We're going to help you." He sighed and warm air surrounded her. She looked behind her to Naro. "He won't hurt you." Raffel carefully laid down as Blāzzer and Naro walked over to his rear leg.

"He's going to bleed a lot once that's removed," said Naro.

Blāzzer nodded, grabbing bandages from her medical pouch. She looked over to Raffel's head. He was watching them. She said gently, "Shift immediately when it's pulled out." He looked away, dragging his head against the dirt and leaving a smear of blood. "Okay, Naro... Pull it out straight."

Naro grabbed the spear shaft with both hands and pulled with his full weight. Raffel cried out, digging his claws into the ground. Naro grimaced and tugged, pushing his hooves into the dirt. The spear came free and Raffel shifted, lying on the ground. Blāzzer immediately knelt by him, forcing his whimpers from her ears, and tightly bandaged his thigh. He grabbed her hand and she looked at his face. Exhaustion, pain, and fear contorted his face. He pressed her hand against his cheek and with her free hand she brushed hair off his face.

Blāzzer murmured, "It's going to be okay. I promise."

Blāzzer sighed as she laid on the mat on the ground beside Raffel's cot. She felt exhausted and drained. With the lamp shielded the tent was softly illuminated. She rolled over and pulled the blanket tight around herself. The sound of people talking and crying could be heard through the tent walls.

After a moment she sat up, pressing her hands against her ears and thinking, *When will this end?* A gentle hand touched her arm.

She turned and saw Raffel looking at her with his arm out towards her. She gripped his hand with both of hers. He pulled her towards him until she was kneeling by the cot and resting her head on his chest. She closed her eyes as she listened to his heartbeat. Her breathing and racing mind slowed.

"Will you lay with me?" asked Raffel.

"I don't want to hurt you," replied Blāzzer, looking at the scratches on his skin.

"You won't hurt me... It'd help me sleep."

She nodded and carefully laid next to him. With his arms around her, he held her close. She closed her eyes and felt herself drifting off to sleep. Raffel kissed the top of her head and she smiled softly. Warmth emanated from the liffen, coming in gentle waves.

## Chapter Twenty-Five

Blāzzer followed Raffel out of the tent. The sky was just starting to lighten with the coming of the sun. He wore his armor and had his sword at his side. The other dragons, prepared for battle, were stepping out of their tents as well. She could feel Raffel's hesitation and placed a hand on his arm. He stopped walking and looked down at her. She cradled his jaw and kissed his cheek.

"Everything will be okay," promised Blāzzer. "You'll come back and I'll be here for you."

Raffel nodded, unable to speak. He turned and walked to the other dragons and Cornin, leaving Blāzzer. She watched as they one by one shifted and took to the sky. She watched as they disappeared across the hillside.

Naro stepped to Blāzzer's side and stood there as a quiet presence of familiarity. After a minute she looked up to him and said, "We have work to do."

Naro stood still as healers placed two bags of supplies across his back. Blāzzer sat in the shade of the battlefield hospital canopy drinking water from a cup. Many of the cots under the canopy were occupied, but the cries and whimpers had quieted as the soldiers slept. She got up once the healers secured the bags and swung onto Naro's back, her legs bumping against the swords strapped to his flanks. He began to walk away, heading for the main exit of the camp.

"The dragons were in bad shape last night," said Naro, looking over his shoulder at Blāzzer.

She didn't meet his eyes, but replied, "They'll make it through this."

He nodded and picked up the pace to a canter. Fewer soldiers were moving about the camp. Those that stood guard by the trench had dirt smeared on them and eyes shadowed by exhaustion. Once Naro's hooves passed the wooden bridge he broke into a gallop, following the same path they had the day before. Blāzzer's ears heard the cries and screams of battle, but her brain had stopped processing it. She looked up and saw the dragons diving down at the enemy. Aurora blasted a stream of blue and white ice. Ash slammed through enemy lines, carrying soldiers high and dropping them on their comrades. Lydia swooped low, clawing and biting at any enemy soldier she could reach. Raffel dove towards the enemy and breathed fire into their ranks. Except, the fire was red and thin.

Blāzzer pressed her lips together and looked away. She took a deep breath, thinking, *Focus on my task. Take the supplies to the Sentinel Crows.*

Naro slowed as he approached the camp at the rear of the Nickadian army. He crossed the wooden bridge across the spear-holding trench. Lemay soldiers standing abreast along the trench didn't acknowledge him. There were more bodies covered in sheets and more wounded soldiers. Blāzzer tried to take a deep breath to steady herself, but the sting of blood and vomit stuck to her throat. Naro made his way to Sentinel Crow battlefield hospital, without glancing at any of the wounded or dead.

Blāzzer swung down and helped the healers remove the bags. Soldiers on the raised cots cried and pleaded as their wounds were being treated. She took the papers listing the wounded and deceased before swinging back up onto Naro's back. He turned and began to walk back towards the camp entrance.

"Make way! Make way for the king!" yelled several voices.

Naro stepped aside as Lemay Soldiers rushed through the main path. Blāzzer blinked as Lemay soldiers marched by, carrying a stretcher between them. On the stretcher was Nayax. His face contorted in pain as he tried to breathe, blood dribbling from his lips. An arrow was sticking out of his thigh and another his shoulder. His metal chest armor was crushed on the front. The Lemay soldiers carried him away and Blāzzer looked up at the flap of wings. Ash flew low overhead and landed in the camp.

"Wait," insisted Blāzzer as Naro began to walk again.

"There is nothing we can do," he replied, not slowing as the trench came into sight. She gritted her teeth and felt tears prick her eyes. Naro broke into a canter once across the bridge. His hoofbeats sounded like a racing heartbeat, matching hers.

Blāzzer looked up and murmured, "Lydia."

The dragon was flying low away from the battlefield and struggled to keep her wing beats even. Light enveloped her.

"No!" screamed Blāzzer. Naro broke into a gallop, charging across the gray dirt towards Lydia as she fell from the sky. Her human body emitted no cry.

Blāzzer snarled, her hands tightened to white knuckles on Naro's armor.

With a dull thud, Lydia crashed into the earth. Blāzzer swung off Naro's back before he came to a stop before her. A sob tore from her mouth as she knelt beside Lydia's broken body. Lydia's leg was bent back at mid femur and the bones in her forearm had broken through her skin. The side of her head was bleeding and the same red liquid trickled from her nose. Her fingers twitched as the seizure held its hold. Blāzzer touched Lydia's cheek as frost crept across the ground from the dragon's body.

"No," whispered Blāzzer, tears rolling down her cheeks. "Please." Lydia's eyes stared blankly up at the sky. Blāzzer pressed her ear against Lydia's chest, feeling the cold of Lydia's endar pierce at her skin. The dragon's heart was struggling to pump.

"We have company coming," said Naro, drawing his swords.

Blāzzer looked up to see enemy horse riders galloping towards them. She looked down at Lydia. Her fingers had stopped moving and her chest had stopped rising. Blāzzer pressed her lips together and closed Lydia's eyes, saying, "You were never a burden. You were never broken."

Slowly and shakily, Blāzzer stood up, drawing Flame. She looked at the soldiers charging towards them. She bared her teeth and let out a battle cry. Heat erupted from the liffen, but it didn't hurt. Her nails thickened to a point, her hair became coarse, two horns sprouted from the top of her head, patches of her skin turned red, and her eyes looked like a multifaceted garnet.

*They will not touch you*, swore Blāzzer, stepping around Lydia and placing herself between the oncoming soldiers and the fallen dragon.

One of the soldiers fired an arrow at Blāzzer and without thought she deflected it with her sword. Naro charged the soldiers, striking with both swords. Soldiers and horses fell in a spray of blood. A few of the mounted soldiers made it past and continued their charge at Blāzzer. The first swung a sword. She dodged and slashed. The horse cried as it fell, pinning the soldier underneath. Blāzzer turned and ran towards the next soldier. She jumped into the air, soaring over the horse's head. The soldier's eyes widened in fear. She spun in mid-air with Flame singing. The soldier's head fell to the ground as the horse galloped away. Blāzzer landed in a crouch and snarled at the last soldier. He turned his horse and fled. The dirt crunched behind her.

"Blāzzer!" yelled Naro as she turned, stabbing the fallen soldier that had tried to sneak up behind her. The korsteel blade stabbed through the soldier's chest without hesitation.

Blāzzer met the soldier's eyes. He coughed blood onto her face before the light in his eyes faded. She heaved against him, pulling her sword free. She looked around, seeing the dead soldiers, blood, Naro, and Lydia. She felt the world spin as the heat from the liffen withdrew. She dropped Flame and collapsed to her knees. Wingbeats sounded overhead.

Blāzzer looked up to see Raffel land before her. She smiled softly before falling forward, unconscious.

## Chapter Twenty-Six

Blāzzer blinked open her eyes, feeling a wave of nausea. Her vision was blurred as she rolled onto her side. Drool dripped out of her open mouth before she vomited over the side of the cot.

"Take it easy," said Truity, pushing Blāzzer's hair back. "You're okay."

"Where am I?" groaned Blāzzer, wiping the back of her hand over her mouth.

"You're at the Sentinel Crow battlefield hospital in the main camp. How are you feeling?"

Blāzzer moaned, rolling onto her back and staring at the gray canopy overhead. Slowly the fabric came into focus. She muttered, "My head really hurts." She closed her eyes, pressing the heels of her hands against them.

"You need to sit up and drink this."

Slowly, and with Truity's help, Blāzzer sat up. The healer handed Blāzzer a cup and without hesitation, the young woman swallowed the liquid. Blāzzer coughed at the bitter taste. Truity gave her a different cup of water.

"What do you remember before you blacked out?" asked Truity, taking the drained cups and sitting on the side of the cot.

Blāzzer looked about for a moment, trying to collect her thoughts. Night had fallen and most of the patients were sleeping. She murmured, "We had dropped off the supplies." She rubbed her head, trying to think through the pain. "Nayax was brought by on a stretcher... He was really badly hurt. Ash landed in the camp." She looked to Truity and the healer nodded for her to continue. "And we left. We were heading back here, when... Lydia... She fell from the sky in a seizure." Blāzzer looked down at her hands, her jaw starting to tremble. "She... Her arm and her leg were broken. She died right in front of me." Tears trickled from her eyes. "I couldn't do anything to help her."

Truity held Blāzzer's hand, saying gently, "No one could have saved her. Do not blame yourself." She squeezed the young woman's hand. "Do you remember anything else?"

"I don't know." Blāzzer looked to the table and saw Flame sitting on it. "I killed them... I fought some soldiers and killed them." She shook her head and looked to Truity. "I don't know how I did. I'm not even very good with a sword."

"Your distress went through the liffen," explained Truity. "You were able to pull on Raffel's endar and enter fatorana." She withdrew her hand and gave Blāzzer a kerchief. "It's why your head hurts so bad."

Blāzzer wiped away her tears, her hands shaking slightly. She asked, "Where's Raffel?"

"In his tent resting. Don't worry, healers have seen to his wounds." Blāzzer swung her legs over the side of the cot and the healer grabbed her arm. "You need to rest."

"I need to talk to him," insisted Blāzzer.

Truity walked around the cot and stood in front of Blāzzer, blocking her from standing. The healer said, "Lay back down. You can see him in the morning."

"He has to fight in the morning." Blāzzer moved to stand, but Truity pressed her hands on Blāzzer's shoulders. Blāzzer looked up at Truity. "Please. I have to talk to him." She gripped the blanket on the cot until her knuckles turned white. "Please!"

"You're not going," replied Truity, sternly.

Blāzzer hung her head. "I have to tell him... I'm sorry about Lydia. I have to."

"I can take Blāzzer to him."

Blāzzer and Truity looked up. Naro stood just outside of the canopy. Darkness was under his eyes and there was a tenseness to his lips. He said, "I'll take her. I can carry her. She wouldn't have to walk."

Truity crossed her arms and replied, "You can carry her. Don't let her walk. We don't need her falling over. If she faints or vomits, bring her right back."

"Understood." Naro ducked under the canopy and carefully picked Blāzzer up with an arm under her legs and the other around her upper back. "You good?"

Blāzzer nodded.

Slowly Naro walked towards Raffel's tent, not jostling Blāzzer. He said, "I'm sorry about Lydia."

Blāzzer pressed her lips together.

"I know she meant a lot to you." Naro paused outside the tent. "You may not have been able to save her, but you will save others in the future." He ducked and pushed through the tent flaps.

Raffel was asleep on the cot. Naro gently put Blāzzer down and helped her sit on the edge of the cot. He quietly said, "I'll come by in a little bit to check on you."

"Thank you," breathed Blāzzer. She looked at the ground as Naro walked away. She jumped slightly as Raffel touched her back.

"Hey," whispered Raffel. She wrapped her arms around herself. "You okay?" He slowly sat up. "Blāzzer?"

"Lydia... I couldn't save her."

Raffel blinked and wrapped his arms around her, holding her close. "I know you did everything you could... I don't blame you. Neither does Mom or Dad... Lydia wanted to fight."

Blāzzer looked over her shoulder at him. Her sadness and grief were mirrored in his face. He laid back slowly and she nestled between his arm and chest. She rested her head on his shoulder and hand over his heart. His warmth helped her relax.

"I miss her already," whispered Blāzzer.

Raffel sighed, "Me too."

The lantern had burned out and early morning sunlight filtered through the tent walls. Blāzzer watched the dust motes float through the air. Slowly she sat up, trying to not disturb Raffel. She looked down at him and saw his peaceful face. She smiled softly before standing up and stepping out of the tent.

The stars overhead were winking out of existence as the sky brightened with the rising sun. Blāzzer blinked and looked about. Soldiers walked about calmly and healers tended to the wounded. She saw Naro standing at a nearby cook fire with a few other soldiers. She walked over to him and he held out a bowl of oatmeal.

"If you're going to be out of bed, you should eat," said Naro. Blāzzer took the bowl, staring at the tan mush that had pieces of dried fruit mixed in.

"The battle?" she asked. "There's no sounds of battle."

"Well, see for yourself."

Blāzzer turned and looked to the battlefield. The enemy army was deconstructing their camps and marching away. She opened her mouth to speak, but couldn't find the right words.

"We haven't won," explained Naro. "They're just retreating as of right now. Something must have happened for them to start packing in the night."

"What about the king?" questioned Blāzzer, looking up to Naro.

"No word yet. Let's get you back to the tent so you can eat. I'll grab a bowl for Raffel."

Blāzzer sat on a stool in the shade of the tent, looking out with the tent flaps tied back. Raffel sat on the cot as Truity changed his bandages. The healer said, "You'll need to take it easy, Raffel. Don't need you pulling your stitches."

"I'll do my best," replied Raffel.

"Good." Truity walked up to Blāzzer. "And how are you feeling?"

"My head is a little foggy," answered Blāzzer. "But I'm doing a lot better."

"Make sure you take it easy too. There is no need-"

Truity was cut short as Ash landed in front of the tents. He collapsed under his own weight. Truity and other healers rushed to him as he shifted. Blāzzer stood up and ran to him with Raffel close behind her. They knelt beside Ash as healers brought a stretcher.

"He's gone," gasped Ash, his face in anguish. "He wouldn't let me save him. I shouldn't have let her fight... They're both gone." The healers transferred him onto the stretcher and quickly took him away.

Blāzzer and Raffel looked at each other. She whispered, "Nayax?"

He looked to where his father was taken into a tent and replied, "I think so." She slowly stood and helped Raffel up. For a few minutes, they stood there not for sure what to do. She laced her fingers between his and squeezed his hand. He turned to lead them back to their tent when a horse rider rode into camp followed by an uleakite.

"Listen up!" shouted Shradur. Everyone looked at him. "King Nayax is dead. Before he passed he named Teredana, Captain of the Lemay Army, his heir. The enemy troops have surrendered. The battle is won!"

People smiled and clapped each other on the backs. Blāzzer blinked, unable to join their celebration. She walked over to Shradur as he dismounted his horse and questioned, "Why did they surrender?"

Shradur looked at her in surprise, replying, "The Snerxites never showed up. From what we've heard the nereids threatened to end all commercial trade with them if Snerx continued their support. So the traditionalists had no chance of winning a long drawn out battle." He sighed. "I'm sorry for your loss... both of you." He looked past Blāzzer's shoulder to Raffel, who had remained where he stood. "Lydia was an amazing person and she fought her hardest."

Blāzzer nodded slightly and turned away, walking to Raffel. She wrapped her arms around him and he held her tight. She listened to his steady heartbeat and felt his deep sorrow. She tried to swallow the lump in her throat and whispered, "Help me... Help me change Nickada and make it a better home for us."

Raffel squeezed her and, resting his cheek against the top of her hair, murmured, "I'll help you in whatever way I can. I promise."

The sun was setting and Blāzzer sat around a campfire with the Stone family. Everyone was quiet as they ate rice and chicken. The young woman glanced at Aurora who hadn't taken a bite for several minutes. She murmured, "What next?"

"Tomorrow those that died will be laid to rest," replied Ash, staring into the flames.

"They'll be buried here in Budsta?" asked Blāzzer.

"No, they'll be cremated," answered Cornin, stretching his legs. "Only Nayax's body will be brought back to Nickada to be put in the royal tomb."

"Lydia," breathed Aurora. She dropped her bowl as her hands began to tremble. Her rider got up and took her hand.

"Let's get you settled for tonight," he encouraged, smiling softly. He led her away to the tent she shared with Ash.

*How are you doing?* asked Blāzzer, looking at Raffel. He shrugged and placed his bowl down at his feet.

*Every part of me just aches,* he sighed. *I've never-*

"What are you doing here, elf?" questioned Ash, glaring past the young dragon and rider. Blāzzer looked over her shoulder to see Leggauto.

"Lord Legorin has requested Blāzzer to see him," explained the heir to the leader of the forest elves.

"There's no reason for him to speak with her," growled the elder dragon as he stood up.

"It's in regards to her staying with the Stone family."

Blāzzer blinked, her heart skipping a beat. Raffel stood up and stepped towards Leggauto, snarling, "Tell Legorin to mind his own business."

"As a ward of the Council, Blāzzer is his business," replied Leggauto calmly.

"I'll go," said Blāzzer quickly, feeling Raffel's aggression through the liffen. He turned and glared at her.

"No, you are not," he snapped, ears pinned back. She stood up and met his gaze.

*I'll be fine, Raffel,* she insisted. *You need to rest.* He stared at her as she stepped around him and walked over to Leggauto. "I'll follow you." The elf nodded and led her away.

*If anything happens,* growled Raffel, *then-*

*Trust me, please.* Blāzzer pressed her lips together, waiting for a response, but there was none.

The Nickadian camp was quiet except for the conversations around different campfires. The air became eerily silent as they entered the elven portion of the camp. Blāzzer could feel the elves watching and regarding her as she followed Leggauto through. They came to a large hexagon shaped tent and he held back the entrance flap. She stepped inside and froze.

Legorin sat at a table with Pe'dah while Caratin stood a few yards away. The leaders each had a glass of wine and looked at Blāzzer as she entered. The centaur's forearm was bandaged, and the elves showed no sign of wounds.

"I'm surprised the dragons let you come," said Legorin, leaning back in his chair.

"I don't need their permission," replied Blāzzer, holding her chin up. *Remember what Ash said, chin up and shoulders back.* Caratin scoffed. She regarded him a moment before focusing back on the forest elf. "Why did you call for me to come?"

"Of course, to check on your wellbeing," answered Legorin.

"As you can see I am whole. Anything else?"

"You should watch your tone before leaders," warned Caratin, stepping forward.

"I have two very angry dragons," said Blāzzer, "that don't need any additional reasons to cause violence against you right now, so I suggest not threatening me."

Pe'dah chuckled, "Your bravery is quite foolish." He sipped at his wine.

"How did you enter fatorana?" questioned Legorin. Blāzzer blinked, not for sure how to answer. "Numerous witnesses state that they saw you enter farorana on the battlefield. And you easily slaughtered two men, yet you have minimal swordsmanship."

"Raffel and I have been training, so it's no surprise that it occured," she replied, hoping they didn't see through her bluff.

Legorin's eyes narrowed. "Do it now."

"What?"

"Enter fatorana here, right now."

Blāzzer glanced at Pe'dah and Caratin, but neither of them seemed to be interested in intervening. She shook her head and said, "I can't. We haven't recovered enough yet."

Legorin tapped his fingernail against his glass, seemingly lost in thought. Pe'dah looked at him before saying, "Well, when you've recovered and upon our return to Nickada, we'll see if you can then." He waved his hand dismissively. Blāzzer pressed her lips together and turned to leave.

"On average," said Legorin, freezing her in her tracks, "fatorana takes over a year to be able to achieve. You've been a rider for less than six months." She forced herself to not tense, but her hands had closed into tight fists. "I wonder if it has to do with how close you are to Raffel. Apparently, you two are very affectionate towards each other for just being dragon and rider."

"What's your point?" questioned Blāzzer, unable to withhold sharpness from her voice.

Caratin grinned, saying, "It wouldn't look good for the ward of the Council to be intimately involved with a member of her host family."

*No! They can't!* screamed Blāzzer. She took a deep breath. "Is that all leaders? I would like to get some sleep before Lydia's funeral in the morning."

"Sleep well, little Blāzzer," said Legorin.

She quickly left and headed away from the leaders, not waiting for Leggauto to lead her back. She thought, *Shit! I can't - they wouldn't! The other leaders wouldn't allow it... right?* Her mind raced as she finally made it to the Stone family camp. Only one member sat at the small fire. He looked up and his red eyes glittered in the firelight.

"What happened?" questioned Raffel, standing up. Blāzzer wrapped her arms around herself, stopping a few feet away. "What did they say?"

"Nothing," she whispered. "Just checking to see if I was alright."

He narrowed his eyes. *Why are you lying?*

"They're just messing with my head." She wiped at her eyes, gulping down air. *They want to use us being together as a reason to take me away.*

Raffel's ears pinned back and he walked up to her, embracing her tightly to his chest. "They won't, I promise."

Blāzzer watched as wrapped bodies were carried between soldiers to numerous funeral pyres. She sat away from everyone on a hillside in shadow from the morning sun. Slowly torches were used to light the pyres and countless columns of smoke rose up into the air. A gentle breeze caught the ash, tugging it north. Blāzzer blinked, her eyes too dry to allow tears to fall. She looked down at the sketchbook she held in her lap.

*Lydia,* she whispered. *We're going to miss you... I'm going to miss you.* Blāzzer carefully opened the sketchbook, taking moments to look at each drawing and trying to absorb every detail. *You were never broken, never a burden. You were a dear friend to me. I'm sorry I couldn't save you. I'm sorry I couldn't tell you that I was there next to you in your last moments.* Blāzzer paused as she turned to a drawing of Ash and Aurora. They were holding hands and looked serene as they gazed into each other's eyes. *They are proud of you. I know they'll miss you and wish that you hadn't fought, but they're proud of you... we're all proud of you.*

The crunching of feet on dirt made Blāzzer look up to see Raffel walking towards her. He limped with each stride until he was at her side and sat down next to her. Stretching his injured leg, he said, "Tomorrow we leave Budsta."

Blāzzer nodded, continuing to look through Lydia's sketchbook.

"You doing okay?"

She nodded again, replying, *I was telling Lydia how proud we are of her... How she'll be missed and never was broken.*

Raffel pressed his lips together. *She'll be missed. I couldn't have asked for a better sister.* He took a deep breath. *I'm proud of her, and I wish I had told her that.*

Blāzzer looked up at him and took his hand, saying, *She knows.*

He smiled softly.

*Now it's our turn to make her proud, to make Nickada a better place.*

# PART SIX

## EPILOGUE

Blāzzer frowned at her reflection in the mirror as she turned from side to side. She looked over her shoulder at Mae who was in a knee-length green dress. Blāzzer muttered, "I'm not used to wearing dresses."

Mae grinned, replying, "You look beautiful!"

Blāzzer sighed, looking back at her reflection. The sleeveless dress was dark red with golden thread along the hems. It was tight around her torso and the front went up to and around her neck. The skirt was loose and flowed about her hips as she turned around. The back of the dress left her shoulders bare, leaving the liffen visible and stark against her skin.

"Come on, it's not every day a new king is crowned," insisted Mae. "What to do about your hair though?"

"My hair's fine," answered Blāzzer, walking to the window and looking out over Stiggress.

Flags and banners hung through the city in celebration of Teredana being crowned king. Countless people were walking through the streets, visiting vendors and merchants. Several ships were docked in the bay on water glittering with the sunlight.

There was a knock on the door and Mae opened it. Aurora, wearing a flowing purple dress, stepped in and said, "Both of you look very nice."

"Thank you," replied Mae with a smile.

Aurora walked over to Blāzzer and held out a hair comb, saying, "Here, I want you to have this."

Blāzzer blinked, picking up the gold comb. At the head of the comb was a small, ornate butterfly with opals as its wings. She breathed, "It's beautiful." She turned it slightly, watching the colors shift in the opals, and looked up to Aurora. "Thank you."

"It was Lydia's... She would have wanted you to have it."

Blāzzer pressed her lips together, feeling an ache in her chest.

"Let me help you with it." Aurora gently took the comb and Blāzzer turned around. The older woman skillfully pinned Blāzzer's hair back on one side. "There, you look beautiful." They hugged each other and Aurora kissed Blāzzer's forehead.

"Now, we should get going before the to-be king is crowned without us there," said Aurora, forcing a smile.

They walked out of the bedroom and Blāzzer looked about the Stone family's suite living room, asking, "Where'd the guys go?"

"They're going to meet us out there," replied Aurora, leading the way out of the suite and down the hall of the palace.

"Why? Were you hoping to show someone your dress?" teased Mae, hooking her arm around Blāzzer's.

Blāzzer blushed, muttering, "I just was wondering. Raffel had said that he'd wait." At Aurora's laughter, both young women looked to her and Mae raised an eyebrow.

"You two remind me of myself when I was dating Ash," explained Aurora.

As they walked Blāzzer thought, *What will he think when he sees me in a dress? This dress?!*

Soon they could hear talking and laughter echoing against the stone walls. Lemay soldiers stood stationed along the hall intermittently. Other people dressed in fine clothing were also walking the halls towards the throne room. Aurora, Blāzzer, and Mae walked through a double set of doors into a large room with a high ceiling. A stone-raised dais was on the far side of the long room with an empty throne. Many people, of all races, stood about the room talking.

"I thought I was going to be able to find them cause Gryphun's so tall," muttered Mae. "But there's so many elves and centaurs."

*Raffel,* called out Blāzzer.

*You here?* he asked.

"This way," said Aurora, beginning to weave through the crowd.

*You with Cornin?* asked Blāzzer, quickly following Aurora and grabbing

Mae's hand.

*Yeah and Dad and Gryphun,* answered Raffel.

Aurora, Mae, and Blāzzer moved through the crowd until they came to a less packed area by the wall. Blāzzer smiled when she saw Ash, Cornin, Gryphun, and Raffel. Each was dressed in brown pants, a loose-fitting shirt, and a jacket.

Mae ran up to Gryphun and, throwing her arms around his neck, kissed him on the cheek, saying, "You look so handsome!" Gryphun grinned and hugged her back.

Aurora stood next to Ash, taking his hand.

*You're beautiful,* said Raffel, looking at Blāzzer and making her blush.

She walked over to him, saying, *I feel awkward.*

*Me too.* They smiled at each other and she put her hand in the crook of his arm.

"I feel like a third wheel," grumbled Cornin.

"You have always been a good third wheel," said Ash, smirking and looking over the crowd.

"I was with Aurora before you were."

"And here we both are."

"I'm going to leave you two here by yourselves if you don't behave," warned Aurora, looking between Cornin and Ash. The two men glared at each other a moment before Cornin winked at Ash.

*Now I just feel awkward about that,* said Blāzzer, leaning her head against Raffel's shoulder. He chuckled.

A horn was blown and the crowd quieted. Lemay Soldiers walked into the room, parting the crowd to form an open aisle from the double doors to the throne. The leaders walked down the aisle one by one. Foxdur climbed the stairs of the stone dais and moved to the far left side of the dais. Meric followed, walking to the far right. Caratin was next and stood beside the uleakite. Durthuh walked up the steps and took his place next to Meric. Legorin walked across the dais, stopping beside Caratin. Pe'dah followed, but went to the right, standing next to Durthuh. Lastly, Shradur walked up the steps and took his place to the right of the throne. The space to the left of the throne remained empty. Teredana walked down the aisle with his head held high and stopped before the steps.

Shradur turned and picked up a crown from behind the throne. It was the same gold and silver crown that Nayax had worn. The leader of the Sentinel Crows stepped in front of Teredana and said, "Kneel." Teredana dropped to one knee and bowed his head. "Nickada lost a great king, who strived for the unity of his people. King Nayax was a brave man and will be remembered for his noble deeds. Without a son of his own, King Nayax on his deathbed named Captain Teredana of the Lemay Army his heir. Captain Teredana do you swear to protect the people of Nickada with all your strength? To protect all of her people as if they were your own children?"

"I do," answered Teredana, loud enough for all to hear.

Shradur gently placed the crown on his head and said, "Stand, King of Nickada." Slowly Teredana stood. Shradur took his place beside the throne and Teredana climbed the steps of the dais. The newly crowned king turned and faced his people.

The crowd cheered, "Long live the king!"


Blāzzer stood beside Raffel along the wall of the great hall. Musicians were playing a slow, sweet melody and people were dancing. All races, except for ruchos and uleakites, were present. Between Raffel and Blāzzer, hidden by their bodies, they held hands.

*Are you sure you don't want to dance?* asked Raffel, keeping his eyes on the crowd.

She shook her head, replying, *I do, but I'm too nervous about meeting with the Council tomorrow.* She resisted the urge to rest her head on his shoulder. *What if they see us together and decide for me to be removed?*

He squeezed her hand. *So let's go elsewhere to dance. I'll meet you out front in five minutes.*

Blāzzer watched him walk away, feeling the void he left behind. She looked up as a centaur walked towards her.

"I thought you two would be dancing together," said Naro, tipping his head slightly.

"Do you think the Council would separate us if they knew about us?" she asked.

"I don't think so. My father and the elves are the only real sticklers with the dragons. So as long as Durthuh and Shradur show up, you'd be safe."

She pressed her lips together, trying to calm the tightness in her chest.

"Don't let them stop you two from being together."

Blāzzer met Naro's eyes and asked, "Why are you so supportive of us?"

"Because it's time for Nickada to be united, and my gut tells me that you and Raffel will be crucial for that to occur."

She smiled softly. "One day we'll be sitting next to each other in the

Council's chamber, and I look forward to that day."

He grinned. "Same." He looked over his shoulder at the crowd. "I hope you two have a good night."

"Thank you."

Blāzzer slipped out of the great hall and walked down the steps to the main courtyard. The moonlight glittered on Raffel's scales where he laid before the stairs. No saddle covered his shoulders. He reached his head out to her as she got closer.

*You ready?* he asked.

She placed her hand between his nostrils, feeling his warm breath push away the chill of the night. She pulled her skirt up around her thighs before climbing onto his shoulders. A sigh escaped her lips at the gentle warmth of his scales on her bare skin. He watched her with one eye as she adjusted her skirt.

Blāzzer looked up and met his eye, saying, *Take me to the stars.*

Raffel growled with pleasure and quickly stood up. In one fluid motion, he launched into the sky. Blāzzer grinned as the air rushed past her with each powerful beat of his wings. She pressed her feet against his collar bone and squeezed tightly with her thighs.

The dragon leveled his flight and his rider sat upright, holding her arms outstretched. The wind pushed between her fingers and tugged at her hair. She tipped her head back and gazed at the stars overhead. Away from the city lights, they were bright and filled the sky. Blāzzer felt warmth emanate from her liffen and smiled as she met Raffel's eye.

*You look so content and happy,* he whispered.

*I have you to thank for that,* replied Blāzzer, rubbing her hands over his neck. He flopped his ears to the side in a smile before facing forward.

Slowly Raffel descended until he glided over the lake surface with a foreclaw trailing in the water. He gently landed on the shore, the city behind him. Once he crouched, Blāzzer slid to the ground. He shifted, placing a bag on the ground.

"Can you see okay?" questioned Raffel, pulling a small item from the bag.

"Yeah, it's beautiful," murmured Blāzzer, looking at the city, stars, and moon reflected in the lake. She blinked as a heartfelt melody started playing. She looked to Raffel, who was holding a small music box with elven engravings.

"I felt really bad when I said no to you in Palator when you asked me to dance," said Raffel, placing the music box by his bag.

"It's okay," assured Blāzzer, stepping towards him.

He shook his head. "It wasn't okay. I was a jerk." He took a deep breath. "You had just told me that no guy had ever shown interest in you... and I was and I still said no." He rubbed the back of his neck before meeting her eyes. Starlight glittered in the swirls of red in his eyes. He stepped up to her and took her hands in his. "I would pursue you across the world and back."

Blāzzer's throat tightened and her heart swelled. She felt tears prickle her eyes. She stood on her toes and kissed his lips. "I would follow you across the world and back."

Raffel gently wiped away a tear on her cheek with his thumb. Carefully, he put a hand around her waist and led them in a slow waltz alongside the melodic music. She rested her hand on his shoulder, feeling the cool patch of skin through his shirt that mirrored her liffen.

Minutes passed slowly as the music continued to play. When it began to slow, Blāzzer put both her arms around Raffel's neck and rested her head against his chest. He wrapped both his arms around her waist, placing his cheek on her hair.

"I know we have a lot ahead of us," he said, "but I'm really glad we're in this together."

Blāzzer smiled and tilted her head back so she could look into his eyes, asking, "If someone told you when we first met that you'd be dating me, what would you say?"

Raffel shrugged.

*Be honest.*

"Probably wouldn't believe them."

"Why?"

"Would you believe them, if they told you?"

"Hmmm, no, but I'd be excited." She grinned. "Who wouldn't want a dragon boyfriend?"

Raffel laughed. "So you're only into me for my dragon body?"

Blāzzer blushed, remembering when she saw him train shirtless. She shared the memory with him through the liffen. "I like this on a lot too." He rested his forehead against hers. She blinked as he showed her what she looked like in the dress through his eyes.

"You are so beautiful that words can't describe how I feel about you," said Raffel quietly. "After you are free and ready, I want to marry you."

"I'd really like that," breathed Blāzzer, feeling her heart pound in her chest. He kissed her lips, tightening his arms around her. She pushed her fingers into his hair, returning his kiss. "I love you, Raffel."

"I love you too, Blāzzer."

The following morning, Blāzzer walked down the hall with Raffel at her side, holding each other's hand. She felt nervous, thinking, *What does the Council want? They aren't going to go back on their vote from before, are they?*

"Hey," said Raffel, squeezing Blāzzer's hand. She looked up at him. "Don't get lost in your head. It'll be okay." She nodded.

They continued to walk down the halls until they came to a set of double doors where Lemay soldiers stood guard. Raffel squeezed her hand and she smiled softly. Letting go of his hand she walked to the soldiers. They opened the doors and Blāzzer stepped inside the chamber. The leaders sat in a half-circle with Teredana in the middle. She walked till she was in the center of the half-circle.

"Blāzzer, the Council has been discussing you're situation," said Teredana. She did her best to keep her face neutral. "We have decided that you are no longer a ward of the Council. You are now free to choose what you do and where you live."

Blāzzer blinked in shock and took a deep breath, trying to keep her composure.

"Of course, we'll be checking in on you," added Legorin.

"In two years," clarified Shradur.

Blāzzer nodded slightly.

"Unless there is something you want to add, Blāzzer, then you are free to go," said Teredana.

"Thank you," replied Blāzzer, holding her arms rigidly by her sides. She turned to leave, but paused and looked at the Council. "In three years I will be here, but as Leader of the Dragons."

Shradur smiled, Legorin frowned, and Caratin scowled. Blāzzer turned and, as the Lemay soldiers opened the doors, walked out of the Council chamber. Raffel stepped forward in question. Her suppressed grin came out in a fit of giggles. She threw her arms around him and laughed, "I'm free!"

A soft breeze rustled the green grass outside of Palator. Small yellow, white, and purple wildflowers speckled the hillside. The summer sun overhead was warm with fluffy clouds lazily floating across the blue sky. Blāzzer walked between the stone gravestones. She felt nervous and held the bouquet of lavender close to her chest. At first the stones she past were worn with moss growing on them. The stones slowly became less worn until they were smooth as if shaped within the last few months. Blāzzer knelt before a stone, reading the engraving:

*Angel Kinsela*
*A Gardener of Souls that Nurtured All*

"Hey, Angel," breathed Blāzzer, feeling tears brim in her eyes. "I'm back... I'm sorry it took me so long to come back. It's been kind of crazy." She placed the flowers at the foot of the gravestone. "I've learned a lot and seen a lot. I learned who my parents were, but you still feel like my mother... I'm going to move to Keeko with the Stone family, with Raffel - we're dating now. He's going to help me build a garden there. Then I'll be able to use what you taught me." She ran her fingers over the engravings on the stone. "I won't forget you, and I'll come visit whenever I can. For now though I have something I need to do... I'm going to become the Leader of the Dragons and make Nickada a better home." Slowly she stood up, brushing off the grass that clung to her knees. "I'm really glad that I got to spend those months with you. I couldn't have asked for a better mother."

Blāzzer wiped the tears from her eyes with the back of her hand before turning and walking back between the stones. She sighed at the feeling of a weight being lifted. She looked ahead and saw Raffel standing there watching the clouds pass overhead. His red hair caught in the breeze. She walked to his side and laced her fingers between his. He looked down at her and smiled softly.

She said, "Let's go home."

# Part Seven

## Appendices

## *Appendix 1. Name Guide*

AncientTime: One of thirteen household spirits of the farnircks. Those that have her as their personal household spirit wear a clothing item of the color brown. She is the spirit of knowledge and wisdom. Item of choice for an offering is sand.

Angel Kinsela: Middle-aged, mortal female living in Palator. Married to Xavier (deceased), son is Lenny, brother is Gorvi, and adopted daughter is Mae.

Argon One-Eye: Middle-aged, mortal male living in Gilzar and member of the Sentinel Crows. Has a large scar on his cheek.

Ash Stone: Elder, blackish red, male dragon living in Keeko. Married to Aurora Stone and children are Lydia and Raffel. Breathes fire.

Aurora Stone: Middled-aged, purplish blue, female dragon living in Keeko. Married to Ash Stone, bonded to Cornin, and children are Lydia and Raffel. Breathes ice.

Blāzzer Ozol (blazer oh-zool): Female ward of the Shadow Council and living in Maro.

BrokenDream: One of thirteen household spirits of the farnircks. Those that have him as their personal household spirit wear a clothing item of the color maroon. He is the spirit of orphans and widows/widowers. Item of choice for an offering is flowers.

Budsta (bud-stuh): Country to the south of Nickada with thirteen tribes and one tribe leader voted as Lord of the Tribes. Capital Du Vent. People called Budstarians.

Caratin (care-uh-tin): Middle-aged, centaur male and leader of the centaurs in Nickada. Son is Naro.

Centaur: Race of Nickada that has the upper body of a human and below the waist looks like a horse.

Chamdal (cham-dale): City in central Nickada. Primary resident forest elves.

Cornin (core-nin): Middle-aged, mortal, male living in Keeko and bonded to Aurora Stone. Member of the Sentinel Crows. Liffen forms a large, horizontal scar across his stomach.

DarkNeedle: One of thirteen household spirits of the farnircks. Those that have him as their personal household spirit wear a clothing item of the color pine green. He is the spirit of unseen guardians and warriors. Item of choice for an offering is ore.

DirtHound: One of thirteen household spirits of the farnircks. Those that have him as their personal household spirit wear a clothing item of the color gold. He is the spirit of trackers and hunters. Item of choice for an offering is bones.

Dragon: Race of Nickada that looks like mortals except for moveable jagged ears, an extra pair of ribs, and ears and eyes of a variety of colors. At puberty, they are able to change shape into their namesake reptilian form. Their hair and eye colors match their scale color. They can breathe fire or ice.

Draig (dray-g): Country to the far south of Nickada. They have been waging war repeatedly against Traig due to differences in views on dragons. Draig views dragons as demons. The primary language is Drakken. People are called Draigites.

Drakken (drack-in): Language of the dragons.

Du Vent: Captial of the country Budsta and located in the east.

EbonyShadow: One of thirteen household spirits of the farnircks. Those that have her as their personal household spirit wear a clothing item of the color black. She is the spirit of loners and hermits. Item of choice for an offering is seashells.

Endar (end-are): The internal energy source that allows dragons to shift and breathe fire/ice. It is the Drakken word for ember or internal heart.

Farnirck (far-nirk): Race of Nickada that looks like mortals except for gray skin and red eyes. Persecuted throughout history by other races and countries.

Fatorana (phat-tore-on-uh): A heightened state that a dragon and rider can enter when bonded long enough. The heightened state includes increases senses, strength, and agility. In this state the rider's hair and eye color match that of the dragons. Nails thicken and small horns protrude from the head. During this state the line between dragon and rider's individual minds tends to blur.

Flame: One of four swords belonging to the Fire Compass. The blade is made of korsteel and the hilt designed to look like a dragon. Etched into the blade is the inscription, "To the north a Flame burns".

Forest Elf: Race of Nickada that look like humans, except for pointed ears and high cheekbones. Compared to their mountain counterpart, forest elves have pale skin with light hair and tend to be very slender.

Foxdur (fox-dure): Middle-aged, golden red, uleakite female living in Wildwood Forest and leader of the uleakites.

Gilzar (gill-zar): Town in the southwest central area of Nickada. In the middle of dry, rocky plains and headquarters for the Sentinel Crows.

Gorvi (gore-vee): Middle-aged, mortal, male living in Palator. Sister is Angel, brother-in-law is Xavier (deceased), nephew is Lenny, and adoptive niece is Mae. Captain of the Palator guard.

Grimsbrothren (grims-broth-ren): Elder, brownish green, male dragon living in Minda Mountains. Son is Gryphun. Breathes fire. Member of the Sentinel Crows.

Gryphun (gry-fun): Teenage, purplish green, male dragon living in Gilzar. Father is Grimsbrothren. Trainee of the Sentinel Crows. Breathes fire. Dating Mae.

HumbleStride: One of thirteen household spirits of the farnircks. Those that have her as their personal household spirit wear a clothing item of the color pink. SHe is the spirit of teachers and counselors. Item of choice for an offering is mirror fragments.

Inks: Middle-aged, mortal male living in Gilzar and member of the Sentinel Crows and their Council.

Inuwa (in-oo-wa): Language of the Shadow People and Shadowfaire.

Keeko (key-co): Town in the southwest part of Wildwood Forest. One of three towns that farnircks reside in. Stone family resides here.

KindredHearth: One of thirteen household spirits of the farnircks. Those that have her as their personal household spirit wear a clothing item of the color orange. She is the spirit of grandparents and other extended family members. Item of choice for an offering is food items.

Korsteel (core-steel): A unique metal that is very difficult to forge. It is notable due to the red swirls in the silver metal. The metal uniquely absorbs dragons' endars and shadow people's mirazhs.

Leggauto: Young, male elf living in Chamdal and heir to the leader of the forest elves. Father is Legorin.

Legorin (leg-or-in): Elder, male elf living in Chamdal and leader of the forest elves. Son is Leggauto.

Lemay Army: King of Nickada's personal army.

Lenny: Nine-year-old, mortal male living in Palator. Mother is Angel, father is

Xavier (deceased), uncle is Gorvi, and adopted sister is Mae.

LightRock: One of thirteen household spirits of the farnircks. Those that have her as their personal household spirit wear a clothing item of the color white. She is the spirit of healers and caretakers. Item of choice for an offering is pieces of quartz.

Liffen (lif-in): The bond between a dragon and their rider. Also refers to the mark on the rider's body from gaining a portion of a dragon's endar.

Lydia Stone: Twenty-four-year-old, reddish blue, female dragon living in Keeko. Brother is Raffel and parents are Ash and Aurora. Breathes ice and has seizures.

Mae (may): Sixteen-year-old, greenish-white, female dragon living in Palator. Adoptive mother is Angel, adoptive father is Xavier (deceased), adoptive uncle is Gorvi, and adoptive brother is Lenny. Dating Gryphun.

Maro (marrow): City in central west Nickada.

Meric (mayor-ick): Middle-aged, albino, male rucho living in Wildwood Forest and leader of the ruchos.

Mirazh (mer-oz-uh): A black energy that all people of Shadowfaire have, though to varying amounts. The energy cannot enter other bodies, but can stop a blade. At all times it must have a tether to the user.

Mountain Elf: Race of Nickada that look like humans, except for pointed ears and high cheekbones. Compared to their forest counterpart, mountain elves have dark skin and hair and tend to be rather stocky.

Naro (narrow): Young, male centaur and heir to the leader of the centaurs in Nickada. Father is Caratin

Nayax (nay-ax): Middle-aged, mortal, male living in Stiggress. King of Nickada.

Nereid (nare-E-id): Race of Nickada and surrounding waters. They look like a human from the waist up, except for their long ears. From the waist down they have the hind legs of a horse and a long tail with a fin. The lower half of their body is covered in thick fish scales.

Nickada (nick-uh-duh): Country with a monarchy and a ruling council made of representatives of different races. Capital Stiggress and king Nayax. People called Nickadians.

Palator (pal-uh-tore): Town in central west Nickada focused on horticulture.

Pe'dah (pee-ed-uh): Middle-aged, male mountain elf living in Crystil and leader of the mountain elves.

Raffel Stone (raf-fell): Twenty-two-year-old, red, male dragon living in Palator. Sister is Lydia and parents are Ash and Aurora. Breathes fire.

RoaringSpring: One of thirteen household spirits of the farnircks. Those that have him as their personal household spirit wear a clothing item of the color purple. He is the spirit of singers and artists. Item of choice for an offering is artwork or writing.

Rucho (ruch-oh): Race of Nickada that looks like large elk. Capable of human speech.

Shadow People: Race of human found in Shadowfaire. They look human except that their eyes can be any color. They all have a mirzah.

Sentinel Crow: An elite organization of warriors that were founded at Nickada's birth. Any person of Nickada may join their ranks, and forfeit any ties to their race.

Shadowfaire (shadow-fair): Country to the north of Nickada. The primary race is shadow people and primary language is Inuwa. People called Shadowfairites.

Shinda (shin-duh): Town in southwest Nickada. One of three towns that farnircks reside in.

Shradur Shadow (sh-ray-dure): Older, shadow person, male living in Gilzar and leader of the Sentinel Crows.

SilentMeadow: One of thirteen household spirits of the farnircks. Those that have him as their personal household spirit wear a clothing item of the color red. He is the spirit of scouts and frontline soldiers. Item of choice for an offering is arrowheads and metal shards.

Snerx (sn-erk): Country with a monarchy. Northwest of Nickada. Capital Varen. People called Snerxites.

Stiggress (stig-gress): Captial of the country Nickada and located in the southwest.

SwiftWind: One of thirteen household spirits of the farnircks. Those that have her as their personal household spirit wear a clothing item of the color lavender. She is the spirit of horse riders and archers. Item of choice for an offering is feathers and horseshoes.

Teredana (ter-dan-uh): Middle-aged, mortal, male living in Stiggress. Captain of the Lemay Army.

Tetricus (tetri-cus): Young, barrun, male who has been missing since the age of fifteen years.

Thornsten Fire (thorn-sten): Middle-aged, half-blood, male living in Gilzar and member of the Sentinel Crows. He is the head blacksmith and is a member of the Shadow Council.

Traig (tray-g): Country to the south of Nickada. They have been waging war repeatedly against Draig due to differences in views on dragons. Traig views dragons as angels. Primary language is Drakken. People are called Traigans.

Truity Heart (true-it-ee): Middle-aged, mortal, female living in Gilzar and member of the Sentinel Crows.

Tsunami: Middle-aged, bluish-white, male dragon living on Whale Island. Bonded to Ecorda.

Uleakite (you'll-eh-kite): Race of Nickada that look like large wolves. Capable of human speech.

WildFalcon: One of thirteen household spirits of the farnircks. Those that have her as their personal household spirit wear a clothing item of the color sky blue. She is the spirit of craftsmen and tradesmen. Item of choice for an offering is worked wood or metal.

Wildwood Forest: A large forest in the middle of Nickada. The forest is home to several of the Nickadian races, including mountain and forest elves, uleakites, and ruchos.

WitheringCloud: One of thirteen household spirits of the farnircks. Those that have him as their personal household spirit wear a clothing item of the color yellow. He is the spirit of elderly, wounded, disabled, and diseased. Item of choice for an offering is withered plants.

*Appendix 2. Map*

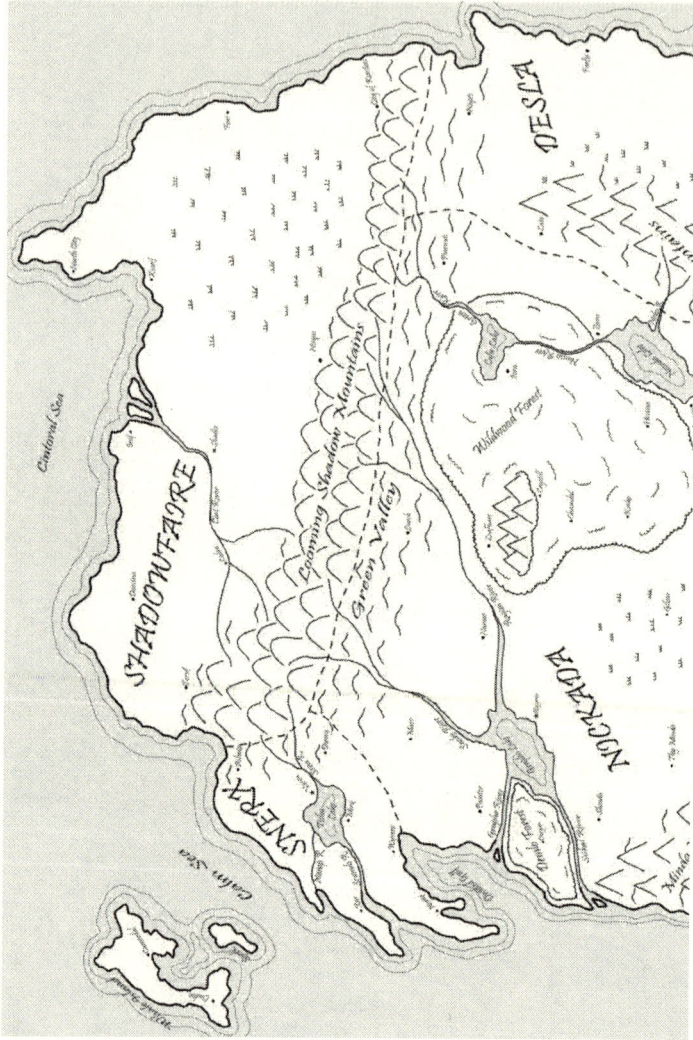

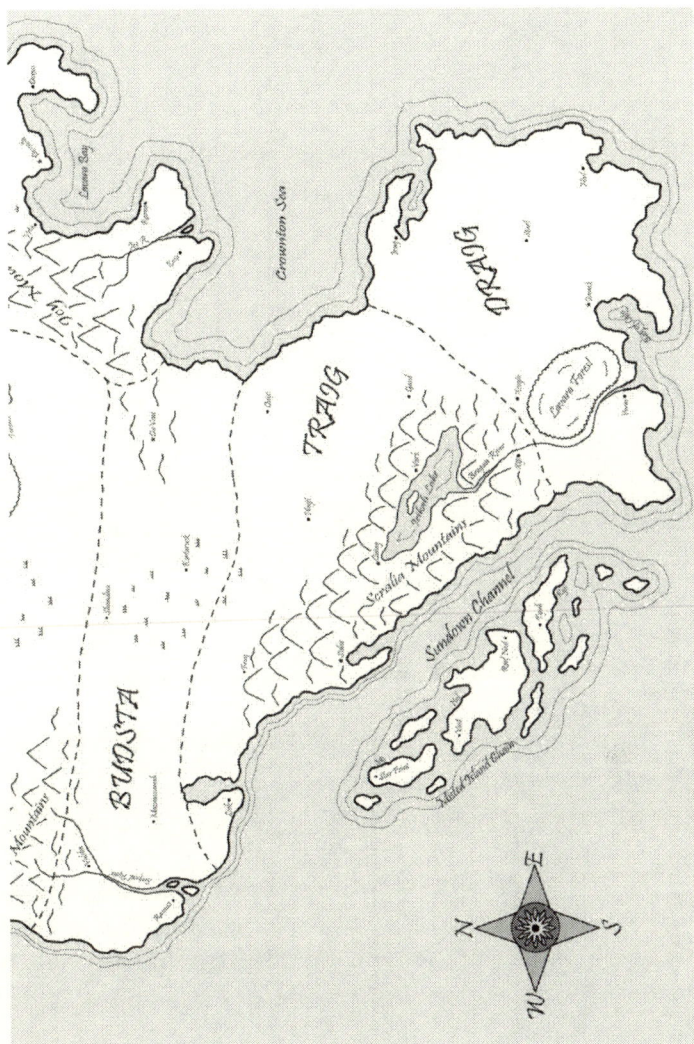

# Appendix 3. Dragon Anatomy

The dragons in the Stories of Nickada have some unique qualities about them compared to the other races. Simply put, they are humans that can shape change into flying, reptilian, beasts. This ability only becomes present during puberty when their endars, an internal energy source located beneath the sternum, begins to increase in strength. As their human body grows, so does their dragon body. Typically the human body is fully grown between 18 and 20 years old where the dragon body can continue growing until they are 25 years old. Dragons can live to 150 years, outliving most other races.

As a human dragons have rather large ears that are mobile, allowing them to express emotions. An extra pair of ribs increases the size of their chest cavity for their enlarged lungs. They are missing a pair of upper incisors, which are switched out for a secondary pair of canines. Female dragons have a three month menstrual cycle. When pregnant they are unable to shift due to the dragon forms lacking genitalia. This is typically the first indicator for a pregnancy. A dragons gestational period is the same as a humans at nine months.

The coloration of a dragon's scales is matching to their human's form hair and eye color. Whenever the coloration is described, the secondary color is written before the primary. For example, Ash is blackish red, meaning he has primarily red scales with some black ones. Dragons typically only have two horns between their ears though some can have an extra set

Below is a diagram of size comparison for the dragons in Nickada.

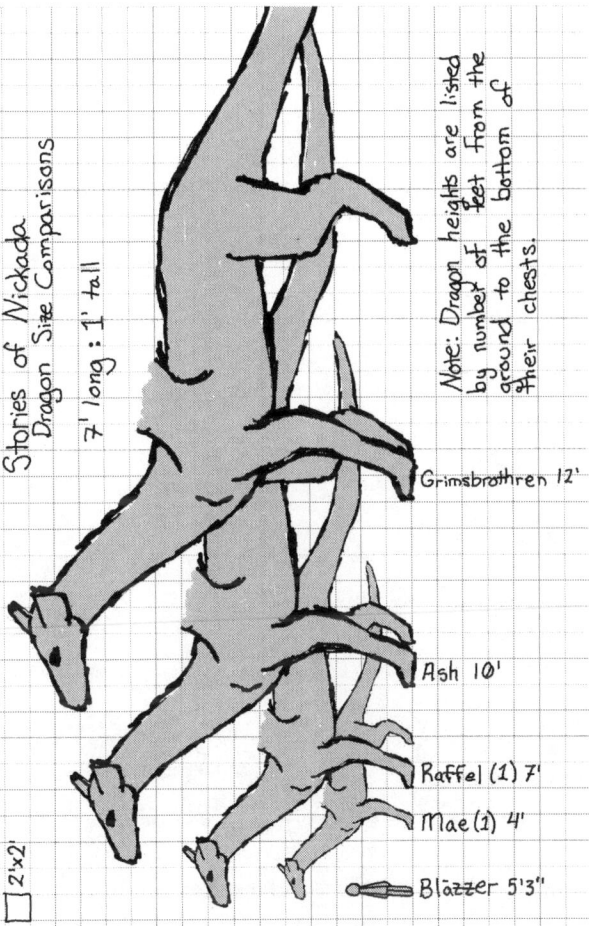

Stories of Nickada
Dragon Size Comparisons
7' long : 1' tall

Note: Dragon heights are listed by number of feet from the ground to the bottom of their chests.

Grimsbrothren 12'

Ash 10'

Raffel (1) 7'

Mae (1) 4'

Blazzer 5'3"

2'x2'

## Appendix 4. Author's Note

Hello Reader,

Thank you for reading the first book in the Stories of Nickada series. It's been a dream to publish this story since I was in fifth grade. Took a while to get to the point of publication, but the journey has helped the story mature and develop into something I am very proud of.

My love for dragons started in second grade when I read *Dragon Rider* by Cornelia Funke. It was then that I created Blāzzer and Raffel (though he had a different name). In fifth grade, I read *The Hobbit* by JRR Tolkien and *Eragon* by Christopher Paolini. These two books inspired me to write my own.

As Nickada developed in my imagination, it became a safe haven for me from the world. I hope that for others that are looking for a book to escape reality, that this story can ease your stress and anxiety.

Below are some fun/interesting facts about the Stories of Nickada:

1. Raffel's original name was Ruby Fire, Ash's was Ash Flame, Aurora was Icy Wind, and Lydia's Winter Blossom.

2. Raffel originally had four sisters.

3. Dragons couldn't shift into humans until the development of the second book in the series.

4. Blāzzer's name has two Zs because I'm too stubborn to change it to the singular Z and have added the proper notation for pronunciation.

5. Blāzzer was originally supposed to be sixteen years old at the beginning of the series.

6. In total, I hand-wrote six books within the Stories of Nickada series, but there are more tales I would like to add in other books.

7. Originally there was a magic system in the world of Nickada, but this was quickly scrapped. The dragons are the closest to magical beings with the

ability to shapeshift.

8. The world maps are not computer-generated designs. It is all hand-created and painted with watercolor paints.

9. Blāzzer was originally the child of Blazen (first Leader of the Dragons), not Tetricus.

10. My favorite group of people in Nickada is the farnircks due to their extensive culture.

11. Cornin and Raffel are late for training in Chamdal, because Raffel was purchasing the music box seen in the epilogue.

I'm excited to continue to share the Stories of Nickada books with you.

Sincerely

Emily Boyd

## Appendix 5. Perseverence

Blāzzer blinked open her eyes at the early morning light peeking through her curtains. She moaned and pulled the blanket over her head. *She thought, Why can't I just sleep the days away until you're back?* With a huff, she sat up and looked about the bedroom.

It was a small room with a single wardrobe and bookcase. A sliding door led to the washroom and another door led to the living room. Blāzzer looked down at the empty space in the bed beside her thinking, *I don't like waking up without you here. It feels like I'm back to before.* She got up and dressed before looking at her reflection in the mirror. She quickly grabbed a brush from the nightstand and combed out the tangles in her hair. *It's been three years since we became rider and dragon. I didn't think then that these years would be spent mostly apart.* She sighed, looking down at a sketch secured to the bottom of the mirror. The drawing was detailed but somewhat faded. It showed Blāzzer and Raffel sitting back to back.

"Just another week and a half," she muttered, placing the brush down.

Blāzzer walked into the living room. A corner of the room was a kitchen with a small iron stove. The rest of the space was filled with a table, four chairs, and a couch. She grabbed a slice of bread and smeared jelly on it before sitting at the table. As she slowly ate she looked over the numerous papers and open book, thinking, *Right... leader proposal to Teredana in three months.* She rubbed her cheek. *I've rewritten this thing so many times that all the lines blur together.* She sighed and looked up at the empty vase at the end of the table.

"If you weren't in Minda Mountains training then you'd bring me flowers," murmured Blāzzer. "Even if they were from the garden." She got up and, grabbing the vase, walked outside.

In front of the house was a large garden with a simple wood fence around it. In a corner of the garden was a shed and firewood stack. There was a five-yard area around the outside of the garden where there were no trees or bushes. Beyond that were the trees of Wildwood Forest and through them, the town of Keeko could barely be seen. Blāzzer walked along a small dirt path between the budding flowerbeds and growing vegetable and fruit plants. She placed the vase under the water pump near the shed and filled it. Using a dagger, she cut different flowers and placed them in the vase one by one. When she stood up, holding the vase, she saw a man walking from Keeko to her house.

"Morning," called Cornin with a grin.

Blāzzer waved before turning and walking back into the house, leaving the front door open. She placed the vase on the table and sat in front of the papers again.

"How's the writing been going?" asked Cornin, walking in. He closed the door behind him and sat across the table from her.

"I think at this point I'm going in circles," grumbled Blāzzer, gathering her polished writing in one stack. "I keep trying to think if there are any other key points I'm missing."

"Well, from what I saw last time it looked like you had everything." Cornin leaned back in the chair with a yawn. "Mind if I make some coffee?"

"Help yourself."

He got up and walked to the kitchen, saying, "You mentioned finances, internal political standing, lack of dragons and riders, other country politics, and a bunch of other important things."

"But?" questioned Blāzzer, turning so she could face him.

"But the only downside you have is lack of experience," replied Cornin, placing a kettle on the stove before working on lighting it. "You haven't been in any battles besides Budsta. You haven't worked on any international affairs... Basically, you're just young." He leaned against the counter, meeting her eyes.

"I know. I'm just hoping that Teredana can put those facts aside." Blāzzer looked back down at her papers.

Cornin nodded. "I think he will. Luckily, it's up to him and not the Council, but he still has to hear their advice on the decision. You just got to impress him enough that no matter what some of the leaders say he'll accept you as Leader of the Dragons."

A few minutes of silence passed before Cornin asked, "Has it gotten rougher without Raffel here?"

"Yeah," breathed Blāzzer, looking out the window at her garden. "His training trips have gotten longer and his home visits shorter. In three years we've only been together for a total of eight months. I don't want to sound whiny, but it just sucks. I know his training is important."

"No, it does suck and you aren't being whiny. Raffel's training should all be over soon. He's gotten a lot stronger through this and will have the skills needed for battle."

Blāzzer nodded. Cornin turned and took the kettle off the stove. He made a mug of coffee before sitting at the table and saying, "I'm guessing you two are still unable to enter fatorana."

She pressed her lips together, thinking, *We can't enter fatorana and we can't even be that intimate. The liffen overloads and we just faint.*

"As close as you two are I was hoping it wouldn't be a struggle," muttered Cornin, looking down at his coffee. "It took Aurora and I a few years to be able to be in fatorana on command."

"How were you able to get to that point?" asked Blāzzer.

He sipped at his coffee. "Honestly, we just had enough adventures together that gave rise to extreme emotions. Those emotions then draw out fatorana. We just had to learn how to coax it without getting all worked up. You were able to do it in Budsta, so you should be able to do it now."

"Yeah," sighed Blāzzer. "I'm hoping that once Raffel is back permanently then we can figure it out."

"I'm for sure you two will. No worries there."

"Except that we have that going against us with the proposal."

Cornin shrugged. "Why don't we take a look at it and see what we can do to encourage Teredana to not be concerned?"

Blāzzer nodded and began to read her proposal out loud.

The next morning Blāzzer sat out in her garden pulling weeds. She worked carefully, making sure to not pull any wanted sprouts. The sun was just over the treetops, letting light fill the garden. Birds and squirrels chattered as they moved between the branches. She looked up at approaching footsteps. A man with gray skin was walking towards the house. He carried a satchel at his side and an envelope in his hand.

"Hello," said Blāzzer, standing up and walking to the entrance of the garden.

"Morning," replied the farnirck. "I have a letter here for Blāzzer."

"That's me."

He handed her the envelope before saying, "Have a good day."

"You too." She watched him walk away for a moment, feeling her heart pound against her chest. She looked at the address and smiled at Raffel's handwriting. She quickly went to the bench under the shed eve and sat down. She opened it and blinked at the two pages, thinking, *He normally only writes one. Something happen?* Blāzzer glanced at the two papers and saw that each was its own letter. One read 'Read First' along the top. She pressed her lips together and slowly read:

*Blāzzer*

*I hope you're doing good and not stressing too much... I'll go ahead and get to the bad news. Though I hope it can be seen as good news, but I know you'll be upset. Grimsbrothren and Dad think I'm almost done with my training like just need a bit more time. So I've decided that I'm going to stay in Minda Mountains a bit longer. I'm sorry. Hopefully, it won't be too much longer, but more likely between a month or two. After that, though I won't need to come back out this way, which would be really nice. I hate the feeling I get when I leave you...*

*So I'll see you soon, just not as soon as we originally planned. I love you.*

*Raffel*

Blāzzer felt tears of frustration brim her eyes as she gripped the papers tighter. She got up and walked quickly into the house, thinking, *I know this is only a small setback, but... why?!* She sat on her bed, pulling her knees to her chest and placing the letters in front of her. *I held onto those dates that you were to come back. You were five days away from returning and now it's farther away.* A painful heat came from her right shoulder. Blāzzer gritted her teeth at it and forced herself to breathe evenly. She thought, *I can't do this alone. I need you here with me. This proposal to Teredana is so daunting. What if I can't do it? What if I'm not meant to be the Leader of the Dragons?* She winced as the pain flared again and her vision blurred. *Breathe!*

For several minutes she focused on her breathing and nothing else. Slowly the pain subsided, but there was still a dull warmth from the liffen on her shoulder. Blāzzer reached under her shirt and rubbed her shoulder, moving the second letter towards her and reading it:

*Blāzzer*

*I really am ready to come home. My muscles are so sore every day. Gryphun drives me up a wall a lot too. He keeps wanting to take a day off and go on an outing. Whether that be going swimming or out to Thy Minda. Also, he's way too nosy about you and me... I thought having him out here for training was going to be nice... and it kind of has been, but he's not you. God, I miss you.*

*You'd like it out here. The mountains are pretty and there are a ton of flowers in the meadow. Hummingbirds and butterflies too. The sea isn't far and the beach is full of*

*seashells. I promise that one day I'll take you out here. We'll spend the whole time together.*
*Just you and me... And maybe then I could propose... I know you want to wait until you're*
*Leader of the Dragons so we'll go there in celebration. How does that sound?*

*No matter what, when I get back we'll do something special. Just you and me. So try*
*not to get too worked up. I know you don't like it when plans change, but this will be the*
*last of my training. Make sure to take care of yourself and not just sitting there and staring*
*at your writing. I'll be back as soon as I can.*

*I love you, beautiful.*

*Raffel*

Blāzzer laid back holding the letter to her chest and smiling softly. She
whispered, "I love you too, handsome."


It was warm in the shed even with the door and window propped open.
Blāzzer sat on a stool in front of Raffel's saddle. She rubbed a cleaning lotion
into the leather of the saddle with a cloth, thinking, *I can't believe how much dust*
*gets on this.* She looked over the saddle and saw her flight harness hanging on
the wall. *That'll need to be cleaned too.* As she worked she checked the straps and
buckles.

"You look like you're keeping yourself busy," said a voice.

Blāzzer looked up at the open door and smiled, saying, "Naro, what are
you doing out this way?"

The centaur grinned. "I'm just running some errands out this way for my
father, so I thought I'd stop by."

"It's good to see you. How have you been?"

Naro shrugged, replying, "Alright. I've begun work on becoming Leader of
the Centaurs."

"Really? I'm so happy for you." Blāzzer placed the cloth over the saddle and
walked out of the shed. Naro followed her around the side to the bench she sat
at. Carefully, minding the plants, he lowered himself till his lower half was
laying down.

"You have enough support from the other centaurs now?" asked Blāzzer.

"More than Caratin," answered Naro, crossing his arms. "Just got to start
work on the proposal to Teredana. How's that been going for you?"

"I feel like I've done all I can to prepare." Blāzzer leaned back against the
shed wall and looked up at the clouds. "I just have to wait and see."

"I think you'll be accepted. Teredana would be doing wrong to Nickada if
he turned you away... My father and Legorin aren't happy about it."

"Yeah, I kind of guessed that. What about Pe'dah? He tends to follow along with them."

"Don't know. Haven't heard much about him of late."

Blāzzer nodded. "My only concern is that Teredana will say no, because Raffel and I can't enter fatorana."

Naro snorted and said, "You can too. I saw you do it back in Budsta."

"Except since then I haven't been able to and Raffel not once."

Naro tapped his arm in thought.

"We'll figure it out," muttered Blāzzer. "Just have to wait for Raffel to get back."

"Remind me again why you two are training independently," mumbled Naro.

"I needed to focus on studies in history and politics along with sword fighting. Raffel though needed to get stronger in flying and fighting as a dragon. Also to work on strengthening his endar. A forest isn't the best place for draining that with breathing fire. Grimsbrothren also refused to leave Minda Mountains to assist with training. Except there's no city in the mountains so I wouldn't have access to any books."

"So training separately was the only option?"

Blāzzer nodded solemnly.

"Well if how you two were in the battle camp in Budsta is still true," said Naro, "then I think you two will figure it pretty quickly."

She blushed slightly and looked away. After a moment she asked, "Would you like to stay for lunch? I need some help with a few chores around here. Since Raffel isn't getting back as soon, I'd greatly appreciate the help."

"Of course. What do you want me to start on while you make lunch?"

"Splitting firewood."


Gray clouds filled the sky overhead as Blāzzer walked along the dirt path away from her house, thinking, *Hopefully Raffel doesn't get caught up in this rain.* Soon Keeko could be seen through the trees. The buildings, filling the sprawling town, were made of wood and plaster. None of the buildings were right next to each other, allowing the trees to grow in between. Farnircks walked about, many of them working. They smiled and nodded as Blāzzer passed. She returned the warm greeting to each one. She headed north along the main road.

At the end of the road was a small fortress, poking above the trees. It was dilapidated with part of its roof missing and holes in the wall. Blāzzer turned down a side road and to a house with a flowerbed out front. She knocked on the door and waited.

After a moment the door opened and Aurora stood there, smiling, "You're here. I was hoping you'd make it before the rain. Come on in."

Blāzzer followed the older woman into the house, asking, "Have you heard from Ash since they told us about their delay?"

Aurora shook her head, leading Blāzzer into a small sitting room that had open glass doors. Beyond was a well-tended garden with high stone walls. Blāzzer and Aurora sat down in cushioned chairs opposite each other.

"How have you been?" questioned Aurora, leaning forward and pouring ice tea from a pitcher into two glasses.

"I've been okay," replied Blāzzer, taking her boots off before sitting cross-legged in the chair. "I'm just ready for Raffel to be home."

Aurora nodded solemnly, sitting back with her glass of tea.

"A part of my mind pesters me that they should have been back by now, but I know that Raffel needs to finish his training."

"Just because something needs to be done doesn't mean it doesn't suck... and this does." Aurora sipped at her tea. "I'm not used to Ash being gone so much. If it wasn't for Cornin I would be lonely. But for you, Raffel is your Ash and Cornin combined."

Blāzzer, feeling a blush rise to her cheeks, looked out at the garden. Most of the plants were from the forest, including ferns and some flowering bushes.

"Cornin mentioned that your proposal is finished," said Aurora.

"Yeah, at this point I don't think me staring at it any longer will improve it," muttered Blāzzer, fidgeting with her fingers.

"You don't seem happy about that."

"Cornin said that the Teredana and the Council will very likely ask to see us enter fatorana on command."

The dragon inclined her head slightly.

Blāzzer looked down at her hands in her lap.

"But you did in Budsta," said Aurora, "and you've never mentioned having trouble before."

"Budsta was the only time one of us was able to," murmured the young woman. *I feel like I've disappointed her. Like I've let her down.* She looked up and met Aurora's purple eyes. "I'm sorry."

Aurora blinked in surprise. "For what, sweetheart?"

"I might not be able to become the Leader of the Dragons," whispered Blāzzer.

"You will be! It may not be this year, but you will become Leader of the

Dragons." When the young woman didn't answer, Aurora continued, "Blāzzer, you will become the Leader of the Dragons. I know you will. You have nothing to apologize for. We know how hard you and Raffel have been working. You two have come so far from when you two first met... try not to be too hard on you."

Blāzzer nodded slowly. She reached forward and grabbed the remaining glass of tea. She drank it as she watched the garden blur with the start of the rain.

After a few moments, Aurora questioned, "Do you want to talk about the trouble you two have been having with fatorana?"

"Yeah," sighed Blāzzer. She tucked her hair behind her ear. "We've tried but we just faint."

"You faint!?"

Blāzzer nodded shakily and pressing her lips together.

Aurora looked about a moment, trying to think. "How long has this been going on?"

"A while... I think it was two or three months after Budsta."

"So over two years. Why didn't either of you mention this?"

"Because it doesn't just happen when we try to enter fatorana," Blāzzer said, hunching her shoulders slightly. "When we're intimate, we faint too." She glanced up at Aurora, seeing the dragon's blank stare. Blāzzer looked away. "We can't do much... nothing down below."

Aurora sighed and placed her glass down, saying, "I'm for sure that has caused a strain on your relationship." Blāzzer didn't meet her gaze. "Have you figured out why this is happening?"

"No... All we know is that it has something to do with the liffen and his endar. We haven't had a chance to speak with any healers about it. We want to talk with Lillian or Truity."

"You'll have a chance to speak to Truity at the summer festival."

"That was my thought too."

"Well, till then keep trying... on both," encouraged Aurora. "You two will figure it out."

Blāzzer, wearing only one of Raffel's shirts, sat on the edge of the bed, brushing her hair. A single candle on the nightstand illuminated the room with the curtains drawn against the night. The sound of crickets and an owl filtered through a window that was cracked open. She placed the brush beside the candle and stood up, pulling the blankets back.

She blinked at the sound of the front door knob being turned. She held her breath, listening closely. The sound of the lock turning made her rush across the room and grab her sword from where it hung on the wall. She quickly drew Flame and tossed the scabbard onto the bed. The front door hinges creaked as it was pushed open.

Blāzzer quietly slid over to the bedroom door and gently opened it a crack before calling, "Whoever is trespassing in my home needs to leave! I am armed!"

There was a thud of something being dropped and the front door being closed. She threw the bedroom door open and stepped out, her sword ready to strike.

Keep a watch for book 2, *Perseverance*, of the Stories of Nickada.

Made in the USA
Columbia, SC
26 February 2022